Felix Moscheles

Fragments of an autobiography

Felix Moscheles

Fragments of an autobiography

ISBN/EAN: 9783743349841

Manufactured in Europe, USA, Canada, Australia, Japa

Cover: Foto ©Raphael Reischuk / pixelio.de

Manufactured and distributed by brebook publishing software (www.brebook.com)

Felix Moscheles

Fragments of an autobiography

FRAGMENTS OF AN AUTOBIOGRAPHY

EARLY IMPRESSIONS

 well remember the terrors of a certain night when the wind was howling and the rain was beating down in torrents over the arid plains of the Lüneburger Haide; between them they had blown or blotted out the flickering lights of a heavy, lumbering travelling carriage such as one used to hire in the so-called good old times. The horses were plunging in the mire, the postillion was swearing, and a very small boy was howling. That boy was I, and the incident marks my first entrance into that conscious life which registers events in our memories. Not that I exactly remember what happened, and how we got out of the ankle-deep mud, and finally reached our destination; but I have no doubt that my father and the "brother-in-law," as the German postillion was addressed in those days, had to get the wheels out of the ruts as best they could without assistance, for there was

no traveller, weary or otherwise, of the regulation first-chapter pattern, to come to the rescue.

No—I remember but little of it, but I have lived it all over again every time I have heard the dramatic strains of Schubert's Erl-king. Great artists, gifted with the power of song, have depicted the whole scene to me in thrilling accents; dear old Rubinstein, the friend, alas, I lost all too soon—grand old Rubinstein, the master whose magic touch swept the keyboard as the hurricane sweeps the plain—could conjure up visions of a misty past in my mind. "My father, my father," I could have cried, as the Erl-king of Pianists pursued the doomed child with his giant strides and unrelenting touch, alternately letting loose the elements to rage in maddening tumult, and drawing uncanny whispers from his weird instrument.

Whatever I may have been prompted to cry when under the spell of Rubinstein's art, I do not think I invoked my father's aid on that night upon the heath; it was more likely "My mother, my mother," I called, and she just protected me, and so, fortunately for me, it all ended happily, and: "In her arms the child was *not* dead, but cried itself to sleep, and was put back into the little hammock that was slung across from side to side of our old-fashioned vehicle, and that temporarily replaced my cradle in 3 Chester Place, Regent's Park, London, the house I was born in.

My father was on a concert tour in Germany, reaping laurels and golden harvests, such as were rarely heard of in those days. From his wife he never parted if he could help it, even for a short time, and by way of an encumbrance he had on this occasion taken, besides the necessary luggage, us children—I think there were three of us then—and a little dumb keyboard on which he used to exercise his fingers to keep them up to concert pitch when pianos were out of reach. I hadn't seen any of those little finger-trainers for years, when I came across one on Robert Browning's writing-table; he always kept it by his side, and I wondered whether he used it to stimulate the fingers that had to keep pace with the poet's ever-flowing thoughts. But my earliest recollections are connected, not with dumb keyboards, but with very full-sounding and eloquent ones. My father was ever happiest when at the piano or composing. He was in-terested, oh yes, much interested in the sister arts, in science and politics, but he had a way of disappearing after a while when such matters were being discussed, or of getting lost when we had set out conscientiously to do museums or churches in Venice or Antwerp, or to visit crypts, shrines, bones of ancestors, and other historical relics above and below ground. We knew we should find him at home at the piano, or pen in hand composing, that is, if he had not perchance been stopped on the way by the sounds of music in some attractive shape. It was quite enough for him to hear such sounds proceeding from an open window, to make for the door, ring the bell, and ask for the " Maestro " or the " Herr Kapellmeister." He would introduce himself, and presently be making friends on a sound musical basis with his colleague. It would sometimes lead to a continental hug of the warmest description, when the surprised native would discover that his visitor was *the* pianist.

Sometimes my father did not wait for that finishing touch, as when on one occasion he invaded the room of an ill-fated lover of music. It was at Tetschen, on a journey through Saxony and Bohemia ; we arrived one evening at the little hotel of that place, tired and hungry, and thinking only of supper and a good night's rest. Scarcely had we settled down to the former, when, separated from us only by a wooden partition, a neighbour commenced operations on the piano, slowly and carefully unwinding one bar after the other of that most brilliant of pieces, Weber's " Invitation à la Valse." " Dass dich das Mäuserle beisse !" exclaims my father, in terrible earnest. " May the little mouse bite you !" That was a favourite expression of his, when he found himself suddenly impelled to denounce somebody or something, and, as he accentuated it, it always seemed amply to replace those naughty words which are not admissible in daily life, and may only be used—and that, to be sure, for our benefit—on Sundays by the exponents of the Christian dogma.

The servant-girl was summoned, and she explained that the neighbour usually began at that time, and was in the habit of playing several hours. " Dass dich das Mäuserle " muttered my father with suppressed rage ; " Dass dich " . . . and with that he rushed out of the room. What would happen ? We were about to tremble, when a meek, respectful knock at the neighbour's door happily reassured us. "Herein"—Come in. Enter my father suavely apologising for the interruption—we hear it all through the thin partition. He, too, is a lover of music; may he as such be allowed to listen for a while. Much pleased, the other offers him a chair and resumes his performance; my father listens patiently, and waits till the last bars are reached. "Delightful!" we hear him say, "a beautiful piece, is it not? I once learnt it too; may I try your piano?" And with that he pounces on the shaky old instrument, galvanising it into new life, as he starts off at a furious rate, and gives vent to his pent-up feelings in cascades of octaves and breakneck passages; never had he played that most brilliant of pieces more brilliantly. "Good-night," he said as he struck the last chord; "allow me once more to apologise." "Ach! thus I shall never be able to play it," answered the neighbour with a deep sigh, and he closed the piano, and spent the rest of the evening a sadder but a quieter man.

But it was not often my father was allowed an opportunity of watching over his own comforts. That was a duty my mother would not willingly share with him or with anybody else; quite apart from the affection she lavished on the husband, there was the tribute of respect she paid to the artist. His was a privileged position, she held, and his path should be kept clear of all annoyance. Petty troubles, at any rate, should not approach him, nor the serious ones either if it was within her power to shield him from them ; if not, she would contrive to take the larger share of the burden upon herself.

From our earliest days, we children were trained to be on our best behaviour when our father came home, whatever our next best might have been previously. We were mostly happy little listeners when he was at the piano, and if he stopped too long for our juvenile faculties of enjoyment, why, our happiness gradually took the shape of respect for the musical function. It even turned into something akin to awe when he was composing. At such times I would not have whistled within his hearing to save my life. A wholesome fear of the Mäuserles that would assuredly sweep down upon me, if I disturbed the peace, would, I daresay, in a great measure account for my praiseworthy attitude, but, apart from any such practical considerations, it was the mystery connected with the evolution of the beautiful in art, which, from the first, held me in subjection.

The whooping-cough with which one of us children started, rapidly communicating it to the others, was also regulated in its outbursts with due regard to my father's peace. Whilst the fit was on us, it was a source of particular enjoyment to my sisters and myself, but we never freely indulged in it when my father was near. At other times we would come together, and wait for one another till the spirit moved us to whoop. Then I would wield the bâton in imitation of my betters at the conductor's desk, and we would have our solos and ensemble-pieces, our ritardandos and prestissimos, producing unexpected effects, and with the limited means at our disposal, making what I recollect as a very attractive and interesting performance. Edifying as it should have been to a parent, my mother could at first not see it in that light, but she had finally to give in, and to acknowledge that it was a bad cough that whooped no good.

I was an only son—an elder brother died some years before I was born—and it was but natural that my mother should look with indulgence on my delinquencies. I must sometimes have tried her and those around me sorely, as, for instance, when I hanged my little sister's favourite doll Anna Maria, from a knob of the chest of drawers, there to remain until she be dead.

Clara—that was my sister's name—was of a warm temperament, and fought for the release of her wax baby with all the passionate energy of the maternal instinct. I had to give way and cut down the victim, and then, all other means to pacify her having failed, I appealed to her imagination, and persuaded her to play at my having killed her in the battle we had just fought; it would be such a surprise for mamma. Ever sharp and quick as she was, she at once saw the far-reaching possibilities of my scheme, and allowed herself to be wrapped up in a bedsheet, as in a shroud, and to be laid out stiff and rigid as a corpse. I pulled down the blinds and shut the shutters; then I lit a candle which I placed by her side; when all was ready, I hid in a cupboard and set up a dismal wail that soon brought my mother to the spot. The effect upon her was all I could have desired, perhaps more so, for the first surprise once over, she expressed her disapproval of my conduct in terms suitable to the occasion, and thus quite spoilt the pleasure I had taken in the whole thing.

My mother was a remarkable woman,—a " lovely " woman, to use the word as the Americans do when they want a single epithet to describe alike the beauty of the body and the beauty of the soul, a word that shall tell of the brightness of the intellect and suggest the qualities of the heart. —

There are those who think that when it comes to the selection of epithets applicable to a mother, however distinguished or worthy she may have been, the son is not the person to entrust with that selection.   Perhaps they are right, and if in this case they care to do so, they must look round for corroborative evidence in her books.   It is just their fault if they have never read them, or if they have never heard of her as Felix Mendelssohn's grand-mother, a character in which she appeared with great advantage to the grandson when she was twenty-four, and he as a young man of nineteen paid his first visit to England.   And it is just their loss if they never saw the jet-black plaits as she wore them coiled around her head when she was young, or the mass of silky, snow-white hair of her later days that, when set free, would cascade over and far below the shoulders that bore the weight of fourscore years. On her face Time had left its mark.   Every line, every wrinkle gave character and expression to her features, and bore testimony to the truly beautiful life she had led.   The picture reproduced on the first page of these reminiscences I painted when she was in her 83rd year.

But the story of my mother's life must be written in another volume. For the present I return to earlier recollections.

When I was ten years old, I was dubbed a big boy, too big to be tied to his mother's apron-strings, and I was sent to King's College to rough it with other boys Opportunities were not wanting for the roughing it. On one occasion a boy called me a German sausage, and I retorted by punching his head ; and on another I met a University College boy, called him a stinkermalee, and got my head punched in return. What the appellation precisely meant, I didn't know, nor do I now, but it was then the particular term, opprobrious and insulting, we King's College boys had adopted to express our unbounded contempt for the hated rivals in Gower Street.

I was generally allowed to walk to school and back by myself, for it formed part of the scheme of education mapped out for me by my parents, that I should start fair and see life for myself. My way lay through St. Giles's and the Seven Dials, and there I did see life and did hear English too, English as she was spoke in those parts, perhaps as she is to this day ; but as I pass that way now, I don't come across it ; the hand of Time has been moving across the Seven Dials, and all the old landmarks are gone. Where in these degenerate times can a schoolboy hope to see a bear, a real big brown bear, in a cage just in front of a barber's shop ? only a penny-shave place to be sure, but bold in its advertisement, a notice in sprawl-

ing big characters proclaiming the superiority of the
establishment's bear's grease over any other grease,
whatever its kind might be. Where is the schoolboy
to-day who can realise the pleasurable excitement of
approaching such a caged bear in a public thorough-
fare close enough to test the beast's good nature
under circumstances of provocation, and his own
adroitness in making good his retreat in case of
retaliation ?

In the streets and alleys of St. Giles's I was first
initiated into the horrors of warfare, especially into
the kind of warfare considered quite legitimate in
those days. A quarrel first;—passions roused—
words leading to blows. Coats off, fists clenched,
and there, whilst two savages were trying the issue
as to which could knock the other into a jelly, or,
if luck would have it, into a coffin, we, the enlightened public, formed a ring and stood round,
nominally to see fair-play, but virtually to back one
or the other of the combatants, goading both on to
fight like devils, and finally rejoicing over the sur-
vival of the fittest.

That kind of thing has been stopped in St. Giles's,
but the devil doesn't mind ; there is so much legitimate warfare, slaughter and massacre nowadays on
a larger scale, that he is said to admit himself that
he gets over and above the share he originally
claimed ; and as for the ring, why, that has grown
apace ; thanks to scientific progress, it is iron-bound
now with telegraphic wires, and is known by the
euphonious name of " the Concert of Europe."

How good man is, and how tender in his concern

for his brother! More than once I saw him pick up
the battered jelly and carry it with fraternal solici-
tude to the neighbouring chemist. How good we
all are, stitching at Red Cross badges, chartering
ambulances, and sending the hat round at the
Mansion House and elsewhere to save the surviving
fittest from starvation!

The question of woman's rights—and wrongs—
was also occasionally raised and illustrated for my
benefit in one or the other of the Seven Dials, the
object lesson sometimes delaying me and getting me
into trouble for being late at the *hic-hæc-hoc* business in the Strand. I particularly recollect a female
fiend rushing after her wretched husband, who fled
down the street from her, and from the blood-stained
poker she savagely brandished.

But there were quieter corners too, not far from
the lairs of the vicious, a dear old printshop for one,
just by St. Giles' Church. The most tempting
pictures were displayed in the windows: coloured
prints of stage-coaches, cockatoos, prize-fighters, and
racehorses; lovely female types, as originally published in Heath's Book of Beauty; there were fashion
plates next to Bartolozzi's, not in fashion, and I daresay many an undiscovered treasure besides. I used
to spend my pennies on views of London, little steel-
plate engravings, printed on a sort of shiny card-
board. Was it my innate love for London that made
them so attractive, or my equally innate love of
architecture? Probably both. I always was, and
am still a cockney at heart, and as for the building
craze, that has been on me from that day to this.

Certainly no boy ever had such a collection of bricks as I had, and such a table to build on, specially constructed with drawers and divisions for all sizes and forms of my materials.

"I'm going to be an architect," I informed the old Duke of Cambridge on a gala occasion when he rode up to our house. "Right you are, my boy," said the Duke. "You'll be too late to build me a house, but you can build me a mausoleum." I've been planning mausoleums ever since, but unfortunately, not being an architect, I never have had a commission in that line. The Duke, who was an enthusiastic lover of music, had come on that occasion specially interested to hear Bach's Concerto in G minor, which my father played from a copy of the original manuscript he had received from his friend Professor Fischhof, of Vienna.

But to return from Royalty to the plebeian quarter of St. Giles, I must state that whatever of my pocket-money may have been invested in views of London, it was not that printshop, but the Lowther Arcade, which usually wrecked my finances. I could not resist the temptation which that short cut from the Strand to Catherine Street offered; my money went to the purchase of most fascinating articles, unfortunately at best of a twopenny - halfpenny character, things of beauty irresistibly suggesting themselves as presents for my sisters, things no girl should be without, wax angels under glass globes, bottle imps, china shepherdesses, or jumping frogs, the latter to be sprung upon the recipient unexpectedly. I brought them home and confided to my mother what bargains I had got. Unhappily the angels, frogs, imps, and the rest, however effective at first, were not long lived, or they proved themselves otherwise disappointing; so they were soon forgotten. Not so their cost.

My mother had carefully kept account of my wasteful expenditure for some weeks, and one day she confronted me with the sum total it had reached. It actually came within measurable distance of half-a-crown, an amount I had as yet never been able to call my own. I was overwhelmed by such proofs of my recklessness, and henceforth resisted the wiles of the Lowther Arcade. So the lesson was not lost on me; it sank deep into my heart, whence I have on more than one occasion been able to bring it to the surface. But I am bound to confess that I never was radically cured. I have periodical relapses when the old craving comes upon me, and the taste for beautifully fashioned angels, for china and for glass, and I revel in a bargain, and exult when I have picked up something every girl ought to have. Whilst the glorious fit is on, I am privileged to forget all I learnt in the sum-total lesson.

My experiences in the Lowther Arcade were soon to be suddenly interrupted, and for a long time it was even doubtful whether I should ever again be able to put in an appearance in that place or anywhere else. I caught the scarlet fever, not in the slums as it might be thought, but at school, where a regular epidemic had broken out. Our class-rooms in King's College were down in the basement, and those who knew said that the outbreak was due to the fact that

the filth-laden river came right up to the feet of the
grand old building, and washed them dirty day and
night; other wiseacres contended that it was more
likely to be the churchyard of St. Mary-le-Grand just
opposite which had done the mischief. As far as I can
remember, nobody mentioned the drains, which in
those days had not yet come into notice and fashion,
and could do their level best for the multiplication
of bacilli without being hampered by meddlesome
sanitary inspectors. Well, whatever may have been
the malignant source which poisoned me, it had done
its work thoroughly, and developed my scarlet fever
in its most virulent form. It was a terrible time I
went through. I was at death's door, but fortunately
that sombre portal remained closed, and I was not
bidden to cross the grim threshold.

No, I was destined to live and to fight the battle
of life with whatever fighting powers I might possess.
Later on I was to wrestle more than once with the
grim immortal who only spares each of us mortals
till his hour-glass tells him it is time to use his scythe.
And if I wrestled well and am here to tell the tale,
it is because by my side watched day and night that
best of nurses, my mother.

I was never what is called a good patient, and to
this day I am very much averse to sending for the
doctor. I quite feel he indeed is a friend in need, and
I do not wish to disparage his power for good, or to
underrate his skill and judgment, but as a rule I
make a point of not calling him in till I know
what I want him to say. I think that doctors
nowadays are more agreeable than they were for-

merly; the great and fashionable doctors, I mean.
A man, to be up to date, had to be brief, brusque,
and bumptious. He seemed to have learnt his
stronger English from Dr. Johnson, and generally
to have been trained in a Johnsonian atmosphere.
He had to say smart things that could be quoted
and hawked about, and to enunciate wise saws in
imitation of the master whose sayings are so unmercifully inflicted on us to this day. He was in
a hurry; he drove up in a big yellow carriage,
and before the horses could pull up, his tiger had
sprung from the footboard, and was giving the most
tremendous double-knock, one evidently meant to
awaken the dead, in case medical assistance had
come too late.

To pass muster, the doctor's natural kindness
had to be concealed beneath an outer coating of
apparent roughness. Sometimes it was the roughness that was concealed only by a transparent veneer
of amiability. Certain it is that in those days no
doctor could look at a boy's tongue without at once
declaring that he stood in immediate need of a black
dose, and if that vile compound did not exceed every
other mixture in nastiness, he did not believe it
would be efficacious. He revelled in blue pills, and
was happiest when he could pull out a little lancet
and bleed you, or send round a man with a complete set of sharp blades, to do the thing wholesale,
jerking them into some part of your precious self,
and pumping a given number of ounces out of it and
into his cupping-glasses.

All this is very ungrateful of me, for Dr. Stone

was the best and kindest of men—and very undutiful, for he was my godfather (Felix Stone is my full name). To be sure he had a big yellow carriage, and a tiger whose main ambition in life it seemed to be to knock his master's patients up. To be sure Dr. Stone came coated with a veneer of roughness, but it was skin-deep; true, he gave me as many black doses and blue pills as he thought my robust constitution could stand, but in addition to these he made me many beautiful presents—a silver mug emblazoned with our family crest and the motto "Labore," a splendid family Bible of about my own weight and size, a costly edition of Byron's "Childe Harold" and ditto of Milton's "Paradise Lost and Regained," and a number of other things doubly delightful and gratifying to my juvenile mind, because they always came at least three or four years before I knew how to use them.

My good godfather had ushered me into this world, from which unfortunately he was himself called away before he had had many opportunities of performing the duties he had undertaken when he pledged himself to see to it that I should "renounce the devil and all his works."

When after many weeks of hard fighting with the scarlet enemy, and after having passed through various relapses and complications, I emerged from the sick-room, I was taken to Brighton for a complete change of air. There I soon found new life and strength. Dear old Brighton! I was to find new life and strength there once more, thirty years later, when I met the young lady who said she would—when I asked her to marry me.

My next station was Hamburg. I was sent there to get the benefit of a thorough change of air, and to improve my German. It was shortly after the terrible conflagration which had laid low a great part of the city.

The jagged walls, springing in fantastic forms from immense piles of crumbling masonry and charred timber, had a weird fascination for me. I was deeply in sympathy with my beloved friend Architecture, and deplored the fate that had overtaken some of the best buildings, but at the same time I was lost in admiration of the beauties, now picturesque, now awe-inspiring, which the caprice of the destructive element had stamped on crazy walls and tangled masses of wreckage.

I have since been similarly impressed; in Pompeii first, and again in Paris, after the Commune ; only to be sure the former scene of devastation I saw neatly put in order and made presentable for the visitor, whereas the latter was yet smoking and all besmirched with the blood of the sorely visited Parisians.

My father had given a concert for the benefit of the sufferers in Hamburg, and was able to contribute a sum of £643 to the relief fund raised.

On my arrival I was received with open arms by my relatives. My grandfather, Adolf Embden, had been staying with us more than once, and he was particularly partial to his grandson, because he had a marked predilection for England and everything that was English. He knew more about British politics than most men born and bred in the country; he read all the big speeches delivered in Parliament, identified himself with the Whigs, and was a fervent disciple of Cobden and Bright. He did his best to train me in the way I should go, and his methods were quite congenial to my taste. We often took long walks together, and his peripatetic teachings are pleasantly blended in my mind with the half-way house at the corner of the Jungfernsteg and the Alster Bassin, then occupied by Giosti Giovanoli, the confectioner. He trained me just once too often, but that was in London, in a shop near Oxford Circus, and it was a Bath bun that made me restless. That shop was painted green and gold, and to this day I would not eat on green and gold premises if I were starving.

In Hamburg I was welcomed, too, by uncles and aunts, first and second cousins, male and female, and by a strong contingent of grandaunts. I am aware that most people have quite as many relatives of their own as they need for home consumption, and that being so, they are not pleasantly disposed towards the family history of their friends. So I mean to use my relatives sparingly, and only to bring them in where they are associated with things I well remember. My mother has penned most characteristic sketches of many of those worthy personalities in a MS. she has entitled "Early Recollections," and the grandaunts hold a prominent place in those papers; but for the reason just given, I refrain from transcribing her graphic descriptions of their doings. I would, however, record my own boyish impressions, to the effect that one or two of my grandaunts were a caution to rattle-snakes. I have learned since to see that they were nothing of the kind, but just old ladies of marked originality. It took some time before I could get to like being loved by them; I preferred making faces behind their backs, a pastime which I was joined in by a cousin about my own age. Cousin Carl got into trouble oftener than I did, and had more reason to regret it, for in one of the drawers of an old-fashioned mahogany secretary his father kept an orthodox cane which he would produce on special occasions—such were the un-challenged methods of training in those days. My uncle was the best of men, anxious only to chastise for the good of the young delinquent, whom he tenderly loved, but he might have saved himself the trouble, for poor Cousin Carl was never to reap the benefit of his training. He had at no time been robust, and was not to live long. That winter of 1842 was looking about for victims. The fearful mornings, when we had to get up in the dark, and wash by the flicker of a tallow candle—wash, that is if we succeeded in hacking up the ice in the jug, and in finding some water at the bottom of it—those fearful mornings proved too much for him. Poor Carl's faces, as he made them behind people's backs, grew longer and longer, his cough grew hollower and hollower, and he soon went to rest where there are no canes and no tallow dips, and all is peace, and even one's grandaunts are seraphs.

The sad event did not, however, take place during my stay in Hamburg. I spent some six or eight months with my uncle and aunt. She, my Tante Jaques, was my mother's only sister, and was deeply attached to her; on me she lavished unvarying kindness and affection. My cousins, all older than myself, were delighted to have the "little Englishman" in the house, and the friendship we struck up then has lasted through life.

One of the grandaunts was a sister of Heinrich Heine, the poet. She had married into the Embden family, and so Heinrich was a sort of cousin of my mother's. They saw a good deal of one another when my mother was in her teens, and he was a dreamy youth whom she and the other girls of the family circle delighted to chaff. His frequent head-aches they not incorrectly ascribed to his mode of living; to be sure, they said, he looked pale and interesting, but that was only because he had eaten too much at yesterday's dinner party. "Now, what *is* the matter with you again to-day?" said my mother as he sat down opposite her one morning and watched her shelling peas. "How pale you are! it's that head again, I suppose?" "Yes, Lottchen, I am ill; it is the head again." "That is what you are always saying, but I'm sure it is not as bad as you make it out to be. Come now, am I not right?" "O Lottchen," he said, "you do not know how I suffer;" and as he sat there musing, she had not the heart further to chaff him. When the next volume of his poems appeared shortly afterwards, she knew what had passed through his mind on that occasion, and perhaps on others when she had shown him friendly sympathy.

He writes :—

> " When past thy house at morning
>   I take my way, to see
> Thy face, child, at the window
>   Is deep delight to me.
>
> Thy dark-brown eyes seem asking
>   As my sad, pale looks they scan,
> Who art thou, and what ails thee,
>   Thou strange and woe-worn man ?
>
> ' I am a German poet,
>   Through Germany widely known ;
> When they name the names that are famous,
>   With them they will name my own.
>
> ' And what I ail, oh many,
>   Dear little one, ail the same.
> When they name the worst of sorrows,
>   Mine, too, they are sure to name.' "

Sometimes he was in livelier moods, as one day, when he, my grandfather, and my mother were walking through the fields together, and were joined by a remarkably dull doctor of philology, whose company was particularly distasteful to Heine. Pointing to half-a-dozen cows and oxen that were grazing close by, he said in an undertone : " I say, Lottchen, now there are seven doctors on the meadow."

Salomon Heine, the poet's uncle, was a millionaire who spent his money right royally and philanthropically ; a man who owed his fortune to his own exertions, and who, when he had made a million of marks for each of his children—I forget how many he had—devoted the next million he amassed to the foundation of a hospital. He was a delightful specimen of an uncle, too, for he would spend his money philonepotically as well as philanthropically. The nephew was ever ready to dive into the uncle's purse ; equally ready to make literary capital out of him and his friends. Gumpel, another rich banker— we know him as Gumpelino—was his pet aversion, and specially suggestive to him as a butt for his satire. Gumpel, too, was a self-made man, a fact of which, however, he did not like to be reminded, quite unlike old Heine, who loved to bring up the subject to the annoyance of his friend, shouting across the table stories of the early days when they came to Hamburg with their bundles slung across their shoulders. To his nephew he was ever indulgent ; he was proud of his rising popularity, and as a rule was not appealed to in vain when the young genius had got into money troubles. On one occasion, though, he lost patience when he had given him a round sum wherewith to defray the expenses of a journey to Norderney, a summer resort on the coast of the North Sea. Instead of devoting the money to the purpose of improving his health, he managed in one night to roll the round sum into other people's pockets at the gaming tables. This time the uncle was indignant, and Heinrich would probably never have gone to Norderney, and consequently never have written the " Nordsee-Lieder," had not the well-known firm of Hoffman & Campe come to the rescue with the necessary funds, in consideration of which they stipulated he should write a volume of songs for them.

In Hamburg I was sent to the Johanneum, a

large public school. It was rather hard, after having been called a German sausage in England, to be derided as an English " Rossbiff" or " Shonebool," which was meant for John Bull. The whole class roared with laughter when I rose for the first time to decline $\dot{\eta}$ Μοῦσα, pronouncing the defunct Greek language as it was spoken in King's College, and the jeers of that whole class so galled and stung me that I wished I could kill all German boys at a stroke, or at least maim those despicable ones within my reach for life. It was well I could not act upon the impulse, for many a German boy of that day was to be a staunch friend to me in after life. I had my troubles in those Teutonic school-days, and I thought the proceedings monotonous, but still there was pleasurable excitement to be had occasionally, as when old Hummel came along — a half-witted water-carrier whom every bad boy in Hamburg knew and hooted. Three words we would shout in his face, three words that meant absolutely nothing, but that sounded worse than any bad language i had ever heard. He was a shaky old man, and the water-pails suspended from his shoulders prevented his running after us, and so we could indulge with impunity in the exhilarating sport of mocking him to the fullest extent our wicked little human hearts desired.

I have also a pleasant recollection of caterpillar-hunting; we were spending the summer near Hamburg in a rustic retreat, and a regular plague of these insects made life a burden to some members of the family. They were larger than ordinary caterpillars and more hairy, and they were so numerous that much thought and care had to be bestowed on the methods of protecting ourselves against them; for they did not confine themselves to the garden, they made no difference between vegetable produce and grand-aunts, and would mistake the best bonnets of those worthies for cabbage leaves. There was even a rumour that one of these slimy crawlers had been crushed out of existence by my grandest-aunt, who chanced to be the heaviest one too. How that caterpillar found its way between that lady's bed-sheets, and whether it did so with or without assistance, was fortunately never ascertained, and as discreet silence has been maintained on the subject for years, it is not for me to solve the mystery to-day.

After an absence of some six or eight months I returned to London, to that 3 Chester Place so full of memories, personal and artistic.

There were quite as many infant prodigies in those days as there are now; little exotic plants, forced in artistic hothouses, artificially developed, and prematurely produced in drawing-rooms and concert halls; glittering little shooting-stars, nine-days' wonders, to be soon forgotten, and ere long to be buried.

But then, there were also wonder-children, as the Germans call them, who thrived and lived, and who seemed to combine in themselves all the qualities that had belonged to the little victims of forced training. Such a one was Joachim. He first appeared in public when he was seven; five years later he played in Leipsic at Madame Viardot's concert;

and when he was not yet fourteen he gathered his first laurels in London at the Philharmonic. That year—it was 1844—Mendelssohn was in England, and mightily interested in the young violinist. One evening, after singing at our house, Mendelssohn wanted to take him to a musical party; a pair of gloves were deemed necessary to make him presentable, and we two boys were sent out to get them; we had a walk, and a talk besides, and I remember thinking what a nice sort of sensible boy he was; no nonsense about him and no affectation; not like the other clever ones I knew. The gloves we bought in a little shop in Albany Street, Regent's Park, and as these were the first pair of English gloves that Joseph wore, I duly record the historical fact for the benefit of all those who have at one time or the other been under the spell of the fingers we fitted that evening.

When two years later we met in Leipsic, it so happened that I was suddenly fired with the desire to play the violin too. My friend Joseph was quite ready to teach me, and we started operations, but two or three lessons were sufficient to convince him and me, that mine was an unholy desire, which, if gratified, would give me the power of inflicting much suffering on my fellow-creatures, and which therefore was calculated to lead me into trouble. So we gave it up, and Joachim has had to rely on other pupils for his reputation as a teacher.

Liszt too had been a juvenile phenomenon, but had long arrived at full maturity at the time I first remember him. I was then about ten, and he some twenty years older. I think I never knew anybody so calculated to fascinate man, woman, or child. He generally spoke in French, which I did not understand, but I had to listen to every word. His voice alone held me spell-bound ; it rose and fell like a big wave, and I could tell that something unusual was going on ; that voice was evidently scattering thought as the big wave scatters spray, and those clear-cut features of his were each in turn accentuating and emphasising his words. His grand leonine mane fascinated me as it started from the lofty forehead, and bounded Niagara-like with one leap to the nape of the neck.

My early recollections of his playing are rather limited. As a boy I was mainly impressed by his long chord-grasping fingers, contrasting as they did with my father's small, velvety hand. To *see* him play was quite as much as I could do, without particularly attending to what he played, to watch his hands fly up from one set of notes and pounce down on another, and generally to lie in wait for the outward manifestations of his genius. Later on I grew accustomed to the grand young man's ways, and just knelt at his shrine as everybody else did.

My father was not the least outspoken of his admirers. In the early days he mentions him as "that rare art-phenomenon," and tells how "he played Hummel's Septet with the most perfect execution, storming occasionally like a Titan, but still in the main free from extravagance." Later on, at the Musical Festival held in Bonn, he describes him as "the absolute monarch, by virtue of his princely gifts, outshining all else."

Half a century ago playing *à quatre mains* was much more popular than it is now; more pieces were written and more pianoforte arrangements were made for two performers. The full-fledged pianist of to-day thinks he is quite able to do the work of two, and sees no reason why he should share the keyboard with another; so he prefers to keep the whole function in his own hands. Formerly he was satisfied to give a concert; the very word implied concerted action of several artists; now he announces the one-man show called a Recital, in which he stars and shines by himself. He scorns assistance, for he wishes it to be understood that he can get through the most formidable programme without breaking down, and that he can rely on his ironclad instrument to hold out with him and lead him triumphantly to the finale.

Well, the great virtuosi of my early days certainly loved playing together, and many are the instances of such joint performances, both in private and in public, which I recollect. How my father enjoyed playing with Liszt he records when he says: "It was a genuine treat to draw sparks from the piano as we dashed along together. When we are harnessed together in a duet we make a very good pair; Apollo drives us without a whip."

If, as my father assumes, Apollo was really the driver on occasions of that kind, I feel sure that his favourite team must have been Mendelssohn and Moscheles; they certainly enjoyed being in harness together, sometimes playing, and sometimes improvising. Occasionally the humour of the moment would lead them to compose together, as when one evening they planned a piece for two performers to be played by them three days later at a concert my father had announced. The Gipsies' March from Weber's "Preziosa" being chosen as a subject for variations, a general scheme was agreed upon, and the parts were distributed. "I will write a variation in minor and growl in the bass," said Mendelssohn. "Will you do a brilliant one in major in the treble?" It was settled that the Introduction and first and second variations should fall to Mendelssohn's lot, the third and fourth to my father's. The finale they shared in, Mendelssohn starting with an allegro movement, and my father following with a "piulento." Two days later they had a hurried rehearsal, and on the following day they played the concertante variations, "composed expressly for this occasion," as the programme had it, "and performed on Erard's new patent-action grand pianoforte." Nobody noticed that the piece had been only sketched, and that each of the performers was allowed to improvise in his own solo, till at certain passages agreed upon, both met again in due harmony. The *Morning Post* of the day tells us that "the subject was treated in the most profound and effective manner by each, and executed so brilliantly that the most rapturous plaudits were elicited from the delighted company."

Mendelssohn himself in a letter gives a graphic account of a rehearsal held at Clementi's pianoforte factory, when the two friends played his "Double Concerto in E."

"It was great fun," he says; "no one can have an idea how Moscheles and I coquetted together on the piano—how the one constantly imitated the other, and how sweet we were. Moscheles plays the last movement with wonderful brilliancy; the runs drop from his fingers like magic. When it was over, all said it was a pity that we had made no cadenza; so I at once hit upon a passage in the first part of the last Tutti, where the orchestra has a pause, and Moscheles had, *nolens volens*, to comply, and compose a grand cadenza. We now deliberated amid a thousand jokes whether the small last solo should remain in its place, since, of course, the people would applaud the cadenza. 'We must have a bit of Tutti between the cadenza and the solo,' said I. 'How long are they to clap their hands?' asked Moscheles. 'Ten minutes, I daresay,' said I. Moscheles beat me down to five. I promised to supply a Tutti; and so we took the measure, embroidered, turned and padded, put in sleeves *à la* Mameluke, and at last, with our tailoring, produced a brilliant concerto. We shall have another rehearsal to-day; it will be quite a picnic, for Moscheles brings the cadenza and I the Tutti."

That golden thread of "great fun," as he calls it, goes through the history of Mendelssohn's life. It intertwined itself with the sensitive fibres of his nature, thus becoming an element of strength, a factor that illuminated his path and spread bright sunshine wherever he went. In fact I always thought one of the most delightful traits of his character was a certain naïveté, which enabled him to appreciate the humour of a situation, and thoroughly to enjoy it with his friends. He would turn some trivial incident to the happiest account, and in his own peculiarly genial way, make it the starting-point for a standing joke, or a winged word, to be handed down from generation to generation in the families of his friends.

Amongst the many drawings of his we treasure in the family is one humorously illustrating my father's works. It takes the shape of an arabesque, artistically framing some lines written for the occasion of his bithday by Klingemann. A second verse was composed for a subsequent birthday.

When in later years, and with a view to publication, I ventured to ask Robert Browning for an English version of those lines, he, with his usual kindness, sent me the following letter :—

"29 DE VERE GARDENS,
Nov. 30, '87.

"MY DEAR MOSCHELES,—Pray forgive my delay in doing the little piece of business with which you entrusted me : an unexpected claim on my mornings interfered with it till just now. Will this answer your purpose anyhow ?—

> "'Hail to the man who upwards strives
> Ever in happy unconcern :
> Whom neither blame nor praise contrives
> From his own nature's path to turn.

> On, and still on, the journey went,
> Yet has he kept us all in view,
> Working in age with youth's intent,
> In living—fresh, in loving—true.'

"Were my version but as true to the original as your father's life was to his noble ideal, it would be good indeed. As it is, accept the best of yours truly ever, ROBERT BROWNING."

Having started on my recollections of Mendelssohn, I am somewhat perplexed to know how many or how few of them I should record here. So much has been published about him, first by my mother in "The Life of Moscheles,"[1] where she has used my father's diaries and correspondence, and then by myself, when I translated and edited Mendelssohn's letters to my parents,[2] that perhaps I ought not to run the risk of telling what is already known. But, on the other hand, Mendelssohn plays so prominent a part in my early recollections, that I cannot write these without attempting to portray the principal figure, my father's most intimate friend and my very dear godfather.

I shall, at any rate, have to exercise due discretion and care, for Mendelssohn, and what he said and did, was such a constant theme of conversation in our family, that I grew up knowing my parents' friend nearly as well as they did themselves, and I may

---

[1] "Life of Moscheles," by his wife. (Hurst & Blackett, 1873.)

[2] "Letters of Felix Mendelssohn to Ignaz and Charlotte Moscheles." Translated and edited by Felix Moscheles. (Houghton & Mifflin, Boston, U.S.A.)

consider myself fortunate if, in recording my earliest impressions, I do not find myself remembering things that happened before I was born.

The very first letter which connects me with Mendelssohn is the one in which he congratulates my parents on the arrival of a son and heir. He heads it with a pen-and-ink drawing, representing a diminutive baby in a cradle, surrounded by all the instruments of the orchestra.

"Here they are, dear Moscheles," he says, "wind instruments and fiddles, for the son and heir must not be kept waiting till I come—he must have a cradle song, with drums and trumpets and janissary music; fiddles alone are not nearly lively enough. May every happiness and joy and blessing attend the little stranger; may he be prosperous, may he do well whatever he does, and may it fare well with him in the world!

"So he is to be called Felix, is he? How nice and kind of you to make him my godchild, *in formâ!* The first present his godfather makes him is the above entire orchestra; it is to accompany him through life—the trumpets when he wishes to become famous, the flutes when he falls in love, the cymbals when he grows a beard; the pianoforte explains itself, and should people ever play him false, as will happen to the best of us, there stand the kettle-drums and the big-drum in the background.

"Dear me! I am ever so happy when I think of your happiness, and of the time when I shall have my full share of it. By the end of April, at the latest, I intend to be in London, and then we will duly name the boy, and introduce him to the world at large. It will be grand!"

In a later letter he announces himself as arriving in June, "ready to act as a godfather, to play, conduct, and even to be a genius."

He came, and I was duly christened Felix Stone Moscheles in St. Pancras Church. Barry Cornwall wrote some lines commemorative of the occasion. Alluding to the date of my birth, he begins :—

1. (*February*).

Speak low ! the days are dear,
  Sing loud ! *A child is born !*
Music, the maid, is watching near,
To hide him in her bosom dear,
  From sights and sounds forlorn.
     Happy be his infant days !
     Happy be his after ways !
     Happy manhood !   Happy age !
     Happy all his pilgrimage.

2. (*June*).

Breathe soft ! the days grow mild,
  The child hath gained a name !
Now sweet maid, Music ! whisper wild
Thy blessings on the new-named child,
  And lead him straight to fame.
     " *Felix* " should be " *happy* " ever,
     And his life be like a river,
     Sweetness, freshness, always bringing,
     And ever, ever, ever singing !

Well, the "sweet maid, Music" never led the new-named one "straight to fame," nor did the child ever get there by any circuitous route, but Felix was certainly "happy ever."

In this, my case, there certainly must have been something in a name, for my good godfather endowed me with my full share of happiness.

In later years Berlioz wrote that well-known line of Horace's in my album :—

"Donec eris Felix, multos numerabis amicos."

(As long as you are happy you will number many friends.) And when I reflect how much friendship I have enjoyed from the day of my christening to the present hour, I feel certain that the name was of good augury, and that Horace and Mendelssohn were right.

If the complete orchestra was the first god-father's present, the little album was the second. It measures only six inches by four, but that small compass holds much that is of interest. The book is full now ; it required about half a century to cover its pages, for they contain only the autographs of such celebrities as were my personal friends. Mendelssohn had appropriately inaugurated it with a composition, the " Wiegenlied " (slumber-song), now so popular.

There are also two drawings by him, one of 3 Chester Place, Regent's Park, and another of the Park close at hand. Mendelssohn must have sat out of doors to make these very faithful transcripts of nature, and I sometimes wonder how the street-boys of those days took it. Looking at those contributions, one cannot help being struck by the care which he bestowed on everything he did. His handwriting was always neat and clear, with just enough of flourish and swing to give it originality. His musical manuscripts vie in precision with the products of the engraver's art, and again there is a marked analogy between his style of drawing and the way in which he forms the letters of the alphabet, or the notes of the scales. As one peruses his manuscripts, one finds oneself admiring the artistic aspect of his well-balanced bars, and on the other hand, the harmonious treatment of his drawings recalls the appearance his pen gives to his scores. In the view he took of the Regent's Park, the leaves, so delicately and yet so firmly pencilled, seem to sway and rustle in unison with the sprightly melody of the scherzo in the "Midsummer-Night's Dream," and just as that melody is discreetly accompanied by the orchestra, so in the drawing, the houses, the old Colosseum in the background, and the trees in the middle-distance, are, one and all, made to keep their places, and deferentially to play second fiddle to the rustling leaves.

In due course of time, and after full enjoyment of the Slumber Song, I got out of my cradle and on to my legs, and it is from that stage in my development that I really date my recollections of my godfather. Some are hazy, others distinct. I am often surprised when I realise that he was short of stature; to me, the small boy, he appeared very tall. I looked upon him as my own special god-father, in whom I had a sort of vested interest, and I showed my annoyance when I was not allowed to monopolise him, or at least to remain near him. Being put to bed was at best a hateful process; how much more so, then, when I was just happily installed on my godfather's knee ; occasions of that kind are connected in my mind with vociferous protests, followed by ignominious expulsion.

There were, however. happier times soon to follow, times which recall to me our exploits in the Park. He could throw my ball farther than anybody else ; and he could run faster too, but then, to be sure, for all that, *I* could catch him. There were pitched battles with snowballs, and there was that memorable occasion when I got my first black eye. I remember it came straight from the bat, but—to tell the truth —I was never quite sure that Mendelssohn was in any way connected with that historical event, correctly located though it is, in the Regent's Park.

Our indoor sports must have been pretty lively too, for on one occasion my mother records how " in the evening Felix junior had such a tremendous romp with his godfather, that the whole house shook." And she adds : " One can scarcely realise that the man who would presently be improvising in his grandest style, was the Felix senior, the king of games and romps."

One of my achievements, when I was a little boy in a black velvet blouse, was the impersonation of what we called " the dead man "; the dying man would have been more correct. From my earliest days I evidently pitied the soldier dying a violent death on the battlefield. Since then I have learnt to extend my commiseration to the tax-payer, and to the many innocent victims of a barbarous and iniquitous system. Well, the dying man in the blouse was stretched full length—say some three feet—on the Brussels carpet.

Mendelssohn or my father were at the piano improvising a running accompaniment to my performance, and between us we illustrated musically and dramatically the throes and spasms of the expiring hero. I was much offended once, because they told me I acted just like a little monkey ; I did not know then, but I am quite sure now, that behind my back they said in a very different tone, admiring and affectionate : " He is *such* a little monkey."

That black velvet blouse I particularly remember, because John Horsley, now the veteran R.A., then but a rising artist, painted me in it ; and also because Hensel, Mendelssohn's brother-in-law, made a sketch of it in my album, at my particular request, representing me on horseback.

What honours that garment might not further have attained I do not know, had I not once for all checked its career by climbing over some freshly painted green railings in the Park, and thus irreparably spoiling it.

The dead-man improvisations remind me of the marvellous way in which my father and godfather would improvise together, playing *à quatre mains,* or alternately, and pouring forth a never-failing stream of musical ideas. I have spoken of it before, but it was in a preface, and who reads a preface ? So I may perhaps once more be allowed to describe it. A subject started, it was caught up as if it were a shuttlecock ; now one of the players would seem to toss it up on high, or to keep it balanced in mid-octaves with delicate touch. Then the other would take it in hand, start it on classical lines, and develop it with profound erudition, until perhaps the two joining together in new and brilliant forms, would triumphantly carry it off to other spheres of sound. Four hands there might be, but only one soul, so it seemed, as they would catch with lightning speed at each other's ideas, each trying to introduce subjects from the works of the other.

It was exciting to watch how the amicable contest would wax hot, culminating occasionally in an outburst of merriment, when some conflicting harmonies met in terrible collision. I see Mendelssohn's air of triumph when he had succeeded in twisting a subject from a composition of his own into a Moscheles theme, while the latter was obliged to second him in the bass. But not for long. "Stop a minute," said the next few chords that my father struck. "There I have you, you have taken the bait." Soon they would be again fraternising in perfect harmonies, gradually leading up to the brilliant finale that sounded as if it had been so written, revised and corrected, and were now being interpreted from the score by two masters.

Besides my godfather there were many of my father's friends who were kindly disposed towards me. Malibran is one of those I associate with my earliest days. Perhaps I remember her, perhaps I but fancy I do, for I was only three or four years old when she died. But I have impressions of her sitting on the floor and painting pretty pictures for us children ; a certain black silk bag, from the depths of which she produced paint-box, brushes, and other beautiful and mysterious things, had an irresistible charm for us, as had also her big dark eyes, and that wonderful mouth of hers, which she showed us could easily hold an orange. And then she would sing to us Spanish songs by her father, Manuel Garcia, and other celebrities. In my album she wrote, " Nei giorni tuoi felici ricordati di Marie de Beriot," and the flourish appended to the signature takes the shape of an apocryphal bird. For my father's album, one of the completest of its kind, she composed an Allegretto, a song which I believe has never been published. The words, probably by herself, run thus :—

> " Il est parti sans voir sa fiancée
> Lorsque le bal était prêt à s'ouvrir ;
> Si pour une autre il m'avait délaissée,
> Malheur à moi, je n'ai plus qu'à mourir."

It is dated July 16, 1836 : she died on the 23rd of September following.

Thalberg was also a children's man. He was not much of a romp, but always full of jokes, musical and otherwise. Interested as I was in the outward appearance of my home pianists, I was duly impressed by Thalberg's rigid appearance at the piano, contrasting as it did with the lively ways of Liszt and others. He had trained himself to this truly military bearing by practising his most difficult passages whilst he smoked a long Turkish chibouk, the cup of which rested on the ground.

Another source of wonder, not unmixed with awe, was the bulky frame of Lablache, the great singer. It was indeed a basso profondo which emerged from the depths of his ponderous figure. The beauty of his voice, the perfection of his style, and his unconventional deportment on the stage, I learnt to appreciate in later years. I particularly recollect him as Bartolo in Rossini's "Barbiere," on an occasion when Sontag and Mario took the other leading parts. As a small boy I just liked to walk round him, and thought the hackney-coach driver, as they called the cabby then, was not far wrong when he inquired whether his fare expected to be conveyed in one lot.

One of the friends of those early days was Dante Gabriel Rossetti. His father was giving my elder sisters Italian lessons, and that led to most friendly intercourse with him and his two sons. I mention Gabriel's name with a twinge of regret, for the chief records of that intercourse, a number of drawings by his hand, are irretrievably lost. There were—I see them still—knights in armour, fair ladies, and graceful pages, bold pen-and-ink drawings, illustrating a story that ran through several numbers of our own special paper the "Weekly Critic." What, or by whom the story was, I do not recollect, probably by Chorley, who was a frequent contributor to that weekly publication of ours. The drawings in no way foreshadowed Gabriel's later manner; they were just what an imaginative young fellow of seventeen or eighteen would draw, but I feel sure there were no beautiful peculiarities or other poetical deviations from the natural in this his early work. I often wonder where the "Weekly Critic" is in hiding. If this should meet the eye of anybody who knows, I trust he will come forward and receive my blessing in exchange for the drawings which we will give to an expectant world.

When I was about twelve I made my first appearance on the stage under peculiar circumstances. My father had announced a concert in Baden, where we were spending the summer, he the centre of a musical circle, I a schoolboy enjoying my holidays, and specially devoted to the climbing of trees and the picking of blackberries. The impresario of the Court Theatre in Carlsruhe (he seemed to me a sort of Grand Mogul) had graciously permitted the stars of his Opera to sing at that concert of my father's. At the eleventh hour, however, there was a hitch, and the stars were needed to shine on their own Grand-Ducal boards. In the hope that matters might yet be settled in his favour, my father sent me to him with urgent messages. On my arrival I made straight for the theatre, and entering by an unguarded back door, I soon found myself in a maze of dark passages. The sounds of music guided me to the stage, where a rehearsal of the " Vier Haymons-Kinder " was going on, and from the wings I found my way into a rustic arbour destined for the trysting-place of the lovers in the particular scene which was being rehearsed ; there I was biding my time when I was discovered by the lady who had come to meet the tenor. The performance was abruptly stopped ; the lady was no other than the great prima donna and our old friend Madame Haizinger. Rushing at me with a cry of dramatic exultation, she seized me and carried me triumphantly on to the middle of the stage. " Here," she cried, holding me up to the assembled company, my arms and legs dangling in mid-air—"here, ladies and gentlemen, you see Felix, the son of my old friend Moscheles." The Grand Mogul sat at a table covered with papers to my left, and happily looked upon the interruption and the rapturous outburst as nothing uncommon. As soon as I was replaced on my feet, I delivered my messages, but my influence as a diplomatic agent was not proof against untoward circumstances, and I failed in my mission.

That same Court Theatre was destined soon to become the prey of flames; it was the scene of a terrible catastrophe when many lives were lost.

I was soon to see more of Carlsruhe. Chiefly with a view to improving my German, I was put to school there. Now Carlsruhe was in those days one of the dullest places rational man ever condescended to inhabit. I think it was Heine who said that the dogs came up to you in the street and begged as a favour that you would tread on their toes, just to relieve them of the intolerable monotony of their lives. How it is to-day I don't know; probably they now have music-halls and motor cars, jingoes and pickpockets, but in my time all was slow, sure, and safe. The Grand-Duke sat in his palace like a royal spider in his web; all the streets radiated fan-like from the centre he occupied. In the forest, at the back of the palace, the avenues were cut out so as to form a counterpart to the city, one and all converging towards the abode of the Ruler. A fine spacious market-place there was, however, with a town-hall and a church and a monument to a departed Markgraf, round which clustered on certain days quaint old apple-women whom we school-boys patronised to the fullest extent of our limited means. We were close at hand, for the "Gymnasium" was happily situated in this most attractive part of the town. For all that, it took me some time before I could get accustomed to my new home.

Professor Schummelig, to whose care I was entrusted, was good in his way; I give him a fictitious name, as I have to record that he could also be bad in his way. I don't think he made my lessons more tedious or my tasks more irksome than any other ordinary German professor would have done; but he was pedantic and I was imaginative, so we did not always give one another satisfaction. We had one or two grand rows, in which the wrongs cannot have been all on my side, for, as soon as convenient, he granted me a free pardon, in consideration of which I was required not to mention the unpleasant incident in my letters to my parents (my father paid a hundred florins per quarter). I acquiesced, and so we were soon on good terms again.

But I always felt he was an egoist. He would carve the daily little piece of boiled beef just so as to give himself the particular portion which I coveted. The bread, too, was under his control: he would never take much of it at a time. but he would just cut himself little titbits, crisp corners, and knotty excrescences, until the loaf took the appearance of a dismantled wreck. He also squinted, not with that broad outside squint, ever ready to see both sides, to embrace all things, but with a narrow selfish inside squint which slid down his nose, and from there watched the focussing and absorption of the titbits with keen interest and an irritating show of gratified tastes.

And not only was the professor's field of vision thus distressingly limited, but there was also some moral obliquity in his composition. He mistook certain piles of fire-logs, which had been stocked for the use of the public school, for his own private property. When this was discovered, the authorities, happily for the professor, winked at his delinquencies with an eye to avoiding a scandal—a course they might be well justified in taking, as Justice herself is admitted to be blind.

There were two female servants to minister to our wants—two female drudges, I should say. In lieu of their real names they had been dubbed " Die grosse Biene " and " Die kleine Biene "—the great bee and the little bee—with a view, I suppose, to encouraging them in the delusion that they were not born white slaves, one large and the other small, but busy bees whose nature it was to improve the shining hour, whether it shone by the light of the day or the oil of the night.

The German language, as spoken in the Fatherland, its irregularities, vagaries, and varieties, gave me much trouble. In Hamburg I had learnt to pronounce the words " stehen " and " stossen " with a sharp and incisive *st*; in the south, all the stiffness and stubbornness was taken out of it, and I had to say " schtehe " and " schtosse." Then the words

themselves changed, and " laufen " stood for "gehen,"
"springen" for "laufen." This surprised me, as I did
not know then that the Southerner generally calls
running what the Northerner calls walking.

Titles, too, puzzled me, especially when applied
to ladies. The first time I heard the " Frau Professorin" mentioned, I looked so blank, not to say
shocked, that I evoked general mirth. (It is surprising how well one remembers the occasions when
one was laughed at.) But the " Frau Professorin "
seemed a strange creature to me in those days, and
I little thought that for many a year I was to hear
my own mother called by that title.

I had my first skirmishes with the French language too, and I certainly thought I was being
made a fool of when I was told there was no word
in French for our verb, " to stand." I had learnt
the German "stehen" and the ditto "schtehe," and I
had conjugated every tense of the Latin " stare," and
now I refused to believe that the French language
could have a *locus standi* amongst civilised nations
without an equivalent for those words. I did not
know then how much civilisation can put up with,
and it took me a long while to overcome my mis-
trust of a language so evidently unsound at its
base.

We all know to what wearisome length an average schoolmaster can draw out a single hour, and
my teachers were no exception to the rule. Time
went slowly, as did all things fifty years ago in
Carlsruhe.

What a blessed relief it was then when a holiday

came round! Perhaps it was when we were liberated in honour of our glorious Grand-Duke's birthday, perhaps when we were to join in the commemoration of some great deed or greater misdeed of one of his ancestors, or perhaps—best of all—when once or twice Mother Earth was clad in so much loveliness, that it was just impossible to keep masters and boys indoors, dissecting dead languages and putting historical bones together. Nature herself seemed to proclaim a free pardon for us prisoners and for our warders : off we went all together to the woods.

How we ran and shouted when we got into those avenues of trees behind the Grand-Ducal Palace, how madly we raced, how heroically we fought the boys we hated, and how solemnly we swore eternal friendship with the ones we loved! We climbed trees, cut sticks, and did what little harm we could to exuberant prolific Nature ; we chased butterflies and deprived spiders of their legitimate prey, and then— selfish little lords of creation that we were—we settled down where the grass grew thickest, to discuss large haunches of bread and red-cheeked apples, and to crack nuts and jokes in true schoolboy fashion.

The masters forgot for the while that they were German professors, with spectacles on their noses and Latin quotations on their lips. They were just human, and felt themselves as much at home in the woods as we did, gratefully inhaling the same balmy air, and greedily swallowing the same glittering dust. They knew something, too, to tell us about God's creation, and in those blessed hours taught us wonderful and beautiful things that stirred our little souls, and made us glad to live and wonder and worship.

Oscar—I have forgotten his surname—was not a professor, and did not even wear spectacles, but he was a sort of monitor, had long silky eyelashes, and he certainly was in love. He never told me so, but I am sure he was, and remembering him and his eyelashes as I do, I can easily reconstruct the simple story of his love. She was a Gretchen, a sweet German maiden, blue-eyed and golden-haired. They first met at a Kränzchen where their feet waltzed to the same step and their hearts beat to the same tune. Then on two ever-to-be-remembered Sunday afternoons they took coffee together in the " Restauration zum blauen Stern," and on the second occasion, as they were going home through the pine-woods, he said something to her she had never heard before ; her answer was inaudible, but I know she left her hand where he wanted it to remain, and the good old moon did the rest. They soon received the paternal and maternal blessings, and now they were happy in the knowledge that in six or eight years nothing would stand between them and their fondest hopes, when he probably would have passed his examinations and have secured his first appointment.

I must have caught the loving mood from Oscar, or else some wood-nymphs or sprites must have been trying their hands on me, or perhaps I was only tired and lagged behind. Certain it is that a new sort of feeling came over me, a semi-conscious yearning for an unknown quantity that was waiting for me somewhere ; and as I lay on my back under the trees, my imagination shot upwards, starting from the gnarled roots by my side, along the mast-like perpendiculars the pines, past jolly little squirrels, patches of moss and garlands of creepers, right to the top where the sky's blue eyes were winking at me.   Nature was whispering some secret and I was dreaming my first Midsummer-Day's Dream.

All around there was humming and buzzing, piping and singing ; mysterious sounds, joyous notes, and pensive ditties.   Some bird with a flute-like voice sang a pretty little musical phrase, just a bar of five or six notes, and kept on repeating it at intervals.   Another little bird, deep down in the forest, answered it—birds of a feather flirt together —only there were so many chirping chatterboxes about, enjoying themselves in their way, that the warbling flirtation was carried on under difficulties. For all that, the flute-like voice never tired of saying its say, and putting its question, pleased as it evidently was with its mate's reply.   I dare say it knew a good deal better than I did at the time what it was all about, and what was the grand and glorious answer inexhaustible Nature held in store for it.

For my part, I gazed upward at the patches of ultramarine, and longed for them, but it was not till years afterwards that they vouchsafed to come down. Then, when they took the shape of a pair of real blue eyes, it all dawned upon me, and I knew what Nature had been whispering, and understood that stately pine-forests, jolly little squirrels, and loving little birds, were only created to guide and direct good little boys to realms of joy and happiness. :—

Whilst I was sitting on school-forms puzzling over nouns and verbs, or lying on the grass communing with the birds, things were happening in my London home that were once more to lead to a change in my surroundings.

Another pleasant day-dream, one that my father and his friend Mendelssohn had for some time past been indulging in, was about to be realised. The frequent correspondence between them, delightful as it was, the exchange of views, musical and personal, and the occasional meetings in England or Germany, had only more saliently brought out the points in favour of a long-cherished scheme which should enable them to live and work together in the same town.

Mendelssohn had for some time been planning the formation of a School of Music in Leipsic, and his letters of this period are full of the warmest and most eloquent appeals to my father to give up his position in England, and to take up his residence in Leipsic. The outcome of it was, that the Conservatorio in that city was founded, and that my father was offered a professorship. In answer to his assumption that Mendelssohn would act as director, the latter answers: " I am not, and never shall be the director of the school. I stand in precisely the same kind of position that it is hoped you may occupy. The duties of my department are the reading of compositions, &c., and as I was one of the founders of the school, and am acquainted with its weak points, I lend a hand here and there until we are more firmly established."

In the summer of 1846 my father migrated to Leipsic. He gave up his brilliant position in London, and, actuated by the love of his art and his desire to be in daily touch with Mendelssohn, he had no hesitation in accepting a salary of 800 thalers (£120) per annum. In a letter to a relative he speaks of the dear and kind friends he leaves behind. "Parting from them individually," he says, "and indeed from the English nation generally, will cost us a bitter pang, for twenty-four years of unswerving kindness have laid upon us obligations which we can only pay with life-long gratitude."

And Mendelssohn wrote: "How could I tell you what it is to me, when I think you are really coming, that you are going to live here for good, you and yours, and that what seemed a castle in the air is about to become a tangible reality; that we shall be together, not merely to run through the dissipations of a season, but to enjoy an intimate and uninterrupted intercourse! I shall have a few houses painted rose-colour as soon as you really are within our walls. But it needs not that; your arrival alone will give the whole place a new complexion."

Not by such words only, but most practically did Mendelssohn show his friendship. With the precision of a courier and the foresight of a brother, he goes into the minutest details of the cost of living in the German city: "A flat, consisting of seven or eight rooms, with kitchen and appurtenances, varies from 300 to 350 thalers (£45 to £50). For that sum it should be cheerful ; and, as regards the situation, should leave nothing to be desired. Servants would cost 100 to 110 thalers per annum (£15 to £16, 10s.), all depending, to be sure, on what you would require. Male servants are not much in demand here, their wages varying from 3 to 12 thalers per month (9s. to £1, 16s.). A good cook gets 40 thalers a year (£6), a housemaid 32 (£5). If you add to these a lady's-maid who could sew and make dresses, you would reach about the above-mentioned figure. Wood—that is fuel for kitchen, stoves, &c.—is dear, and may amount to 150 or 200 thalers (£22, 10s. to £18) for a family of five with servants. Rates and taxes are next to nothing ; eight or ten thalers a year would cover all."

Those were indeed the good old times, when the Fatherland was not yet weighed down by blood-and-iron taxes. The most gifted member of the International Arbitration and Peace Association could not speak more eloquently than do those figures. A family of five with servants ; 24s. to 30s. a year would cover all rates and taxes !

Soon, then, the suitable flat was found and my father migrated to Leipsic, entered on his new duties at the Conservatorio, and became a good citizen and ratepayer. The "intimate and uninterrupted intercourse" became a reality, and there was scarcely a day when the Mendelssohns and Moscheles did not meet. They could not do without me, however (remember I was an only son, and a well-beloved godson), so I was recalled and soon left Carlsruhe, I am afraid, with a wicked sense of ingratitude for all the care bestowed on me by Professor Schummelig and my other teachers.

It was terribly cold that winter, and travelling was fraught with difficulties, if not with dangers. Our diligence was a heavy one, and when it got stuck fast in the drifting snow, as it did more than once, the passengers had to get out, whether it was by day or by night, and literally put their shoulders to the wheel. It was only thanks to a very kind and provident "conducteur," that my much-tried little spark of vitality was preserved. He kept a never-to-be-forgotten straw-plaited brandy flask suspended from his neck by a green cord, and when my spirits flagged, his did good office.

It was midnight a day or two before Christmas when we arrived at the "Post" in Leipsic. My luggage was put on a diminutive sledge and dragged along the snow-bound street, I running by its side to keep body and soul together. Nobody knows till he has tried it how hot a run in the bitter cold can make one, particularly when one's heart beats at the thought of a welcome, and one's mind is all ablaze with the brilliant images of those one loves. There I was at last in the new home and folded in the old embrace.

Once settled, the question soon arose what was to be done with me next, and a decision was come to, to send me for a short time to the Bau Schule (School of Architecture). Those wooden bricks of my early boyhood, and the table with the many compartments, had gone the way of all good bricks and tables, but my love for architecture remained, and I now sometimes regret that I was not to continue my studies in that direction till I had had the regular classical education ; but so it was. By the time I had learnt how to stretch a sheet of paper on a drawing-board, and how to handle the compasses and T-square, and just when I was getting to know something about the price of tiles and the mixing of mortar, I left the Bau Schule, and was entered at the Thomas Schule. That was a famous old institution. The whole upper storey of the school was occupied by a number of free pupils, the "Thomaner" choir-boys. They were celebrated throughout Germany as the best singers of sacred music, trained as they had originally been by no less a master than Johann Sebastian Bach, the famous "Cantor." His rooms in that building were now occupied by his successor, Hauptmann, who knew how to maintain the highest standard of excellence in his pupils. He was a man of learning and an erudite musician, and as such, one of the pillars of strength on which rested Leipsic's reputation, that city standing quite unrivalled as the centre towards which all musical aspirants gravitated.

He spoke little ; but when he did, it was to say much. His criticisms could be severe, as when a new orchestral piece was being rehearsed, he said, "That sounds quite Mendelssohnian, it must be by Sterndale Bennett."

His boys sang on many occasions—at church, at weddings, funerals, or birthdays. I made great friends with some of them, and formed a regular class to teach them English; but although they were very willing pupils, I did not obtain as brilliant results in my line, as my predecessor, Johann Sebastian Bach, had achieved in his.

Herr Magister Hohlfeld, the Professor of Mathematics, was a wonderful old man—how old no one knew. He was a figure that belonged to the middle of the last century. Clad in a long grey cloth coat, which reached to his feet, he looked a curious relic of bygone times; cares and calculations, worldly and scientific, had worked deep furrows all over his lofty forehead, and had left their impress on every feature. A rich crop of white hair fell over his shoulders; his hands on his back, and his head slightly bent down, he would solemnly address the boards he was treading, as he paced up and down between the two lines of school-benches; it was given to few of us to catch the words of mathematical wisdom that fell from his lips.

"The Frenchman" was another figure I look back to with interest. Not that there was anything remarkable in his appearance, but that, when judiciously roused to anger, he would never fail to make a fool of himself. He was not a Frenchman, but a German born and bred, who taught French, and happily for us he was so constituted, that it was a real pleasure, unchecked by any fear of possible consequences, to take advantage of his weaknesses. We did so, exercising our indiscretion whenever we had a chance. A good opportunity presented itself during the cherry season. We paved the particular part of the class-room he was in the habit of promenading, with bad intentions in the shape of cherry-stones. After the first few steps he had taken, he stopped short, indignantly apostrophising us. " I tell you, boys, it's just a piece of impudence when the master treads on cherry-stones." We thought so, too, and howled with delight. At that time I had a beautiful big dog named Hector, and one afternoon I thought it might prove effective if I entered the class-room with him when the French lesson had begun. I did so, to the terror of " the Frenchman," on whom Hector had at once made a friendly rush. The dog was expelled, and then I was severely taken to task. " Ah," said the Professor, " you think you can take liberties with me, but I tell you, sir, you can't take liberties with such a big dog."

But it must not be thought that I was always worrying poor innocent Magisters, and rejoicing in their discomfiture ; some of my teachers I think of with gratitude. There was Stallbaum, the rector himself a great man of learning : he took great pains to cram us with our full share of Latin and Greek, and to make us periodically contribute to the wealth of the classical literature handed down to us, by writing essays and composing verses in the dead languages.

The love of fighting was early instilled into us by the works of Homer, Herodotus, Julius Cæsar, and other historians ; and if, as some think, my pugnacious instincts have not been satisfactorily developed, it was not the fault of the Rector. But he taught me to revere that grandest and most powerful of tragedians, Sophocles.

Nor must I forget to mention the lasting impression that Ovid's "Metamorphoses" made on me. The gods of mythology have ever remained dear to me; they are so accessible, so free and easy as they come down from Olympus quite unceremoniously, to roam about and make love; you meet them in the woods and on the waters, above ground and below ground, sometimes enjoying themselves at your expense, but mostly showing you, by their example, how you should enjoy life. To be sure the methods of a Jupiter or a Venus are quite inapplicable to the social restrictions, and generally to the changed conditions of the present day, but they were dear old gods and goddesses all the same, who condescended to be human, and sanctified our frailties. I, for one, am grateful to them, for they taught me the love of poetry and the poetry of love.

My first drawing-master, Herr Brauer, was a good old soul too : I owe him one of the foremost pleasures of my life, the exercise of my profession as a painter. His own work, although very clever in its way, was niggling and minute, but his ideas and teachings were broad, and whilst encouraging a taste for form which had made the study of architecture so attractive to me, he knew how to awaken a love of colour, that was eventually to lead me to the sister art.

The old masters, too, had their full share in making me long to paint. There was a certain picture by Murillo, a Madonna and Child, in the Schletter Collection which afterwards formed the nucleus of the Leipsic Picture Gallery; that picture so filled my imagination that I was fired by the desire to go forth and do likewise.

I have since frequently found that that kind of *anch'io* feeling is by no means confined to those in whom it would be justifiable. In a masterpiece the artist betrays no effort; all looks so easy that one fancies it *is* easy. The lines of the composition flow so naturally, the colours strike so complete a chord, that one is deluded into the belief that it could not be otherwise, and that it is just what one would have done oneself had one been in the painter's place. So I was gradually settling in my mind that, as soon as I had passed my Abiturienten Examen (equivalent to our matriculation), I would, without much delay, begin to paint like the old masters.

Of Mendelssohn and the many friends, musical and otherwise, who made my stay, and later on my visits to Leipsic, interesting, I must speak afterwards. But an incident which has left a lasting impression on my mind, finds its place here, as being connected partly with my school-days and partly with my art studies.

 well remember, and I shall ever remember with gratitude, the man who in my German school-days helped me along the thorny paths of the Latin and Greek grammar, Herr Magister Dr. Traumann. I suppose I got into trouble, as much as any boy of sixteen, with the so-called regular, and those disgracefully irregular, verbs the old Greeks tolerated. But Dr. Traumann was always kind and helpful; in fact, he was not only a first-rate teacher but a lovable man. I had, soon after my arrival in Leipsic, been put under his care, and thanks to his coaching, I got so well ahead of myself, that although my scholastic antecedents would really have fitted me more for the "Tertia" class, I could be pitchforked into "Secunda."

During a temporary absence of my parents from Leipsic I was for some months staying in the Magister's house; three flights of stairs brought one to his door. I usually bounded up those stairs with the elastic step that leads to a happy home, but to-day—a certain to-day that seems but yesterday—my tread was slow and diffident. How could I face the Magister, the man above all others whom I had treated with disrespect—I had libelled! What reception awaited me? Whether I took two steps at a time or one at half-time, the result was much the same; I got upstairs, rang the bell, and went in.

This is what had happened during the morning's lesson at the Thomas-Schule. The learned doctor was expounding the subtle meaning of some lines in Virgil's "Æneid." I found that the top layer of the poet's meaning would do for me, but, as is the way with the erudite, Dr. Traumann went down very deep, backed by an army of commentators; in fact so deep that I did not care to follow. So I took to a more congenial occupation, and, under the cover of a friendly desk, I began to compose what seemed to me an interesting subject. How long I was about it, I do not know. The Doctor had walked up and down dozens of times between the forms, when suddenly a hand reached behind the desk and quietly annexed and pocketed the composition. The hand was the Doctor's. He walked on quite unconcernedly, prodding and probing old Virgil's defunct thoughts as before. And all the while he had that wicked caricature of himself in his breast-pocket, and presently he would see it and read the legend that relegated him and the commentators to the Dantesque depths of their own seeking.

I was eating a green apple, to give myself courage, when the Magister came in. What would he say? How would he take it? Well—he took it just as if nothing had happened, and smiling pleasantly, he said, "Look here, Felix, I have got a splendid specimen to show you," and with that, he fumbled in his pocket and produced a small piece of quartz. "I have got another piece, so you can have this for your collection."

"Oh, thank you, Herr Magister," I said; "I am sure you are too kind. I—I don't deserve it."

He cut me short with: "Not at all, my boy; we are just on a footing of exchange. 'Eine Hand wäscht die andere,' as the proverb says."

What has become of my minerals I don't know, but to this day I often think, soap in hand, of the proverb that says, "One hand washes the other." As for the caricature, he never said anything about it, but I know now he treasured it and loved me all the more for being a bad one.

If he was kind, she was still kinder; she, the Frau Magisterin. I had by this time got initiated into the mysteries of German usage as regards the participation of the wife in her husband's titular advantages. Without an effort I could address Frau Schmidt as Mrs. Lettercarrieress, or Frau Müller as Madame Chimneysweeperess. So the "Frau Magisterin" came quite naturally to me. She called me "Mein Lixchen," a tender variation on my name. In fact, tenderness prevailed between her and me from first to last, maternal on her side, filial on mine. She was under middle size and of slight build; her bright little eyes, beaming with benevolence, attracted you so much that you saw but little else in her face. Everything was small about her. A tight-fitting cap hid the best part of her hair, and the plain dress without puffs or ruffles, or any of the other digressions dictated by the fashions of the day, seemed to make everything else subordinate to the love - beaming eyes. She was then in the prime of life. When I last saw her she was an old lady of fourscore years, and her dear little face had become so very small, that, although I am sure I did not mean to be irreverent in my thoughts, I could not help being reminded of the immortal Cheshire cat, that vanished leaving naught behind but a smile. Time, I felt, might deal with her as is its wont, contract here and pinch there, lay out in folds and wrinkles what were round and smooth surfaces; but that particular twinkle that goes straight to the heart, the smile of the eye, would ever remain intact.

The Magister and his wife were a truly happy and devoted couple, and closely wound around their hearts were Bella and Frida, their two daughters; one was about sixteen, the other fourteen, at the time I was staying with them, good girls and pretty, with brown hair inclined to curl on Bella's head, very smooth and Priscilla-like on Frida's. With a view to securing for them the best possible education under the maternal eye, classes had been formed at their home, and consequently a bevy of young girls came up and went down those three flights of stairs on certain days and at given hours. I was always interested in curious coincidences, and so, to bring them about, I frequently found myself in the way at the given hours. On such occasions I tried to look unconcerned, or surprised at the meeting, but unfortunately I was yet too honest and truthful, so I signally failed and blushed like a girl. Not like those girls though; they didn't seem to blush, the little fiends. With the exception of just one, they tittered right over the banisters, whispered, and shook locks and dangled satchels until I was quite discomfited. I suppose they thought it rich fun, for they knew, long before I was aware of it myself, that I was desperately in love with Helene. It was the tittering, I am sure, that finally put me on the track, and the whispering that opened my eyes to the blindness I was stricken with. That was one day when those rosy, mischievous, young amorettes must have said something particularly unkind to their sister, for she bounded past me and her tormentors, like a deer, to get rid of the lot of us. After this I felt an ever-growing desire to see Helene, but took a dislike to the staircase as a meeting-place.

About this time, as luck would have it, I came across her two brothers, fair chubby boys about my age. We struck up a sort of friendship, and I took care the sort should be improved upon, interested as I was in securing their good-will. It was, above all, important to get reliable information as to where and when *she* could be met out skating, and my new friends, I found, were particularly sympathetic and communicative when under the influence of a certain kind of "apfelkuchen," an open apple tart, dispensed on most advantageous terms in the Barfussgässchen. There the Frau Bakermistress often had to open for

me a little shutter in a shutter and hand out, on
a piece of newspaper, large segments of the Kuchen,
bidding it God-speed with a parting jerk of the per-
forated tin sugar-box.   Perhaps to show that there
was no bribery or corruption in my standing treat, and,
perhaps too, as one's appetite at the age of sixteen
is rather stimulated than blunted by love, I took my
fair share of the segments.   These symposia led, in
the most natural of ways, to our making appoint-
ments to meet on this or that frozen pond or river,
and I was sure to be punctual, knowing as I did,
from information received, that Helene would be
there.   More than once I skated along that narrow
river, the Pleisse, for miles, pushing before me the
" Stuhlschlitten," with its precious many - locked
burden.   Helene was comfortably ensconced in that
elementary specimen of a sledge, a sort of easy-chair
on skates, and was wrapped up in furs and covers,
every inch of her carefully protected, excepting her
little nose and lips, which would get linked to her
veil by cobweb threads of ice, as King Frost welcomed her cherished breath.   And didn't his Majesty
just rule supreme that year !

I may have been a fair example of a boy lover,
but I fear a diary which I kept and have preserved
goes far to prove that I was a most precocious—you
might call it priggish—young meteorologist, making
his observations with pedantic regularity, morn, noon,
and night, on thermometer and ombrometer, and
publishing the results in his own name with the
proud prefix of " Herr Gymnasiast."   We often hear
of exceptional winters, but the one I speak of beats

the record. Siberian cold visited us all through January; on the 21st of that month I find noted:

8 A.M.	12.M.	10.P.M.
− 19.7	− 14.2	− 21.4 Réaumur;
equal to 35,	26, and	39 degrees Fahrenheit below freezing-point.

A bitter cruel time to many;—a very Godsend to hardy skaters. I was of the latter. Off with overcoat and on we went—left, right—left, right —in long curved lines, the sledge flying ahead on the frozen waters of that puny river that had swallowed up thousands of Napoleon's followers on their retreat after the lost battle of Leipsic. On we went till we landed on the very spot where one of the last decisive encounters took place, and there we, some dozens of us, fought bravely for an adequate supply of coffee and Kaffeekuchen (you know by this time that "Kuchen" means cake, and that it meant a good deal to us in those days). In the meanwhile the girls of our fancies had time to thaw, and usually came in a melting mood to the little tables at which they would graciously accept the chivalrous attentions dear to the bread-and-butter Miss.

As for Helene, to be sure she was of the ripe age of seventeen, and I had a sort of feeling that she would expect me to speak to her parents if I had anything definite to say. Till then the indefinite would do, and she made it quite easy to me to say all I wanted in that deliciously tentative way that marks our first attempts at disguising our feelings, whilst we are burning to proclaim them. It was all smooth sailing as long as I only had to minister to her creature wants, and I got as far as—

"O Fräulein, you must come out every Sunday; I do hope you will."

But when I wanted to explain that this my wish was mainly owing to the fact that her hair started in most fascinating wavelets from her temples, there was a kind of barrier that arose to stop me, a halo that came in the way to form a magic circle into which I could not penetrate. I wanted to say something about Helen of Troy, but I did not know what conclusion to draw from her history, and besides it would sound so foolish and priggish. So I said nothing about her, and by the time we got up to return home, I had not done much to improve the opportunity.

Our skates were once more firmly secured to our feet, and our young ladies comfortably settled in their Stuhlschlitten. We all started together, but soon we broke the ranks, each one taking his own time. I was in a mood to go ahead and struck out at full speed. In fact it was not long before I was dashing past another sledge at such a close-shaving pace that Helene gave a start and a little cry of "Ach, don't, Herr Felix, please don't." But I was reckless and only went at a madder pace. She was in my grip; I had her to myself right away from the other boys. How I triumphed over them all! What did they know about love? With them it was all giggling and window parade, and meeting on the Promenade, and doffing caps, and then taking a short cut, to meet again and have another chance of cap-doffing. To be sure I had done all that kind of thing myself, but I was much too full of the present to think of the past.

She was mine; I held her in my—or at least my sledge held her in its—arms; it was the most glorious consummation of my wishes. I had carried her off into some new atmosphere, that did all the propelling automatically, some new element where weight counted for nothing. So on I went. Danger! Nonsense, there was none. I had got my treasure well in hand. Never mind if she fancied there was danger and was nervous; all the better if she was right. Was not I there to save and to protect her?

Such a swing round to get out of the way of that lumbering skater, hanging on to a sledge with a woman and two children. No, I certainly wouldn't dig my heel into the ice and pull up.

"Ach, don't, please don't, Herr Felix," she cried; "I'm sure there'll be an accident."

"Don't be afraid, please don't, Fräulein Helene," I rejoined; "can't you trust yourself to me?"

"Oh yes, yes, but really, please, do stop, *dear* Herr Felix."

I slackened a little as I said, "Why *do* you always call me Herr? It does sound so formal."

"Well, isn't that the right thing?" she answered. "You only call children by their Christian names. Don't grown-up people always call one another Herr, or Frau, or Fräulein?"

"Not always; you don't call Julius, Herr Julius."

"To be sure not, you silly; who is Julius? He is only my cousin."

"That's just so unfair. He's a benighted ass, who, I'll be bound, doesn't know the colour of your eyes, or which side the dimple is, and you treat him better than those who do—(a pause)—yes, who do—who do quite well."

"Oh, I hate my dimple ; my brothers are always worrying me about it."

"I'll stop that, but you must drop the Herr."

"No, I certainly *won't*. Do you want to be a child ?"

"No, Helene, you are the child and I am the man ; that I will show you "——

And with that I started off again viciously.

"Ach, Herr Felix—no, I mean Felix, I didn't say I wouldn't."

Another diabolic spurt that made the sledge twist and quiver. She clutched its wooden sides for safety, and cried out to the young fiend behind :

"I never said I wouldn't, Felix ; do please stop—Felix—dear Felix."

This time my heel went deep into the ice, grinding out its order to pull up. In a moment I was round to the front, on my knees to pick up one of the rugs that had got loose and was dragging. The footstool was half off, and poor Helene's little feet were exposed to the biting frost. They were just lumps of ice, and I felt very guilty, for it was all my zigzagging and swinging about that had done it. "Wait a minute, I know what will warm them in no time. My fur gloves are the very thing."

And with that I popped one foot into each glove, and gave her the cord to hold that connected both, and that was usually slung round my neck."

"Oh, that is glorious!" she said, as the heat from *my* gloves, my heat, passed into her veins. "You are too kind, dear Mr. . . . I mean, my dear Felix. But you will want them yourself. You must take them back."

"Nonsense," I answered, as I tightened the gloves round her feet and tucked her up with the rug that had kindly played truant.

"But I am sure you will get your fingers frost-bitten."

"Not likely; you just look out they don't set the back of your sledge on fire."

And with that we started at a moderate pace. I was in no hurry to get home, and in fact we had to give the rest of the party time to come up with us.

Fancy having to sit down and prepare for to-morrow's mathematics and Virgil after that! This time I was one of the commentators, and marginal notes in the shape of initials and scribbled profiles got in where they shouldn't.

But on the whole I did not find that the new development interfered with my studies. It was rather the other way, for I felt it would be positively ignominious to be snubbed by a professor, a school-master. I was filled with overweening self-confidence, and fired with ambition. The things I thought and planned! Just the things you would laugh at now that you know so much about love and love-making. You shouldn't laugh! Is not the boy's first budding love the very best bit of the Creator's work, the

tenderest shoot He grafts on the old tree of life?
Nature likes to hear her own voice as it comes truly
and purely from the boy's lips, tired as she is of
man's false vows. The boy's heart holds the divine
spark of love, the same that will light the flame
of his later days, only it is minus the bacilli that
threaten to creep in, sooner or later, and crowd it
with doubt and disappointment, or poison it with
selfishness and passion. Nature, consistent as she
is, repeats her processes wherever she is at work.
For a while the rosebud remains closed, and is
safe; then it opens its unsuspecting leaves, and
in walks a wary worm and says, "This is just
the place for me." The snow falls white, even in
grimy cities—how soon to mingle with soot and dirt!
The world changes, but the fountain source of all
things remains pure; we can return to it, recuperate
and restore ourselves in its waters; there alone we
may find the mythical baths that, in olden days,
promised health and youth. Harking back, we
shall hear voices that once touched us, and may
yet guide us.

But whilst my aspirations were soaring higher and
higher, the fates were taking me and my lady-love
into their old meddlesome hands, and just shaping
our course at the dictates of their irresponsible
caprice.

A grand sledge-party had been organised for the
following Sunday,—a big affair, with a band to start
us and torches to light us home. It was a glorious
prospect, and I for one was duly excited. On Friday,
at 10 P.M., I went as usual to take the reading

of my thermometer. The mercury had risen by six degrees. I went out into the garden, consulted the wind and sniffed the air, and my meteorological soul was filled with the greatest misgivings. I felt it, I knew it; nothing could save us. The thaw had set in; there would be no band, no torches, no Helene!

Such an opportunity I was never to have again. The river that had befriended me had lost its strength, and was no more to carry her or me; soon it would flow its natural course. Thoughts alone and words remained icebound, and my hopes sank below zero. Henceforth I should meet her only on *terra firma*, and—alas!—*terra firma* was not as friendly an element as *aqua firma* had been.

The first time I saw her was about three weeks after the "My dear Felix" day. She was walking with her mother along that beautiful promenade that encircles the old city of Leipsic. On her other side was a middle-aged man—he must have been at least twenty-five—and he—oh! I could see it at a glance —was all smiles, doing the amiable. *He* was not like Julius; *he* knew which was the dimple side and had taken it.

To be sure I had to pull off my cap and salute, what they call bow and grin; but I felt like a bird with clipped wings, a string tied to its leg and fastened to a bar of its cage.

After that I did not see her for a long time. I heard she had gone to Dresden on a visit to friends. Once or twice I met her brothers, but, although I quite intended to do so, I could not summon courage to ask them who was the middle-aged man; nor did

they seem inclined to talk about him or about her.
But the truth gradually leaked out. He was the
acknowledged suitor. Soon the news came. They
were engaged. She was going to Switzerland in the
summer to meet his parents, and in the autumn they
were to be married. It was true, then : Helene had
preferred a man to a boy !

Once more I met her before she left. It was
on the Neumarkt, close to the old Gewandhaus. I
bowed stiffly and was passing on, for I had swallowed
the poker of resentment, but she stopped short
and stroked my big dog Hector, and said to him :
" *You* wish me all happiness, I am sure, don't you ?
We have been friends, and we shall always remain
friends, shan't we ? "

And as the dog didn't answer, I had to say,
" Yes, Helene, always."

And then the poker began to lose substance,
and gradually it melted away. But it was only
gradually.

It is many years ago now, but I still adhere to
my original proposition, " Helene was of a lovable
type," and I am sure Leonardo da Vinci, if no one
else, would say that I am right.

I must admit, though, that shortly after that
interview on the Neumarkt, I became painfully aware
that I was not as unhappy as I should have liked to
be. This is such a world of compensations, and they
do so flood in upon one in the spring-tide of life !
Not that I at once met with any new and revised
edition of Helene, handsomely bound ; but true
friendship came to heal the wound, and sisterly

affection to take the place of love. Bella and Frida were my friends. Bella so restful and soul-soothing, with her far-away look ; Frida so sympathetic and affectionate. They did not say much about Helene, as it was an awkward subject to discuss, but through all their tact and reticence I could plainly see that they disapproved of Helene's conduct, and thought her worldly and heartless. At that time I was much with those kind sisters, but I soon after left the Magister's house to live under the paternal roof, my parents having returned to Leipsic after a prolonged absence. But there was constant and pleasant intercourse between the two families, and my friendship with Bella and Frida flowed on peacefully and serenely, as if nothing could ever impede its progress through life.

All the while Time, in a quiet, unobtrusive way, was doing his wondrous work, taking the school-girls in hand and making young ladies of them. Pinafores had long since been relegated to the dust-hole or the paper-mills, but there were frumpy aprons to be exchanged for dainty ribbons, dresses to be elongated, and something dangling or jingling to be added before the young ladies could be considered presentable in a ball-room. And Time had done just the right thing, not scamping the work, as he will sometimes, or hurrying it and putting in touches that would come so much better a little later. So the result was that the newly developed young ladies remained young girls still, natural and unsophisticated.

And the schoolboy was being transformed too. It was noticeable that the left-hand side of his right hand middle finger-nail now rarely showed the inroads of an inky pen; a looking-glass, too, had evidently been consulted in some important matters, and the hands were observed frequently to twist and twirl some imaginary growth on the upper lip.

There is more in the eagerness with which the youth welcomes the advent of a beard than is at first apparent; he feels intuitively that the time is approaching when that mobile feature, the mouth, may possibly want a little disguise. It is easier to control the eyes, where there is an emotion to conceal, than the lips with their tell-tale quiver: they need protection. Bold indeed is the man who dares to shave, and reveal, say to a young and confiding wife, who has known him only with a beard, all that underlies the hirsute mask, thus laying bare his true nature, whatever that may be, good, bad, or indifferent. We may safely assume, I think, that under the beard she will find a man she does not know.

But all those considerations are, at best, after-thoughts. When my time came to twirl the first threads of my moustache, I suppose I did not feel anything intuitively, but greeted the badge of manliness with satisfaction. Then, to be sure, I was not going to be an actor, who wants every square inch of his face for his work, nor a priest who has nothing to conceal, nor a lawyer who is not worth his salt if he cannot conceal anything or everything. I was going to be an artist, and as such, I meant to look my part, at any rate as regards the beard.

My school-days had come to an end; some

dreaded examinations were satisfactorily passed, and I sallied forth, backed by a grandiloquent Latin document describing me as " F.S.M. Londiniensis," an " honest youth " who had never done anything " reprehensible," and who was now " omnino " worthy to be admitted to the higher universities.

Instead of accepting the advantages thus offered to me, I disposed of some of those old school-books I hated, and packed up others that I loved, in a green carpet-bag, which was adorned with a worsted-work presentment of a shepherdess tending her sheep under a very small tree. This bag was of a style much admired in the Fatherland of those days, and had been presented to me by a very dear friend. Another parting gift I much prized was a woollen comforter knitted by Bella's own hands. Thus equipped, I started for Paris. The Traumanns saw me off. They were characteristic in their parting words. The Magister said—

" *Felix qui potuit rerum cognoscere causas.* Never look at things superficially, my boy, go deeper for the cause of things."

The Magisterin said—

" Remember, mine Lixchen, wear those woollen socks and keep your feet dry."

Bella said—

" You will write, won't you ? I shall be so anxious to know all about—I mean something— about what you are doing."

Frida said—

" Ach, Felix, do see if you can't get me one of those lovely black cats they have in Paris."

What a change from Leipsic to Paris, from home to the unknown, supervision to independence ! When I speak of Paris, it must be borne in mind that it is the Paris of 1850–51, not the one we evoke when we think of the Imperial capital of later days. It was the old city with its high houses and crooked streets, with its nooks and rookeries, suggestive of revolution and barricades ; not the Paris we know with its gloriously disciplined palaces, standing shoulder to shoulder, and with its splendid military avenues that can carry conviction in the straightest and most direct of lines from the mouth of the cannon to the heart of the canaille.

The first restaurant I went into—it was a " Marchand de vins, Traiteur "—I was addressed as " Citoyen," rather a startler for a newly imported Leipsic schoolboy ; but those were the days of the Republic that had followed Louis Philippe's flight, and there was a great show of " Liberté, Égalité, Fraternité," on walls, churches, and other public buildings ; whilst, as far as I could see, everybody seemed to be just as anxious as before to be fraternally equal with his neighbour in the matter of taking liberties, and whilst Prince Louis Napoleon and his friends were looking round for a favourable opportunity to daub out the foolish words and replace them with a capital " N," protected by an imperial eagle with rather sharp claws.

The *coup d' état* came. I saw it all; first the soldiers bivouacking on the quais and in the streets, eating and drinking to their hearts' content ; then the Prince President riding across the Place de la

Concorde on a proudly prancing horse, followed at some distance by a brilliant staff of officers on more modestly prancing horses (according to the rules of etiquette), and I heard the troops shouting "Vive Napoléon! À bas la République!" and the crowd hooting "À bas Napoléon! Vive la République!" and saw the future emperor bowing impartially left and right, to the loyal and to the disloyal, and fulfilling his destiny with the imperturbable passiveness of the fatalist. He really looked the picture of Fate in the uniform of a General, and adorned with a moustache waxed to inordinate lengths and culminating in sharp points.

Then I was run in, not for shouting, but because I was with a friend who carried a stick with a lead-weighted knob. At the police-station they proceeded to "dresser procès verbal," as they call it, and we were temporarily released; that process, however, within the next few hours, got so mixed up with human blood, ashes, and brick-rubbish, for the station had been fired, that when I called a few days later there was no trace of it left. So I was never sent to Cayenne or any other penal settlement.

On the contrary, Prince Napoleon had saved France, and he could not do without me to consolidate it. Achille Fould was his Chancellor of the Exchequer, his right hand, and as Madame Achille and her sister were old friends of my parents, and had been amongst the first to welcome me into this big world, it was but natural they should now take me in hand and wish to introduce me into their particular world. So wherever golden dust was to be thrown into the eyes of the pleasure-seeking Parisian, my presence was politely requested. On my side I accepted favours with princely condescension, and got into the Tuileries, when there was a ball or a fête on, hours before other poor mortals of inferior clay. The coachman of our ministerial carriage holding a card with the injunction, " Laisser passer, s'il n'y a pas empêchement de force majeure," we had not to wait our turn in the interminable queue that stretched through Paris for miles. I might be dancing at the Tuileries one night in the same room with the Prince President, who would perhaps be walking a quadrille with the wife of the British ambassador, and the next night—there comes the other side of my life—I was accoutred in a blouse and a workman's cap, and was diving into the haunts of destitution and misery, into those privileged places where unpoetical license reigns supreme. I learnt French argot, the thieves' language, at the fountain-source, and studied political economy under Communists—some of them philosophers, some firebrands. All that, to be sure, I could not have done alone, but I had some trusty friends amongst my studio comrades who initiated me and taught me French, as according to them she should be spoke. I had to learn a poetical effusion by heart of which I just recollect the two lines—

> " Le jour viendra ou le père éclairé
> Donnera sa fille au forçat libéré."

One of the highest officials I met at the Tuileries, the type of a perfect gentleman, was the biggest scoundrel I ever came across ; whilst on the other hand, the man who more than any other taught me to love humanity, was a scoundrel whom I met in a low wineshop in the Belleville quarter, the hotbed of irresponsible revolution.

Memories are rather troublesome friends to deal with. They will not form into line after the example of the Parisian *queue*, but crowd around the pen with the cry of " Laissez passer." One ought really to have one's little brains divided into thought-tight compartments, so that one could turn on perfect gentlemen, biggest scoundrels, or would-be Emperors, without being flooded by the immortals of the Institute, or those gods of the day representing the arts and sciences, whom it was one's good fortune to have known. Some special bulkheads or barriers should be provided to restrain the lovely types of womanhood that memories evoke.

I have to get back to Bella and Frida, and tell of heavy clouds that arose to darken our path, and of how I came to draw a portrait that has left a lasting impression in my mind. So I will but cursorily mention that there were one or two of the above-named lovely types that commiserated the unlicked cub, and set themselves the difficult task of raising him, if not to their level, to within measurable distance of it. It was rather an awkward position for the cub when one of them more than usually warm-hearted and liberal, foreshadowed the bestowal of a first prize if the unlicked one proved himself an apt pupil. Of this I said something in a letter to Bella, for I occasionally remembered that she had wished me to tell her "all about—I mean something about" what I was doing. I gave the incident in a diluted form, merely hinting that the lessons might be learnt in Paris, but could be better applied elsewhere. Yes! When I come to think of it, I am sure Bella was my guiding star, shedding a ray of light just when I particularly wanted it to show me the right way.

It was now more than a twelvemonth since I had gone to Paris, and the time was drawing near when, in accordance with the good old fashion, I should spend Christmas at home. Notwithstanding all the attractions of upper and lower Paris, I had been working hard, drawing from morning to night, and sometimes from night to morning. Those were the days when a humble student might still worship at the shrine of a Vandyke or a Rembrandt, when the war-cry, " Nous avons changé tout cela," had not yet sounded, and the Messiahs of modern art were not yet busy proclaiming their newly-found truth from the house-tops, and painting there, too, lest a particle of light should get lost. So I was still quite naïvely addicted to drawing portraits by lamplight, putting in deep shadows and deeper accents, and picking out high lights on the breadths of foreheads or the tips of noses.

At last I was in the train and we were approaching Leipsic. I was thinking of parents and friends, and as I mentally rehearsed our meeting and greeting, I am sure my lips moved unconsciously, and the subtle smile of anticipation must have played around them. It was 3.30 P.M., I had travelled forty-five hours, but at last the old familiar landmarks appeared.

There was the row of poplars, the distant spire. Out came the pocket-comb—a final touch, and in a few minutes I was in my mother's arms. She had come upon the chance of my arriving by that train; time-tables did not pretend to give much information in those days. It is a long while ago, but I well remember that particular meeting and embrace. The two separate parts of one whole were re-united and were being welded together. Words had to wait. When they came—it does seem absurd—they were the most trivial ones, and rushed out buzzing like froth from the bottle. "Where's the green carpet-bag?" "I've got the parcel;" "All right, here is my passport;" "And when did you leave? to be sure, you must be hungry, poor boy;" and so on, till home was reached, where other loving arms awaited me. As we sobered down, the froth was brushed aside, the right words came, and we drank deep draughts from the phial that contains the very essence of love.

My first visit was for the Traumanns. That tailor at the corner of the Passage d'Orleans in the Palais Royal—he is there still—had made me a waistcoat of blue velvet, dotted with little yellow spots; it was of the very latest Paris fashion, and in it I went to make my call.

Once more a joyous meeting, a warm welcome. Herr Magister and the Frau Magisterin were just the same as I had left them. Frida had grown, but was little changed otherwise, just as bright and happy as ever; but Bella I could not see; she was not well. That was disappointing; I kept looking at her desk, just opposite me, with the glass inkstand on the right, and the little bust of Mendelssohn I had given her, on the left.

"Well, good-bye, Frida," I said at the door, "tell Bella she must be well by Friday; she's got to dance at least two waltzes and the cotillon with me."

Now dancing at the Tuileries is a very good thing in its way; elbowing a future emperor, and hobnobbing with a scoundrel disguised as a gentleman, are things to brag of. But it is nothing to having a dance at one's own home, with one's sisters, and one's sisters' friends, with one's friends and one's friends' sisters.

I was surprised to find several "Impériales" on the programme of our little dance, and was told that was the latest craze all over Paris. Now nothing of the kind had ever been heard of in the terpsichorean circles I had just left, so naturally I had no notion of what the step might be like. When I attempted it, however, it mattered little whether I danced it correctly or not, for, coming straight as I did from the French capital, I was supposed to know all about it; so the good Leipsickers soon adopted my rendering, and my step became the fashion.

I wanted those two waltzes and the cotillon because Bella was the best dancer in Leipsic. She must have been born under the star of rhythm; some fairy must have beaten time with a magic wand, pronouncing a *One*-two-three, *One*-two-three blessing upon her. One would never have imagined that that reserved girl, with the far-away look, was the queen of the ballroom; true, her figure was perfect, but it was not till she waltzed that its

F

graceful and subtle lines revealed themselves. Curiously the far-away look never left her when dancing; she seemed to be undulating towards some distant goal, wherever that might be.

How few fairies there are to beat time at the baby's cradle ! and is it not curious how seldom they go to the little boys ? Dancing humanity has had to invent the valse à deux temps, that bids us close our ears to the strains of the syren, Strauss, and take two steps where there should be three. Perhaps there is some malignant fairy to visit the cradles of the little boys. One would think so, to judge by the expressions on the faces of many dancers, expressions varying from that of painful uneasiness to that of abject misery. Poor souls ! Some rushing wildly to destruction, others doomed to crawl out their ballroom existence, gravitating within the narrow circle of the chandelier !

*   *   *   *   *   *

Friday came, and the ball.

But I have nothing to tell about it. Bella was not there. No, Bella could not be there—she was ill.

Ill—then very ill—dangerously ill. Soon she was dead !

It all came so rapidly, it must be told rapidly, breathlessly.

When ? How ?—She died on Sunday night at eleven o'clock—It can't be true !—It was true.

How incredulous we are when first called upon to realise the truth ! how slow to understand and believe that what was but yesterday a living form must be accounted dead to-day! Anguish rises rebellious: It cannot be.—It is a dream, a grievous mistake, to be explained away presently. Love's giant strength would wrench its victim from death's grasp. Hope, the very last to yield—or is it but an afterglow of hope?—will catch at shadowy straws, ere it submits and sinks to rise no more.

None but the father, mother, and sister were at the bedside when the young life ebbed away. Poor tortured souls! May they be strong enough to bear the heavy trial. That night the father never shed a tear, nor the next day, nor the next. It would have been better had grief found a natural channel. He spoke but little, and mostly sat by the bed as if in deep thought, until they carried her away.

The white wreaths had come,—and the black hearse; and graceful lilies, their long stems bound together with white ribbons. Black crapes too, and sable hues, to harmonise with a world of sorrow and darkness.

Then the blinds went up, and the world went on as before. I looked out of the window; I recollect a boy's cap had got cast adrift on the branch of a tree just opposite the house of sadness; a little crowd had collected to do justice to the incident. "Would it get off, or gradually perish where it hung?" was the question of paramount interest to that particular little world.

But does the world really go on as before? Not quite. A fraction of our globe has been disturbed, a balance lost. The blow that struck down one brother or sister wounds many hearts, reverberates in circles small or large, and it will take time to restore that fraction's equilibrium. It is as when we break the peaceful surface of the water. First a thud, a gash; next a circle, small, but broken and restless; then a larger one and a larger, each and all gradually calming down to be at rest, with the smooth untroubled waters beyond.

When a link in the chain of existences, near and dear to us, is snapped asunder, we instinctively seek to close up the gap, to join hands and succour one another. So Frida's heart went out to her father as he sat brooding, with his eyes fixed on the desk with the little bust. It was not till much later that I knew what she had suffered. She wished to throw her arms round his neck and cry her little aching heart out, and love him with her dead sister's love and her own, and let him cry too, that love and sorrow could mingle. But he sat there, so forbidding, so strange, that her arms fell, and her tears flowed back to the aching heart. Then she went up to him and stood by his side. The word "father" quivered on her lips; she knew not why, but she dared not pronounce it. Her mother came in and stood waiting too, hoping he would turn round, but he did not move. "Dearest mine," she said, "speak to Frida."

He lifted his head slowly, as if it were a great weight, his lips moved with an effort, and looking vacantly at his poor love-seeking child, he said, "Never, never!"

Days passed, and melancholy settled deeper and

deeper on the sufferer. He would occasionally show something of the old tenderness for his wife, and sometimes a spark of gratitude would for moments light up the darkness of his moods. But mostly he sat brooding, prostrate, heart-stricken. If she spoke to him of Frida he would wave his hand as if to beg her to forbear, and would keep on repeating to himself the words, " Never, never!"

She had insisted one day; she had hoped to break the spell, when he rose angrily, he the mildest of men. "Never, never mention her name to me again," he said sternly, then, gradually recovering himself, he returned to his seat and relapsed into silence.

The well-known physician and psychologist, Dr. Reclam, was in daily attendance on the patient. He was an old friend of the Magister's, and put heart and soul into the task of restoring him to health. He had said, " No, she must not show herself for the present, it would be to no purpose ; but you must not let a day pass without mentioning her name in some way or other ; we must not allow the blight to settle upon him undisturbed." Soon he advised change of air and surroundings. So the Magister and his wife left for Sonnenthal, a place far away in the country, where a cousin of his owned a large farm. He had spent part of his childhood there, and it was hoped that early associations, and the soothing influence of some old trusted servants who would be around him, might go far to restore his mind to peace and rest.

Frida remained in Leipsic ; she left the darkened

home, and went to stay with an uncle, a well-known lawyer. He was a good man at heart, but one of those whose hearts lie so deeply hidden away that there is no getting at them. He had a boy we all hated; his heart-strings must have been hopelessly knotted and tangled, or he would never have tortured that poor kitten as he did. With the assistance of his friend, the carpenter's son, he— But no, I will not tell, for I am firmly convinced that the very mention of evil begets evil. Such is man; moulded perhaps after the Divine image in some respects, he has in his composition quite as much of his brother beasts as of divinity. Curious lord of creation! As if there were not enough misery in the world as it is, he must needs go out of his way to torture kittens.

In this crisis of her life Frida found two friends, absolutely devoted and sympathetic : Helene and her husband. They, more than anybody, helped her through those first sad weeks. How mistaken the girls had been when they thought Helene worldly and heartless. My little flirt was then, and has proved herself through life, the most steadfast and reliable of us all. Her two brothers, the chubby boys, were now students at the Leipsic University, qualifying themselves for future town-councillorships and civic honours, coupled, I presume, with some German substitute for turtle soup.

Frida spent much of her time in the congenial atmosphere of my parents' house. We had always been devoted to her; how much more now! She loved music, and that, with us, was a sort of staple commodity to be found as surely as the daily bread.

It was not an easy task to divert her thoughts from her trouble. All her girlish brightness had vanished, and she seemed, without a warning, to have had womanhood, suffering womanhood, thrust upon her. But she loved to be soothed by music, and more than once I remember my father improvising strains of consolation on his grand Erard, that seemed to go straight to her heart and strengthen her.

"Will you sit for me, Frida?" I asked one evening. "I should like to draw a portrait of you."

I had known Frida for four or five years, and had never asked her to sit, so the question surprised her, and it startled my mother, who was seated at the other end of the drawing-room on a little raised platform, surrounded by palms and a variety of plants with curiously shaped and fancifully speckled leaves. Her spinning-wheel, that had been going round with the regularity of clockwork, suddenly stopped—perhaps the thread had snapped. Catching my eye she reproachfully signalled behind Frida's back: "How can you, my dear? Surely this is not the time to use the poor girl as a model?" Frida evidently thought so too; she was at a loss for an answer, and there was an awkward silence. For an instant I wished I had not spoken; my request, I felt, was really ill timed; but, once out, I adhered to it, insisting, "Do, Frida; if nothing else, it will keep me out of mischief this evening."

She knew the thought of mischief was far from my mind, and she simply answered:

"Very well, Felix, if you wish it, I will sit." And with that she gave me an encouraging look.

I was anxious to get her to sit, for a picture of that girl in her sadness had gradually been ripening in my mind; it was so complete that it seemed only to want putting down, and no more difficult of accomplishment than the writing out of any lines that I might have learnt by heart. It was a case of "Don't begin till it's finished." That I have often since found a good maxim, but one not so easily lived up to. The picture, then, such as I had conceived it, I was wedded to, for better or for worse. I must draw her all but full-face. The light from above, and slightly from the left, will model and bring out the delicate beauty of her features. It was all ready to be transcribed: the smooth hair with the black ribbon tied in a large symmetrical bow on the top of the head, the plain dress, the background, and, above all, that expression, reflecting the yearnings of a poor chilled soul. On the surface, bewilderment, helplessness; beneath, a substratum of trust, of faith; and far below, hope, the spark of life that glimmers and glows on, even under mountains of despair.

We got the lamp that had served my purpose more than once, and the two candles, with the little special shades I had brought from Paris (I have them still), and Frida sat. Not once, but often, for the more I drew the more I was eager to pursue that will-o'-the-wisp, the realisation of an idea. Many a time I had to point my crayons, Conté No. 2, and to blacken the little paper stumps, the classical tortillons, before I could make up my mind to admit that I had finished.

And what was the result? Perhaps it was very poor; probably it was; certainly, if you like—but I don't want to know it if it was. I want to think it was good and true, like the knight that serves the lady. If it is an illusion, bear with me and let me keep it.

I had a grey mount put round it and a cheap little black frame; and then—may the gods forgive my presumption!—I felt as if the crayons and the humble tortillons might possibly have been working for the ends of Providence; I packed up the picture and sent it with all my love to the Magisterin.

"Try it," I said; "he may like it." And she tried it, and—to that poor little drawing of mine it was given to work a miracle—gradually, but surely, it rent asunder the veil that obscured my dear Magister's mental vision.

It was not till long afterwards that I learnt what had happened on that critical day. The Magisterin told me all as we sat on a stone bench in the garden at the back of their house. It was a hot day and the Magister was in shirt-sleeves, pruning and tending his rose-trees, perhaps removing the blight that had settled on some leaf to warp and waste it. For once in the way the good Hausfrau vouchsafed to stop knitting, and took my hand as she began :—

"Your drawing came in the morning, my Lix-chen. It was as I had fancied it, for Frida had well described it in her letters. It touched me deeply, but I could not even give a stray thought to my own feelings. 'Try it,' you had said, and a wild rush of conflicting emotions quite overcame me. How should I try it? I wished you were there, you or

Reclam, to tell me what would be best. Might it not give him a shock and do him harm? I never felt as utterly helpless as all that morning. I waited. At one o'clock he was lying on the sofa and resting; he seemed to slumber more peacefully than usual. You know he had the desk with the little Mendelssohn bust sent from Leipsic; it was the only thing he had asked for. I stood the drawing up against it. He would be sure to see it when he awoke.

"Then I sat down and prayed.

"He rose as usual and seated himself at the table. Hours passed. His face was turned away from me, but I could see his hands as they lay clasped before him. At last he got up and went to the bookcase. 'They have changed everything,' I heard him say to himself. 'Where is my Sophocles? Ah! to be sure, to be sure.'

"He sat down, but got up again directly, found paper and pen, and laid out everything, just as he used to do at the old writing-table before beginning work. He took up the pen, but he did not write; occasionally he passed the quill over his forehead. I dared not move or speak. Oh, how long the hours seemed!

"The daylight was fading. Martha came home with the cows, and old Günther made his rounds and bolted the front gate. After that all was quiet. Yes—all was quiet,—quite quiet for a while.

"Suddenly he rose. He turned round and stood still. He looked at me,—a look I knew. My heart beat fast and the clock ticked so loud.

"He looked, and, ach, mein Lixchen, he smiled

at me, just a little feeble smile, and an instant afterwards he rushed up to me and he burst into a flood
of tears as he buried his face in my lap.

"'O Hannerl, my heart's treasure, tell me:
Where is my Frida? Why is she not with me?'"

The dear old Magisterin could say no more;
tears of gratitude choked her voice. I pressed her
hand with my right, and with my left hand I brushed
away something that had got between my eyelashes.

CHAPTER III

I well remember that first year of my stay in Leipsic, when all our interests seemed to centre in the friend we were to lose so soon.

At all times I was proud of my godfather, inordinately so, perhaps, when conversation turned on the great kindness which Goethe had lavished on his young friend Felix. To know a man who had known Goethe seemed to me like knowing a man who had known Shakespeare, and I was accordingly proud of my godfather. It is not surprising that Goethe, the great dissector of human nature, should, with a few masterly touches, have portrayed the boy of twelve, and forecast the character of the man. "You know," he said to his friend Rellstab, "the doctrine of temperaments; every one has four in his composition, only in different proportions. Well, this boy, I should say, possesses the smallest possible modicum of phlegm, and the maximum of the opposite quality." Whatever that "opposite quality" was which Goethe had in his mind, it was one which kept Mendelssohn on the alert; it was the very essence of life that he was drawing on, alas! too prodigally.

Thus, of his own compositions he says in a letter to my father: "How I am to set about writing a calm and quiet piece (as you advised me to do last spring) I really do not know. All that passes through my head in the shape of pianoforte music is about as calm and quiet as Cheapside; and when I sit down to start improvising ever so quietly, it is of no use— by degrees I fall back into the old ways."

But if Goethe noted the boy's extreme sensibility, he also appreciated his sound intellect. "He is so clear-headed about his own subjects," he says, "that I must learn a great deal from him." And Mendelssohn relates how, seated at the piano, he familiarises the poet with the work of Beethoven, how the grand old man is overwhelmed by the beauties and mysteries revealed, and sits all the while in a dark corner, like a Jupiter Tonans, with his eyes flashing fire. "I felt," he says, "that this was the very Goethe of whom people will one day declare that he is not at all one person, but is made up of several smaller Goethes."

The house we lived in stood in its own grounds, and very picturesque they were; some parts delightfully kept, others still more delightfully neglected. Wild tangles blocked disused paths; weeds and creepers climbed up the legs of classical statues, and wound round their arms when they had any. There was a Kiosk too, a little museum in which had been collected relics of the great battle which had raged furiously in those grounds. It was dedicated to Prince Poniatowski, who, during the disastrous retreat of the French army, was drowned with scores of other fugitives in that rapid little stream, the Elster, which flowed at the bottom of what was in my days called "Gerhard's Garten," the same stream in which I now used to take my daily swim.

There were only two houses in that "Garten." In one of them lived the Herr Legationsrath Gerhard, our landlord, a personal friend of the great Goethe, and himself a gifted poet, and so good a scholar, that he was able to make an admirable translation of Burns's poems. The good people of Leipsic appreciated his talents, but were very angry with him because he was unmistakably a poet with an eye to business, and he charged five neugroschen (sixpence) for admission to the historical site and to the Poniatowski Kiosk.

In the other house we occupied the second floor, and on the first lived Madame Mendelssohn's sister, Madame Schunck, and her family. The ground-floor was the private residence of a wealthy wine merchant; perhaps Schmidt was his name. The latter nearly got us into very serious trouble in the days when the tide of revolution, set in motion by the French rising in 1848, had swept all over Germany, and when even the Leipsickers, usually so peaceful, were up in arms. The standard of insurrection had been raised throughout the Fatherland, dynasties were threatened, and thrones shaken. Some of the Saxon patriots had gone to help their brothers in the Austrian capital, amongst others Robert Blum, one of the most popular leaders of the democratic party. The barricade he was defending was taken, and he was made a prisoner. Popular feeling in Leipsic ran high, and when the news came that he had been tried by court-martial and shot, it reached fever heat.

Interested as I always was in the doings of man, woman, or child, especially when they had come together in the name of mischief, I was naturally anxious to watch as closely as possible the process of history-making they were about to engage in. So I was to be found where the crowd was thickest and the mob most threatening.

An indignation meeting was improvised; the more rabid fire-eaters were hoisted on some handy box, or took possession of a passing cart, from which they addressed the rioters. The Austrian rule, its Kaiser, and its leading statesmen, were held up to execration, and a shout was raised, "To the Consulate!" Sticks and stones appeared on the scene, one knew not whence, and soon we were on our way to the Consulate, where it did not take long to smash every window in the house. The arms of Austria were torn down and carried in triumph to the market-place, where they were ignominiously strung up to a lamp-post amidst yells of exultation. The mob had by this time worked itself into a frantic state of excitement, and was thirsting for action. "What next?" was the cry. "To Gerhard's Garten," shouted a voice; "let us hang Schmidt next. He bragged that he would stand a dozen of his best champagne if it were true that Blum had been shot. We'll drink it to the scoundrel's health—to his perdition—hang the dog!"

"Save the dog," was naturally my first impulse, and I ran off at full speed to give warning. I arrived in time to raise an alarm, and the place was speedily prepared to resist at least a first assault ; the massive iron gates that protected us on the river-side were closed, and the heavy wooden doors on the land-side were barred and bolted. The rioters were soon on the spot, and threatened to make matchwood of them if they were not opened. In true mediæval fashion the old Legationsrath parleyed with the enemy through a grated opening in the door, asseverating that the man wanted was not in the house or anywhere on the premises. He was so successful in his diplomatic efforts that a compromise was agreed to, and a few of the most clamorous were admitted to satisfy themselves that the object of their search was not in hiding. The wine merchant had plenty of time to escape, the crowd, baffled of its prey, moved on to seek fresh fields of action, and our house escaped with only a few panes of broken glass. As for myself, I was warmly complimented on having acted the goose and saved the Capitol.

The next day matters wore a graver aspect, and attempts were made to raise barricades. During the short conflict which ensued, a friend of ours, Herr Gontard, was shot through the heart, as from his window he was pointing a rifle at the insurgents. He was a prominent citizen, and his death created a profound sensation. When a short time afterwards I accompanied my father to the house, to inquire after the bereaved family, we were shown by the servant into the room where his master lay in the stillness of death, a service which we were expected to acknowledge by handing him the customary

"Trinkgeld," the tip which a German servant considers his due, whenever his master practises hospitality. On this occasion it was a weird entertainment we had been bidden to.

In Dresden the insurrection was of a much more serious character. Civil war raged fiercely in the streets of that capital, and the Saxon army proving insufficient to subdue the people, the assistance of the Prussians was invoked or had to be accepted.

Great was the excitement when the first batch of soldiers passed through Leipsic, but it led to no demonstration. By this time the restless spirits knew that the cause of liberty was lost. The new *Zündnadel Gewehr* just introduced into the Prussian army, a rifle that was shortly to prove its superiority in the Danish campaign, seemed a very strange-looking piece of mechanism to us. What would be the English for *Zündnadel Gewehr* I do not know, nor will I ascertain, for I object to showing an interest in lethal weapons manufactured for fratricidal purposes.

Richard Wagner's active participation in the revolutionary movement was at the time severely commented upon by many of his friends, for he had every reason to be personally grateful to the king, who, it was said, had acted very liberally towards him, and had generally distinguished and befriended him. Accounts varied as to the actual part he took in the fighting, but at any rate he had to flee the country, and took refuge first in Paris and then in Zurich.

After a prolonged conflict the barricades were

taken; from the front they had been made all but impregnable, so the Prussian troops cut themselves a road through the party walls of the adjoining houses, and attacked them in the rear; they did terrible execution, and it was once more crowned autocracy which scored a victory over struggling democracy.

When all was over, a deputation of so-called loyal subjects waited upon the King of Prussia to do homage to the victor.

" I wish all my subjects were now here before me, to do justice to my august sentiments," were the concluding words in his Majesty's answer. And the royal utterance was suitably quoted beneath a drawing published shortly afterwards, in which the king stands, fuse in hand, by the cannon, ready to fire a well-directed charge of grape-shot into the midst of his faithful subjects.

*   *   *   *   *   *

All this happened some months after Mendelssohn's death, and it was well he was spared experiences which would have made the most painful impression on his sensitive nature. Indeed, so impressionable was he, that even trifling incidents would sometimes visibly affect him, and then he could make it very trying for those who had the misfortune to incur his displeasure. He had strong likes and dislikes, and would not always take the trouble to conceal them; as on one occasion, when he very pointedly showed his dislike to Miss F., an Irish girl, who was studying at the Conservatorio in Leipsic.

I think he was prejudiced against her because she had a mass of fluffy reddish hair, which would break away from the rule of the hairpin and escape in a spirit of rebellion; just the sort of thing we admire nowadays, but that was thought positively improper then.

She once appealed to me, when my mother was reading her a homily on the wicked ways of that hair. "Now, Felix, you who have an artist's eye; is it really so dreadful?" she asked. To be sure I told her that I, for one, thought it mighty fine, and she triumphed, but I was ever after chaffed as the one who had "an artist's eye."

There were tears shed on the evening of the Pupils' concert at the Gewandhaus. When Miss F.'s turn came, it was found she had forgotten her music, and Mendelssohn, behind the scenes, was in a rage. There was an awkward pause whilst the music was being fetched and the audience was waiting, but my father called up the tuner to officiate and fill the gap, and so appearances were saved. But Mendelssohn never forgave poor Miss F.

A passage in a letter to my mother, dated September 3, 1832, I must transcribe, if only because I think it my duty to quote it as a warning to such bachelors as may be inclined to make rash vows of celibacy. Mendelssohn, who was then twenty-three, wrote of his friend Klingemann: "If Klingemann flirts, he is only doing the correct thing, and wisely too; what else are we born for? But, if he gets married, I shall just die with laughter; only fancy Klingemann a married man! But you predict it, and I know you can always tell by people's faces what they are going to say or to do. If I wanted bread at dinner, you used to say in an undertone, 'Some bread for Mr. Mendelssohn;' and perhaps your matrimonial forecast might be equally true. But on the other hand, I too am a prophet in matrimonial matters, and maintain exactly the reverse. Klingemann is, and will ever be, a Knight of the Order of Bachelors, and so shall I. Who knows but we may both wish to marry thirty years hence! But then, no girl will care to have us. Pray, cut this prophecy out of the letter before you burn it, and keep it carefully; in thirty years we shall know whether it proves correct or not."

Klingemann married in 1845, and Mendelssohn became engaged to Cécile Jeanrenaud in September 1836, just four years after his prophecy.

He writes in a very different strain shortly after his marriage :—

" All that is good," he says, " has become doubly dear to me; all that is bad, easier to put up with. Your wife must not visit my sins on Cécile; on the contrary she must be ready to like her, and to love her a little when she becomes acquainted with her. And truly my dear Cécile deserves it, and I think I need not make any appeal to your wife, but simply introduce her and say, 'This is Cécile'—the rest will follow naturally." He was right; they met the same year and became friends.

Cécile was in many respects a contrast to her husband; she was calm and reserved, where he was lively and excitable. Hers was a deeply emotional nature, but she rarely showed outwardly what moved or impressed her, whereas his emotions would ever rise to the surface, generally to overflow and find expression in words.

My father, after first meeting her in Berlin, says: " Felix's wife is very charming, very unassuming and childlike. Her mouth and nose are like Sontag's. Her way of speaking is pleasing and simple ; her German is quite that of the Frankforter. She said naïvely at dinner, ' I speak too slowly for my Felix, and he so quickly that I don't always understand him.' "

I remember thinking her exceedingly beautiful. Her appearance reminded me of a certain picture of Germania by Kaulbach ; but she was not the typical fair-haired German ; she was dark, and wore her hair not in classical waves, but according to the fashion of the day, in many ringlets.

The daily intercourse between the Mendelssohns and the Moscheles was a source of real happiness to both. They were constantly meeting to make or to discuss music, to take long walks together, or short ones along the Grimmaische Strasse to the Conservatorio. The work there was particularly congenial to my father's taste ; after the many years of feverish activity he had spent in London, Leipsic was truly a haven of rest to him, and he could well say, " I am beginning to realise my dream of emancipation from professional slavery."

Following the example of the parents, the children of the two families soon fraternised too. I recollect a very lively children's party at our house. Mendelssohn came in and joined in the games ; then he went to the piano and set us all a dancing as only the rhythm of his improvisation could. When he ended, we clamoured for more. Give any child a Mendelssohn finger and no wonder it wants the ten. We got another splendid waltz that glided into a galop, but when that too came to an end, we insatiable little tyrants would not let him get up from the piano.

"Well," he said, "if all the little girls will go down on their knees and beg and pray of me, I may be induced to give you one more dance." A circle was soon formed around him, and they had to beg hard, harder, and hardest, before he allowed himself to be softened.

David, the violinist, also belonged to the intimate circle of our friends. He had come to London in 1839 with a warm introduction from Mendelssohn, and had soon endeared himself to all of us. He was a musician of the good old kind, practising and loving music for its own sake; he was a man of high culture, ever entertaining and genial, and took special delight in smoking innumerable cigars with his friends. In one respect he was much like my father and Mendelssohn. He could not understand how anybody could get through twenty-four hours without playing some Sonata or Trio. I recollect he was quite indignant on one occasion when he was in London and was staying with Sterndale Bennett. "Would you believe it?" he said. "I have been in the house now for more than a week, and we have not once sat down to make music." Poor Sterndale Bennett, who had probably been giving his eight or ten lessons a day in London or Brighton!

Rietz, too, the conductor of the Gewandhaus Concerts, was a friend and a *music-maker* in the German sense—a musician of the highest order, and a brilliant virtuoso on the violoncello.

For Mendelssohn's birthday, the 3rd of February, we had been getting up theatricals, and great excitement prevailed amongst old and young, for all were to take part in them. I feel pretty sure that my mother had planned it all, for, amongst a good many other things, she was the family poet and playwright. The performance began with a scene acted in the Frankfort dialect by Madame Mendelssohn and her sister, Madame Schunck; then followed a charade in four parts—"Gewandhaus," the name of the famous concert hall, was the word to be illustrated.

For the first syllable, " Ge," Joachim, then sixteen years old, appeared in an eccentric wig, and played a wild Fantasia *à la* Paganini on the Ge-Saite, the G string. Then the stirring scene from " A Midsummer-Night's Dream," when Pyramus and Thisbe make love through the chink in the wall, stood for " Wand," the German for wall. The lion, I need not say, roared well.

To illustrate the third syllable " Haus," my mother had written a little domestic scene, to be acted by herself and her husband. When the curtain rose, she was discovered knitting a blue stocking, and soliloquising on the foibles of female authoresses; whereupon enter the cook. The cook was my father, and his bearing on this his first appearance in the part, his female attire, as well as his realistic get-up, so tickled Mendelssohn's fancy, that he broke into a fit of Homeric laughter; Homeric, with this reserve, that that historical outburst was not produced in a wickerwork chair, and therefore cannot have been as effective as Mendelssohn's. Under his weight the chair rocked to and fro, and creaked till one thought it must break its bonds. But it held out, and gradually found its balance; it was not till then that the cook was allowed to proceed with her part.

Finally "Gewandhaus," the complete word, was represented by all the juvenile members of the company; each of us had to blow or play some instrument of a primitive character. Joachim led with a toy violin, and I wielded the bâton, and did my best to take off the characteristic ways of my illustrious godfather. Some of my imitative faculty must have survived the dead-man period of my early days, for the wickerwork once more shook with the sympathetic laughter of its occupant, and it reached a climax when Joachim made some pointed remarks in imitation of the master.

After the performance actors and public gathered round a festive board. In the centre of the supper-table stood the birthday cake, around which burned thirty-seven candles, one for each year, according to the good old German fashion. My mother had written a few words descriptive of the year each represented—from the cradle to the piano and the conductor's desk—from his first attempt at composi-

tion, to " St. Paul," " Elijah," and the opera to come.
In the centre stood the Light of Life, that, alas! was
so soon to fail. We little dreamt that it was his last
birthday we were celebrating.

The sounds of mirth, as the chords of harmony,
were ere long to be silenced. A few months later
Mendelssohn's dearly beloved sister, Fanny Hensel,
suddenly died. It was a heavy blow from which he
never quite recovered, for the brother and sister were
bound together by the closest ties of affection, and
the most striking artistic affinities. He spent the
summer in Switzerland, but returned enfeebled in
health and depressed in spirits. "His step is less
elastic than before," says my father, "but to see him
at the piano, or to hear him talk about art and
artists, he is all life and fire."

The evening of the 8th of October was the last
I was to spend at Mendelssohn's house. He, my
father, Rietz, and David had been playing much
classical music. In the course of an animated conversation which followed, some knotty art question
arose and led to a lively discussion. Each of the
authorities present was warmly defending his own
opinion, and there seemed little prospect of an immediate agreement, when Mendelssohn, suddenly
interrupting himself in the middle of a sentence,
turned on his heel and startled me with the unexpected question—

" What is the Aoristus primus of $\tau\upsilon\pi\tau\omega$, Felix ? "
I was at that time a schoolboy in my fifteenth year,
and so, quickly recovering from my surprise, I gave
the correct answer.

"Good," said he, and off we went to supper, the knotty point being thus promptly settled.

*   *   *   *   *   *

I well remember the 9th of October of that year. From our windows we saw Mendelssohn walking slowly and languidly through the garden towards our house. As he came in, my mother inquired after his health, and he answered, "*Grau in grau*" (Grey on grey). My father suggested a walk in the Rosenthal, that beautiful park, in those days scarcely touched by the hand of the landscape gardener. Mendelssohn acquiesced listlessly. "Will you take me too?" asked my mother. "What do you say? shall we take her?" broke in Mendelssohn in his old genial manner. Well, she was taken, and so was I, or, at any rate, I went. The walk seemed to do him good; he brightened up, and was soon engaged in lively conversation. My mother said, "You have not told us enough about your last stay in London," and that started him talking of our mutual friends there. Then he gave us a graphic account of his visit to the Queen.

It will be remembered how, on a previous occasion, he had spent a delightful hour in Buckingham Palace, and was charmed with the Queen's singing of some of his songs, and struck with Prince Albert's musical talents. How, between them, the three had set to work to pick up the sheets of music which the wind had blown all over the room, before they settled down to the organ and the piano, and how Mendelssohn carried out the parrot in his cage, to the amazement of the royal servants. The pleasant incident of his last visit, which he related to us as we walked along the Rosenthal, was this. He had been once more making music with the Queen, and had been genuinely delighted with her rendering of his songs. As he was about to leave, she said—

"Now, Dr. Mendelssohn, you have given me so much pleasure; is there nothing I can do to give you pleasure?" To be sure, he answered, that he was more than amply rewarded by her Majesty's gracious reception, and by what would be a lasting remembrance of the interest she had shown in his music; but when she insisted, he said—

"Well, to speak the truth, I have a wish, and one that only your Majesty can grant."

"It is granted," she interposed.

And then he told her that nothing could give him greater pleasure than to see the nurseries and all the domestic arrangements connected with the royal children. The most consummate courtier could not have expressed a wish better calculated to please the Queen. She most cordially responded, and herself conducted him through the nurseries. Nor was the matter treated lightly; she had to show him the contents of the wardrobes and give him particulars of the service, and for the time being the two were not in the relative position of gracious sovereign and obedient servant, but rather of an experienced materfamilias and an enlightened paterfamilias, comparing notes, and giving one another points on the management of their respective children.

Mendelssohn left us about one o'clock in the most

cheerful mood. The same afternoon he was taken ill in Madame Frege's house. He had gone there to persuade her to sing in his "Elijah," which had as yet only been performed in England, and was now to be heard in Leipsic; he also wanted her advice and help in putting together a new book of his songs. I pass over the anxiety of the next weeks, the partial recovery, to be followed only by relapse and aggravated symptoms.

From the 1st of November we knew that the worst was to be feared. My parents were not often away from the house of sickness. In the morning of the fatal day, at four o'clock, I went to the Körner-strasse to get the latest news; I had to return hopeless through the dark and foggy night. Later in the day I was again for some hours in the house, but was not allowed to see the dying man. From two o'clock in the afternoon, the hour when another paralytic stroke was dreaded, he gradually began to sink. Cécile, his brother Paul, David, Schleinitz, and my father were present, when at twenty-four minutes past nine he expired with a deep sigh.

The next day Cécile wrote to my mother asking her to order the mourning for the children; she would let her know when she could see her. Some days elapsed, the funeral service had been held and the remains had been transferred to Berlin, when she wrote again asking my mother to come and to bring me. We went. Outwardly we found her calm and resigned, but one could read in her countenance that she was mortally wounded. She talked of him she had lost and showed us a deathbed drawing that his brother-in-law Hensel had made.   For a time his manuscripts remained untouched; the door of his study she kept locked.

"Not a pin, not a paper," she wrote, "could I bring myself to move from its place. That room must remain for a short time my sanctuary; those things, that music, my secret treasure."

It was with feelings of deep emotion that I entered the room when, shortly afterwards, she opened its door for me. I had asked and obtained permission to make a water-colour drawing of that study, whilst all yet stood as the master had left it. On the right was the little old-fashioned piano on which he composed so many of his great works; near the window the writing-desk he used to stand at. On the walls water-colours by his own hand—Swiss landscapes and others. On the left the busts of Goethe and Bach, placed on the bookcases which contained his valuable musical library.

Whilst I was painting, Cécile came and went. Not a sigh, not a murmur escaped her lips.

She died just four years after her husband.

CHAPTER IV

MY FIRST COMMISSION

 **well remember** how I got my first commission and earned the first money in the exercise of my profession. It came about in this way.

I was down by the Quais of old Paris, close to the Pont des Aveugles, drawing the Parisian workman as he took his midday rest. The Quais had not yet got as strait-laced as they are now, and the river flowed its pleasant course without much police supervision. There was the loveliest of buildings, the Louvre, but it had not made more than a start towards the Tuileries, with which it was in but a few years to join stones.

I was often down there sketching, and I always found willing models amongst the friendly natives in blouses. The Parisian has an ever-varying way of asking you to take his likeness. "Tirez ma binette," "Fixez moi cette frimousse," or, "Relevez moi le plan de mon image," are amongst those I recollect. "Draw my mug," we might say, although translation does not go far to render that sort of colloquialism. —"Fix my phiz," and "Just you give me the map of my image."

I never accepted coppers on the occasions when I

presented my models with a sketch, but such ready-money payment was often proffered. It was not till a man had insisted on my accompanying him to his home with a view to artistic business, that I was led to accept my first commission. He lived near the Temple, quite a little distance from the Quai Voltaire, and as we went along, my companion became very communicative. He began about himself, then gave me a bird's-eye view of the family history, and soon came to "Ma mère," a theme he stuck to as only a Frenchman can. "She was," he said, "une maîtresse femme," and he would just like to see the man "qui pourrait lui tirer une carotte" (who could extract a carrot from her). This was not an allusion to the fruit and vegetable shop she kept, but meant that she was not an easy one to get over in money matters. I found the old lady as my friend had described her. She was stout and determined, and she kept her money jingling in the two or three capacious pockets of her apron. She could see I was an artist; why, *she* could recognise one within a radius of a league; and if I would draw her the portraits of her two granddaughters for five francs, I might set to work at once; they both had the eyes of *her* family, the Roufflards,—not a trace of the Tusserand look—an advantage I was not to overlook. The girls were about fourteen or fifteen, and I thought I could make rather a telling picture of the two heads together in medallion shape. But the old lady was after me at once. She didn't believe in pinching and cheeseparing, and didn't want the thing rounded off in any of those circular frames. "No," she said.

"*Allez-y franchement;* you just draw them as they are, hands and feet and all, *comme qui dirait:* there they are, those two girls, *les fillettes à la mère Tusserand.*"

To this I answered that we hadn't bargained for all that, and I was right from a strictly professional point of view, but I wouldn't have lost the five francs for the world, and I daresay she guessed as much, and stuck to her guns. She, as an old materfamilias, knew that people were not born in bust shape; then why should they be thus represented? *She* always gave good measure, and if she didn't, her customers would soon keep her up to the mark; so why shouldn't she have her money's worth? I felt that I ought to insist on better terms, if only for the dignity of my profession, but I was no match for the old lady, so I started work on her conditions, only, to save appearances, bargaining for a plentiful supply of *reineclaudes* during the sittings.

A sort of staircase, that had just missed being a ladder, led up in a straight line to the room that was to serve as a studio. A bed of imposing dimensions took up the greater part of the room; the bedstead of polished mahogany was an old-fashioned structure, that you could see at once had been handed down from one generation of fruiterers to another; similarly suggestive was a queer old roccoco looking-glass, and a faded portrait of a tom-cat sitting on a middle-aged spinster's lap. "Who are you, young man?" these worthy relics seemed to say; "have *you* got a pedigree?"

The latest offshoots from the genealogical tree of the Roufflard-Tusserand family had to be enthroned on the bed. I could otherwise not get sufficiently far away from them to overlook my group. It was desired that their arms should be interlaced with a view to emphasising their sisterly affection, and this gave rise to a new difficulty as to the presentment of one of the hands, which, being in perspective, did not show the full complement of fingers. When Madame Tusserand came to inspect my work, she particularly insisted that no part of the thumb should be concealed. She had noticed such imperfections in other pictures, and had always looked upon them as instances of the artful way in which painters sought to scamp their work. But here I struck. I swore by the holy Raphael that I could and would not alter it, and gave the old lady a lecture on the glorious Madonnas, who, even with incomplete thumbs, had been the means of regenerating the world. She was so pleased with the mention of the Madonna, and more especially with that part of my argument which she did not understand, that she gave in, and so perspective scored a victory.

The two girls, my models, were neat little types of the bourgeois class. I did not think much of them or the type; in fact I thought the generality of Parisian girls plain; but experienced friends told me I knew nothing about it, and taught me that if I wanted to judge of a woman (that unripe fruit, a girl, to be sure was not worth mentioning), I must study not her face or her figure, but her general appearance and one or two essential parts of her toilette. "What is the use of features," they asked, "to a woman who can't dress, or who is *gantée* and *chaussée* as if she *revenait de l'autre monde*." Which other world they meant, and how they wear their gloves and shoes there, they didn't explain. "And why should you give undue importance," they wound up, "to beauty where there is the *tournure* to observe and the *chic*. No, *mon cher*, if you want to form a correct estimate of a woman, study her ankles and her *bottines*."

Whilst I was taking stock of my models, and arriving at the conclusion that they were plain, pert, and precocious, they had evidently lost no time in deciding that I was green, and that it would take a good deal of teaching to give me the more attractive tinges of ripeness. They told me all about the Bouzibon, a familiar name by which they designated their favourite Bal de Barrière. They took it for granted I couldn't dance, but I might come and learn there next Sunday evening. It was a most respectable place, and nothing was ever lost or stolen there. La mère Bouze was a widow; to be sure I had noticed that elegant place in the Faubourg St. Denis, the fried-fish shop; well, that had originally been started by the late Monsieur Bouze years ago.

In return I told them my old yarn about Prince Poniatowski being drowned in the river Pleisse, just at the bottom of our garden in Leipsic; but I let out the point too quickly, and once they knew the Prince was drowned, they did not care for the rest. They behaved very well on the whole, and, as far as I am aware, did not make ugly faces at me when I was looking the other way. I am sure they did not like me though ; their fancy men were two *garçons coiffeurs* in a barber's shop close by, and so I hadn't a fair start.

That was my first experience as a portrait-painter. From that day to this I have truly loved my profession, undeterred by the fact that the course of true love does not always run smooth. At any rate that five-franc piece which Madame Roufflard-Tusserand took from the depths of her apron pocket and handed to me, gave me more satisfaction than many a " Pay to F. Moscheles, Esq.," that has since followed.

I wonder whether my drawing still exists, and, if so, whether it is going down as an heirloom from generation to generation with the bedstead, the looking-glass, and the middle-aged tomcat lady.

CLAUDE RAOUL DUPONT

 well remember the first words of French that I mastered, and the sensation I created when I, a very small boy, irrepressibly burst forth with my declaration :

"O Madam, kay voos aite bell !"

This was addressed across the friendly supper table to Madame de R., who with her husband, the well-known portrait-painter, was spending her honeymoon at Boulogne.

To Boulogne we too had gone, as people went then when they wanted a change of air, or as they go now to Africa or the antipodes.

On this occasion our party consisted of my parents, three sisters, myself, and an English nurse, who, from first to last, was unutterably shocked by what she called the outrageous proceedings of the foreigners, and by the fearful language that parrot used, who always gathered a little sympathetic crowd in front of the shell and wooden-spade shop.

My sisters had a French governess of the approved type.

"Maitre Corbeau sur un arbre perché," she recited to me with conventional emphasis and genuine affectation. On such occasions I stood staring at her, surprised at the amount of mouth-twisting and wriggling it took to talk French. Then I tried to do as much, and said :

"Mayter Korbow sure unn ahber per Shay."

"Perrrché," she interposed, and

"Pure Shay," I repeated.

"Mais non, mon petit chéri, perrrr—ché!" and so on, till we got to "apeuprès ce langage," the "a pew pray" being, I recollect, a terrible stumbling-block.

I was about eighteen when I met that handsome Madame de R. again in Paris. She reminded me of my early appreciation of her beauty, and was anxious to know whether I was still inclined to express my admiration as warmly as I did formerly.

"To be sure," I said. "Yes. *Mais oui certainement, madame.*" But, oh dear! how little female French I must have understood in those days, and how little male French I must have had at my command! for—I must confess—I said no more.

The de R.'s became great people under the Empire : he and she—or perhaps more correctly she and he—got into the inner Court circle, where she soon distinguished herself as a leader of fashion, and he as a very successful painter of life-size fashion-plates in oils. Both his works and her personal charms were graciously smiled upon by the imperial master himself.

Apropos of my French, I may say that I had every opportunity of improving it. I soon entered the Atelier Gleyre, that studio we have heard about in reference to Du Maurier, Whistler, Poynter, and others, who there learnt to draw their first bonshommes, and to spoil their first canvases.

I had made a sort of mental vow to speak nought but the language of the country for the first year of my stay in Paris. In the beginning I found it rather tough work, but a French studio is a good school. I plunged in head foremost, and soon got on swimmingly. From the first I was attracted by the brilliancy of Parisian slang, and by the terseness of French argot (that is, the thieves' language). As for the genuine article, real French, as spoken by real Frenchwomen in real salons on a "*Madame reçoit*" day—nothing could exceed my admiration for it. But the Quartier Latin, with its studios and garrets, its *crémeries* and little restaurants, all bedecked with clever works from the brushes of the *habitués*, was the high school in which I graduated and which in due time turned me out a fair specimen of the classical *Rapin*—the art student as Paris alone produces him. In a word, I soon felt quite at home in that delightful haven of unrest we call Bohemia.

And the friends of those days! I made many and lost few. There is one who stands out prominently from amongst the rest, and he is connected in my mind with a thousand and one incidents of my Paris life. His name was Claude; Claude Raoul Dupont.

At our first meeting I felt that I should like to make friends with him. He was what the Italians call *sympatico* — not quite the same thing as sympathetic ; just the sort of man whom little girls would unhesitatingly request to ring the bell they couldn't reach, or boys would call to their assistance with a " Please, sir, lend us your stick to get down that cap from up there," or " to fetch out that ball from inside them railings ;" the sort of man with whom you or I would at once have got into conversation, if we had met him in a railway carriage.

My first acquaintance with him was in that Atelier Gleyre.   We were just fellow-students at the beginning, then chums, *bons camarades*, soon friends, and finally we got linked together by the most lasting of ties, that of brotherly love.   So it comes that the story of his life is most vividly impressed on my mind.   It is uneventful, perhaps, and differs little from any other story that pictures the artist's life, with its hopes and aspirations, its sprinkling of love-making and its glorious consummation of love-finding, but I must attempt to give an outline of it, if but in memory of my friend.

To begin at the beginning, let me sketch our days of good comradeship, and put in a wash of background here and there, and a few touches of local colour in illustration of the life we led.

You could tell at a glance that Claude was a " Rapin," but that was not surprising, for in those days it had not yet become the aim and end of the young artist to conceal his profession and to walk through life incognito, with a well-groomed chimney-pot implanted on the top of his head. So you must fancy Claude with a soft felt hat of a species even now not quite extinct, although, as we all know, superseded by the boiled apple-pudding-shaped dome, ornamented with a gutter, which we have universally adopted, and which we call a pot hat, a bowler, a billycock hat, or as the coachman or groom says, a bridle.

It was quite appropriate that Claude should wear a wide-awake, as being in keeping with an expression that showed him always on the *qui vive*. He was tall, rather too much so for the breadth of his shoulders, but he moved with great freedom and ease, and as he was mostly on the move, he also mostly showed to advantage.

In the Atelier Gleyre he was the leading spirit. That studio was situated in the Rue de l'Ouest, flanking the Luxembourg Gardens. It was a large, high room with the regulation studio window, and was furnished with one model table on wheels, one iron spitfire of a stove, and a lot of three-legged easels and four-legged stools, not to forget a large screen behind which the models undressed; all things bearing traces of the perilous lives they led, and showing picturesque seams and scars where they were begrimed with the scrapings from perennial palettes. The professor very liberally gave his instruction gratis. For the working expenses of the Atelier the students clubbed together, each contributing ten francs per month to the "masse." At the time I entered, Claude was "Massier," that is, a sort of secretary, treasurer, and boss combined. He occupied that exalted position with much distinction, for he could be alternately serious and absurd, weighty and trivial. Common sense on the one hand; an uncommon amount of nonsense on the other. In fact his character was a curious compound of elements seemingly opposed, but working in harmony together. He was *facile princeps* as a *blagueur*, that is, he could chaff unmercifully, talk tall, make a fool imagine himself wise, and a wise man feel foolish. It takes a double-distilled Frenchman to make a full-blown *blagueur*, and such a man was Dupont.

We were a lively set, and the jokes that were bandied about, coupled with the most unparliamentary, not to say vituperative language, at first startled me. But the Rapin's bark is worse than his bite. "Il est défendu de chahuter la religion et la famille" was an unwritten law, that excluded those two delicate topics, the family and religion, from the field of word-battle. Another law bade you keep your temper. We might have hurled the most obnoxious of epithets at one another, but when the available catalogue of abuse was exhausted, we would wind up with some good-humoured trump card, like "C'est égal, je suis plus bête que toi," which, freely translated, says, "Never mind, I am the bigger fool of the two."

One of the first things that struck me in the atelier was a large felt hat forming a sort of centre on the ceiling. That was Gobelot's hat. It was there just because some of the boys had taken a dislike to it; in fact it was a priggish hat, and as Gobelot had a twitchy sort of a face that would work well under feelings of surprise and resentment, they thought they would like to watch him, from the first moment when he would miss his hat, to the last when he would discover its whereabouts.

It had got fixed on the ceiling with some difficulty, whilst its owner had fallen asleep by the stove. The model table was placed in the centre of the room, and the ladder held upright upon it by half-a-dozen sturdy arms; a light-weight clambered to the top and did the nailing. The result proved pre-eminently satisfactory to all except Gobelot, and even he, I think, after the lapse of a few months, got to be rather proud of the excelsiority accorded to his headgear.

This was by no means the first experience he had had of studio life. On his entrance into the Atelier Gleyre, he had set himself to draw the figure of Sinel, one of the leading models of the day, and had betrayed more self-confidence than was compatible with his position as a *nouveau*. He had been working for a couple of days, when Monsieur Gleyre came to visit his students. The bear-garden was suddenly transformed into a grave academy. Respectful silence and order prevailed, as the master passed from easel to easel, criticising here and encouraging there, and generally enunciating wise artistic saws for the benefit of the students. When Gobelot's turn came, he paused a while before he expressed an opinion on his work. At last he said kindly but firmly: " Young man, you have come to study with me, and it is my duty to advise you honestly and straightforwardly. Believe me, devote all your attention to the human foot; learn to draw that correctly,—and then perhaps you may be successful as a bootmaker." Therewith he passed on to the neighbour. Shortly afterwards the real Monsieur Gleyre came in, for the whole thing was a plant, and Gobelot was officially introduced as the *nouveau* by the sham professor.

It is not a sinecure to be the *nouveau*. One is the butt of endless jokes, and has to take them meekly; one is at everybody's beck and call, to pick up a brush, or to run for a ha'porth of bread or a penn'orth of fried potatoes. When I was the new boy, I knew resistance was useless, so I served my time cheerfully, swallowing snakes, as the French call it, with apparent relish.

But one day I was caught napping. I had joined in the general conversation, and had so far forgotten myself as to make a joke, and, what was worse, they said, not a bad one. This was adding insult to injury; a storm of indignation broke forth, and the cry of "À l'échelle" ("To the ladder") was raised. I should then and there have suffered the penalty of my rashness, had not Dupont interposed. He mounted the rostrum, *i.e.* the model table, and made an eloquent appeal on my behalf. I was an Englishman, he pleaded, and as such I had been reared on raw beef and bran puddings; he would himself now see that I was kept on lighter food (I suppose he meant frogs). Yes, I had presumed to trespass on the domain of "esprit," the exclusive property of Frenchmen in general, and of the duffers now before him in particular—he would not offend them by calling them gentlemen. My joke, he admitted, was a good one, but then, what could you expect from a benighted foreigner, who did not know the value of a bad one. And so on. However feeble his defence may appear to us as we read it in cold blood, it had the desired effect, and I was saved from my impending fate. But I was not to get off for long. Only a couple of days afterwards, an incident led to my punishment. It was luncheon time and I was studying the greasy paper that my potatoes had been wrapped up in, probably a leaf from some old register, so many tons of which are issued daily by bureaucratic Paris. I had got to my second course, roast chestnuts done to a T, when I had a sort of secret forewarning that a certain long stick with a hook, one of the studio properties, was stealthily approaching towards the stool I was sitting on. A sudden jerk, and the stool was pulled from beneath me; but being fully prepared, I failed to collapse, and remained as if seated, continuing my meal as if nothing had occurred. Such independence could not be tolerated. Stop, the well-known caricaturist, now formally moved that I be " mis à l'échelle," and the resolution was unanimously carried. So the ladder was laid on the floor, and I was bound to it hands and feet; then it and I were hoisted up and placed against the wall. Next Stop proceeded to bare my breast, and to paint thereon a highly coloured picture representing several pigs and their doings. In the meanwhile the poker was being made red-hot in the stove. The occasion must be marked by a scar, I was given to understand, and I can assure those who have never gone through a similar experience, that a touch from a red-hot poker is very painful, even if the red is only vermilion and the heat imaginary. I was informed that I should have to preserve the pig picture for a fortnight, after which time I should be called up for inspection.

When a *nouveau* is entered at an atelier, he is expected to pay "la bienvenue," his welcome. Gobelot had preceded me as the new boy, and as we had both been pretty liberal, a sum of about fifty francs was in readiness to be used for some sociable purpose. After some deliberation it was decided to invest our capital in donkeys, to be hired in the Bois de Boulogne. So one fine afternoon we found ourselves in full force, selecting our mounts at Père Delaborde's well-known stables. His donkeys were always the best fed and best kept, and to us, who had never been to the East, and therefore did not know what a donkey was really like, they seemed quite decent and cheerful specimens of their kind. Here and there, to be sure, there was one who had not become resigned to his fate, and who would stiffen his neck with an emphasis that showed that he would have used strong language, had he been endowed with the power of speech. But on the whole Monsieur Delaborde's donkeys were quite docile and manageable, and accustomed to be ruled by the little shouting savages known as donkey-boys.

There were two horses in the stables, and it was decided that Gobelot and I should mount them and take command of the donkey brigade. The responsibility of leadership soon, however, devolved on me alone, for Gobelot's horse had, I suppose through long-standing habits of companionship, taken to the ways of its mates; so it kept step with them, and stretched its ears full length, and took all things philosophically. My steed was made of very different metal. He started off at a lively pace, giving me an opportunity of showing off my horsemanship, acquired at the riding-school in Leipsic. I felt pleasantly aware of my superiority over my donkey-mounted friends, especially over Dupont, whose long legs were dangling very near the ground, he having left his stirrups, or they him, and over Gobelot, who was ineffectually trying to break into a canter.

Very suddenly and unexpectedly my horse stopped as if it had divined that I thought it time to inspect my followers. It was my intention to form them into column, and then to execute one or two strategical movements that seemed well adapted to the occasion. As a first step towards this, I wanted to wheel round and face my men, but my steed was evidently in a meditative mood and would not be disturbed. I applied my heels to its flanks, and pulled its head round, till its eye met mine, but its body remained stationary. When it had thought out whatever it may have had on its mind, it started off again as suddenly as it had stopped, before I had had an opportunity of commencing operations. This capricious starting and stopping, over which I had no control, was, I need not say, a source of annoyance to me, and of hilarity to my friends. It was to be more than this presently.

I had got pretty far ahead of the others, when my mount came to one of its dead stops. I contented myself with hoping it would soon have done staring vacantly. Looking round, I noticed some commotion in the distant donkey group, and an opening in its ranks to let a carriage pass. As it approached, it proved to be a well-appointed phaeton, and I recognised Louis Napoleon, who was driving himself, accompanied by a gentleman and by two servants in green and gold livery. I made every effort to get out of the way, but in vain. The prince took in the situation at a glance and considerately deviated from his course, seeing that I could not keep it clear for him. A smile flitted across his face and enlivened his rigidly waxed moustache, as he turned to his companion and made some remark. I did not catch it, but my horse probably did, and must have taken it as encouraging, for it started off in an uncontrollable fit of loyalty, and whether I liked it or not, I had to ride by the side of the phaeton, acting, for the time being, as equerry to the future emperor. He took it kindly ; the two green and gold ones were amazed and indignant, but too well trained to lynch me, and so I galloped on till once more my quadruped stopped and again became absorbed in thought.

When my companions came up, they gave expression to their unbounded delight at my discomfiture, and generally treated me, their appointed leader, with every mark of disrespect. This time the horse must have mistaken their vociferous hooting for a signal to return home, for it started off in that direction, and took me back without once indulging in the usual hiatus.

I dismounted, and whilst, on the one hand, I was glad to be now able to regulate my own movements, on the other I was smarting under the recollection of

my ignominious failure, and the jeering and hooting
still rang in my ears.

A couple of *sergents de ville* were on duty
close by, a circumstance which suggested to me the
opportunity of getting even with my insubordinate
men.

" Well, Messieurs," I said to the policemen, " I
think there might be a few more of you along the
principal avenues.   It is positively disgraceful.   I
don't mind a bit of a joke myself, but in my country
we don't play practical jokes on royalty, as that
young chap with the brown felt hat did on your
Prince President."

" What he did ? "

" Why, ride alongside the prince's carriage, giving
himself airs and posing for *son Altesse's* aide-de-camp.
And, following him as fast as they could get along,
a band of asses on donkeys, braying like *imbéciles*.
Well, *bon jour*, Messieurs ; after all, it's no business
of mine.   I only thought you might care to know."

On the arrival of the band, I learnt afterwards,
they were confronted by four *sergents de ville*, the
two original ones having been reinforced. Gobelot,
the man with the brown felt hat, was asked for his
passport, and, not being able to produce it, was
looked upon with suspicion and closely cross-questioned.   Dupont rather entered into my joke and
let things go wrong, till it was high time to set them
right.   Then I was denounced, and it was not without some difficulty made clear to the authorities that
the informer was the real culprit.   So Gobelot the
innocent was only warned to be more careful another

time, and my name is probably inscribed on some black list at the *Préfecture*.

*　　　*　　　*　　　*　　　*　　　*

Claude was a most indefatigable worker; as an artist ever severe and uncompromising, studying on the lines of Ingres and Flandrin, loving a bird, a stone, a woman for the sake of the outline they imprinted on his mind, and ever seeking an ideal contour, whether he held the pencil or the brush. His enthusiasm was quite catching; so under his influence I soon began to love drawing for its own sake, and we spent many an evening together studying Dante's stern features from the cast or working from the living model.

He had inherited his classical predilections from his father, who himself had started life as an artist, but had found that large historical landscapes *à la* Poussin were not easily convertible into bread and butter, and had therefore wisely abandoned art as a profession, and had embraced the administrative career, in which he rose and prospered. His leisure hours he still spent at the easel, but his canvases were not as large as formerly; in his productions he always gave me the impression that he could use more emerald and olive greens, to the exclusion of other colours, on a given space, than any man I had ever known.

He was quite touching in his love for Claude.

"What I have dreamed of and struggled for in vain," he would say, "that boy is going to realise. He is born with *du style*. Believe me, my child, outside *le style* there is no art. From the time of

Raphael down to the present day, nothing is worth recording, nothing remains or will remain, that is not *de l'école*. *La grande école*, my child, *le style, la ligne, voilà le salut*, believe me."

I winced, for I loved, above all the colourists, the Spaniards, the Dutch; but he was so sincere, so convincing, that for the time being I felt as if I could have sold my birthright for a line of beauty.

"He is quite right," Claude would afterwards say to me, "but he puts his finger in his eye, if he thinks he can flatten your bump of colour. Every man is born with his own bumps, and they are bound to grow with him just as his hair does."

And with that we would plunge headlong into the famous discussion *sur la forme et la couleur*, each doing battle for his god with the energy of youthful fanaticism, and feeling all the while that we would have given anything to be able to exchange bumps with one another. How much further his bump would lead him, I thought, and how admirably he was organised to use it in the service of high art! And he, on the other hand, would say—

"What am I, my dear fellow, as compared to you, born in the purple of art as you are? You hold the trump cards, and will," &c. &c.

Then there was an uncle of Claude's, *l'oncle Auguste*, whose views clashed fearfully with the artistic aspirations of my friend and of his father. He was a tanner, at the head of a large establishment which he had founded—a self-made man, with a lot of cleverly-grabbed money. In his social intercourse he had so carefully surrounded himself with inferior intellects, that he could not but shine as a bright light amongst them—a circumstance which led him to form a most exaggerated estimate of his own wisdom and mental powers.

"My dear Jean," he would say to his brother, "I should really have thought your own experiences with those blessed paints would have made a wiser man of you. Surely one victim to the mania in the family should have been enough, without dragging that poor boy into it; a splendid fellow, sane and sound, if it weren't for the rubbish you put into his head. He was cut out for the business; never happier than when he was pottering about at the works. Why, when he was a mere child, he very nearly got drowned in the tan vat." And turning to Claude: "What have you to say to it, you young rascal? Ah well, I know you are hopelessly lost, since you got out of those plaster casts and those bones and muscles into that—What do you call that place, where able-bodied young men, strong and fit for work, sit all day drawing mannikins! *Une vraie fabrique de bonshommes! En voilà un métier!*"

The same evening l'oncle Auguste was holding forth to some friends he had invited to sit at his feet and at his whist-table—

"Now mark my words, messieurs; we are going to make an artist of that nephew of mine, and one who will surprise the world. He has been received first on a list of I don't know how many hundreds of students at the Life Class of the École des Beaux Arts. *Oui, messieurs*, art is an heirloom in our family; we hand it down from generation to generation."

But differences of opinion on the merits of the artistic career led to no more than skirmishes; the real tug-of-war between the Duponts, father and son on the one hand, and l'oncle Auguste on the other, came when they exchanged their views on matrimonial alliances. The former to be sure looked upon the tying of the nuptial knot from the ideal point of view; the latter very strongly held the belief that a young man should marry money, and should do so early in life.

"Suppose now," he would argue, "you mean to marry 100,000 francs, why put it off till you are twenty-six or twenty-eight? Why lose the interest of your money for so many years?"

"But perhaps, uncle, my lady-love is still in the nursery, and I must wait awhile till I can declare my undying affection. Yes, I believe she is only just beginning to play the piano, and I really cannot take her till she has done practising her scales, you know. Besides, her father has only lately started collecting the 100,000 francs, and I think he has not got further than 3500."

"God forbid, unhappy boy, that you should be led away to paint one of your classical haloes round the head of some such unfledged chicken, blessed with a fond and shabby father. Remember, young man, you have two things to look forward to that can set you up in this world—matrimony and expectations; expectations and matrimony—and don't forget that in my mind they are very closely connected."

"Don't be angry, my dear uncle, and don't worry till there is cause. As for the 'dot,' I suppose I could do with 100,000 francs as well as any other fellow who has got to take a *bel appartement orné de glaces*, and to put himself into his furniture. But surely you, who know the value of skins, you wouldn't want me to sell mine, with what is inside in the way of body and soul, for that price!"

"See that you get 200,000 then, or three or four; you're worth all that. Lady-love, indeed! so beautiful, I suppose! Sentiment—romance— eternal love! Eternal fudge! Remember this, Uncle Auguste's fortune was not made to encourage tomfoolery."

Now there was really no reason why Uncle Auguste should deliver himself of that speech. There was no lady-love, no classical halo, and no centime-grabbing father. But the fact was, the uncle trembled lest he should be disappointed in the boy he loved so well. He was already scheming for him, and telling one or two friends of his confidentially, that it was quite worth while treating Claude with respect, as he was the nephew of a very rich uncle. It was not to be long before the uncle was deemed well worthy of respect, as being able to boast of a very clever nephew.

Whilst he was still painting studies at the Atelier Gleyre, and attending classes and lectures at the École des Beaux Arts, Claude started a picture in a queer little studio he had taken for the purpose, at the top of a very tall house in the Rue de Seine, Quartier Latin. Somebody, with an eye to artistic possibilities, must have converted what was originally a garret into a studio by adding a big projecting window. It had a top light into which all the prying cats of the neighbourhood used to peer, whilst the less inquisitive ones merely made the loose tiles rattle as they prowled along the roof.

There was a second studio of the same kind up there, which was occupied by Giacomo Irmanno, an Italian boy of about seventeen years, with jet-black curly hair. That peculiar underglow of rich bronze colour, so characteristic of the Southern type, lit up Irmanno's perfectly chiselled features. Dupont and I made great friends with him, and I often enjoyed helping him with his work. He could be very morose and look Italian daggers, but that was probably because in his desire to become an artist he was waging war at fearful odds against poverty. He was quite out of his element under northern skies, and spoke French in a way that taught me much Italian.

His only means of support were derived from painting what is called " Les Stations de la Croix." These pictures, destined to decorate the village churches in France and generally in Catholic countries, are produced in a more matter-of-fact than artistic way. The employer with an eye to the advantages of division of labour, has the subjects printed on canvas. Then a batch of Station No. 1, perhaps some six or eight canvases at a time, are given out to artist No. 1, who puts in the landscape and surroundings; from there they go to artist No. 2, who paints the draperies, and finally to No. 3, who fills in heads, hands, and feet. Irmanno was No. 2. We placed the pictures ready for treatment all round the room. Then we started with one colour, say dark red, for the shade of a certain drapery; when that had been repeated on all the canvases, came the turn of the middle tint, and finally of the light red. Then came the next colour—I need not say they were all prescribed—and when we had made the round with that, the next, and so on until all the draperies were satisfactorily disposed of.

The proceedings were only varied when Irmanno lay down on the red brick floor and groaned, and pretended to have a sort of attack. I did not mind, because when the evil spirit was upon him, he always looked particularly interesting.

Next door, in the twin garret, Dupont was putting heart and soul into the production of his first picture; it was still in its initial stages, but studies small and large, in pencil and in chalks, were gradually covering the walls. His subject was " The raising of the daughter of Jairus," and he would never tire of talking to me about the grand opportunities it afforded to the artist. He would question me too on things connected with mesmerism (I was mesmerising in those days), and would want to know all about the first symptoms of awaking from a trance, of the action of the hand as it makes passes, and the dictates of the eye as it bids the subject sleep or wake. " Christ, the God," he wrote to me in a letter of a later date, " can never be depicted, translated into human forms, but Christ the Healer, Christ the Helper, and He, the lover of children, is perhaps approachable. Give me a lifetime, and possibly I may decipher a little of what is to be read between the lines of the New Testament."

The summer had set in early and rather savagely, as it will do sometimes in Paris, and the heat in those ex-garrets of the Rue de Seine was stifling.

Rosa Bonheur Sinel did what she could to mitigate the evil. Rosa Sinel was her real name, but somebody had nicknamed her Rosa Bonheur, and in course of time her father had worked himself into the belief that the great artist had been her godmother. She was a precocious little woman, somewhere between the age of ten and fifteen—who can tell the real age of a Parisian child? *Le père* Sinel was one of the best known models in Paris. He was a living *écorché*, a creature designed for the study of anatomy, for he had a most extraordinary faculty of showing the action of any and every muscle; in fact he could, if the circumstances required, give himself the appearance of having been skinned, scalped, or flayed alive. He was ever boasting of his participation in the great pictorial and plastic works that had made a mark in his days, and always claiming his full share of the laurels awarded to them.

"It is not so much my exceptional figure that has inspired my friends, as it is my experience that has guided them," he told us. "Did not the great Monsieur Delacroix say with his characteristic modesty, when his plafond in the Galerie d'Apollon was uncovered: 'Where should I be without the assistance of my friend Sinel?' *Oui*, messieurs, he was right, and such a plafond is not produced in a day. ' Art is short and sittings are long,' as the poet says; *Voyez*, Monsieur Ingres!   Many an hour was I nailed to the cross as a thief, before we could get the true agony.   I well remember his saying ' Sinel, *mon ami*, till I knew you, I had no idea what the flexor of a third and fourth toe could do, nor did I know what acting was till I heard you.'"

" Allons donc, blagueur"—from the students—" what do you know about acting?"

" Moderate your language if you please, messieurs.   You would not laugh if you knew the position I hold in the theatrical world—"   With much dignity—" I am of the Théâtre Français."

" Shut up, *tais toi*," cries one,

"'To be sure you play the fool," shouts another.

" *Il n'y a pas de tais toi*, messieurs ; but I must be off and study my part.   To-night I am on with Mademoiselle Rachel.   I am cast for ' Le peuple murmure.'"

To return to the daughter, I must say she was the most useful little studio drudge I ever knew. Her appearance was against her, for she was plain and generally unkempt and untidy; the cleanest parts of her apron were the holes, but for all that she was an ever-handy little monkey of all work. She would roast chestnuts on the stove according to her own particular system, and would feed that stove with heterogeneous fuel that it would not have taken from another hand.   She would water the garden—a sort of shelf suspended outside the window—would drench unsuspecting but indiscreet cats, and was generally of an aquatic turn of mind.   One very hot day we came upon her unexpectedly, and found her perched upon a high stool, her dress tucked up, and her bare feet on the chair rail. She was contemplating with evident satisfaction what she called *le reservoir*. It looked very much as if she had been utilising it as a footbath, by way of refreshing herself, but that may or may not have been the case. There was an empty pail that told the story of the reservoir. She had sprinkled part of its contents over the studio floor, forming a quantity of little quivering black pearls, as the water licked up the dust; the rest she reserved to make a pool where the hand of time, or the foot rather, had produced a deep hollow in the red brick floor. The cement of time must have been at work too, to weld the bricks into a compact mass, for the water did not seem to percolate through to the neighbour's ceiling, but stood its ground to bear witness to Rosa Bonheur's aquatic genius.

After this success she had visions of gold-fish and fountains and of *les grandes eaux de Versailles*, and she wanted more snubbing than ever.

But water or no water, the heat in the studio remained intolerable. It soon began to tell on Claude. who was not of the most robust, and who was simply overworking himself. He did not like being told so—artists never do; he had got into difficulties with his picture, and now that it was in distress he would not leave it.

It really needs as much patience and perseverance to mature a picture as to rear a child. All goes smoothly for a while, and one's offspring, picture or baby, is a source of happiness. Then comes a hitch, an illness, and everything seems darkness. But just as a father does not give in and say, "Oh, this baby is no use, pitch it aside," so a true picture parent does not gash the canvas of his own painting with a knife, or cast it away because it has the scarlet or yellow fever, or because it tells of a crooked leg or a deformed limb. On the contrary, he sets to work and tends the patient with soothing oils, and with the whole arsenal of remedies his palette affords. Wonderful are the cures that have been effected on canvas, and little does the public know, when it admires the completed work, how desperately the artist has had to struggle at times to preserve even a spark of vitality in it, and how narrowly it escaped destruction at his hands.

Claude had got into a phase of despair. Several studies he had made lately, especially some for the head of the daughter of Jairus, he considered absolute failures.

"Those blessed models," he said, "drive me wild. The rubbish that girl talks whilst I am trying to raise her from the dead, would make a saint swear."

It took a good deal of persuasion to get him away from the studio and the models, but luckily an opportunity for a rest came, when his father had to make an official inspection of some works in the neighbourhood of Lyons and wished Claude to accompany him.

The short holiday that he thus had to submit to would have proved rather dull and uneventful, had it not been for an incident that made a great impression on him. In his rambles through the city of Lyons he had come across a fine old building, the gates of which stood hospitably open; the door too, for, having crossed the picturesque courtyard, at one time probably a cloister. there was nothing to prevent his entering the main building, and he soon found himself wandering along the corridors of the City Hospital. He seems at first to have chatted cheerfully with some of the patients, amusing and encouraging them in his pleasant way; but presently, as he passed from ward to ward, and witnessed the acute sufferings of some of the sick, and the dull hopelessness of the incurables, he gradually felt his strength failing him. The long rows of beds began to revolve around him; he mechanically clutched hold of something and—fainted.

So much of the incident he mentioned in a letter to me; as also that he was going daily to the hospital to make some drawings, but the more interesting features of his adventure I did not gather till a week or two later, when we met in Orleans, which place was to be the starting-point for a pedestrian tour we had planned. There he gave me full particulars.

"I felt it coming," he said; "the rail of the bedstead nearest at hand seemed to be going round like a wheel, and I had to wait till it was within reach to catch it. What happened then I don't know. I suppose the good sisters helped me to a seat and watered me till I came round. All I can say is, that there must have been a long interval between getting out of the faint and back to life.

It was a curious experience, and one I shall not easily forget. The first thing I became conscious of, was that my eyes were riveted on the lifeless body of a girl laid out on a bed, and covered with a spotless shroud; I thought it was of marble. I saw no one else, and wondered that there was no relative or friend to watch by the corpse; then it occurred to me that they must all have gone to break the news to Jairus. I sat gazing at the girl's large eyelids that lay heavily on the eyes but were not quite closed; at the wax-like features, so beautifully chiselled; and the lock of brown hair, the only living texture, in striking contrast with the cold sculptured pillow and with the stiff rigid fingers that rested on the border of the shroud.

" I felt very tired and leant back, wondering what the colour of her eyes might be. Then—was I dreaming?—I suddenly became aware that they were violet, like the colour of a transparent amethyst. She had opened them, and was looking quietly and unconcernedly at me.

" ' J'ai bien dormi,' she said, and I, at one bound. leaped back to life and its realities.

" ' Tiens, oui,' I said, ' you look all the better for it. Now what have you been dreaming about, if I may ask ? '

" ' Oh, about the bon Jésus : I love to dream of Him, it makes me so strong.'

" ' And what is your name, mon enfant ? '

" ' Madeleine, monsieur.'

" I was truly glad to know, for I always regretted the apostle had not told us the name of the daughter of Jairus.   Well, I got Madeleine to tell me a little of her history, and the good sisters gave me the rest. Her father was a poor labourer, and she had been in the hospital for the last nine months under treatment for hip disease.   She was the sweetest and most lovable of patients, they told me.

" When I went away I said :—

" ' Is there anything you want?   Shall I bring you a book when I come to-morrow ?'

" ' No, not a book ; bring me a rose, please, a red rose.'

" Well, you can fancy I thought of nothing else but the Jairus's daughter I had found.   The next morning I brought her three of the reddest roses I could find, and she beamed with happiness as she fondled them.

" ' Oh, *ma sœur*,' she said to the nurse, ' you will let me keep them just here by my side ; they smell so sweet, and they can't hurt me now the windows are all open.   I want to nurse them myself, and when they are tired of living in a glass, I will keep them between the leaves of my prayer-book,' and presently she added : ' I am going to read them all day.   You know, monsieur, I can't read really; that's why I didn't want you to bring me a book.' "

Here I interrupted Claude with the question—

" How old is she ? "

" How old?   Well, really it never occurred to me to ask her age.   I suppose it's a sort of grown-up age, but then, to be sure, she is quite a child, poor little thing."

And so on, and so on.   Every morning he brought

a fresh red rose for the pale girl. *Sub rosa*, to be sure, was the sketch-book. Now that he had found his long-sought model, he was glowing with the desire to make studies from her, and so he spent the better part of a week by her bedside, pencil in hand. The drawings I thought by far the best things I had ever seen of his; especially one in which he had used a few coloured chalks, and where the amethyst eyes gazed at you wonderingly. I have since sometimes been reminded of those eyes in the work of Gabriel Max.

* * * * * *

We had met in Orleans as I have said, and started on our walking tour in a southerly direction along the banks of the Loire. We were most unconventionally equipped, wearing caps and blouses, and carrying only the artist's knapsacks with a change of clothes and sketch-books.

What can be more glorious than walking, if you have the right boots to tread along in, and the right friend by your side? It was perfect. The river flowed with a will, the birds sang with a soul, and we could not but catch the note and go forward in unison with stream and song. We were in such high spirits that we found it hard to pass a man without hurling a cordial *bon jour* or a thundering bad joke at him. We helped old women with their bundles, and pauperised small children by giving them sous when they never dreamt of asking for such a thing.

Thus we pushed on, till we reached a town, not the first day, but another. What town I have forgotten; nor do I remember what art treasures may have been accumulated within its walls. I only know that our sketch-books were out, and that we had found a corner of the market-place, from which we could, without being too much noticed, catch the characteristic figures that were buying and selling, sitting, standing, or hanging about.

We had been working some time, when a friendly native of the fair sex, who had evidently taken a discreet interest in our work, requested us, with profuse apologies for the interruption, to give her a few minutes' interview at her shop, as soon as we should have finished.

"It is just over the way," she said; "'Leroux, Smith and Carriage Varnisher,' is written over the door."

In due time we went, and Madame Leroux asked us with some trepidation what might be our charge for a portrait of her little girl. Dupont was at once fully up to the situation, and said—

"Ah, madame, it is not quite easy to give you a direct answer. Charges, you see, vary a good deal according to the style. There is the guaranteed likeness at one price, and there is the family likeness at another, considerably lower to be sure; that again fluctuating according to the amount of chiaroscuro the client desires introduced. What shall we say, my friend?" he asked, turning to me. I started a consultation on the subject in gibberish, to which he readily responded in the same tongue. She was much impressed by our mastery over the strange idiom, and exclaimed admiringly—

"Ah, messieurs, anybody could see you were English."

Returning to business, Dupont further explained—

"It is, above all, the colouring, madame, that makes the difference in price. We can do you a drawing—of the first-class quality to be sure—for two francs twenty-five centimes; coloured, madame, it cannot be produced for less than three francs seventy-five centimes."

It was her turn to consider and mentally to review the means at her disposal for art purposes.

"Well, messieurs," she finally decided, "will you please do the drawing part, and"—pointing to the pots and pans on the shelf—"my husband will lay on the colours."

The little girl was pretty, and we had got our full enjoyment out of the joke, so we set to, Dupont drawing her, and I doing the painting, and finally we presented our joint work as a free gift to Madame Leroux. She was deeply grateful, but looked just a trifle alarmed. Were we princes in disguise, she was wondering, or had she been harbouring peripatetic angels unawares? But she only pressed our hands and said—

"Believe me, Messieurs, I felt it, I knew it from the first, that you were English."

I only hope that Monsieur Leroux, when he came home, was pleased with our performance, and satisfied in his mind that I had given the full amount of colour necessary to constitute a complete work of art.

Leaving the city, we shortly had an opportunity of testing our abilities by the attractions they might possess for the rustic population of France. It was in a charming little place, somewhere not far from Blois, an idyllic spot and a very haven of rest, I should think, in times of peace ; but just now it was invaded by a large contingent of visitors, attracted by the holding of the annual fair and of a cattle-market. In ordinary times, I daresay the approaching traveller would have been greeted by the silvery voice of the village church-bell, and the peasants working in the fields would have doffed their caps *à la* Jean François Millet as the Angelus called them to prayer. But we only heard the discordant voices of man and beast, as they rose from the market and the fair, and the devout peasants had left the fields to bow their heads reverently somewhere nearer the centre of festivities.

We found but poor accommodation at the crowded inn, but had learnt by this time not to be particular, and to put up with a bundle of straw for a mattress, and the back of a chair turned upside down for a pillow.

I had left Claude making some studies of oxen that might perhaps some day, under his brush, figure as a background to a sacred subject, and I had sauntered on to the fair. There, having pulled out my sketch-book, I soon became a centre of attraction. An artist was evidently a strange figure in this primitive place, and so a little crowd collected to watch one of the species use his tools. It was on this occasion that I had an opportunity of realising a truth which I have subsequently so often found confirmed—viz., that there are occasions when I am wanted, and others when I am not wanted. In that particular place I was not wanted. So the boss of a theatrical show, close to whose booth I had taken my stand, told me. He put it in the most courteous language. With me it did not mean business, he could see that. With him it did, and his business was suffering from the unwonted attraction I offered. I at once closed my sketch-book, and he improved the occasion by announcing his performance in stentorian voice to my crowd. It was something about the Assassin's Coffin and the Haunted Wreck—grand drama in so many acts and so many more tableaux, performed by his troupe in all the capitals of Europe.

"Entrez, messieurs! on va commencer. Deux sous l'entrée!" and he was up on his platform, prodding a monkey with a long thin stick, and banging on a drum with a short thick one.

I was moving on, when a lady, also gifted with an eye to business, addressed me, this time to tell me that I *was* wanted.

"You will be here this evening, will you not?" she said. "Would you mind coming and doing some of your drawing in front of my booth; you would attract the people, and once they are there, leave me alone for the rest." I agreed, and in the evening Claude and I started operations. She had placed a bench in front of her booth, which was well lit by a couple of large lamps. Claude was in his element. He harangued the open-mouthed villagers in his best manner. Our connection with the court, he explained, generally made it impossible for us to accept any engagements outside Paris, but, hearing that the good lady who presided over the classical game of Loto had the misfortune to be a widow and an orphan, we had felt it our duty to give her the advantage of our presence on this occasion.

"Yes, gentlemen," he added, "not only has she put before you a most remarkable collection of valuable articles, specimens of which the lucky card-holder may carry home to the wife of his bosom or the child of his headache, but the purchaser of the series of five cards is entitled to have his portrait executed in the latest and most approved style, by your humble servant, and his friend and colleague. Deux sous la carte, messieurs; deux sous la carte!"

We did a good stroke of business for the enterprising widow, and at the same time carried off some first-rate types in our sketch-books. For we placed our models in the centre of the bench, and each of us drew a profile from his side. Of the two sketches, we gave one away and kept the other. The people were refreshingly ignorant; a scrap of conversation between two old women was specially edifying. They were comparing notes after having watched our work from both ends of the bench.

"Well, you see," said one, "there are two of them — they each make half; then they put it together, and that makes one."

"Sure enough, that's just the way it's done," answered the other.

It was on leaving this place that we unexpectedly found ourselves "wanted" by the rural police.

We were trudging along, when we met two gensdarmes on horseback.   They pulled up and asked us rather gruffly for our passports.   Dupont handed them his, which was of the regulation pattern and therefore easily passed muster; but mine was a British Foreign Office passport, neatly bound in a leather case and signed by Lord Clarendon, and as I produced it from beneath a time-worn French workman's blouse, it seemed, to say the least of it, out of keeping with my appearance.   It was very explicit, setting forth that: "We, George William Frederick, Earl of Clarendon, Baron Hyde of Hindon, Peer of &c. &c., request and require in the name of Her Majesty, &c. &c. &c."   But the gensdarmes looked in vain for the signalement, the personal description of the bearer, which they considered the very essence of a respectable passport; and so they refused to "allow me to pass freely without let or hindrance." (You see I have the old friend of a document still, and am quoting from it.)   In fact they invited us to follow them to the town we had started from in the morning.   To this we demurred, and it was not without some difficulty that we persuaded them to run us in in the other direction, only succeeding when Dupont said he had an uncle in the gensdarmerie, who had often told him that the men were so badly paid, that they could not make both ends meet, were it not for an occasional tip from those interested in securing their good offices.

In due time we were marched into a pleasant little town—I forget its name—our captors following close on our heels.   We were taken to headquarters and detained, as nobody there could make head or tail of Baron Hyde of Hindon's rescript. It was taken to Monsieur le Maire, before whom we were shortly summoned to appear. He received us courteously.

"I have no doubt, monsieur," he said to me, "that the passport is in perfect order, but I should like to see your signature and any other papers you may have about you that may establish your identity." I produced a washing bill, and the last letter I had received from my father. He looked at these and then selected a thick-set volume from the bookcase. "Mo-sche-les," he said, as he turned over the pages, evidently to assure himself whether my name figured in the register of criminals. Then, turning an inquisitorial eye on me, he sat down to cross-question me, his fingers all the while beating a little bureaucratic tattoo on his knees. I felt as innocent as ever I had felt in my life, and strong in my reliance on Baron Hyde and the British fleet.

"So you are an Englishman?" he asked. "And where was your father born?" "In Prague," I answered. "Quite right," he said, with a glance at the book; "in Prague, in 1794. You are the man;" and before I could say anything, he had got up, and calling to a young lady in the next room, he said, "Just come here, my dear, and look. This is Moscheles' handwriting. Is it not a curious coincidence, just when you are studying the Rondo brillant and the Sonata? This is Monsieur Felix Moscheles, his son.—My daughter, Mademoiselle Julie, messieurs."

It was a very pleasant and timely coincidence.
My blouse blushed, I suppose, but Mademoiselle
Julie was too polite to notice it. Monsieur le
Maire said—

"Well, as I have been officially called upon to
find you a lodging, I may as well walk with you
to the Hôtel de la Poste, and see that you get a
comfortable one. When you have rested, you must
come round and take a little supper and music
with us."

Our arrival, escorted by the gensdarmes, had
caused considerable excitement amongst the natives;
our reappearance under the wing of Monsieur le
Maire, with whom we were evidently on terms of
easy familiarity, at once dispelled all doubts as to
our character, and not only were first impressions
wiped out, but we took position as the recognised
heroes of the day. Besides thus rehabilitating us,
Monsieur le Maire profusely apologised for the gensdarmes' blunder.

"The fact is," he said, "they have instructions
to look out for two young men who are wanted,
and who are supposed to be in the neighbourhood,
so they are all on the alert." To which Dupont
added—

"Yes, I quite see; if they just weed out all
the wrong ones, they can then easily lay hands
on the real culprits."

"Il y a de cela," said the Maire good-naturedly.

We spent a very pleasant evening with our friend
and his family. The daughter played me the Rondo
brillant and the Sonata, both early works of my

father's that I was not quite as familiar with as I felt I must pretend to be. Dupont did a little pretending too, I think, for he got on splendidly with the mother by taking a lively interest in the pedigrees of the leading families in the neighbourhood.

Neither of us fell in love with the daughter, as one of us, if not both, should have done, to make a good story of it; nor, to the best of my knowledge, did Mademoiselle Julie lose her heart to either of us.

*   *   *   *   *   *

Just one more little incident of the road, to close the record of our excursion. It would not be worth mentioning, had not the future given it significance.

It was towards evening; the sun had gone down behind one set of heavy clouds, and the wind was whipping up another set to join them. We were anxious to get on, and if possible to find a short cut to our destination, so we consulted a man who was mending the road. He had evidently not been talked to for some time, and wanted to make the most of his chance, for instead of a simple answer, he gave us a long yarn about his father's road and his brother's road, and about how his was so smooth we could play at billiards on it, but we couldn't on theirs. When we replied that we didn't want to play, but to walk it, he said we were only chaffing him. "I know you well," he added; "you are the two young men who are staying with Monsieur le Docteur."

We should have done better not to take our cue from this specimen of a billiard-table road-maker, for he misdirected us, and we must have got on to the father's road when we should have been on the brother's, or *vice versâ*.   And the rain came on and drenched us, and soon there was a good deal of big cloud-rolling above us, and enough of light-flashing to show us there was nothing worth seeing—no house, no shelter of any kind.   But we didn't mind; we knew that in an orthodox thunderstorm a friendly beacon of light shining from the window of a cottage is sure, sooner or later, to come to the rescue of the belated traveller ; and so we pushed on till we discerned its twinkle.   Then we made for it.

We were soon being hospitably received by the three inmates of the friendly cottage—an old man, an old woman, and a dog in the prime of life.   The old man made up the fire on the brick hearth for us to dry our clothes by, the woman stirred something that was simmering in the caldron, and the dog sat down and stared at Dupont.   He was a beautiful shaggy creature, a sort of shepherd-dog, I think; they called him Rollo.   His pedigree might perhaps not have passed muster, but for all that, one felt sure that his sire and his sire's spouse must have been good dogs.   I have never forgotten the deep mysterious look in that creature's eyes.

There were some pigs, too, somewhere in immediate proximity to us, but more heard than seen, consigned as they were to a dark corner, where they lustily grunted, whilst some of their relatives, already dismembered, hung up inside the chimney-breast, to be gradually smoked and cured.   The old woman fetched a saucepan, and put something in it that bubbled and fizzed, and presently one could see floating, quivering particles come together and solidify, and finally emerge in pancake form. Good solid pancakes they were, like counterpanes, not like those flimsy kid-glove sort of pancakes we get in society. We fully enjoyed them, and the coarse peasant's bread and the home-made cider.

Then we went to bed—to palliasse rather, for two big bags filled with straw were laid down for us, and we turned in, or rather on. Our hosts had made us as comfortable as they could, and we felt that all we could do in return was to sleep well and to forget a few francs on the table when we left. The old man was so kind; he knew from the first that we were itinerant painters, and that no discredit attached to our calling. "C'est un métier comme un autre de faire des images,"[1] he said encouragingly. They were a cheerful couple, those two old people, and looked as if they had not known much trouble or worry, and had just collected their wrinkles, as time went on, for what they were worth.

One does sleep soundly on a bag of straw after a thunderstorm and a rustic supper, and I should have done so till sunrise if, some time in the middle of the night, Rollo had not poked his nose into my face. I woke up with a start, and looking round, was surprised to see Dupont standing at the window, gazing into space.

"What's the matter?" I said.

"Nothing," he answered. "It's a wonderful night."

I turned round to go to sleep again, but Rollo

---

[1] It's as good a trade as another, that of making-up pictures.

was very restless, and a glorious full moon was flooding the kitchen with light, her silver rays forming fantastic patterns on the stone floor, broken as they were by the little lead divisions of the casement and by the flower-pots, bottles, and various nondescript articles on the window-sill.

"I wish you would come to bed, and not stand there as if you were moon-struck," I said at last.

"That's just what I am," he replied. "I wish you would come and be so too."

"As-tu fini?" I growled. "Va te coucher, imbécile,"[1] and with that I dozed off.

But Rollo, I dreamed or I felt it, was sitting gravely by my side and wondering how I could be so rude, his tail all the while beating the ground at regular intervals. I roused myself once more; there stood Dupont as before.

"Hang it all," I said, "I do wish that blessed dog and you would shut up and turn in."

"I wish you'd open up and turn out," he answered. "Come along, don't be an *épicier*;[2] get up and let's tramp it. It's a splendid night."

"What's the matter, messieurs?" here broke in the old man, whose head and nightcap appeared at the glass door which separated his sleeping-nook from the kitchen, and—"What's the matter?" echoed the wife's voice. When he saw Claude, he simply said, "Oh, c'est ce jeune homme qui souffre de la lune; c'est tout comme Rollo."[3]

---

[1] "Shut up," I growled, "and get to bed, you idiot."

[2] Philistine.

[3] Oh, it's that young man who is upset by the moon; just like Rollo.

I burst out laughing, and—I suppose lunacy is catching—I too felt that I could not lie still, and that a moon that could make that pattern on the floor was not the Philistine orb of the Boulevards, but a heavenly body well worth getting up for.

Soon we were on the move. Every cloud had vanished; Nature was in her most peaceful mood; all was at rest. We walked on, Dupont a little ahead of me, whilst Rollo, who had come with us, never budged from his side. We must have gone some miles when the moon, gradually descending towards the horizon, went down behind a potato-field. We sat on the banks of a ditch and watched it.

"A true circle," said Dupont, "a true circle!"

When it had quite disappeared, we went on. For a while Rollo stood staring after Dupont, then he started off at a slow trot in the direction of home, and was soon out of sight.

"Drole de chien cela,"[1] said I.

"C'est égal, il a du flaire,"[2] rejoined Dupont. Beyond that he was not inclined for conversation, so I relapsed into silence.

And that is all. But I was to remember the moon of that night when once more Dupont and I sat together and watched "the true circle."

New-Year's Day in Paris is, as everybody knows, the most soul-foot-and-purse-stirring day of the year. Everybody has to conciliate everybody

----

[1] Queer dog that.
[2] That's all very well, but he knows what's what.

else. Emperors and kings move their oracular lips to dispel any "black specks" that may be visible on the horizon, and to proclaim the fact that, under their paternal guidance, everything is for the best in the best of States—winding up in all humility, with a filial appeal to the Father of all, and praying that He may devote Himself specially to the interests of His chosen people.

The telegraph boys rush from the palace to the office, and soon the high-priests of the Press trumpet forth the words of the mighty, and explain their oracular utterances to the gaping crowd that stands ready, all the world over, to be gulled, and is ever proud to wear some master's livery and be crushed under the glorious weight of the fetters he forges.

Sometimes the first day of God's new year is specially selected to accentuate the Divine Right of Temporal power enthroned on earth. With breathless expectation we await a sign — it comes — Jupiter has not deigned to wink, or worse still, Jupiter has frowned; he should have turned to the left, and he turned to the right, or—ye other gods protect us!—he did not turn at all! Then suddenly there is a great commotion in the human ant-hill. It is Neptune's ambassador who has been slighted! The courtiers stand aghast, the High Press priests shriek prophetically, and spill vicious inks all over their papers. Vulcan with his big bellows fans the ever-glowing embers of distrust, just to oblige his noble friend Mars, who looks forward to glorious work and fresh laurels. A howling mob of human ants breaks out into rabid patriotism, and calls upon the State to lead its armies, and on the Church to bless its banners.

To be sure Neptune at once calls for an unlimited credit, to satisfy the ever-neglected claims of the Panic Fund. Up go some things, by leaps and bounds; down go others; bears and bulls hug and gore one another to death, the dogs of war strain on their leashes, whilst the devout ant sets to, and works with a will for six days in the week to fill the arsenals, and then spends the seventh solemnly invoking the aid and the blessings of the Prince of Peace.

How petty the little incidents I can record appear when compared to the fratricidal aspirations of the faithful! Yet I must return to my own little lambs. I had only mentioned New-Year's Day to speak of cards and letters exchanged, and of the tribute of sweets to the sweet, and of tips to the tipsters. All that to tell of a particular letter Claude received on that day. The address was in his own handwriting on an envelope which he had left the summer before with Madeleine.

"When you can write, you let me know," he had said. "The good Sisters have promised me to teach you." And here was the letter:—

"Monsieur,—I have learnt to write now, and I am so happy because I can write to you. I have prayed to the Bon Jésus to give you health and all happiness in the new year. And I am still in the hospital, and the sisters are so good to me.—Your grateful   Madeleine."

To be sure he answered, and that most cordially and sympathetically, and at the same time he wrote to the Économe, the Secretary of the Hospital, asking for information concerning her health, and her prospects of recovery. He received in return full particulars both from the secretary and from the doctor who had been attending the case for the last fifteen months. Her life had been despaired of, nor was she yet out of danger; she would have to undergo another operation shortly. Further anxious inquiries from Dupont elicited bulletins stating that the operation had been successful, but that for some time afterwards the strength of the patient had been at its lowest ebb. She was improving, and the only thing that might eventually restore her to health would be to send her into the country, where pure air and careful tending might possibly effect a cure. Situated as she was, there seemed no prospect of her securing that advantage, so Dupont volunteered to defray the cost of placing her in a convalescent home, as soon as she could leave the hospital. The country air worked wonders, and, one thing leading to another, in due time he placed her in a school, a convent, where she was in every respect well taken care of, and where she still enjoyed the full benefit of healthy surroundings. Under these circumstances she made rapid progress, both physically and intellectually.

In the meanwhile Claude was busy all through the winter. After our return from the pedestrian tour he had set to work on the picture for which he had accumulated so many studies. It was original in more than one respect. He had selected a canvas of a peculiar shape, about twice as wide as it was high, but his composition seemed to fill the space allotted to it quite naturally and spontaneously.

His figures were half life-size; the main group, somewhat to the right, was enveloped in the haze of a mysterious chiaroscuro. On the extreme left, at the entrance to the primitive dwelling, the figures of three children stood out dark against the bright sky, a beautiful silhouette and true to nature, for he had taken it from life, noting it during a halt in a peasant's cottage near Orléans. He knew the text tells us that none but the apostles and the child's father and mother were allowed to follow the Master; but children were children all the world over, he said, and they might well have disregarded the command.

The picture was destined to remain on the easel for a long while, for whilst devoting much of his time to it, Claude continued his studies with unabated energy, attending lectures, making a series of elaborate anatomical drawings, and I fear, generally burning the artistic candle at both ends.

But towards the close of the winter, the picture, being very far advanced, Claude showed it to some friends whose opinion he valued. They were evidently much struck by his rendering of the subject.

Some very eulogistic remarks must have reached l'oncle Auguste, for, on the strength of them, he resolved to visit the studio. He had hitherto not condescended to show any interest in his nephew's work, but, as others were speaking of it, he felt it desirable to be posted up to date.

It happened that when he called, Claude was out, but Rosa Bonheur Sinel was there, and at once took it upon herself to do the honours of the place and to expatiate on the beauties of the canvas.

"*I* sat for the foot of the daughter," she said; "she is supposed to have pushed off the drapery. You see, my big toe is fine; it is quite apart from the one next to it; there is room for three pieces of twenty sous between them. Sit down this side, so you don't get the varnish; now if you look through your hand, like that, you will see a large earthenware thing in the background. That's a big water-bottle; it's what they used before they were Christians. It has *du style*, you know, and keeps the water cool. Next week we shall get the frame, then you will see it plainer; and look at the figures; they are just what is wanted, and the draperies; monsieur never uses the mannequin, that's what makes them so natural; that's just how people look when somebody gets risen from the dead."

And so she went on, assisting Uncle Auguste in arriving at a due appreciation of the picture, and giving him points he used afterwards for the enlightenment of his friends. Looking round the studio, he said, more to himself than to the young lady who had taken him in hand—

"What a garret! Never saw anything like it! Why, there isn't a creature comfort in the place. I must really send him up some"——

"That you should," broke in Miss Rosa; "I know what he wants."

"And what may that be, Miss Saucebox?" he asked.

"Goldfish in a bowl, and a net with a handle," she said. "Four goldfish."

"Bosh!" said the tanner; "fiddlesticks!"

But this remarkable young person knew her own mind and would not take "Fiddlesticks" for an answer, and before many minutes had elapsed, she was escorting l'oncle Auguste to a neighbouring shop, and superintending the purchase of a long-coveted bowl resplendent with gold-fish.

"They're just right," she said; "he will like something live, I know; he's tired of his models. They are all nowhere now, since he has had that girl, that daughter of Jairus. Oh yes, monsieur, I know all about it. She's a young person in Lyons, and he wants his father to send for her, and do I don't know what besides. But I don't want her here with her big staring eyes and her Sainte Nitouche airs."

L'oncle Auguste raised his eyebrows in a way peculiar to himself. Who was this girl in Lyons? How was it that a man of his importance in the family should be reduced to picking up his information in this stray fashion?

Rosa was quick to read his thoughts, and saw her opportunity. Tossing her head so energetically, that the last hairpin gave way and those obstreperous red locks of hers came tumbling over her eyes, she said—

"It's no business of mine. Besides, *I* never speak

of young ladies who write letters," and another shake of the locks emphasised her meaning.

That was all. It would have been *infra dig.* for *l'oncle* to have cross-questioned her, so he said nothing, but his eyebrows went up a little higher, and remained there quite a while after the little female Iago had left the stage triumphantly minus hairpins, but plus goldfish.

I say stage advisedly, for Rosa was a consummate little actress, and as the père Sinel of the Théâtre Français used to tell us, there was no doubt her talent was inherited from him.

The uncle went home in a reflective frame of mind. He could see no particular objection to some short-lived intrigue.

"A good-looking young fellow like Claude," he muttered to himself. "To be sure. We all know what's what—but that's not that, or his father would not know of it, or at least not be asked to bring her to Paris. There must be something more serious at the bottom of this. *Petite guenon va!* (You little she-monkey!)" and he growled as his thoughts reverted to Rosa; but being himself something of a bully, he rather appreciated her impudence. So when he later on related the gold-fish incident to some friends at his club, he wound up with his favourite phrase—

"Now mark my words, gentlemen" (he always insisted on having his words marked at the club), "mark my words, that girl will go far; and when she finds a comb to keep that crop of hair in order, she'll find a carriage and pair too."

As I have said before, the subject of matrimony, applied to his nephew, was of all others the one that the uncle was touchy about, and anything that threatened to delay or obstruct the ambitious plans he had formed for that nephew must be combated. He had more than once expounded the true principles of worldly wisdom to him, but had always been nonplussed by Claude's independent spirit and his ready wit, so he did not go straight off and make a scene ; he must get at the truth though, but he must bide his time and watch his opportunity.

The facts of the case were simply these : There had been some question of finding Madeleine occupation in Paris, for it had become desirable that something should be done to give her the means of earning her own livelihood, and Miss Rosa, who had caught scraps of conversation between the father and son, had just put two and two together in her fanciful way, and had jumped to her own conclusions not complimentary to the Sainte Nitouche.

It so chanced that at the time Madeleine's future status was under consideration, I was able to visit Lyons, so I had at last an opportunity of seeing my friend's protégée. It had been arranged that I should meet her at the hospital in the Économe's Office, and I was not a little anxious to see what she would be like. In the office I found Monsieur Tamiasse, a small man, seated at a disproportionately large table. I was struck, too, by the size of the fine old room, and somewhat overawed by its contents.

There was an air of systematic order and bureaucratic rule about it that did not fail to impress a frail

Bohemian like myself; there were many books, boxes, and cases about, labelled, ticketed, and docketed, and I felt sure I was going to be placed in safe custody somewhere in a pigeon-hole, neatly linked to Claude, Madeleine, and the doctors. But Monsieur Tamiasse soon put me at my ease. He was a bright, genial little man, a first-class Économe, wearing a second-class wig, and probably in receipt of a third-class salary. I was Monsieur Dupont's ambassador and plenipotentiary, and as such I was received with a warm welcome, and officially thanked for all that had been done for Madeleine. I could but return the compliment, for Monsieur Tamiasse had quite constituted himself her guardian, and had proved himself a most practical and useful friend, ever ready to smooth any little difficulties that came in her way. We soon got to the object of my visit, and talked over the next step to take in Madeleine's interest.

An extensive business in ecclesiastical embroideries is carried on in Lyons, and it had been suggested that she should enter an *atelier de broderie*. Claude had already expressed his approval, so nothing remained but to find a suitable opening for her. An excellent lady, who was at the head of such an atelier, was a personal friend of the Économe's, and so all could be soon satisfactorily settled.

When our little consultation was at an end, Madeleine was called in. I was rather formally introduced to her, and to the Sister of Mercy who accompanied her; the latter one of those excellent Sœurs de Charité who devote their lives to the tending of the sick and helpless.

" You have been Madeleine's ministering angel, ma sœur," I said—" I am sure we are deeply grateful to you. *N'est ce pas, mademoiselle?*" I added, turning to Madeleine.

" *Ah oui, monsieur*," she answered.

" And you are the good fairy who taught her to read and write," I went on, " and there again, I am sure we are very grateful to you. *N'est ce pas, mademoiselle?*"

" *Ah oui, monsieur*," she once more answered.

She was decidedly shy, and only raised her eyes for a moment, by way of seeing those three words safe on their way.

The eyes were the amethyst eyes of the picture. I had at once recognised those, but in all else I found Madeleine quite different to what I had expected. In fact, at this, our first meeting, I was rather disappointed. Instead of the delicate poetical creature I had always fancied her, I found a strong and hearty girl, with fresh red lips and rather sunburnt cheeks, but without a suspicion of Biblical halo encircling the several coils of brown hair that were loosely wound around her head.

She, I think, was disappointed too in me. Whether, in her mind's eye, she had also pictured me surrounded by some sort of halo or blazing glory, I do not know. It is as likely as not, for Claude had mentioned me in his letters to her, and he was never impartial in his judgment when speaking or writing of his friends. And wisely too, I think, for whom can a man look to for partiality, if not to a friend ? David and Jonathan, I feel sure, were not unbiassed in the estimate they formed of one another. But however pleasant it may be to find one's merits acknowledged and one's virtues extolled, it is decidedly a drawback when one is called upon to live up to the reputation that has preceded one. The Madeleines and others will seek in vain for the halo, and undoubtedly be disappointed.

The good sister took her leave, and Monsieur Tamiasse left me to have a *tête-à-tête* with Claude's *protégée*, whilst he at once wrote off to the lady embroideress who was to take charge of her. I had by this time quite realised that Madeleine and the daughter of Jairus were two very distinct persons, and that the former was none the less attractive for never having been called upon to cross and to re-cross the Styx. I had gone a step further, and looking at her with an artistic eye, I had even noticed that her eyelashes had considerably grown since the days when Claude drew the eyes *à la* Gabriel Max.

So far I did not seem to have hit on a good conversational opening. To be sure, if Madeleine had been an English girl, I might have made a remark about the weather and had a fair start; as it was I went on at random and said—

"I am so glad you liked that book I sent you." (It was Grimm's "Fairy Tales.") "You did like it, didn't you?"

"Oh yes, monsieur; so much I can't tell you."

"But do try to tell me. I so want to know why you liked it."

"Who could help liking it? It's all about the fairies and fairyland."

"Yes, mademoiselle, that is quite a wonderful world to peep into."

"It *is* wonderful. It's *my* world. Things happen there just as they happen to me."

"Well, I hope it was only the good fairies you had to do with."

"I don't know that, but they protected me from the bad ones. And they wouldn't let the dragon devour me, but nursed and cured me, and taught me to pray to the Sainte Vierge."

Here her ologies were becoming somewhat mixed, for she had evidently not attempted to settle in her mind what of gratitude to give unto Theos and what unto Mythos.

"It was one of the good ones, I suppose, that taught you to read and write?"

"Yes, that was Sister Louise whom you saw just now; she's as good a fairy as ever was. Ah, monsieur, you can't understand it, you can't realise what a wonderful thing it is to be able to read and write. You learnt it when you were a child and *couldn't* know; but I was quite a big girl and had made my first communion when I began to learn those wonderful signs that you can say everything with—everything you can possibly think of—and that make it possible to read anything anybody in the whole world ever thought of."

"Well, I am quite glad you told me. Now I can report to Monsieur Dupont that you are both well and happy."

"That you can; and tell Monsieur Claude that I am grateful to him for bringing me those three fairies.

It was that morning, the second time he came——
But I am talking too much," she said, interrupting
herself suddenly, "and that is rude. I hope you will
excuse, monsieur."

"Excuse! Why, my dear child, I love to hear you
talk about all that—I am devoted to Fairyland myself; it is quite the artist's home, you know, and I
must tell you my experience of it presently; but first
I am curious to know how he came to bring those
good fairies to you. And three too; just like in the
tales; everything always goes by threes."

"I never thought of that," she said reflectively,
and then continued, once for all giving up the idea
that talking much was rude. "I've got them pressed
between the leaves of my prayer-book. They were
three beautiful red roses when he brought them; I
never saw such three roses before. I turned them to
the light and tried to make them happy whilst they
were with me, but to be sure I knew I could not
keep them alive long, so when they seemed ready to
die, I put them in the book. They were under my
pillow when I was very, very ill. I must have been
bad, for one night the doctors thought I was going
to die, and Sœur Louise wouldn't let Sœur Amélie
take her turn to sit by me. But I knew I was not
going to die; I even knew I was going to get quite
well, because the three good roses told me so—I
hope you won't laugh at me, monsieur, for calling a
rose a fairy, but I——"

"Now really, mademoiselle, you couldn't for a
moment imagine that I should be so matter-of-fact
and heartless as to laugh."

"Well, what do you think of her, monsieur?" broke in Monsieur Tamiasse. "What does she look like now? There's her record in that third Division, Casier G, No. 721. There we have her from the first day when she was brought to us, to the day when we thought she was going to be carried away from us, and so on up to date. She is not a bad specimen of the sort we turn out at the Lyons City Hospital, is she? Not that we always succeed. We are beaten more than once by the grim old gentleman with the scythe. But we are always ready to fight him, and we manage sometimes to get hold of his hour-glass and turn it upside down. Well, to-morrow we hand this young lady over to my friend Mademoiselle Chevillard. She will be here at twelve o'clock. Will you come and give your sanction to the transfer?"

"Certainly," I said, and took my leave.

And as I went home I thought the world was not so bad after all, with its Sisters of Charity, its bright, devoted little Économe, and its Madeleine with her friends the fairies.

To-morrow came, and with it the transfer. I sanctioned it with all my heart, for Mademoiselle Chevillard at once struck me as just the person we could entrust our ward to. She and the Économe were settling the business part of the transaction, and I turned to Madeleine and asked her whether she was pleased to learn the art of embroidery.

"Pleased!" she said, "why, it's the very thing I have always been longing for. That's just why I am going to get it. I told you that things happened to me as they do in the fairy tales. So my wish is to be fulfilled, and I'm going to paint pictures like the one Monsieur le Curé showed me, all done with a needle."

I wanted to know more about Monsieur le Curé and the picture, and so she told me he was her great friend and instructor at the convent. He had one day taken her into the sacristy of his church, and there she had seen the most lovely piece of embroidery one could imagine. It was under glass and in a gold frame, and represented the Madonna surrounded by little lambs with silky curls; one of them she was fondly petting. Over her head two little angels were holding a large crown, all of intertwined gold threads, and at her feet l'enfant Jésus was seated on the grass amongst flowers, every one of which was a combination of glossy silks and sparkling beads and spangles. I remember it all so well, for I am sure that girl taught me, if not to admire, at least to analyse the beauties of ecclesiastical embroidery.

By this time we had got quite confidential, and she said, "You were going to tell me about your fairyland."

So I told her that I too was one of those privileged creatures to whom all good things seemed to come without much waiting. I could not lay claim to a fairy godmother, but my godfather was quite a match for any good genius of either sex.

"Yes, mademoiselle, every Thursday evening, as the clock struck half-past six, he would appear in a hallowed place called the "House of Robes."[1] There

---

[1] The Gewandhaus in Leipsic.

he stood, every inch a ruler, the centre figure in a group of loyal vassals, waiting for a sign from his hand—I see him now—He raises his magic wand; a great rite is about to be performed, and spell-bound we listen for the coming sounds. Then onwards, upwards he leads us, into realms of un-fathomable mysteries, where Music rules supreme."

"Who was that, monsieur? I cannot follow you."

"A magician, Maddalena! He could conjure up to your vision the dream of a Midsummer night, and his were the Songs that needed no words. Now, he has left us for the very realms his fancy had created. When he arrived there, the gate was opened wide to admit him, and Elijah the prophet stood ready with St. Paul to receive him. No wonder you are mystified, my dear. I'll explain it all to you another time. I really only meant to tell you that his name was Felix, and that means happy, and with the name my good god-father gave me happiness. Yes, good things seem to come to me as they do to you. May it last! At any rate we will hold on to the fairies as long as we can, and if ever the wicked dragon crosses our paths, we will stand by one another, won't we?"

"Well, I can't do much," she said, "but I'll run a needle through him, if he means mischief."

And the offensive and defensive alliance thus ratified, we parted, each the richer for a new friend.

In my letters to Claude I gave very full parti-culars of my conversations with Madeleine, and of the practical result of my visit; in fact it is from these letters, now in my hands, that I have been largely quoting. More than a twelvemonth was to elapse before we met again, for I had left Paris to pursue my studies under Kaulbach in Munich. The numerous letters Claude wrote to me during the interval, mostly treat of the two subjects uppermost in his mind, art and love. As I once more read them over after many years, I am aware that the history of his loves really offers no very remarkable features, and I approach the subject with some diffidence on that account. But on the other hand I remember that we all like the old story that always assumes a new shape; we like it perhaps, because, in this wicked world of ours, hatred and evil influences so constantly cross our path, that we are always glad to turn aside when the opportunity offers, and to listen to tales of love and devotion. And there were gold and silver threads that ran through Claude's life, as they do through most people's.

He was very impressionable, but he never treated love lightly; he often would see beauty where I, for the life of me, saw no more than ordinary good looks; in fact his artistic temperament would lead him to evolve a perfect Venus or a paragon of virtue from very slender materials. But he was too honest, and too much of an idealist, to indulge in the popular pastime of flirtation. Love skirmishes he might be drawn into, but they were not of his seeking, and he usually remained on the defensive. The Venuses and Paragons might rule supreme for a while, but when— as would soon happen—they were found wanting in some of the perfections his imagination had endowed them with, his idol had to step off its pedestal. Nor was he particularly humbled when he had to acknowledge his mistake. He would often say that it was quite a different thing to be " amoureux d'une femme," and to " aimer une femme "—to be in love with, or to love a woman. And then, dear old mystic that he was at the bottom of his heart, he would conjure up a " Vision of Love," as he called it, a vision to be "divined, not defined." Was he ever to marry and be happy? I often wondered.

When I arrived in Paris, I found Claude at the station, and we embraced in true continental fashion. I had been invited to stay with him and his father, and I was soon established under their hospitable roof.

The first twenty-four hours we slept little and talked much. I knew all about the picture and all about a new star in his horizon, Mademoiselle Jeanne, but what is *all* when it is crammed into the few pages of a letter? Very little as compared with what can be made of it in conversation.

Of the picture later on; first about the girl. Mademoiselle Jeanne was the daughter of the *grand Roule;* so we had called her father, for no better reason than that his charming residence was in the Faubourg du Roule.

He was one of the leading physicians in Paris, more particularly known by his writings, which treated of some pathological speciality, I forget which. Her mother was an Englishwoman. During a twenty years' residence in Paris she had added to the sterling qualities of her race the graceful attributes of a Parisian. She was not only a charming hostess, but a woman of great literary attainments, and indeed she must have been more than that, an erudite scholar, if, as the world said, some of the best pages in the doctor's books came from her pen. He gave colour to the assertion, for by word and deed he showed that he held her and her judgment in the highest esteem. It was quite a pleasure to see this united couple together, a pleasure I often enjoyed, for during my first long stay in Paris I had been made quite at home in their house.

Jeanne, or, as her mother persisted in calling her, Jane, was about sixteen when I first knew her. She was reserved and diffident; happiest when allowed to remain unnoticed in the background, positively distressed when dragged into broad daylight, or obliged to take her share in gaieties. I soon discovered the cause of her shyness. She suffered from the consciousness that she had red hair; in fact that consciousness seemed to have sunk deep into her heart and mind, and to have made her morbidly sensitive.

In those days red hair evoked nothing but a pointed reference to carrots — that from the ill-natured; the good-natured would feel compassion for the poor girls who were thus afflicted. I wonder sometimes whether the red of those days was the same we admire now, whether those carrots of my youth can have been transformed into the lusciously lustrous locks of to-day. Were they formerly only under a cloud and crushed under the weight of unanimous condemnation? Could the molten gold have been hidden away, and the deep-toned brass notes silenced, and were they only waiting to be combed and coaxed to the front?—Well, the trials of the sandy-hair phase are over, and I, for one, am grateful to live in the Renaissance period, and to witness the triumph of woman's loveliest crown.

Poor Mademoiselle Jeanne did what she could to conceal the luxuriant crop Nature had given her. She wound it in tight coils round the back of her head, where at least she could not see it if she chanced to come across a looking-glass. She brushed it off her forehead with a determination to show as little as possible of it in front, and if a few spiteful stray hairs would not lie down with the rest, she cut them off, much to my distress, for, when talking to her, my eyes were always wandering to the little border of reddish stubble that remained, and I saw her see me seeing, and that made it awkward for both.

Her extreme sensitiveness no doubt originated in the unkind comments made upon her in her childhood. As she grew up, it seemed impossible to efface these early impressions. She had got it into her head that she was the ugly duckling, and neither parents nor friends could persuade her to the contrary. But she gradually accepted what she considered the inevitable, and at the time Claude appeared on the scene (I introduced him to the family) she had sufficiently overcome her shyness, to perform the duties of a young lady of eighteen in her mother's salon, without betraying how much she would have preferred keeping in the background. It was very characteristic of that young lady that, when she did emerge from the background, she would do so with a rush; whether she offered you a chair or a cup of tea, she came upon you unexpectedly, firing as it were, at close quarters, and retreating before you could capture her.

"I know I'm a coward," she said to me one day when we were talking of heroes, "and it's just because I'm a coward that there is no virtue I admire more than courage. If I were a man, I would, I could "——

There she stopped short, and left me to guess the rest. I often noticed that when her thoughts were about to come to the surface, she would get alarmed at her own boldness, and take refuge in some commonplace remark, or relapse into silence, leaving your curiosity ungratified as to what was really going on in her mind.

With Claude she was more at her ease than with any of the other young men that came to the house. This was not to be wondered at, for Claude, as I have said, was the sort of man who would inspire even little street girls with confidence. I don't think he ever made any comments on her hair, but perhaps his eye too sometimes rested unconsciously on the stubbles, and thus exercised its influence; certain it is that an influence was at work. The little refractory hairs that had been a source of so much trouble, were allowed to follow their natural bent, and began to wave and frizz. That was a symptom: others were to follow. One evening conversation had turned on skulls and brains, and the doctor had given us some interesting facts relating to the comparative sizes of the brains in man and in the inferior animals. Claude, who had made quite a special study of anatomy, took up the subject from the artistic point of view, and showed the relationship between brains and beauty.

"The great artists," he said, "have ever given due predominance to the cranium over the eyes, nose, and mouth. The receptacle of the brains must lord it over the representatives of the senses. That is, too, why they have made so much of the hair, using it to give full development to the upper part of the head. It's a most fascinating art, that of the hair-dresser," he wound up, "and I sometimes feel that *Anch'io* might have been *Parruchiere!* I think I missed my vocation!"

These observations of Claude's had a remarkable effect. The coils were loosened, a little at first, then by degrees more; and the material at hand, one could not help noticing, was being reconstructed after the style adopted by the immortal Venus of Milo. At that time Claude was but moderately interested in Jeanne, but, much as a gardener looks with satisfaction at the fresh shoots of a plant that seemed doomed, so he looked with pleasure on the rising waves which he knew had come at his bidding. His eyes had a way of indicating a little in advance what his lips were going to say; it was a case of light travelling faster than sound; so first came the twinkle and then the words. Jeanne got the full benefit of the approving twinkle, and was relieved when she found that it was not followed by a congratulatory speech. He only said—

"I see your brain is struggling for space," and then changed the subject.

It is surprising how symptoms have a way of begetting symptoms, and what striking effects they are apt to have on sensitive natures like Claude's. He became more and more of a gardener, and brought beneficent sunshine into the life of the budding flower.

On the 15th of August he and Jeanne were together at the Turkish Embassy. They were amongst the guests invited to witness the grand spectacle provided for the pleasure-seeking Parisian on that day, the *Mi-Août*, as it is called. It was the great Napoleon's birthday, henceforth to be consecrated as the National Holiday. The newly founded Empire spared nothing to organise fêtes in general, and this one in particular, on the grandest scale. All the resources of the decorator's art had been brought to bear on the Champs Elysées, and with such success that no fields could have looked more Elysian. The sculptor had contributed colossal figures, the architect triumphal arches, and an untold number of *lampions* were suspended in festoons which reached in gradually ascending curves from the Place de la Concorde to the Arc de Triomphe de l'Étoile.

A grand review, a military pageant, such as only a Napoleon could call into existence, was once more to show an admiring universe the unrivalled superiority of the French army, when marshalled by the Emperor now representing the greatest of Cesarian dynasties.

The Parisian was overflowing with patriotic emotions; his heart beat fast and vibrated with legitimate pride, as drums and bugles summoned him to witness the glorious spectacle. From all sides the people were streaming towards the Place de la Concorde. There, to your left, if you turn your back on the Obelisk and the fountains, you see the garden of what was then the Turkish Embassy (now a club). It is considerably raised above the level of the Rue Boissy d'Anglais on the one side, and the Avenue Gabrielle on the other. It was a point of vantage from which it must have been quite pleasant for the privileged beau-monde to look down on the struggling plebeian.

Jeanne and Claude had been walking up and down that garden absorbed in earnest conversation. He was bitterly opposed to these military pageants, and with the natural eloquence of conviction, he had been inveighing against the delusions of mankind that culminate in fratricidal warfare. He was particularly hard on Horace Vernet, that panegyrist of the *piou-piou*, as he called him.

"How can a man lower his art to the level of tunics and red breeches?" he asked. "He's at best a stump orator on canvas, using his brushes to tickle the national pride of the Frenchman! 'L'Empire, c'est la Paix,' indeed! Does it look like it?"

"Well, so far it does," said Mademoiselle Jeanne. "Surely this is a peaceful fête. See how the people enjoy it."

"Yes, mademoiselle, poor blind deluded people! Look again, and fancy that man shot through the heart with a bullet, and that boy on his shoulders pinned to the wall with a bayonet."

"Oh, don't speak like that, Monsieur Claude; you know I'm an abject coward. I should fly to the ends of the earth rather than face danger."

"You are right. I beg your pardon; I know I ought not to conjure up ugly visions, least of all before your eyes, Mademoiselle Jeanne."

"I dare say you think me very foolish, Monsieur Claude, but——"

"Not foolish, mademoiselle; on the contrary, I am grateful to you for pulling me up when I fly off at a tangent as I did just now."

"Yes, monsieur," she answered, "I know you are always indulgent. That is, I suppose, why I venture to pull you up, as you call it. You see, I can't always follow you, and I don't want to be left behind."

That was a long sentence for her.

Whilst the ambassador's guests had elbow-room and to spare, the crowd below got more and more densely packed; it had so far surged hither and thither to the accompaniment of good-natured jokes, banter and *blague*, but suddenly a cry of alarm was raised :—

"*Nom d'un nom*, stand back ! *Pour l'amour de Dieu*, don't push; you'll crush the child ! The woman is fainting. Keep her head up or she's lost !"

Those are terrible moments when a crowd first realises imminent danger, and the instinct of self-preservation overrides all fellow-feeling, shows no mercy, gives no quarter. Yes, indeed, keep your head up, or you are lost. In the garden above, the festive gathering was suddenly changed into a scene of confusion. The ladies shrieked, and one or two of them swooned in sheer sympathetic terror. Men thundered words of command to the crowd below, that were lost in a sea of noises. At the first indication of danger, Jeanne had darted away like an arrow into the house; Claude was to the front trying, but in vain, to reach the child that was being held up by a pair of strong arms. A few instants more and Jeanne was back, carrying a chair. Not a pin could drop to the ground that crowd covered, but the chair did, and, with its aid, the work of rescue began.

"Get another," she called to Claude, "that one will be broken up directly," and off she was again. Another minute and she appeared at a window overlooking the Rue Boissy d'Anglais, brandishing the first thing she chanced to lay hands upon—a large Turkish sabre. The shy girl with the red hair, the abject coward, was transformed into a modern Jeanne d'Arc, mowing the air with the curved blade of the Saracens; a curious picture, that arrested the attention of the crowd beneath, at a point some two hundred yards in the rear of the dangerous corner of the Avenue Gabrielle, thus holding in check for a moment the seething mass of people who were pressing forward, unconscious of the danger to life and limb they were creating.

"En arrière!" she cried. "On s'écrase la bas! Barrez la rue!" An officer of the Gensdarmerie took in the situation. He backed his horse on the advancing crowd, orders were given to stop the influx from the Rue du Faubourg St. Honoré, and a catastrophe was averted.

The story of the timely relief of those besieged

garden walls rapidly spread amongst the guests, who were gradually recovering from their fright. The ladies had ceased shrieking, and had completed the elaborate process of swooning, and of being brought round by the polite attentions of the gentlemen; they were now extolling Jeanne's presence of mind.

"My dear," said one old lady, "without you they would have stormed the house, and with my wretched health, I should not have survived it."

"Yes," added her son-in-law, "single-handed she beat the rabble back. She ought to have the Légion d'Honneur."

"Take me away," Jeanne said to Claude; "anywhere, into the house."

"Do you mind my stopping with you?" asked Claude, but not till they had settled on a many-cushioned divan in the coolest and quietest room of the Embassy.

"Do stop," she said, "to protect me from the rabble. I might not be able to beat it back single-handed."

Claude thought he had never seen her hair so beautifully untidy before.

"I am sure I said nothing; no, *nothing*. But I can't help fancying she thinks I said *something*, and that's what makes me miserable."

So Claude assured me as I closely cross-questioned him on the subject of that day's conversation. Something had happened since to make him revert to the many-cushioned divan with uneasiness. He had gone, much against his inclination, on a visit to his uncle's.

"I know it's a guet-apens, a trap," he had said to me. "The old story ; he wants to marry me to some money-bag. Anyway, he's too late now ; I'm not in the market. For all that I wish I had Jeanne down there to help me beat off the enemy with her Turkish scimitar. Bother matrimony ! Why must we always be thinking of it ? As if loving and being loved wasn't heavenly enough by itself. And why must we always go a-hunting in so-called society ? Don't you think we ought to stick to our Quartier Latin and take a spouse of our own Bohemian type, instead of pottering about in swell salons and falling in love with some fine lady who will expect a fellow to go about disguised as a gentleman for the rest of his natural life ? "

Such were his sentiments before he started. Four days afterwards he returned in love with a beautiful woman, and quite disposed to make a gentleman, or even a fool, of himself for her sake.

I happened to know her. Her name was Olga Rabachot. Her father was a Pole, one of those ill-fated noblemen who died for their country, whose estates were sequestrated, and whose fortune went to swell the coffers of the Russian Treasury. The mother and daughter settled in Paris. I suppose they lived in a garret, and gave music lessons, after the style of good Polish refugees ; but I really know nothing about it, and probably only derive my impressions from the circumstance that the mother sang and the daughter played one evening when I was introduced to them at the house of Hittorff, the famous architect of the Place de la Concorde. A short time afterwards it was rumoured that a Monsieur Rabachot, an elderly gentleman who had made a fortune in business, had become much attracted by the charms and graces of the mother, Madame Somethingiska. This proved to be true, but only inasmuch as he saw in her an eligible mother-in-law. We soon heard to our surprise that his hand and his fortune had been accepted by the daughter, the younger *iska*.

The curiously assorted couple enjoyed but a brief term of matrimonial bliss, or whatever else it may have been. Before a year had gone by, the wealthy manufacturer was suddenly struck down by heart disease, as he stood by the open grave of a friend. The incident made quite a sensation in Paris at the time.

It was the bereaved widow, then, that Claude met at his uncle's. The late husband had been on terms of close friendship with the tanner, and had appointed him one of the executors of his will. But all business connected with this had been settled nearly a twelvemonth ago, and now l'oncle Auguste thought it about time to put his abilities in the matrimonial agency line to the test. So, as Claude had correctly guessed, he had prepared his little guet-apens.

With Claude it was love at first sight—that is, if we may apply the term love to what is begotten of intense admiration for the creature beauties of woman. She had eyes, so it seemed to me at least, that might rest when off duty, but would ever be on the alert where they could be used to advantage. Her mouth, I must say, was most attractive. The lips were carved, curved, and coloured to perfection, and I cannot recollect ever having seen any of their kind better fitted to be met by other lips. Her pallor was interesting, her hair jet black, and her manners fascinating; but for all that I could never have worshipped at her shrine. Not so Claude. He saw everything in her that a man sees when he is struck blind by the God of love.

As we walked home together, on his return from that first meeting, we talked it all over. When we got home we talked it all over again. First it was daytime; then came the night; then the day broke again, and we were still talking—always on that inexhaustible theme that, since articulate sound was created, has used up more language than all other themes put together.

It must have been thus, I feel confident, that Orestes and Pylades talked by the hour when one of them or both were in love, and so too all the O.'s and P.'s, and, for the matter of that, all the other initials of the alphabet, ranging from the Alpha to the Omega.

At first I was not sympathetically inclined, and put spokes into the wheels that were running away with Claude. After a while I merely tried to apply the brake, lest he should rush down hill too rapidly, but I finally found myself running and rolling along, doing my best to keep pace with him.

The fact is his enthusiasm was catching. He described that woman so vividly that, for the time being, I could not help seeing her as he painted her. To be sure the thousand and one little details that made up our conversation do not bear repetition. The facts that I elicited were these : At his uncle's bidding Claude came, Claude saw, and Claude was conquered. Was she conquered too? That was a question not easily answered. During the four days they were together she sometimes accepted his attentions very graciously ; at other times she was anything but encouraging, and even showed so marked a preference for the uncle that it seemed as if the young widow had preserved a taste for elderly husbands. He, l'oncle Auguste, inclined as he was under ordinary circumstances to lord it over friend and foe alike, was unmistakably cowed in the presence of the Polish fascinator. She not only showed interest in the tanner's work, but also fearlessly indulged in criticism ; this more especially in reference to the ventilation of some of the workshops. That she should have selected this particular subject for her adverse comments rather surprised me, for I had been brought up in the belief that the Poles might ventilate their grievances, but not much else.

The subject led to a rather lively discussion between Madame Rabachot and Claude's uncle, she being of the very advanced opinion that a man, even if he only worked from ten to twelve hours a day in an enclosed space, was entitled to a fair amount of pure air, whereas the distinguished head of the concern, who was of the good old school, maintained that in his experience of many years' standing he had always gone by the golden rule that the amount of fresh air provided for the workman should be in exact proportion to the wages he is paid. The fair advocate of man's rights, however, stood her ground so well that the unfortunate employer had to give way, and promise the desired reforms.

This episode made a great impression on Claude, as well it might. Perhaps, though, he went a little far, when he said she was a noble creature, the champion of the great cause of suffering humanity, and the like. To be sure the chief factor of her strength was the splendid gift she possessed of using her eyes.

I elicited that even whilst skirmishing with the uncle she always had at least one eye on the nephew; that one was evidently enough to hold him in subjection, for with it she had condescended to say many pleasant things that she did not deem it desirable to entrust to the indiscretions of the lips. Taking it all in all, I came to the conclusion that she was, to say the least of it, very much interested in Claude, but that, being of a kittenish disposition, she had coquetted with the uncle in the playful way so frequently practised by women when they look sweet upon one man with a view to quickening the pulses of another, whose affections they aspire to secure.

If Claude said he was miserable, it was not so much because it was yet an open question whether the young widow could reciprocate his feelings, but because the image of Jeanne stood between him and his new love. He knew that Jeanne was more than partial to him, and he felt that he had been slowly but surely drawn towards her.

How much or how little had he really shown the interest he took in her was the question that exercised his mind.   Had he ever said anything that she could have construed into an acknowledgment of a deeper feeling than that of friendship, anything that would be at least morally binding?   No, certainly not in words ; but then, to be sure, much can be said without the use of spoken language.   Of all the songs without words the love song is the most legible. Besides, the most harmless of words can make mischief if they are taken in connection with what has preceded.   The statement that twice two makes four is innocent enough in itself, but it may, under given circumstances, be made to say that she has two eyes and so have you, and that, if she could only vouchsafe to see with your eyes as you see with hers, twice two in this particular case would make one.

Nor need you propound subtle solutions of arithmetical problems ; you need but admire the humble cottage as you go across fields with her, if you want to commit yourself irrevocably, and so too, the mere mention of the moon has been enough to dispose of a man for life.

Claude may not have strictly avoided every opening of this kind, but I certainly do not think he had any cause for self-reproach.   I felt sorry for Jeanne, for it was evident that, for some time to come at least, there was little prospect of her regaining whatever hold she might have had on him.   There was nothing to be done in that direction ; so we shelved Mademoiselle Jeanne *sine die*, and talked of the other one.

That other one had been particularly sympathetic in her appreciation of Claude's picture; it had at last been completed and sent to the Salon. On the varnishing day it was sold to a dealer for two thousand francs.

"That goes to the Madeleine fund," said Dupont, who was always planning great things for the girl's future.

"That goes to me," said the dealer, as he resold the picture and pocketed a profit of fifteen hundred francs.

The "Daughter of Jairus" could not fail to attract much attention. Original as it was in its composition, and independent in its conception of a religious subject, it led to much heated controversy in the leading papers of the day. In some of them the artist was lauded to the skies; in others, roundly abused. Those three poor dear little innocents standing at the open door of Jairus's house, more than any other incident in the picture, gave rise to brilliant argument, vigorously attacked as they were on the one hand, and heroically defended on the other.

Virtually the able art-critics were divided into two camps, from which they issued grandiloquent manifestoes, and passed judgment on art and artists, past, present, and future. I have not preserved cuttings from the papers, but I think I can give a pretty correct idea of the opposite views taken by those heaven-born wiseacres, the art-critics of the day, only apologising to them for my poor rendering of their doctrines.

"Monsieur Claude Dupont," said one set, "is a young man of great promise; he is a powerful draughtsman, and his gifts, if turned to account, may prove him to be a worthy champion of that severe and chaste school that gave us a Lesueur, an Ingres, and a Flandrin. Whilst prognosticating so bright a future to Monsieur Dupont, we feel, however, that we should not be doing our duty, if we did not warn him against the perverse influence that the apostles of the so-called Realistic school have already begun to exercise over his brush. We allude to the three children most unseemingly intruding on the grand scene that is being enacted in the house of sorrow. Let us hope that the danger that threatens the young artist may yet be averted, and that so much talent may be applied to perpetuate the traditions of a great past."

"Monsieur Claude Dupont," said the other camp, "has a great future before him, if he wisely utilises his gifts. We welcome in him a painter who, in his treatment of a religious subject, breaks with the traditions of an effete school. The introduction of those three children, peering with wondering eyes into the house of mysteries, we consider a stroke of genius. But for all that, the fetters forged by the past are still clinging to him. We heartily congratulate him on the step he has taken towards emancipation, but we would have him fully realise, that if he is to fulfil the brilliant promise of this his first picture, he must abjure once for all the errors and conventionalities of a school destined to perish at the hands of triumphant Realism."

These newspaper comments affected different people in different ways. Rosa Bonheur Sinel resented anything short of unqualified praise, and was simply indignant with one writer who had ventured to criticise the drapery she had sat for. The article commenting on the masterly drawing of her foot, she kept in a discarded hatbox with other treasures, prominent amongst which was a defunct goldfish preserved in a glass bottle.

Madeleine was supremely happy. She had seen a very sympathetic notice in the leading paper of Lyons.

"I am proud of the picture," she wrote to Claude, "and I can think of nothing else. I am sure I am quite glad I was so ill, if that helped you at all. The man who wrote the article was kind enough to say he liked the way I opened my eyes so much, that he was glad I had come to life again. I thought that rather flippant. Don't you think so, too? But then he described the whole picture so beautifully, that I fancied I could see it; he seemed to like it all, only he wanted some more 'impasto.' What can that be? May I tell you about a dream I had? You know I am always having dreams; you won't mind, will you? It's quite short, and it is all about you. I saw you in a large looking-glass, but not all of you; only from your neck to your feet; I could not see your head. Besides, I should not have noticed it if it had been in the looking-glass; I could only look at your feet. You had those slippers on I embroidered for you last year, and I was so unhappy, because they were so ugly; so unhappy, that I woke up quite upset. And since then I've been thinking, how could I ever have sent you such a stupid flower pattern, all so hard and stiff? I do feel ashamed of it now.

"Madame Chevillard is so kind. She says I am her daughter, and I feel as if I really were. In the evening I go up to her room, and she unlocks her treasure cupboard, and takes out something to show me and tell me about. She has got beautiful books, and she lets me read them to her; she sits in her big armchair and looks sweet, and she seems to know everything that is in the books. There is one that just tells all about the artists; there are lots of hard words in it, and one can only read a little of it at a time. Sometimes she laughs at me, because I say I should like to be an artist, too. I don't mean painting, but making some kind of thing beautifully.

"And often, when I read to her, I begin to wonder again how the thoughts get into the book, and I can get them out again.

"I ought to leave off writing, Madame Chevillard says, so adieu, Monsieur.—I am, your grateful friend,
"MADELEINE.

"*P.S.*—Please throw away the slippers; do. I am making you a surprise, and madame says it is going to be a much better piece of work this time. I should so much like to tell you what it is, but then, to be sure, it would not be a surprise.

"How nice you have Monsieur Felix staying with you; he is good.

"I am glad your cough is better, but do take care of yourself."

Ah, yes! we all wished he would take care of

himself; but, alas! that is just the thing he could not be induced to do. One would think that to be in love with one woman, and just out of love with another, would be fairly enough to occupy one man's mind; but it was not so with Claude. He was working in his studio, in museums and libraries, all day long, and of an evening he would study anatomy, as if he had been qualifying for a doctor. Pictures seemed constantly coming to him, like so many mocking Will-o'-the-wisps, flitting before his eyes when they were open, and twitting his worried brain when they were closed.

Madeleine's letters were always particularly quieting and soothing to him, and he used to say that, when he wanted a rest, he liked to sit down and write to her.

Not long after Claude's momentous visit to his uncle I had again to leave Paris. It was a wrench to part with him just when he needed a friend to help him through his joys and troubles, but duties of various kinds called me back to Munich, so there was nothing for it but to say good-bye. We felt it doubly, for we knew we were not to meet for some time. Write we should, to be sure, we were always good correspondents; and this time there was no need to assure one another that we should do so often.

I started from the Gare du Nord.

"Good-bye then, old fellow! *Au revoir—adieu!*" —lightly said, deeply felt.

I rolled on, thinking of Claude and Jeanne, the

widow and Madeleine, till I got to my destination,
my queer little studio in that ramshackle old house,
Schützenstrause No. 5/3 links. The address is no
use now, for that abode of mine is pulled down, as
are its dear decrepit brothers and sisters, and the
primitive old station opposite.   All to make room
for new buildings more suitable to tenants with sensitive noses and rectilinear tastes.

The first letter that reached me from Paris was
not, as I expected, in Claude's handwriting, but in
his father's.   It told me that Claude was too ill to
write.   He was to have gone down to his uncle's on
the Saturday (1 had left on the Tuesday), and he
was looking forward to what only a short time previously he had called a trap, a guet-apens, with the
greatest impatience, for amongst other guests would
be Olga Rabachot.   But before the day came he
caught a severe chill, and was peremptorily ordered
to bed.

The fascinating widow he was never to see again.
Not only the old cough had returned, but with it
symptoms sufficiently grave to make it desirable he
should winter abroad.

I had foreseen, and so has doubtless any one who
has cared so far to follow Dupont on the love-path,
that it was not he who would marry the fascinating
widow, but the uncle, and so I may as well state that
such was the case. How it came about I either never
knew or have forgotten, and as I should only be getting out of my depth if I attempted to fill the gap
with scraps of fiction, I will confine myself to the
simple narrative based on my recollections, and will

merely add that I trust the uncle and the aunt lived happily ever after, and that the workmen at the dyer's works got as much ventilation as was procurable at that time and in that particular part of the world.

Claude soon left for Mentone. Then came my turn; was it sympathy or was it coincidence? About the same time I too was taken ill, and that seriously. The cause was not far to seek : a component part in the great scheme of creation is a certain vicious north-east wind that seems to live and thrive on annihilation. This Boreas is a kind of ogre who feeds not only on fat babies, but on any mortal thing that he can turn into dust. Not satisfied with his legitimate prey, the autumn leaves, he explores every nook and corner seeking whom he may devour. He found me out one evening after a day of unusual heat, as soon after sunset he suddenly came sweeping across the mountains that lie to the north-east of Munich. For months to come he laid me low, very low, and thus all the fine plans that Claude and I had made for a regular correspondence, that would keep us linked together at least mentally, came to naught. Letters dictated to the kind and anxious watchers by our respective bedsides were but poor substitutes for the minutely detailed accounts of our doings that we usually exchanged, or for the heartfelt effusions that our friendship prompted.

But to talk of one's illnesses is really a most unpardonable offence. For all the purposes of description one can find quite enough of weakness in man when he is strong and hearty, without going out of one's way to ransack the sick-room for further evidence of his frailty. So I will merely mention that I was and remained an invalid throughout the greater part of the ensuing winter.

The truth concerning Claude's health was kept from me. I since knew that he had passed through an alarming crisis; when the fever was at its height, his mind had been wandering, and in his disconnected talk he had alternately appealed to Olga in the tenderest language, and had shrunk from her imaginary presence with aversion and terror. When calm returned and comparative health, he would not speak of her. Something of the shrinking remained.

"With you I could talk about her," he said in the first letter he could write from Mentone, "but I must wait till I am stronger, and particularly till I hear better accounts of you. It was an unpleasant dream that — well — that Erlkönig dream. Again and again I cried out : 'Mein Vater, mein Vater !'— no help came—*her* voice pursued me—On we dashed fever-spurred, till I lay dead in *her* arms.

"But, to be sure that is all 'such stuff' as dreams are made of.' To you, my dear fellow, I should only send pleasant visions, like those I am revelling in here. A new world is every day unfolded before me, a world vibrating with light and glowing with colour. I have seen the woods and the hills and the waters before, but never in their gala uniform, and I am simply dazzled. Where are my beloved outlines ? They seem merged in harmonies and swamped in colours so glorious, that even I lose sight of them. Do you know, my dear Felix, since I am here I feel there is in me the making of a colourist, a germ somewhere hidden away so far down, that perhaps it may never thrive and reach the surface, but a source of happiness it is to me all the same. When I get strong enough I am going to nurse the little stranger, and see whether I can coax him on to the canvas; but I shall do nothing till I have made careful drawings of a couple of hundred olive trees. Why, every trunk is a weird fantastic subject in itself, and every branch as it twists and writhes in titanic agonies. It is as if all the lines of the universe had taken the olive groves for their place of rendezvous.

"Literally so; for there as I sat wool-gathering the other day, I descried approaching me the unmistakable lines of Gobelot's hat, a direct descendant of the one we punished in the glorious old Gleyre days; and under the hat was the man himself, walking through life as placidly as ever. He has evidently not yet learnt to draw a foot, so he has not fitted himself for a bootmaker. Nor need he, for his father, who died not long ago, left him quite a little fortune, *rien que cela!* Amongst other properties he inherits a villa in the best part of Mentone, with a beautiful view on to the sea, and so many acres of land; the very olive tree I was sitting under belongs to him. He has come down here to take possession, and was glad to find in me some one whom he could talk to. The fact is, he wanted to unburden himself of a secret. He is in love. He is engaged; you will never guess to whom. Wait; don't look to the end. She was a young girl whom you knew before she was beautiful, as he assures me she is now. She always loved the theatre, and one day, it appears, she was irresistibly attracted by the bills that announced the performance of that lovely opera of Cherubini's, 'The Water-Carrier.' That she must see. So she treated herself to a very good seat, and went off all by herself to witness for the first time in her life the performance of an opera. Then and there she was stage-struck, and swore by her illustrious godmother that she could and would be a singer. She asked some one to teach her, and wouldn't take 'No' for an answer. She next asked some one to bring her out, and made him do so, and got the public to applaud into the bargain. I'm not sure she didn't ask Gobelot to marry her; but so much is certain—he's going to, and we shall soon hear of Madame Gobelot, *née* Rosa Bonheur Sinel. Qu'en dis tu? L'oncle Auguste was right. Didn't we one day have to mark his words, 'When she gets a comb to keep that mop of hers in order, she'll find a carriage and pair too.' Now she'll have it, and a good deal besides; and you can be sure she will be the Queen of the Regatta, and win all the prizes.

"I wish I had you here to tell you more, but I must break off, I am so tired.   CLAUDE."

The generally cheerful tone of Claude's letters, as of some I received from his father about this time, was, as I know now, only adopted because I was considered far too unwell to be told the truth.

In reality, Claude's condition gave cause for grave anxiety.

I was not a little surprised to learn that Madeleine was installed as Claude's nurse in Mentone. It was all the uncle's doing. He who had always resented the mention of her name—and it was often on Claude's lips—had been instrumental in bringing her to his side. The invalid was told that Madame Chevillard and Madeleine were on their way to Genoa, where the former had been appointed to superintend the formation of a school of embroidery. There was no truth in the story; it had only been concocted to explain their presence to Claude.

His uncle had himself gone to Lyons, and had induced Mademoislle Chevillard to bring her ward to Mentone. How matters stood there he told them with tears in his eyes. They must come at once, and——stop to the last.

A month had elapsed, and every day had brought Madeleine nearer to the friend she tended. Her long enforced stay in a hospital had naturally qualified her to nurse the sick; but it was not her experience alone, but her devotion to Claude, deep-rooted and untiring, that came to wrestle with the messenger of death. And the invalid who had been so restless, even so querulous, before her arrival, was now soothed by the mere sound of her voice, and as he looked into her amethyst eyes, an unknown happiness dawned upon him.

Thus I found him and her when I arrived. I had set out for Mentone as soon as I was strong enough to travel. It was in April; God's Nature was bright, but sad was the journey, sadder the meeting.

I was fully prepared to find my friend much changed, but when we met I had difficulty to conceal from him how shocked and distressed I was by his appearance. I could not but see that he was rapidly wasting away, a prey to that terrible disease, consumption. The matted hair clinging to the moist forehead, the pulses on the temples beneath marking life's ebb ; the sunken cheek and the hollow soundless voice, all foreshadowed the approaching end. As I sat by his side and held his emaciated hand, I felt I had come none too soon.

Yet he sought to appear cheerful.

" Where are my birds, *ma petite?* " he asked Madeleine. " Give me the ' surprise.' Look here, Felix, isn't she an artist ? " he said, holding up the surprise ; the same his *petite* had announced as being in preparation. It had taken the shape of an embroidered mat to put under his lamp.

Yes, she was an artist. Her subject was simple enough. Four birds representing the four seasons filled the corners of a grey silk square. There was the crow, the swallow, the nightingale—the fourth I forget ; each beautifully modelled with many-shaded threads of silk, and linked together by a cleverly - contrived garland of flowers, appropriate to the seasons they were to illustrate. In the centre, entertwined with a bunch of evergreen, a ribbon, on which were embroidered the words—

<blockquote>
" Les saisons qui changent
L'amitié ne dérangent."
</blockquote>

Yes, she was right. True friendship will not change with the seasons that come and go. But had she thought, as she plied the needle, of the friendship that ripens and grows, expanding till it is merged in affection of a deeper nature?

" Stop with me another ten minutes, then let me rest," Claude said, as we sat by the window, waiting for the moon to rise. " Perhaps I shall see it; or if not, I shall know it has risen."

" Where must I look for it?" I asked.

" Over those hills. It will hide behind the mists. Wait, to - morrow perhaps; Thursday — Thursday, Friday, Saturday. Wait."

He was exhausted; I would not let him speak more, but left him to rest, watched by the pale girl that was ever by his side.

The next day he seemed so much better that he surprised us all. Could it be possible that a crisis was passed, that the illness had taken a favourable turn? One dared not think so, but yet the balmy air of Mentone had ere this worked wonders.

" O Felix," he said, " I feel happier than I have ever been. Every day brings me new life and light. The world is more beautiful than I thought; not all drawing; colour too, such colour!" After a pause, he continued—

" I must tell you all, Felix. I was blind, and she —slowly, gradually—led me out of the darkness. I thought I knew what love was—Paris—you know —all passion, pain; love is peace, happiness. It is she who taught me. I have peered into the deepest of all mysteries, too great to be solved in this world." And he fell back on his cushions, and gazed as if in a trance, murmuring " Ma petite."

High winds had been blowing for the last few days, whipping up the waves of the blue sea and chasing the clouds across the path of the moon, but now nature was returning to its pleasanter mood, and the clouds were gradually dropping into line, and taking up positions just above the horizon.

Saturday had come.

" Good-night, father ; good-night, uncle. I feel much better."

Madeleine and I remained. Vigils and anxiety had told upon her. The bloom had left her cheeks, and her eyes were heavy. We wheeled his chair to the window and propped him up with pillows.

" Over that hill," he said, " at 11.59 ;—curious— just a minute before midnight—I watched it grow ever since it was a tender crescent."

The full moon rose, a red disc, blood red, emerging from this world of strife ; it ascended, taking its hues from man's yellow gold ; then on—freed from terrestrial mists, excelsior to purer skies.

" See," he said, " a true circle ; no beginning and no end. The emblem of eternity !"

Madeleine was resting her weary head on her arms as they lay folded on the window sill. Silvery rays fell through the window and played around her hair.

" Hush ! let her rest. Ma sainte ! See now— that halo of light around her head—a vision." He spoke with an effort, but on that early Sunday morning he told me how deeply he loved Madeleine.

The sun rose once more on Claude; never again the moon. He was still sitting on that chair when his head dropped to move no more. We were all present. Madeleine knelt by his side and buried her face in the grey rug she had so often laid across his knees. She held his lifeless hand and wept in silent anguish until we led her away.

*　　*　　*　　*　　*　　*

Did she know, poor Madeleine, that she too had but a few years to live? that the germs of the unrelenting disease which had carried off her friend, her lover, were at work within her?

I was with her when she too closed her eyes,— so peacefully, serenely. It was a vision of love that passed away from amongst us.

"I am quite happy. You will lay me by his side?"

"Yes, Madeleine,—yes."

And now that I have said what I wanted to say about those friends of my early days, and followed them to the closing chapters of their lives, I ought perhaps at once to turn over a new leaf and record a fresh impression. But it is hard to dismiss memories which one has evoked. Why should one? Nothing in good old Nature is abrupt; the sun sets and day fades into night; in the rainbow yellow merges into green, and green into blue, and it seems but in keeping with the ways of Nature that there should be something to read between the lines of a slightly sketched life-story, and something to be thought out between heterogeneous chapters. They cannot but be varying if they are to depict the motley crowd of figures that go to make up one's own experiences. Such chapters are like the various pieces on the programme of a musical recital. There we are taken from a fugue to a notturno, from a grande valse to a moonshine sonata; and the pianist, if by some chance he happens to be a musician, leads us with a few improvised chords, from one mood to another, from flats to sharps, major to minor.

So then my starting-point is once more Dupont, and before I think of other friends, I find myself speculating as to what he might have achieved, and to what honours he might have attained, had he lived. What would he have thought of to-day, and what would to-day have thought of him? To be sure he would be wearing a bit of red ribbon in his button-hole, as all distinguished Frenchmen do; and who is not distinguished? By this time he would have been an Academician, royal or national, a Membre de l'Institut, perhaps even one of the forty "Immortals," if he had taken to the pen, as we know painters will sometimes do. In the eyes of the rising generation the Immortals mostly take rank with any other old fogeys, and Dupont would have fared no better than his contemporaries at the hands of the *Nous avons changé tout cela's* of the day.

It could not have been otherwise; for, alas! (and I have not sought to disguise it) he had none of their distinctive qualities. He never loved the un-beautiful for its own sake, nor was he a man of the prominent-wart school. In his compositions elevated thought and subtle expression had a fatal tendency to eclipse the non-essentials; his luminary rays were painted without regard for the laws of decomposition, and his atmospheric vibrations, if he attempted them at all, were not worth speaking of. Besides, the least prac-tised art-student of to-day would not fail to notice that his careful drawing of hands, or the grace-ful lines of his draperies, would monopolise atten-tion, to the detriment of the backgrounds, which had a way of receding, so that the main interest of the picture could never be said to concentrate upon them.

The enchantress, Art, is ever making new victims. Just now she is wedded to the new master, the variety painter, and is on her wedding-trip, fully equipped with new fashions of tone and colour, rich too in new values; and she travels along happily uncon-scious—some ignorance is bliss—over the treacherous roads designed by the "new" perspective, past totter-ing towers, over warped planes, and down steep inclines, pluckily standing her ground where those fallen angels, the old masters, would have feared to tread.

It's the old suit once more before us; young folks versus old fogeys, the traditional battle-royal, to be fought to-day, as it will be fought to the end of all time. I say, Hurrah for the young ones! Perhaps they are leading us a step or two backwards, but I verily believe it is only to *reculer pour mieux sauter*, to back, we should say, the better to jump. So let us keep the line clear for youth and strength; we can't do without their vigorous onslaughts. Where would the old tree of art be, if it were not for the new shoots?

A TRIP TO AMERICA IN 1883

 **well remember** a chance remark of mine which led to my crossing the ocean.

"Well, if I can get a cabin in your boat, we'll go too, but I'm afraid it's too late now, at the eleventh hour."

That was said to Irving and Ellen Terry, who were preparing to leave on their first visit to the States in 1883.

I had never given a trip to America a serious thought; a consultation at Cook's office and subsequent trunk-packing usually meant a flight to the sunny South or the glorious East; but a new country, and a civilised one into the bargain, had failed to attract me. I had heard over and over again that the Americans were a practical people, and that, to be sure, meant inartistic, and I knew they could talk, build, and make money-piles bigger than we can, and that again did not predispose me in their favour. In fact I may say, without boasting, that I cherished about as many prejudices as does the average Englishman when he seeks to form his opinion regarding those unhappily not included in the magic circle to which he belongs, and I felt that, if ever I visited my

young American cousins, it would be to give them
the benefit of my superior old-world experience.

I may say at once that I had not been in the
country long, before I found it desirable to climb
down, discovering that it was quite as much as I
could do to keep my footing at all on one or the
other of the scaling ladders I had tried to ascend.
But for all my ups and downs, one thing is certain:
it was a happy thought that led me to take my
passage to New York, and a specially happy one to
cross with Irving and Ellen Terry.

> " I count myself in nothing else so happy
> As in a soul remembering my good friends."
>
> —*Richard II.*

So wrote Irving in my album, dating the lines from
the "Atlantic Ocean, 20th October 1883."

It was indeed a time of good and friendly relations we had on that Atlantic, meeting at a sort of
poet's corner of the captain's table at dinner-time,
and later again, when we could discuss the merits
of the nocturnal Welsh rarebit, or of the comforting
nightcap. Those expressive legs of his, with which
we are all so familiar, were a constant source of
delight to me. In the smoking saloon he would
know how to stretch them till they gave you a sense
of absolute rest; and when he got up, you felt they
must originally have been designed for sea-legs.
When sometimes I paced the deck by their side, I
felt I could now really boast of being in the same
boat with my illustrious friend, and of more than
that: for once in a way, I was actually treading the
same boards with him.

I think he thoroughly enjoyed what was to him an unknown experience, a ten days' rest; but I doubt whether he took it as a holiday; he had books and papers to keep him company that looked suspiciously like business, and when he reclined full length on his steamer-chair, contemplating the rolling sea through his eye-glasses, he looked as if he were meditating a revival of "The Tempest," and consulting with Neptune and Æolus as to the best way of producing it.

As for Ellen Terry, she was *facile princeps* on our floating city, fascinating everybody, from captain and crew, *viâ* first and second class passengers, down to the emigrant's crowing baby. There had been a grand gathering to see her and Irving off. Friends had come, laden with parting gifts; golden-haired children were there, bringing baskets full of flowers that should intertwine themselves with their dear Ellen's existence, till others could be gathered to greet her on her arrival.

When the bell sounded, recalling the visitors to the tender that had brought them, the process of leave-taking went through its acutest stage; there were the cordial grips and moist eyes, the crisp, resonant kisses, and the long, silent embraces. "Good-bye; take care of him, take care of her, till I come back! Good-bye, again!"

Ay! some of us had taken return tickets, some had not. Which of us would return?

We got sorted at last; all the good clothes on our side; the new suits, ulsters, and dresses to be bodily introduced into the country that produces the like only at ruinous prices. We all looked brand new, as if we were equipped for our respective honey-moons. Soon we were passing the last outstretched arm of land, that seemed to bid us one more fare-well; but the greeting only came from Cinderella, the Emerald Isle, and we, I suppose being an English vessel, refused to hug the coast, and made for the open sea, whence for some time we could see her knowingly wink her revolving Cyclopean eye at us.

The moon had risen majestically; it could not do otherwise with those Lyceists on board. We had achieved something like order in our cabins, and were reappearing above to have a look at one another. Ellen was leaning over the bulwarks with one of those flowers in her hand, which by any other name would smell as sweet. She was still gazing shorewards, as if she would keep on saying Good-bye until to-morrow; a living picture, long lines of beauty flowing from her shoulders to her feet, such as natural grace will evolve even from the slender material of a travelling dress.

But for all that, she must not be imagined as addicted to mooning or posing; just the reverse, she was the most practical soul on board, ever active and thoughtful. Before the first twenty-four hours had passed, all those hothouse grapes the old friends had brought had found their way to the new friends, the steerage passengers; so, too, what of shawls and wraps she could lay her hands on. " I have hidden away one or two warm things," said her maid, " or there would be nothing of the kind left for her."

For a day or two we had very rough weather, and the attendance at poet's corner was small; our first night in particular set many of us wishing that Columbus had minded his own business and not gone out of his way to discover a new continent. If a ship would only roll and pitch, an average land-lubber might have a chance, but it has a nasty trick of seceding from beneath you when you are lying on your back, and leaving that back to follow as best it can. This particular hiatus was not new to me, but such a multiplicity of noises as made that night hideous I had never encountered before. The wise-acres said that a cargo of pig-iron had been badly stowed in the ship's entrails, and was trying to knock a hole in its side, and so it sounded. The drillings of the screw I could recognise as it doggedly worked its way, occasionally writhing in impotent rage as it was lifted out of the water; but all the other squeaking, grating, bond-bursting sounds I could not analyse. As for my cabin, it soon pre-sented the appearance of a Pandemonium. There was no provision for securing anything, so port-manteaux were colliding with one another, and with various articles of furniture and crockery that had put in an appearance; my dressing-case was sliding along the floor like a schoolboy on the ice, and in fact every mortal thing was on the alert, trying to find its ever-shifting centre of gravity. For all that I went to sleep, to dream of alligators and lifebelts, and of the list of the saved, amongst whom I could not find my name.

That chivalrous White Star Company had con-structed a special state-room on deck for their guest, the histrionic star, and had furnished it comfortably, as I know full well, for when, after the demoralising experiences of that night, I had crawled to the surface limp and crushed, a ministering angel at once took me in hand, laid me out in full state in that room of hers, propped me with cushions, tended me with creature comforts, and finally willed me to sleep. When after some hours I came out vivified and refreshed, I found her squatting on the deck in true schoolgirl fashion, writing letters in her big handwriting. Later on what on *terra firma* I call my better half had also emerged from below, and was organising a personally conducted five-o'clock tea, made attractive by certain canisters in her private possession. Full justice was done to the popular meal by the small but select circle of friends come together on that occasion.

As we proceeded, many an incident occurred, partly connected with the vagaries of the Atlantic, partly with the thousand and one social and humanitarian interests awakened on board a floating city. They seemed noteworthy then, but to-day, and to make a long voyage short, I will only say that it's an ill wind that can't leave off blowing, and it's a long water-course that has no landing stage, and that consequently, after a good deal of boisterous weather, the sea calmed down and we arrived safely in New York harbour. On the morning when the pilot came on board, we were most of us still in our berths; but Ellen was up and on deck, and the first to shake hands with him, and greet him with a hearty "Good-morning, Mr. Pilot!"

The first thing that happened to me on arriving

in the free country, was that I was most courteously but resolutely deprived of my liberty by the interviewers. Hobnobbing as I was with Irving and Ellen Terry, they had evidently taken me for somebody, and, under that mistaken impression, at once proceeded to extract copy from me.

What a splendid institution that interviewing is! The stranger has from the first a unique opportunity of showing himself just as he wishes to appear. He can drape himself in dignity, or pose for the free and easy; he can borrow good works from his friends and virtues from good books, and throw in as much soft-soap and blarney as he thinks the natives can stand. What I may have said I don't know; but I am quite sure I missed my chance. I was much too innocent then, and probably told the truth.

On Ellen the interviewers must have doted from the first; she was so charmingly impulsive, so spontaneous and overflowing with copy. I dare say she gave them points about Art and the Drama, from Sophocles *vià* Shakespeare down to the last thing out; but I only remember the delightful insight into her personal habits and tastes she let them have when she chose to take the world into her confidence.

"What do I drink?" she said on one occasion. "Very little wine, I am so nervous. The doctor restricts me to milk, but restrictions and doctors combined will never come between me and my tea. I must have tea—tea or death—three times a day, and, as Johnson said about Mrs. Woffington and her tea, 'It is strong, and red as blood.' I take English tea, which I buy by the caddy, and wherever I am,

there are my caddy and my dog—Fussy and caddy.
Without them 'Othello's occupation's gone.'"

At the custom-house I gave the customary tip,
for I had been confidentially informed that no official
on the landing-stage, calling himself a gentleman,
would misinterpret my courtesy, or allow himself to
be unfairly influenced by it. I had fully expected
that, by some ingenious mechanical device, my luggage would be landed simultaneously with myself,
and placed on certain square yards of the American
Continent set apart for our temporary use. I had
imagined the custom-house a many-storied edifice in
keeping with the high tariff it enforced. Instead,
however, of any such expectations being realised, I
found myself in a large open shed, from which I
could watch the luggage as it was being ejected in
a most primitive way from our ship, with a good
riddance shove from above, and a " look out " shout
from below.

An army of porters made a rush for it, and began
strewing it all over the place, getting everybody's
belongings thoroughly mixed, and generally acting
as if they were shuffling a pack of cards before commencing a new game.

The new game took the shape of a free fight,
which was waged with varying fortunes for two or
three hours. By dint of displaying much energy in
the attainment of my own ends, to the detriment of
everybody else's, I succeeded in regrouping the greater
part of my effects; not without sorrow can I look
back, however, to that field-day, and the sad losses I
sustained, the latter conclusively proving to me that

within the carefully guarded precincts of the custom-house no thieves are admitted except on business.

The process of clearing and of being cleared out once terminated, I drove to the " Brevoort," that most respectable of hotels, founded, I believe, by a party that came over in the *Mayflower*, a house second only in antiquity to some " Noah's Ark Hotel " in Philadelphia. I went there because the last, not least, of the Henrys had selected it for his head-quarters. As soon as the rescued trunks reached me I unpacked my writing materials, and, following illustrious examples, at once sat down to write a book about America, and the manners and customs of its inhabitants. But, unlike the illustrious ones, I thought better of it, and got up again. The fact that I have now once more taken up the pen, evidently with the same purpose, somewhat recalls Jean Paul Richter's story of the tippler, who, for once resisting temptation, passes the door of the public-house, and then, proud of his achievement, turns back that he may reward himself for so much self-denial. So, too, do I appear to be tardily, but none the less surely, succumbing to temptation ; and the parallel goes even further, for, as the tippler in all probability did not rest satisfied with one glass, so I feel a morbid craving to write as many volumes on America, as there are kinds of drinks at the bar of a big New York hotel. If such volumes, full of pleasant memories, are destined never to appear, it will only be because publishers are, perhaps providentially, placed as protecting buffers between the public and the author. A few chapters may, however, possibly

be allowed to pass, so I let them take their
chance.

"Dis moi qui tu hantes, et je te dirai qui tu es,"
says the French proverb, which, freely translated,
might be made to say : "Tell me whom you knew
in America, and I will tell you what you thought
of the country." Well, I think I knew just the
right people, and from that you can gather what
my impressions were. I certainly started fair,
equipped as I was with a batch of letters of introduction. These, according to American usage, I
posted to their addresses, and then sat in state at
a given time, waiting for the friends of my friends
to come and make friends with me. One letter,
however, I carefully kept, and only showed to those
who I thought would appreciate it. It was that
best and kindest of men, Robert Browning, who had
given it me, and to this day, when I read it, it seems
more like music than like epistolary prose to me.
It ran thus :—

"19 WARWICK CRESCENT, W.,
11th August 1884.

"To whomsoever it may concern.

" I have received such extraordinary kindness from
Americans, and number so many of them among my
friends, that it would seem invidious if I selected
those whom I ventured to believe would oblige me
were it possible. I shall therefore say, in the
simplest of words, that should my dear friend, the
Painter Moscheles, meet with any individual whose
sympathy I have been privileged to obtain, what-

ever favour and assistance may be rendered to him, or his charming wife, will constitute one more claim to the gratitude of   ROBERT BROWNING."

One of my first visitors was Dr. Fordyce Barker, the eminent physician, and more particularly the idol of the fair sex, which owes him so large a debt of gratitude. He ignored the given time above mentioned, and, calling at some unearthly hour before I was fairly presentable, he was away again before I could find my boots.

" What have you come to America for ? " was his first shot. The question coming suddenly upon me, I found no better answer to it than, " Well, just to have a look round—wanted to see the latest thing out in the way of civilisation."

" But you are a portrait-painter, I understand ? "

" Yes, I am."

" Then you have come here to paint portraits ? "

" Well—certainly," I hummed and hawed—" in case the opportunity should present itself— and if I should find that "—but he cut me short (beating about the bush is not popular in the States).

" How much do you charge ? " he asked bluntly, and without the least regard for the sensitive nature of a British artist, so I had to make a plunge and tell him ; so much for head-size and so much for a three-quarter canvas.

" All right," he said, and was off.

Later on I painted him, and he was ever a good friend to me.

It took me some time to get accustomed to the

outspoken ways of the American. With us the artist is a privileged being, unlike any other producer or vendor, but there everybody takes it for granted that he is quite ready to accept dollars in exchange for his work. The waiter in the café, the artist who shampooed me, or the clerk in the hotel, wanted to know my charges, and it once or twice happened that they turned their knowledge to good account.

" Now, sir," said a clerk in the Hôtel Richelieu, Chicago, where I was staying, to a wealthy senator, also a guest at the hotel—" now, sir, this is Mr. Felix Moscheles, the celebrated English artist, and I guess you had better have your portrait and your wife's portrait painted, whilst he is here to fix them up." That introduction led to commissions as acceptable from the artistic point of view as they were remunerative, and to the most cordial relations between client and artist.

But I am drifting away from New York, where I want to remain for a while. I had not been there many hours before I went for a ramble on Broadway (the American walks *on* the street, not *in* it, as we do). I always loved to explore the busy, bustling thoroughfares of a big city ; it is there you can feel the throbbing feverish pulse of an active community ; in the Park or on the Corso you only get that languid fashionable-doctor sort of pulse, which takes its airing in a landau or a victoria, a correct and well-regulated pulse that knows its duty to itself and to the society it is privileged to beat in.

With such predilection for high-pressure and a

rattling pace, I soon found myself making friends with the Broadway. I always had a weakness, too, for shops, and there were miles of them; stores they call them, and every mortal thing is stored behind their immense panes of plate-glass, or in those outposts of business, the show-cases, that go dodging about the footpath, and look as if they were on their way to some international exhibition. Anything and everything man can desire to smooth the thorny path from the cradle to cremation, he will find in the Broadway.

Talking of the thorny path, I was much struck by the liberty, not to say licence, accorded to the paving stones, each of which acted quite independently of his neighbour. The noise, as the vehicles ploughed their way along the road, and as it was echoed by the massive stone buildings, was really appalling. Infernal, I should say, but that adjective is too good in this case, for the Inferno was at least paved with good intentions, whereas that road meant mischief and strife, and revelled in the purity of its own cussedness.

I could not help speculating as to what dear old mother Regent Street would think of it all; how she would be shocked at the way in which that transatlantic upstart hands up his goods from the basement, and pushes them just under your nose, or piles them up sky-high and block deep, before he consents to put a roof on them. Father Oxford Street, too, would be scandalised, and so would his time-honoured brother-streets, that fancy themselves arteries, as they wind their crooked way from the fashionable brick piles of the west to the golden-calf temples of the east. They do their best, suffering as they are from chronic congestion, and I have loved them since the days of my boyhood. No, I certainly mean no disrespect to the British lion and his partner the unicorn, nor to the griffin at Temple Bar, nor to the bulls and bears farther on, nor to the turtles and plovers' eggs at the Mansion House; least of all to the bank-notes opposite, good company as they always are.

America is a country of contradictions; that is a safe way of putting it, as the same can be said of all countries. Wherever he goes, the stranger sees with his own eyes, feels with his own heart, and above all, judges according to the state of his own liver. One man practises his bump of veneration on all he meets; another travels on the *nil admirari* principle. Golden threads traverse the road of either, and so do rotten threads. The first man seizes the golden ones and is happy; the second picks up the rotten ones and makes himself equally happy with those. Both come home triumphantly to show their threads, and to say, " Behold, that is what I found ! " It must be difficult for the same hand to pick up both sorts of thread, and to present them impartially, weighing one set against the other and judging dispassionately. There are some strong men who can do it, and there would be more of them, I believe, if it were not for that liver. In my case, that organ may have been in a satisfactory condition, and have prompted me to be sociable. So I was rather disappointed when I found that there was more formality in the great

Republic than under the old Monarchy, and that if I wanted to talk to somebody, I had to be introduced first.

Day after day I have sat with my wife in various hotels at some little table laid for four, sharing it with some other Mr. and Mrs., without exchanging a word. Elsewhere we should soon have been playing that stimulating parlour-game of inter-social hide-and-seek, or we might for the time being have formed a pleasant little *partie carrée*. Sometimes my heart went out to my neighbours, I think in a true Christian spirit, but I could have seen them starve, and yet not have dared to hand them the mustard or pass them the butter. I knew they would have looked upon me with suspicion; yet I flatter myself that, with a little discernment, they could have seen that I was not a shady character, and that neither I nor that most artless and guileless partner of mine was capable of playing off the confidence trick on the clergyman opposite, or on the charming elderly lady with the white hair and the two golden-locked grandchildren.

We English are often reproached with our respect for caste. We emphasise the difference of position in the social scale, whereas the American—unless, to be sure, he be a Bostonian—takes every opportunity to emphasise his indifference for such distinction. We think we know a gentleman when we see him; he rather mistrusts his judgment, perhaps because he has seen fewer generations of the species than we have; so he sometimes mistakes a sheep for a wolf in disguise, and only recognises his error when the sheep is for-

mally introduced, and thus guaranteed as the genuine
article.   Perhaps it is that, by dint of proclaiming
that one man is as good as another, the citizen of the
Great Republic finds himself arriving at the conclusion that one man is as bad as another, and so it is
for the stranger to show cause why he should be
allowed to pass the hotel mustard or butter.

All that, I must admit, applies, as far as I know,
only to the few cities I visited ; I had much too good
a time in each of them, painting and lecturing, studying and learning, to go away in a hurry ; so I cannot
speak of the boys on the ranches or the girls in Cali-
fornia ; nor can I say whether the fifty or sixty odd
millions of Americans to whom I was not introduced
would have taken kindly to me or I to them, had we
met.

My first visit to the United States was not the
mere excursion I had expected it to be.   I remained
six months, mostly in New York.   First I made
myself a temporary studio at the Park Avenue Hotel,
but soon finding that I wanted more easel and elbow
room, I took a flat and a studio in " The Chelsea,"
furnished and decorated it *right-away*, and settled
down to a winter's work.   When the spring came, I
just locked my door, told the clerk in the office to set
the burglar alarm, and went off to the other Chelsea,
my home in London.   So, for three years, I divided
my time pretty equally between the two countries.

I look back with pleasure to many an incident
connected with the portraits I painted in America.
So, too, to my experiences on the platform.   Not
only was I allowed to lecture, but I was even listened

to. To be sure, my lectures were only announced as "Studio-talks," and I took care they should be very much varied according to my audiences. The inexhaustible subject of Art had to be presented in one way when addressing the students in Philadelphia or Chicago, in another when speaking to the select circle of the Thursday Evening Club in New York. Considerations that would be appropriate to put before a large gathering of beautiful and gifted young ladies at one of their great colleges, were not the same that would appeal to upwards of a thousand Negroes and Indians, students at the famous Hampton Schools in Virginia. In each case, however, I illustrated my lecture by painting a life-size head from nature, my subject being mostly selected from the audience.

I cannot refrain from mentioning one instance of the warmth with which my efforts were occasionally rewarded. " Thanks !" said one of the gentlemen officially connected with the Hampton Schools, at the close of my lecture, " a thousand thanks ! You cannot realise what pleasure you have given to those young men and women.—Understood it ? I should think so. Why, I can assure you, they have enjoyed it as much as if they had been to a circus."

I have often wondered where I found the courage to undertake what I had never attempted before, and whence came the capacity which saved me from discomfiture. I can only imagine that I took my colour from my surroundings, and that where everybody was going ahead, I could not lag behind. I certainly never knew what I really was, till I had been to America. The gentleman at the schools was right ;

it was clear to me : I was a circus-horse, and America
the man with the whip in the middle of the arena.
As he urged me on I could clear bars and barriers as
never before ; the people all around, I knew, were
keen judges of horseflesh, and could not be hood-
winked. I must do my best. And then, when sympathetic friends applauded, it was an easy matter to
march boldly along on two legs and to hold up my
head with the best ; my nostrils dilated, and I felt
as proud as a man. And when, to reward me, some
of the loveliest women of the great Republic patted
me on the back and fed me with sweets and kind
words, I reciprocated with all my heart, and felt as
if I could once for all shake off the yoke of the slow-
coaches in the old countries, and start afresh on life's
big race in the new one.

I was, from the first, much struck by the cor-
diality with which a stranger is received. Hospitality
is a virtue inherited by the American from his
ancestors, a tradition handed down to him. It has
not yet had time to become blunted, as it has
with us much visited Europeans. One can quite
fancy how delighted the first settlers must have been
to welcome friends from the old country and to get
the latest news, to say nothing of the latest fashions,
from home. Now, to be sure, messages get from
house to house before they are cabled (as the clocks
go) ; and as for the fashions, it takes a fleet to convey them across the seas. Who can tell how much
horse-power is annually needed to convey the creations of a Worth or a Virot to those I would call the

P

loveliest women in the world, were I not afraid of being misunderstood by other sets of loveliest women nearer home. Anyway I do not hesitate to assert that the best productions of the great Parisians become worthier of the fair sex for which they are conceived, by being subjected to the chastening influence of the American lady's taste, and to the subtle touches which she knows how to add.

But however up-to-date the hyper-civilisation imported in dress-baskets and handboxes may be, and however high the hothouse temperature under which the New Englanders force the growths they receive from foreign soil, their good old times are still within easy reach, and many an ancient custom has survived, foremost amongst which, the practice of hospitality.

One of the most practical forms in which it is dispensed is called a Reception, and I most gratefully remember the pleasure and the advantages derived from such gatherings. Introductions are there dealt out wholesale to the individual in whose honour they are held. When a stranger to Chicago, I had delivered a letter to a prominent citizen and his wife from a mutual friend in New York. They knew everybody worth knowing, and kindly offered to introduce me to their circle of friends. On the evening appointed, I stood next to the hostess, and as one after the other of the guests arrived, each was introduced to me by name. " Mr. So-and-so," she said, " Mr. Felix Moscheles." Whereupon I had to shake hands and say blandly, " Mr. So-and-so," whilst he had to repeat " Mr. Felix Moscheles." If he had not caught my name, or had any doubt about its pronunciation, he would make a stand and inquire: "*How was that? How do you spell it?*" and when once enlightened on those points they would be fixed once for all in his mind. It was there he had the advantage over me, for after a short interval I was sure to have forgotten whether Mr. So-and-so's name spelt Homer D. V. Smith or Plato V. D. Brown, and whether Homer and Plato were men at all, or ought to have been connected in my mind with a Mrs. or a Miss.

But notwithstanding such imperfections of my memory, I had no difficulty in retaining the names of many good friends I made in Chicago. Foremost amongst these is Robert Morse.

I had got very busy in the studio I had taken in Chicago, where I was spending the winter of 1887, when a very pleasantly-worded letter reached me, inviting me to transfer my studio to Omaha, two days' journey farther west. I could not accept the invitation, and so it was arranged that at least one of my intending models should be brought to me, to be dealt with according to the severe laws of the portrait-painter's art. Robert Morse was four years of age, and had a distinct objection to be thus dealt with, and out of that circumstance arose a series of difficulties. But, oh, how beautiful he was! I see him now as he was handed out of the carriage on his arrival at the Hôtel Richelieu, his golden curls escaping from beneath his Phrygian cap of liberty, and cascading over his shoulders. We were in the depth of winter, and his sturdy little figure was

warmly clad in the ample folds of the toboggan costume—a sort of ulster made of a deep-toned red
flannel; collar and cuffs of the same material, but
dark blue, and the cap to match. His mother led
him upstairs—or I should more correctly say, speaking of this typical American child, was led upstairs
by him. After forty-eight hours' travelling, that
lady stepped out of the train much as if it were
one of those boxes marked " Worth—Paris." She
was a lovely woman, as I soon learnt; lovely not
only in outward appearance, but in that moral and
intellectual sense which the American language connects with the word.

My stay in Chicago was limited, and I had
written to say that I could only undertake to paint
one picture—that to be a head of the boy. When
we met, however, I at once felt I *must* paint him
full-length, life-size, toboggan costume, cap, snow-
scape, and all; and as for the mother, to be sure, as
she wished it, we must find time for a head-portrait
of her too. There was that in her that seemed to
call for a picture from the artist's brush, and so I
soon enthusiastically set to work, painting on the
two canvases alternately.

But it was not long ere troubles came thick and
fast, growing out of Robert's determination not to
sit for his portrait if he could in any way help it,
and further, on no account to leave the studio when
I was painting his mother. I tried various subtle
devices to make work possible. With a piece of
white chalk I designed a most scientific frontier,
separating his territory from mine, and that was

capital fun as long as I joined in the game and we repulsed one another's attacks, but it fell flat as soon as I returned to the easel.   I fed him from an unlimited supply of "candy," and succeeded after a while in bringing about indisposition of a marked character ; but he speedily recovered, his animal spirits rising with returning vitality.   I sometimes flatter myself that I possess a faculty of inducing docility in my sitters.   More especially in the treatment of children I pride myself on a series of minor accomplishments, mainly connected with a free transcription of Nature's noises, pleasant and unpleasant, such as the animal kingdom furnishes to the observant ear.   But such talents were of little avail. That infinite source of assistance which I usually speak of as " a lady attached to the establishment," also failed on this occasion.   She who accompanies me through life for better and for worse, and whose blandishments European children have ever acknowledged to be irresistible, could gain but momentary influence over this American child.   But—well, I could not help it—I loved that boy ; I admired his spirit.   How should he, at his tender age, know that an artist is a superior, privileged being, to be treated accordingly ?   At all hours of the day Robert was delightfully bright, but his *'cuteness* seemed sharpened as bedtime approached.   Not that he objected, as most children do, to going to bed, but, however sleepy he was, his spirit of resistance seemed somehow to revive when the moment came to recite his simple prayer.   On one occasion all went smoothly as long as he prayed for his father and mother, his brothers and sisters, but when it came to his uncles and aunts and to their numerous offspring, he made a decided stand, putting it plainly to his mother, "I say, *mámma*, why can't they pray for their own crowd?" Another time, there had been in the course of the day a distinct difference of opinion between Robert and his mother on the advisability of his going out sleighing. He gave in with unwonted docility, but when the evening came and the fond mother folded her hands and knelt by his bedside, he shook his head, and said, "No, *mámma*; no sleigh—no prayers!"

It was with some impatience that I expected the arrival of Mr. Morse, for whenever Robert was particularly untractable during what, by courtesy, was called the sitting, his mother would say, "Wait till his father comes; he knows how to manage him." After a fortnight that father came, and he and I at once struck up a friendship which promised to last, and which ever since has kept its promise. He was a fine and prepossessing specimen of the free-born American citizen. Six feet something in height, strong and straight as they are reared under the guiding brightness and the protecting shadow of the Stars and Stripes. Under his eye I was to put the final touches to Robert's portrait. I hopefully started work, but, alas! where was the paternal authority I had relied upon to get a view of that hand that was dragging the toboggan across the snow, and that foot on which rested the main action of the figure? Robert *would* perch on his father's shoulder, and thence look down upon me and the world in general.   Difficulties finally reached a climax.   I protested in the name of correct drawing and the eternal laws of perspective, and, fairly roused by my pleading, the father sternly motioned the son to follow him into the next room. . . . At last, I thought, the "right of the strongest" will be vindicated, and that child will be thrashed.

But if I expected howling and gnashing of teeth, I was to be disappointed.   Nothing broke the silence, until, after some time, the door opened, and father and son reappeared.   Robert took his place, clutched the cord attached to the toboggan, and listened with rapt attention to his father's words; these were spoken slowly and impressively, giving me time to apply whatever faculty for correct drawing I might possess.   As he sought to spin out his words, so will I, for obvious reasons, seek to curtail them, only adding that, to do them justice, they should be read with the characteristic American accentuation which seems to give importance to some words that we should slide over.

"Sir," he began solemnly, "Robert wishes me to communicate to you what has passed between us during our absence from this room.   It did not take me long to elicit from him the fact that he has no desire to see his portrait finished.   He has even assured me that, as far as he was concerned, it need never have been painted at all.   He further stated that he at no time had formed a desire to visit Chicago, and that he much preferred Omaha to that city.   Also, he said—and, I think, with some show of reason—that, having no playmates here, he would like to return to those he has left behind, more especially to his brothers and sisters. Now, sir, you are aware that I, on the other hand, wished him to make it possible for you to finish that portrait, and I could see no cause why I should recede from that position; so I politely but firmly requested him to do as I desire. There are, no doubt, some boys who, when thus thwarted and opposed, would not have hesitated to strike their fathers, but Robert is not a boy of that description, he would at all times respect his father's independence. Still, you see, we were at what you might call loggerheads. We had gotten fixed like in a dark place with no door behind us, the windows left out, and a stone wall in front. Under these circumstances I cast about in my mind, and it occurred to me we should do well to make straight for arbitration. Now Robert said he did not know the precise meaning of the word arbitration, so I explained to him that when two parties could not agree it was usual to call in a third to decide which way things were to be settled. I wanted to nominate you, sir, but Robert put in his opinion that you might not be the right person for our purpose; he said that I myself should do better, so, after giving the matter careful consideration, I decided that Robert should come in and take friendly to that toboggan and that cord, and that he should make himself generally portraitable; I further decided that, as long as it lasted, I should sit here patiently and wait; but that, as soon as you had finished, I might go and procure a horse to have a ride on the road to Omaha, and that I should also hire a pony, so that Robert might accompany me on that ride."

Robert listened intently.   I painted ditto.

They say in Omaha, where the portrait hangs, that it is good.   So, " All's well that ends well."

Of that I am glad, and, as I recall the incident, I am once more lost in admiration of the American child that, from its earliest days, is ever ready to elicit the noblest qualities of patience and forbearance in the parent it is training.   And what a training, too, for the boy !   Will not Robert, who is now growing into manhood, be a staunch supporter of International Arbitration, and help us, if need be, to rescue the Anglo-American treaty from destruction, or, should that be achieved, to uphold and to strengthen it ?

*   *   *   *   *   *

But the mightiest advocate of International Arbitration, I found amongst the friends I made in Albany.   For him I must turn over a new page.

 **well remember** the Governor, as I made my way up into his bed-room, paint-box in hand, and said: "Well, we must make the best of it, and turn this into a studio. May I move the bed a few inches?" "All right," and between us we moved the bed.

The Governor was Grover Cleveland, and the State he governed the State of New York. I had long since learnt that New York was not the capital, but that Albany enjoyed that privilege. In Albany I was making a prolonged stay, painting portraits of some very prominent people, amongst others of Mrs. V. L. Pruyn and the Erastus Cornings, who were notably amongst his warmest friends and supporters.

I was enjoying Mrs. Pruyn's hospitality, and in her house I had exceptional opportunities of being initiated into the mysteries of American politics. I was made very much at home, too, in surroundings which bore testimony to the consummate taste and connoisseurship of my hostess and her late husband. My wishes were not forestalled, or they could never have been so correctly carried out. But, as soon as they were expressed, some magic button would be touched, and some tutelary genius would appear to take my instructions, or some man or woman I had desired to know would be announced. So I made many pleasant acquaintances, and in due time was introduced to Cleveland.

Election time had come with all its excitement and turmoil. Good citizens wearing most picturesque uniforms were mustering by their thousands, and were drilling as if war were imminent; but it was only the true military step and swing they were practising, that they might creditably march in procession with banners flying and bands playing, and outdo the rival party in their show of enthusiasm. Sober, steady-going individuals were transformed into stump orators and agitators; the contagion spread, quickening pulse and heart-beat, till the whole nation seemed delirious. Enthusiasm begot passion, and passion frenzy. Then came the crisis. The returns were officially announced; the President was elected, and—one, two, three, as if by the touch of a magic wand, down went the pulse to its normal beat, the excitement suddenly collapsed, and the electors settled down to a well-earned four years' rest. But before that happy consummation, there was much to see and note that was interesting to a stranger like myself.

Amid all the conflicting opinions and clamourings, there was one point the whole nation seemed to agree upon. Everybody was going about, Diogenes-like, seeking for an honest man. When found, he was to be made a President of. To be sure either party claimed to have discovered that one honest man, and thereupon commenced the main work on both sides, that of vilifying the personal character of the opposing candidate. All the dirtiest sediment at the bottom of the blackest inkstand was stirred up, all the devilry stored in the arsenals of diabolical newspaper offices was brought into action, to prove to the hilt that Mr. Blaine and Mr. Cleveland were the two most dishonest men in the United States. Under the guise of " plain truths " fanciful untruths were circulated, and the mud raked up was used to make mud pies which were greedily devoured by hungry partisans. There were curious war-cries too on either side, the deep significance of which had to be fully explained to the uninitiated, before he could appreciate their strength. In the Cleveland camp they were constantly burning pieces of paper and shouting : " Burn this letter, dearest Fisher." " Oh ! you'd better, better, better burn this letter," or up went the cry in rhythmical measure—

> " James Gould Blaine, James Gould Blaine,
> He's the continental liar from the State of Maine."

Outsiders got a little slap too, where the partisan saw his opportunity, as when one of the Irish banners paraded the sentiment : " We love James Blaine for the English enemies he has made."

I fully shared in the excitement, and wherever two or three thousand people were blocking a space really only adapted to so many hundred, I helped to make ugly rushes, and took my part in the chorus of yelling and hissing. This was in New York, on the principal day of the election. A day or two afterwards I had returned to Albany, and was calling on Cleveland with Erastus Corning.

"No," said the future President in answer to Mr. Corning's proposal to start the illuminations and torchlight procession that night, "don't hurry; I know it's all right, but wait for to-morrow's returns." He was, to all outward appearances, the one man least affected by the issue.

The next day the returns came, and the torch and other lights were allowed to blaze. All doubts had been dispelled by a certain telegram from Jay Gould. His enemies swore that that arch-grabber of millions had manipulated the telegraph wires, withholding or forging the returns expected from various parts of the States, and it was generally understood that the earliest opportunity would be taken to burn down his house and to lynch him. That morning a telegram of congratulation from the great financier, happily unlynched, had just been handed to the President-elect; he showed it to us, deliberating whether it should be communicated to the representative of the *New York Herald*, who was anxiously waiting to carry it away. He decided to do so, and then turned to a dear old man who stood beaming in the doorway, with a little boy clinging to his coat-tails, both looking round the big reception-room with eyes of wonder and bewilderment. There were no servants or ushers to introduce visitors; anybody could walk in unannounced, and the old man, who had tramped up with his grandson from a great distance to see the new Democratic President, found his way into the large hall of the capital. Now he was evidently much puzzled to know which in our little group of eight or ten persons was that President. He soon held the right man's hand, and truly touching he was in his allegiance. He had waited for many a weary year, he said, for the advent of the Democratic party, and at last this happy day had dawned upon him and his beloved country.

I made a rapid sketch of him, for he was a type well worth recording ; Cleveland liked it, so I naturally gave it him.

All this was in the first days of November 1884. It was not till the following February, when I again visited Albany, that I found myself installed in the bedroom above mentioned. The President-elect was living in a very small house in Willet Street, what we should call a bijou residence. The people had nicknamed it the Casket, if I recollect right, and it was certainly not much bigger than a receptacle of that description.

Cleveland had very kindly consented to let me paint a head of him. An opportunity of doing so was only to be found in the little house, and we entrenched ourselves in the bedroom against the intrusions of office-seekers and office-bearers, enthusiastic supporters, cranks and faddists, and, though last not least, young ladies with albums and birthday-books.

"Well, Mr. Cleveland," I said, as I started full speed to cover my canvas, "I'm not going to apologise for troubling you; I'm sure you must be quite pleased to have for once in the way a man come to view you, not to interview you. It must be a relief too, to know that I'm not going to rush off after the sitting, and send telegrams and cables all over the place, to let an expectant public know what you said."

He answered, " I am glad that is so."

Then for a while our conversation ran on art and other peaceful pursuits of man. Seeing a good opening I led up to the question ever uppermost in my mind,—that of international arbitration as against the arbitrament of the sword, and of the institution of a permanent tribunal between the United States and England. And here let me say in parenthesis, it is a glorious profession, that of the portrait-painter ; he can button-hole his man and keep him a fixture, whilst he indoctrinates and prods him with truths, from which, under other circumstances, his victim would seek to escape. Cleveland sat like a brick, and listened sympathetically. Then, he said in a few sharp concise words, that he fully agreed with me, and that he strongly felt it was high time for civilised humanity to abandon the barbarous methods of settling disputes. I told him I was sorely tempted to break my word, and to cable that welcome " message" to my friends in Europe without further delay. That temptation, however, I was not going to yield to. Finding that, as a member serving on the Executives of various Peace Societies, I was well posted up in matters relating to the subject, he began to question and cross-question me like the lawyer that he is.

I had to give him information concerning the various proposals made in Europe (which continent by the way he had never visited), for the constitution of permanent courts of arbitration, and to explain any views I might personally hold. This more especially in reference to my suggestion, that we might take up arbitration where we left it and link the present to the past; that we might do this by resuscitating the last tribunal that had done good service—at that time it was the Court that adjudicated on the Alabama claims—and declare it permanent, as permanent as all national courts and constitutional parliaments.

He expressed no definite opinion on the merits of the scheme, but was sufficiently interested in it to look at it from all sides. He wanted to know how it was "going to be worked out practically," and I had to particularise the provisions according to which the members of the last tribunal were to be replaced in cases of death or retirement, or new members were to be added, to suit the special case to be adjudicated upon. There was a good deal more said about the Dis-united States of Europe, as compared to the United States of America, but as I was the talker, and he only the questioner, it need not be recorded.

Some weeks afterwards I met Mr. Love, Secretary of the Peace Union in Philadelphia, and learnt from him that the President had requested him to furnish particulars concerning the work of the Peace Societies in America.

Such seeking for information is particularly characteristic of the man. I can fancy his saying to himself, "What that artist told me I've put in a pigeon-hole. Now I'll just hear what one or two others have to say about it.   Later on, I'll decide what's worth keeping."

From that day to this he has certainly been a warm supporter of arbitration.   Which is the method he considers best suited to be worked out practically we were only to learn twelve years later, when, under his administration, the Treaty of Arbitration, unfortunately not ratified by the Senate, was signed.

That chapter closed, we turned to more restful subjects than the peace question.   Talking of portrait-painting, I chanced to mention that I liked to give my sitters some characteristic name, to keep before my mind as a sort of password, whilst I proceeded with my work.   By way of illustration, I told him of a certain young lady I had been commissioned to paint.   She was very pretty, had a pair of twitting, soul-tormenting eyes and moisture-sparkling lips. I added, that such arbitrarily coined adjectives, and a good many more that suggested themselves, helped me but little towards the composition of my picture. That only came when I had found my formula ; and my young lady, who had all along been waiting for me to name the happy day of the first sitting, was much pleased when I started with the motto, "Don't you wish you may get it ?"   I painted her peeping out from behind a curtain, holding a lovely red rose in her hand, which, the rose and the hand, you might or might not be destined to get.

Mr. Cleveland listened with that interest which every good sitter is expected to display whilst under treatment, and sympathetically agreed with me that

it was wise not to begin a thing till it was finished.
Then he said, "Have you given me a name, too;
and if so, what is it?"

Now that was rather a poser, for I *had* given him
a name, and it at once struck me that he might not
like it. I admitted as much, and prefacing that he
must take one of the two words used in the good
sense, I said that I had labelled him "Solid and
Stolid"; the "stolid," I explained, meaning that he
was a man who wasn't going to move unless he saw
good cause why. He seemed to think I wasn't far
wrong there. As for the "solid," that needed no
apology. Physically, any weighing machine would
prove his substantial solidity; and intellectually,
even a slight acquaintance with him would show
him to be a powerful man.

All this little by-play did not prevent my getting
on with my picture; nor was I much disturbed by
the business that occasionally claimed the President-
elect's attention. He took things with characteristic
coolness, and gave his instructions without moving a
muscle. Only once he got up, more freely to indulge
in his habit of thinking before speaking. He was to
decide where he would take up his quarters on his
visit to New York; that was a burning question,
warmly discussed in the press. Why, I don't quite
recollect, but anyway his decision was eagerly awaited
by two contending groups of his followers. His Secretary had handed him a telegram, and was waiting for
instructions what to answer. I thought it proper
to be unmistakably minding my own business, and
became deeply interested in the background of my

picture. But I could not help hearing Cleveland's answer :—

"Say the governor has not decided ; he seems inclined to select his own hotel." This in a drowsy undertone. Then, turning to me with a sudden outburst of energy he said :—

"They'll have to find it out sooner or later, and the sooner they find it out the better, that I'm not a figure-head to be put in front of a tobacconist's store."

After the second sitting my portrait was finished, and my kind model asked me to stop and take luncheon with him. I accepted with pleasure, and this little *tête-à-tête* with Cleveland is one of my pleasantest transatlantic recollections. Democratic simplicity ruled supreme. We shared four cutlets and a dish of potatoes, and wound up with some stewed fruit; with that we drank our bumpers of ice water in true American fashion. It was quite a relief to get from Lucullus to Cincinnatus. I had had ample opportunity of appreciating American hospitality, fêted and "received" as I had been by my new friends, but now, it was really refreshing to sit down for once in a way to a meal without having constantly to say "No, thank you," to the bearers of dish or bottle, and without being uncomfortably reminded that you were feasting whilst others were starving within easy reach perhaps of your table, laden with all the luxuries that wealth commands.

The servant disappeared, we helped ourselves, and in answer to a question of mine, Cleveland chatted freely about himself and his antecedents.

"I really do not know how it has all come about," he said. "I began in the smallest of ways as clerk in a store; then I got into a law office" (I think he said at four dollars a week), "and one thing leading up to another, I set up as a lawyer myself. For a while I was Mayor of Buffalo, and then an unexpected opportunity sent me as Governor to Albany. I can hardly tell you why I am President; I was not anxious to be Governor, and not ambitious to be President. When my term is ended, I think, on the whole, that I should like best to be Mayor of Buffalo again."

I answered that I could well understand that desire, as he might not find quite so much left to veto there as in other places. This in allusion to the byname of "the vetoing Mayor of Buffalo" the people had given him on account of his systematic opposition to all extravagant expenditure when Governor of the State. It was said he had saved the taxpayer a million dollars during the first year of his administration.

Then the conversation turned on the responsibilities of statesmen, and I hazarded the remark that they must weigh heavily on them, especially in cases where perhaps the fate of nations depended on their decision. What were Mr. Gladstone's feelings, and how did he sleep, I wondered, after he had signed the paper authorising the bombardment of Alexandria?

"Well," said the President, "I think he would have slept well. When a man has fully and carefully considered all facts and arguments that can help him to a conclusion, and when he has decided to do what he considers right, according to the best of his judgment, there is no reason why he should not sleep as soundly as ever he did before."

Such were the characteristic words meditatively and slowly spoken by the man who was going to be inaugurated, a few days later, in Washington, as President of the United States, and who henceforth was to take many a momentous decision, that would affect the weal and woe of millions of his compatriots—decisions, too, so weighty and far-reaching that on them might depend the fate of nations, the peace of the world.

CHAPTER VIII

GIUSEPPE MAZZINI *

I well remember some great and good men whom it has been my privilege and my good fortune to know, but none do I see so plainly before me as Giuseppe Mazzini. His features, his expression, and his every gesture, all are indelibly engraven on my memory. Is it because thirty-four years ago I painted a portrait of him that hangs here just opposite me, and I reverently look up at it as I am about to speak of him? Or is it not rather that to have known Mazzini means ever to remember him—to hear his voice, to feel his influence, and to recall his outward form?

The portrait was painted in the little studio of my bachelor days, which measured about twenty feet by ten, and had no other appendage but a good-sized cupboard, by courtesy called a bedroom. But it was situated right in the middle of six or eight acres of ground in the heart of London, which for many years went by the name of " Cadogan Gardens," till one day it was "improved" away, and its good name was transferred to a new row of Philistine stone houses. Such as it was in 1862, Mazzini liked it,

* Reprinted from " Cosmopolis."

and would often look in on me and my brother-in-law, Antonin Roche, the only other occupant of those Square gardens.

Roche, who is now of a ripe old age, and is enjoying a well-earned rest, was an old friend of Mazzini. The two took very opposite views in politics, for Roche was a " Légitimiste," warmly attached to the direct line of the Bourbons, and true to their white flag; whilst in the eyes of Mazzini, as we know, all kings were pretty equally black, and no flag acceptable but the white, green, and red one of a united Italy. A long experience had taught him to place no faith in princes, but to centre his hopes in the people, and in the ultimate triumph of Republican institutions. So he and Roche had right royal word-fights when they met, and they were not badly matched; for Roche was quite a living encyclopædia of knowledge, and had the history of mankind, from the days of Adam up to date, at his fingers' ends. And he had every opportunity of keeping his knowledge fresh, for during a period of forty-five years he regularly held his French "cours" on history, literature, and a variety of other subjects, and before he retired he had educated three generations of England's fairest and most aristocratic daughters.

Mazzini and he, then, would often discuss politics and political economy of the past, present, and future, and I sometimes ventured to join in their conversation. To-day I see the presumption of my ways, but then I was younger, and whilst reverencing the master-mind, and feeling infinitesimally small next to the great man, I yet was bold enough to advance where many besides angels would have feared to tread. I had lived in France for some years under the second Empire, and had, perhaps, more respect for the successful than I have now. I had witnessed the rebuilding of Paris, the revival of art, and many evidences of increasing prosperity, and — always allowing for the needs of France and the French of that day—I looked upon Louis Napoleon as rather the right man in the right place.

But Mazzini reviled him, and at the mention of his name would burst forth into a passionate philippic, crushing "the adventurer, the perjurer, the tyrant" with all the weight of his glowing indignation. "But apart from all that," he would say, "we hate each other personally."

He was certainly the most uncompromising enemy of royalty, disdaining threats and blandishments alike, and preferring exile to the acceptance of such favours as the amnesty which at a later period recalled him and his friends to their native land. "He who can debase himself," he said, "by accepting the royal clemency will some day stand in need of the people's clemency."

If he was grand in his wrath, he was grand also in his ideal aspirations ; whether he thundered with the withering eloquence of a Cicero, or pleaded for the Brotherhood of Man with the accents of love ; whether he bowed his head humbly before the power of one great God, or rose fanatically to preach the new Gospel : "Dio e il popolo," God the first cause, the People sole legitimate interpreter of His law of eternal progress.

The conviction that spoke from that man's lips was so intense, that it kindled conviction ; his soul so stirred that one's soul could not but vibrate responsively. To be sure, at the time I am speaking of, every conversation seemed to lead up to the one all-absorbing topic, the unification of Italy. She must be freed from the yoke of the Austrian or the Frenchman ; the dungeons of King Bomba must be opened and the fetters forged at the Vatican shaken off. His eyes sparkled as he spoke, and reflected the ever-glowing and illuminating fire within ; he held you magnetically. He would penetrate into some innermost recess of your conscience and kindle a spark where all had been darkness. Whilst under the influence of that eye, that voice, you felt as if you could leave father and mother and follow him, the elect of Providence, who had come to overthrow the whole wretched fabric of falsehoods holding mankind in bondage. He gave you eyes to see, and ears to hear, and you too were stirred to rise and go forth to propagate the new Gospel, "The Duties of Man."

What he wrote, what he spoke, was something beyond revealed religion, the outcome of a faith that looked upwards to gather a new revelation of the eternal law that governs the universe. Gospel, Koran, Talmud, merged in his mind in the new faith, rising over the horizon to illuminate humanity.

There was another side of his nature that many a time deeply impressed me. The enthusiast, the conspirator, would give way to the poet, the dreamer, as he would speak of God's nature, and of its loveliest creation, Woman; of innocent childhood, of sunshine and flowers.

I have heard much said about Woman and Woman's Rights since the days of Mazzini, from pulpit and platform, from easy-chair and office-stool. It often seemed to me to be said in beautiful prose; but still in prose. Mazzini spoke the language of poetry; not in hexameters or blank verse, but still it was poetry. We of to-day look forward, create a new ideal, a new woman; he looked backward to the days of his childhood, and conjured up a vision of Maria Mazzini, his mother.

He loved children, too, and they him. There were boys and girls of all ages in the Roche family, clever and active, and, consequently, what wise and sapient parents call naughty. Some of these now ex-children tell me they have a distinct recollection of having been on more than one occasion turned out and sent to bed prematurely. "We often got into trouble," they say, "when Louis Blanc was there, but we were always good for Mazzini; that was because he was so kind, and never failed to inquire after the dolls; and then we loved to sit and listen to him. To be sure we sometimes didn't understand a word of the conversation going on, but his voice was so beautiful that it fascinated us."

Overawed, I think, would frequently have been more correct, when I remember how they must have heard him denouncing the Austrian rule, or holding up to execration his crowned enemies. I always looked upon him, as I certainly believe he did upon himself, as the ordained champion of the oppressed, and as a menacing tool in the hands of an unflinching Providence. He was as unflinching as the Fates themselves, and, regarding himself as the embodiment of a good cause, he cared little for the obloquy his opponents ever heaped upon his head. To name but one instance : When Orsini attempted the life of Napoleon III., throwing a bomb at the imperial carriage as it was approaching the Opera House in the Rue Drouot, killing, not the object of his hatred, but so many innocent people, a cry of horror went through the civilised world, and Mazzini got his full share of execration. Nobody entertained a doubt that he was at the bottom of the plot. It could only be he who had organised it ; he had supplied the bombs, and Orsini was but a tool sent to the post of danger, whilst he himself remained on the safe side of the water that separated hospitable England from the realm of the French Emperor and his ever-watchful police.

The world was mistaken. Mazzini may have hatched plots and prepared *coups;* indeed, to do so was his daily task, and sometimes when I asked him : " Eh bien, comment ça va ? Qu'est ce que vous faites ? " he would pleasantly answer : " Je conspire " ; but in this case we knew that he could not have had any communication with Orsini. What had happened between them had led to an irreparable breach. During one of Mazzini's secret visits to the Continent, his friend Sir James Stansfeld, then Mr. Stansfeld, had undertaken to open his letters for him, and to forward what he deemed desirable. Among others a letter from Orsini thus came into his hands, which contained the vilest accusations against two most deservedly respected ladies, friends both of Mr. Stansfeld and of Mazzini. The indignant answer with which the former met the slander led in true Continental fashion to a challenge from Orsini, which, it is needless to say, was treated with contempt. Mazzini, to whom woman was ever an ideal to be looked up to and revered, was deeply incensed. He never met Orsini after the incident, and he never forgave him the libels he had penned.

Alluding to these circumstances, I asked him why he did not publicly contradict the reports that accused him of complicity ; knowing, as I did, that they were untrue, I wondered that he did not repudiate the charge. To that he answered : " It matters nothing, or rather it is well the world should believe me implicated. I never protest. Europe needs a bugbear, a watchword that threatens, a name that makes itself feared. The few syllables that go to make up my name will serve the purpose as well as any others."

Mr. Stansfeld was one of his earliest friends. He has often told me how great was the personal influence Mazzini exercised over him. " What could be loftier," he writes, " than his conception of duty as the standard of life for nations and individuals alike, and of right as a consequence of duty fulfilled. His earnestness and eloquence fascinated me from the first, and many young men of that time have had their after-lives elevated by his living example."

There were two associations of which all the

most active members were young men, Mr. Stansfeld amongst the number: "The People's International League," and "The Society of the Friends of Italy;" the latter especially exercising considerable influence in accentuating and bringing to the front the expression of British public opinion in favour of the emancipation and unification of Italy. At the close of the revolution that in 1848 shook the very foundations on which rested European thrones, many of the most prominent leaders and revolutionary personalities of the period sought shelter in the sanctuary of the British Islands, and it was at this time that Mazzini's more intimate friends found a hospitable and cordial reception at Mr. Stansfeld's house. Mazzini himself had come to London when he was obliged to leave Switzerland in 1841. One or two of the incidents that arose out of his presence in England are worth recalling.

In 1844 a petition from Mazzini and others was presented to the House of Commons, complaining that their letters had been opened in the Post Office. Sir James Graham, under whose instructions as Secretary of State this had been done, defended his action, and roundly abused Mazzini, as did Lord Aberdeen in the House of Lords. They, however, afterwards apologised for their words. A Bill was introduced to put a stop to the power of opening letters by the Secretary of State, but was dropped. It was on this occasion that Carlyle wrote to *The Times* his famous defence of Mazzini. "I have had the honour to know Mr. Mazzini for a series of years, and, whatever I may think of his practical insight and skill in worldly affairs, I can with great freedom testify to all men that he, if ever I have seen one such, is a man of genius and virtue, a man of sterling veracity, humanity, and nobleness of mind, one of those rare men, numerable unfortunately but as units in this world, who are worthy to be called martyr souls."

Twenty years later the subject of Mazzini's letters once more led to heated controversy in the House of Commons. At that time Mr. Stansfeld was a Junior Lord of the Admiralty. His friendship for the champion of Italy's rights had ripened as years went on, and he was ever ready to serve him and the good cause. It happened that the French Procureur-Impérial, while engaged in prosecuting a State conspiracy, discovered that one of the accused persons had been found in possession of a letter telling him to write for money to Mr. Flowers, at 35 Thurloe Square, S.W. This was Mr. Stansfeld's address, and he did not hesitate to admit that he had allowed Mazzini to have his letters addressed there, under the name of M. Fiori (Anglicè, Flowers), to prevent those letters from being opened, while at the same time he knew nothing of their contents. The incident was used by Disraeli to make an attack on the Palmerston Government, for containing in its ranks so dangerous a man as Stansfeld—a man actually engaged in sheltering a conspirator, and "the great promoter of assassination," as he was pleased to call Mazzini. Bright made a strong speech, defending Stansfeld and Mazzini, and declaring that Disraeli himself had justified regicide, as he had in the "Revolutionary Epic."

Stansfeld also spoke, saying that he was proud of the intimate friendship of Mazzini, and denying that the great patriot could be properly described in the scurrilous language Disraeli had used.

It was in consequence of this incident that Mr. Stansfeld resigned office. "perfectly satisfied." he says in a letter on the subject, "in being able by so doing, to reconcile the duties of private friendship with my obligations to the Government, of which I was the youngest member." In his long and honourable career, whether as Mr. or Sir James, Stansfeld was always a good knight and true, labouring with the zeal of the reformer and the foresight of the statesman. In Mazzini he admired not only the patriot who served his own country with passionate devotion, but the teacher who, seeing far beyond the narrow limits of each separate nation, could realise the ideal of international unity, and foreshadow a future, in which the aim of statesmanship among free nations would no longer be to perpetuate the weakness of others, but "to secure the amelioration of all, and the progress of each, for the benefit of all the others."

Thus impressed with the solidarity of nations, and the community of their interests, Stansfeld at all times advocated the cause of international unity and the establishment of tribunals of arbitration ; and, if a powerful figure-head was wanted to represent those causes, be it to preside over a meeting or to introduce a deputation to the prime minister, we looked to Sir James as the man round whom the best and most influential politicians would rally, and whom they would cordially support, confident as they were both of his strength and of his discretion.

From the arena of politics, national and international, to the four walls of my little studio is an abrupt transition ; but with the name of Mazzini as a connecting link, it needs no apology. So I make straight for Cadogan Gardens, in order to mention a pleasant recollection I have of a certain October evening in 1862, when Mazzini unexpectedly dropped in. My cousin, Ernst Jaques, and two friends, Felix Simon and Herr von Keudell, had met there on a short visit to London to "make music." Mazzini and myself formed an appreciative audience, as well we might, for they played Mendelssohn's D Minor Trio in masterly fashion, von Keudell at the piano, Simon taking the violin, and my cousin the violoncello part. Mazzini loved music and was in full sympathy with the performers, so naturally the conversation first turned on the beauties of Mendelssohn's work and on the excellence of its interpretation ; but it soon gravitated to the subjects always uppermost in his mind. Herr von Keudell was particularly successful in drawing him out, perhaps because he held views opposed to those of the great patriot, and was well prepared to discuss them. He was soon to become Bismarck's confidential secretary, and as such to take an active and influential part in the chapter of history that was ere long to be enacted. In later years he rose to occupy the post of ambassador to Italy. There was much in his aspirations that interested Mazzini, and when presently my cousin asked him for his autograph, he wrote, "Ah, si l'Allemagne agissait comme elle pense." Then it was on matters revolutionary that he talked, on the organisation of secret societies, on his clandestine visits to countries in which a price had been set upon his head, and finally, as he got up to leave us, on the detectives he would not keep waiting any longer. They had shadowed him as usual from his house, and would not fail to shadow him back. Very sensational stories were current in reference to those clandestine visits and the disguises under which Mazzini was supposed to have travelled, but they were mere inventions, he told us. To keep his counsel about the end of his journey and the time of his leaving, to shave off his moustache, sometimes to wear spectacles, and to travel quickly, were his sole precautions.

He always carried a certain walking-stick with a carved ivory handle, a most innocent-looking thing, but in reality a scabbard holding a sharply pointed blade. This is now in the possession of Mr. Joseph Stansfeld, to whom it was given by Mr. Peter Taylor, the old and trusted friend of Mazzini. He also preserves a volume of "The Duties of Man" with the dedication in his godfather's hand: "To Joseph, in memoriam of Joseph Mazzini." There is too a portrait of Maria Mazzini (Giuseppe's mother). It is a very poor production, and whilst it may, perhaps, give us some idea of her features, it certainly in no way reflects her lovable nature. When I knew Mazzini he was living in the simplest of lodgings, at 2 Onslow Terrace, Brompton. His room was littered with papers and pamphlets. Birds were his constant companions; the room was their cage, wire netting being stretched across the windows. They flew around and hopped about most unceremoniously on the writing-table amongst the conspirator's voluminous correspondence. He had a curious way of holding his pen, the thumb not closing upon it as he wrote, a peculiarity which accounts for the crabbed character of his handwriting. Being an inveterate smoker, he and the birds were mostly enveloped in a cloud. Smoking cheap, but many, Swiss cigars was the only luxury he allowed himself. He was the austerest of Republicans, had few wants, and but slender means with which to satisfy them. Whatever he may have possessed in early life he had spent for the cause he was devoted to; afterwards he lived on a small annuity which his mother had settled on him.

When he sat for me I always took good care to place a box of cigars, and wherewith to light one after the other, on a little table by his side. Thus equipped he proved an admirable model; he sat, or rather stood, with untiring energy, dictating, as it were, the character of the picture, and enabling me to put every touch from nature; posing for those nervous, sensitive hands of his, for the coat and the black velvet waistcoat buttoned up to the chin —he never showed a trace of white collar or cuff— and for the long Venetian gold chain, the only slender line of light I could introduce in the sombre figure. He was indeed, I felt, a subject to stir up an artist, and to sharpen whatever of wits he might have at the end of his brush.

From Mazzini I first heard of the new enterprise

Garibaldi had embarked on in August 1862. He had once more left Caprera, and had crossed over to Calabria with the avowed intention of driving the French garrison from Rome. Mazzini was most emphatic in his condemnation of the scheme, and used strong and uncomplimentary language in censuring the action of his colleague. "But the die is cast," he said, "and under the circumstances I cannot do otherwise than give instructions to all our groups and societies to support him."

How disastrously the expedition ended we all remember. It was denounced as treasonable by the Italian Government in a royal proclamation, and Garibaldi was wounded at Aspromonte in an encounter with troops sent to stop his advance. Great and spontaneous was the outburst of sympathy in England for the hero of Marsala. A small group of his friends arranged, at a cost of £1000, to send out an English surgeon, Mr. Partridge, to attend him. It was not by him, however, but by the eminent French surgeon Nélaton that the bullet was found and extracted.

More than once Mazzini's impulsiveness, not to say naïveté, struck me. Thus one day he rushed breathlessly into my studio, with the words, "Have you heard the news? We are going to have Rome and Venice." I forget what particular news he alluded to, but remember pulling him up with unwarrantable audacity. "At what o'clock?" I asked. "Ah," he answered, "go on, go on. I am too well accustomed to jeers and epigrams to mind." I humbly apologised for my disrespectful retort, uttered on the spur of the moment; but to do so seemed scarcely necessary, for the lion evidently did not mind my taking liberties with his tail; and presently, when I said, " Well, if not at what o'clock, tell me in how much time you will have Rome and Venice," he answered, " Within a twelvemonth. You will see." I made a note of this date, but never reminded him of the incident. In his enthusiasm he had been over-sanguine. " Id fere credunt quod volunt," says Cæsar in his " De Bello Gallico " (" they readily believe what they wish "), and Mazzini was the man of faith and aspirations. Four years were yet to elapse before Venice was liberated, and eight before the Italians gained possession of Rome.

One of the subjects on which he felt strongly was that of compulsory insurance. I cannot remember that he favoured any particular scheme, but he was wedded to the principle that no man has a right to become a pauper, and that he should be compelled by law to save a fraction of his earnings, to be entrusted to the State. In old age he should be able to draw upon a fund thus constituted, and in doing so he would be under no greater obligation to the State than any man is to the banker with whom he has opened an account.

Some little notes which I received from him mostly refer to the sittings for his portrait. On one occasion I must have written that I was again conspiring against his peace, and wanted him to make an appointment. In allusion to this he answers, addressing me as " Mon cher conspirateur." On another occasion I had put that I was one of the several tyrants who were clamouring for his head, to which his answer commenced, " Mon cher tyran." That autograph I always particularly prized, the juxtaposition of the words " Dear " and " Tyrant " in Mazzini's handwriting being, I believe, unique. In my album he quotes Goethe, " Im Ganzen, Guten, Wahren resolut zu leben," words that strike one as the appropriate motto for the man who ever sought to live resolutely for all that is good and true. His quotation, however, was not quite correct, for he had substituted, characteristically perhaps, the " True " for the " Beautiful."

Some letters addressed to his friend, Allessandro Cicognani, which have recently come into my possession, are characteristic. He writes :—

" Fratello mio,—La vostra lettera mi è giunta carissima ; ora tanto più che io sento il bisogno di riannodare intelligenze coi buoni della città di Romagna e stava cercandone i modi ; dopo tre anni d'agitazione nelle quali abbiamo lasciato fare perchè l'esperimento fosse intero e i fatti parlassero, noi ci troviamo a un dipresso là donde eravamo partiti, colla Lombardia rioccupata, coi principi piu o meno proclivi a retrocedere.

" È tempo che ci dichiariamo in faccia all' Europa inetti a essere liberi, o che cominciamo ad agire da per noi. Noi vogliamo *cacciare lo straniero d' Italia,* e vogliamo *che il paese intero decida liberamente delle proprie sorti.* Guerra dunque e costituente. Se vi è chi dissenta da quegli due punti, merita condanna da ogni Italiano che ama il Paese. Non si tratta più di un partito o dell' altro, si tratta di esistere come nazione e di riconoscere nella nazione la sovranità. In questi limiti noi vogliamo stare, al di qua noi non diamo ormai più tregua ad alcuno.

" Questa posizione che noi repubblicani abbiamo presa io la esprimerò nettamente in un opuscolo, che escirà fra cinque o sei giorni e che vorrei mandarvi ; vogliate indicarmi il modo più conveniente e se io debba via via scrivere al vostro o ad altro indirizzo. Su quel terreno intanto è necessario che rapidamente ci organizziamo per l'azione concentrata a raggiungere il doppio intento. Io vi manderò tra due giorni una circolare della nostra Giunta centrale contenente appunto le norme d'organizzazione generale che dovremmo dare uniforme a quanti consentano in quella bandiera. Voi farete il meglio che potrete.

" Vi suppongo in contatto con Malioni ed amici. Fra qualche giorno giungerà tra voi un amico mio, Lauri di Forli col quale desidero vi teniate in perfetto accordo.

" Addio, possiam noi far davvero un ultimo sforzo che levi il Paese da questa vergognosissima via di ciarle di progetti impossibili e di transazione fra il fianciullesco ed il gesuitico, che ci fanno parere decrepiti all' Europa quando si tratta di ringiovanire ed iniziare una nuova era di vita !—Amate il vostro,

" GIUSEPPE MAZZINI.

" FRONTIERA LOMBARDA.
15 *Novembre* 1849."

Translation.

" MY BROTHER,—Your letter received was most welcome, all the more so, as I feel the want of putting myself once more in communication with the good friends of the cities of the Romagna, and I was seeking for the best means of doing so. After three years of agitation, during which we have let things take their course in order to allow the experiment to be complete, and facts to speak for themselves, we find ourselves about at the point from which we started, with Lombardy re-occupied and the princes more or less inclined to retrogression. It is time that in the sight of Europe we should either openly avow ourselves incapable of being free, or that we should begin to act for ourselves. We are resolved to *drive the foreigner from Italy*, and to let the whole country be the free arbiter of its own destiny.

" This means war. If there is any one who dissents from these two points he deserves the condemnation of every Italian who loves his country. It is no longer a question of one party or another; it is a question of existing as a nation, and of recognising the sovereignty of the nation. Within these limits we will stand; beyond them we will henceforth concede no truce to any one.

" The position which we Republicans have thus taken I shall define in unequivocal terms in a pamphlet which will appear in five or six days, and which I should like to send you. Please let me know which is the best way of doing so, and whether

I should for the present write to your address or to another. In the meanwhile it is, however, necessary that we should rapidly organise in order to attain by concentrated action the two objects in view. I shall send you in two days a circular issued by our Central Giunta, containing definite instructions for general organisation, which must be made uniform for all those who rally round this banner. You will do the best you can.

"I take it that you are in touch with Melioni and friends. In a few days you will receive the visit of a friend of mine, Lauri di Forli, with whom I wish you to hold yourself in perfect agreement.

"Good-bye. May we in full earnest make a final effort that shall lead the country out of that most disgraceful rut of useless chatter of impossible schemes and of compromises between the childish and the jesuitical, that make us appear decrepit in the eyes of Europe when we speak of regeneration and of the introduction of a new era in our lives. Love me.—Yours, GIUSEPPE MAZZINI.

"LOMBARD FRONTIER, *Nov.* 15, 1849."

I have two short letters written to the same friend and dated 1869 and 1871, not of general interest, but the latter concluding with the characteristic sentence :

"Il meglio sarebbe che si aprisse la via cercata per lunghi anni da noi ; e s'aprirà ; ma siamo corrotti e privi di coraggio morale.

"Persisto nondimeno e persisterò finchè vivo."

"The best would be, that the road should open

which we have sought for many years, and open it will; but we are corrupt and devoid of moral courage. I persist nevertheless, and shall persist as long as I live."

The epistles he received he sometimes showed me as curiosities. Some came from his admirers, other from his detractors, either frequently total strangers to him. There were letters couched in terms of most eccentric adulation, others that unceremoniously relegated him to the regions of perdition. One merely requested him to go to the antipodes, in order that he might be well out of the way of regenerated Italy. Another, less urbane, addressed him as "Uomo aborrito!" ("abhorred man"), and continued in a similar strain of abuse. Mazzini took it all pleasantly; the lion's tail was once for all proof against any amount of pulling.

The patriotic dreams of Mazzini were gradually to be realised, in a measure, at least; for although his ideal—a Republic in place of a Monarchy—seemed hopeless of attainment, the hated foreigner was expelled, or had retired from Italian soil, and a united people joined hands from the Alps to the Adriatic.

He had returned to his native land, and there, active and uncompromising to the last, he died at Pisa, on March 10, 1872, in the Casa Rosselli. A private letter in the possession of Mr. Stansfeld gives some particulars of his last hours. He was perfectly tranquil, and free from suffering, but sank into a gradual stupor. During the day, at times, his hands moved mechanically, as if he were holding and smoking a cigar. Madame Rosselli asked him why he did that; but his mind was wandering, he did not understand her, and answered an imaginary question. He roused himself, and looking straight at her, he said, with great animation and intenseness, "Believe in God? Yes, indeed I do believe in God." These were his last words of consciousness.

A friend of his, writing a few days after the fatal 10th of March, tells how the mystery which surrounded him all his life continued to envelop him to the moment when death broke the seals of secrecy. Then, for the first time, the good people of Pisa learnt that the mild and retiring Mr. Francis Braun. who had long lived within their walls, was no other than the redoubtable Mazzini. He had come to their city in the February of the preceding year, and had remained till August, returning from Switzerland with the first frosts of November. The authorities doubtless knew perfectly well who the supposed Englishman was, who spent all his days in study and all his evenings in the company of the self-same small family circle. But they were to let him alone. It was not for the first time that they wisely ignored his presence. The chief difficulty of the Italian Government had been, not to find him and seize him, but to find and not to molest him. On one occasion the Neapolitan police put the Government into much perturbation by telegraphing that it was "impossible to avoid arresting Mazzini."

On another occasion—it was in 1857—the house of the Marchese Pareto, where Mazzini was staying, was surrounded by the police, and a large military force in attendance made a portentous show. The

Quæstor, an old schoolfellow of Mazzini, formally demands admittance in the King's name, when the door is opened by Mazzini himself, disguised as a servant. The Quæstor asks to speak to the Marquis, and is forthwith introduced by the obsequious flunkey. Did the Quæstor recognise his old friend? Our informant believes he did. He tells us that diligent search was made throughout the house; that nothing was found but a stove full of ashes, the remains of papers just burnt; that the Marquis was carried off by the police in his carriage, to make certain depositions, which meant nothing; and that the servant was left behind.

In like manner Mazzini was suffered to remain undisturbed in Pisa. Dangerous though some timorous officials deemed him to be, the Government knew full well that he would be far more dangerous as a captive than as a free man.

To the citizens of Pisa his *incognito* was so complete, that even the doctor who attended him in his last illness did not know his patient.

On the Wednesday before his death he wrote an article for the *Unità Italiana* on Renan's book, "La Réforme Intellectuelle et Morale de la France." He talked rarely about politics even to his intimate friends. Occasionally he would, however, break out into anathemas against the "International"; his eyes would then flash fire, and he would use strong language against Ledru Rollin, Quinet, "e tutti quanti," who, he would say, "might have saved France, but who, by mere inaction, had abandoned her to the most pernicious of impossible delusions."

The news that his remains had been embalmed by Professor Zorini and placed in a metal coffin, into which a glass had been inserted, with a view to exhibiting them on the anniversary of his death, raised an indignant protest from some of his nearest friends in England. They wrote warmly denouncing what they declared would most have wounded and outraged him. " His whole life," says Madame Venturi, in a letter to an Italian friend, " was one long protest against materialism, and they make of his sacred corpse a lasting statue of materialism, and of his monument an altar to the idolatry of matter. Write to the people and tell them that he expressed a wish to lie by the side of his mother."

The truth concerning the matter which led to so warm a protest, is this : Mazzini was only partially embalmed, and lay in state in a small room on the ground floor of the Casa Rosselli. A tricolour flag covered his breast, and a laurel wreath crowned his head. A plaster cast and a photograph had been taken by Alinari. On the birthday of the King of Italy and of his son the remains of their potent adversary were carried on a simple car to the railway station outside the Porta Nuova. The pall-bearers were six of his nearest friends, besides a student and a working - man ; deputations from neighbouring cities, and crowds of sympathisers, formed a procession and lined the streets. Conspicuous on the coffin was a wreath with the inscription, "The Americans to Mazzini"; it had been placed there by the consular representatives of the United States. On its arrival in Genoa, the remains lay in state again, but for one day only. Then better counsels, more in harmony with the patriot's wishes, prevailed, and his body was placed in the sepulchre, where no human eye has seen it since. His burial-place was selected next to that of his mother, and now her tomb is enclosed with his.

It was after his death only that the great agitator's life-work began to be fully recognised by his countrymen. A reaction set in in his favour; the Parliament of Rome passed a resolution expressing the grief of the nation at the death of " The Apostle of Italian Unity"; public meetings were held, and many were the marks of respect paid to him throughout Italy.

This seemed to me an opportune moment to add my small tribute to his memory, so I called on the Marquis d'Azeglio, then Italian ambassador to England, and offered to present my portrait of Mazzini to the Italian nation, that it might be placed in one of their public galleries. But I was to be disappointed, for the marquis bowed me out, very politely, I must say, but fully giving me to understand that it was one thing to tolerate the demonstrations in favour of Mazzini, and another to do honour to him and his portrait. The picture has since gone through one or two similar experiences. What will become of it eventually I do not know, but I am happy to have it with me still.

On the second of November, some ten years ago, I happened to be in Genoa. It was the day of " Tutti Morti" (All Souls' Day), the great holiday, tearful and cheerful, on which all good Catholics make their pilgrimage to the cemeteries where rest their departed friends. A steady stream of visitors was flowing towards the "Cimetéro di Staglieno." I joined it, and was soon wandering through arcades filled with marble tributes to the memory of the dead, some of the sculptors' work being very beautiful. Then, across the Campo Santo—the consecrated field—all bedecked with flowers and garlands, I came to where the path winds upwards to the graves and monuments that dot the hills above. There stands Mazzini's tomb, a mausoleum worthy of the man, severe and solemn. Two short, thickset columns mark the entrance and carry a massive stone, on which is inscribed in plain large characters the name "Giuseppe Mazzini." That day the monument and the surroundings seemed doubly impressive, for a guard of honour had been placed to hold watch by the great liberator's tomb. It was here, then, that the exile and the outlaw had at last found rest in the land he loved so well—in Genoa, the city of his birth.

I sought out a place from which I could make a water-colour sketch, and, as I sat painting, my thoughts reverted with reverence and with love to the master and to the friend.

CHAPTER IX

ROSSINI

 well remember my first introduction to Madame Rossini in April
1854. I was sitting with the Maestro
in his study one morning whilst he
was finishing his toilet; his valet had
selected one of two brown wigs, and adjusted it on
his illustrious master's head, leaving the other, placed
on a little stand, to ornament the mantelpiece. Next
he brought him a silver bowl full of milk and one
or two of those cunningly-twisted rolls or crescents,
the very thought of which conveys to the appetite's
memory a whiff of dainty Paris.

Rossini liked to be informed of the latest news,
meaning the up-to-date incidents in Paris society,
and to be told what the wicked world was saying,
and what *bons-mots* the clever ones had made; so
we young fellows were expected to drop in occasionally at an early hour in the morning and keep
him posted up. His comments on our news were
always much more *spirituels* than the best of *bons-
mots* we could impart, and frequently a good deal more
spicy than our versions of Parisian doings. I dare
say then I was carrying coals to Newcastle, and he
was making them blaze, when the door was abruptly

thrust open, and a bejewelled hand—it was Madame Rossini's—triumphantly appeared, flourishing a ham of unusual dimensions, that she had brought for the master to see and to rejoice over.

A pair of piercing dark eyes next swept the room to see who might be there. Finding there was nobody—a young man like myself not counting—the hand and the eyes were followed by the rest of her. She struck me as every inch a queen—a tragedy queen, off duty. Her black hair hung dishevelled over her shoulders, and she was clad in the style the French call "neglected." The upper part of her classical figure was more or less concealed beneath a loose white garment, which I have since learnt to associate with hair-combing. Her lower limbs showed off to great advantage under a heavy striped petticoat; that at least I think it must have been; if it was meant for a dress, it was certainly cut several inches too short.

Whilst I was contemplating her, she and her husband were examining the ham, and commenting upon it *en amateurs*. I was called upon to admire it, and incidentally introduced to Madame. Disgracefully ignorant as I was of pork-flesh, and being of those honest youths who call a pig a pig, I found nothing better to say than, "Voilà ce que j'appelle un cochon." That seemed about as much as they expected, and I was allowed to pat it on the hip.

And here I cannot help leaping at a bound from 1854 to 1896, and from Paris to Venice. Just as I was sitting, pen in hand, and trying to conjure up a correct image of Madame Rossini, a living biographical dictionary, in the shape of an elderly lady, walked in, who had been sent round to show me some valuable old lace she had to dispose of. The grand race of the *decaduti* (the come-down in the world) is by no means extinct, and Signora Baldazzi was a pleasant representative of it. I welcomed her, and, having made the acquisition of some of her lace, I chanced to elicit, in further friendly conversation, that she was a teacher of music, and had studied for years at the Liceo Bologna, when Rossini was director there.

She had plenty of " I well remembers " to start with, so she was soon telling me how good and kind he was, and how brusque and rude, and how he spared neither teachers nor pupils. Even *il maestro Cappeletti, il professore di timpani,* she said, speaking of him with the greatest respect, came in for his share, when, in a rehearsal under Rossini, he made some blunder. " Asino," cried Rossini. " That sort of thing was not unusual," added my informant; " one always expected something hot from him." " Do I remember Madame Rossini, la Pelissier? Ma che! I see her now in her red corsage and many-coloured petticoat, leading her dog by a string. I knew la Collbran, too; his first wife, you know. They had been married a good many years, when he got tired of her; he told her so, and said he wanted a change. She did not mind the change, but she would not leave the house for him or for anybody else; so she lived in one apartment whilst la Pelissier and Rossini occupied another; but they all took their meals together, and la Collbran did the housekeeping."

This lady, it will be remembered, was the famous singer who created some of the principal parts in Rossini's opera. I thought the story of the joint *ménage* so peculiar, that I subjected the good lady, my informant, to a severe cross-examination, but I did not succeed in shaking her evidence. Future biographers may further look into the matter if they care.

I return to that corner house of the Rue de la Chaussée d'Antin, where the maestro lived. One morning I was there with my cousin, Ernst Jaques, when Rossini's old friend Scitivaux came in.

"There," said Rossini, "there is what I promised you, and I have written all you want to know inside." With that he handed a copy of the "Barbiere" to Scitivaux, who, at the sight of the gift and its precious dedication, broke into raptures of gratitude; I am not sure whether he wept or laughed on the other's shoulder; but I distinctly recollect he was immediately turned out. "Take it, but go," he was ordered; "I don't want you here. Mr. Jaques is just going to play to me. No; you can read that afterwards." A final continental hug, and he and the book were outside. So was I, for I thought it prudent not to await definite instructions, and I was dying to know what was the purport of the exciting inscription.

So we stood in the hall reading it, and I was treated to the after-glow of Monsieur Scitivaux's raptures.

The dedication was in Italian, and related how Rossini had composed the "Barbiere" for the Duke

Cesarini, the director of the Teatro Argentina in Rome, to retrieve for him the fortunes of a bad season. Rossini went on to say that he had written to Paisiello, who had previously treated the same subject, to assure him that he in no way sought to compete with that master, well aware as he was of his own inferiority, and that he had avoided as much as possible to use the same incidents in his libretto. "I thought," he worded it, " that, having taken this precaution, I might consider myself safe from the censure of his friends and his legitimate admirers. I was mistaken! On the appearance of my opera, they precipitated themselves like wild beasts upon the beardless maestrino, and the first performance was a most stormy one. I, however, remained unconcerned; and, whilst the public hissed, I applauded my performers. Once the storm blown over, at the second performance, my ' Barbiere ' had an excellent razor, and shaved the Romans so well that, to use theatrical language, I was carried home in triumph. There, my good friend, I have done what you desired. Be happy, and believe me, yours affectionately,

GIACOMO ROSSINI.

" PARIS, 22 *Apr.* 1860."

The facts related were well known, but here they were confirmed by the master's own narrative, and the recipient's happiness was unbounded.

The Jaques who was going to play to Rossini was my cousin, a partner in one of the old banking firms of Hamburg, and, besides, a thorough artist and virtuoso on that soul-stirring instrument, the violoncello. But it was not to have his soul stirred that Rossini gathered young musicians around him at that early hour of the day. They came to play his last compositions to him, and they remained to practise them at his house. You could often hear the sounds of various instruments proceeding from as many various rooms. The piano predominated, for at that time of his life Rossini was most assiduously composing for that instrument, labouring, as it seemed to me, under the fond delusion that he had discovered a new vein in the old mine which had produced such a fund of musical wealth. Sometimes he reminded one of Hummel's style, sometimes I thought I traced a Weber idea as it would be if filtered through the pen of a Mendelssohn. He would on no account allow his MSS. to leave the house. "Jamais," he said when my cousin expressed the wish to give the violoncello piece a day's practising at home, "Jamais ; je ne veux pas dépendre du public." So the performers had to go to the Chaussée d'Antin, and prepare themselves there for the Saturday evenings at which the latest works of the master were produced.

Amongst those privileged young musicians was the pianist, Georges Pfeiffer, who has since become so popular a composer. Rossini would give him such curiously named productions to study as " Cornichons," " Radis," and the like. There was also a " Boléro tartare," and a certain Rondo in the style of Offenbach, the famous composer of " La belle Hélène," " Orfée aux Enfers," and other operettas that for years drew all Paris to the

"Bouffes." He was universally credited with exercising the baneful influence of the evil eye, and Rossini, being superstitious, had headed his manuscript with a drawing of a *gettatura*, which should act as a charm to protect him. Georges Pfeiffer, no less superstitious—he always asserted he had good reason to be so—had managed to play the opening theme of the Rondo with the two fingers which in the *gettatura* are supposed to lay the evil spirit ; and Rossini so fully entered into this serio-comic solution of the difficulty, that he expressed his warm approval, and added Pfeiffer's fingering to the manuscript.

Henri Wieniawski, the violinist, and his brother Joseph, the pianist, were also great friends of Rossini's. He was present at Henri's wedding. The bride, Miss Hampton, was lovely, the guests distinguished, and the wedding breakfast sumptuous, and all would have gone well if the best man—or the next best— had not unfortunately made an eloquent speech to propose the health of a near and dear relative of the bride's who had been buried not so very long ago.

On those famous Saturday evenings I was a frequent visitor and attentive listener, but my own performances were reserved for those occasions when I was alone with the master.

He knew me to be the unworthy bearer of an honoured musical name, but he had by chance discovered that, however great my deficiencies, there was a little musical vein in me which he thought I might exploit. It is regrettable that one cannot write one's reminiscences without mentioning one's self. Things go so smoothly as long as one records the doings of others, but become so puzzling when one has to introduce the *Ego*. Between self-laudation and mock modesty there is not much to choose, and if you try to steer clear of the one, you are sure to fall into the other. I must take my chance though, and say that that vein of music, encouraged by the kind maestro, has many a time been a source of infinite delight to me, and to my friends too, or they would not have dragged me to the piano whenever they felt that they had had enough good music and now wanted the other thing. I would show them how easy it is to compose a masterpiece if you only know the secrets of the trade, and I would notably convince them that, if they would follow some very simple directions of mine, they could then and there write an Italian opera.

Singing-masters, it is well known, never agree as to the best way of cultivating a voice entrusted to their care. One will work a mezzo-soprano downwards to a contralto, the other upwards to a high soprano. With me the wiseacres never could settle which of my voices I ought to have developed—my bass voice, my tenor, or my soprano. In the meanwhile I alternately used each, distributing them according to the dramatic needs of the situation created, the story, to be sure, being made up to suit the madness of the hour. In the front line came the love duets between tenor and soprano, with moonlight accompaniment; then peasants' dances interrupted by thunder-storms, and drinking songs for the baritone, backed by an approving chorus. And

so on and on till the tragedy business was reached :
"Ye padre furioso e figlia infelice," as Du Maurier
calls them, when he relates his performance at Blank-
enberghe "in imitation of his illustrious friend, Felix
Bobtailo."

I must have been endowed with an extraordinary
amount of boldness and recklessness in those days,
or I never could have given the great maestro an
insight into these my accomplishments. It came
about in this way :—

Conversation had turned on the curious practice
which prevailed formerly, to write the principal
men's part in opera for an artificial male soprano,
and that led to my remarking that Rossini and his
contemporaries had done good service in banishing
that incongruous personage from the stage, but
that they had still left undisturbed some puzzling
anomalies in the distribution of parts. There
remained the fact that a man has a tenor voice as
long as he is a bachelor and a lover, but, when he
becomes a father, he develops into a basso profundo ;
and, by way of pointing to another anomaly, I
wanted to know why, when the prim'uomo and the
primadonna, with whose affections we so warmly
sympathised, have clandestinely met and resolved
to fly from a tyrannic parent, they should compromise their safety by singing a duet of inordinate
length: first warbling tender melodies, then shouting
stern resolves, practising scales, shakes, and dangerous runs to illustrate the course of true love, and
finally proclaiming their immutable determination
to live and die together, in strains so wild and so

powerfully backed by all the brass instruments of the orchestra, that the irate father is invariably brought on to the stage, naturally to wreck the lovers' fondest hopes.

By way of illustrating my meaning, I struck a chord or two, and did my worst in imitation of the lovers' cadenza, and more specially of the effect produced by overpowering brass instruments. That led to further developments, my brass gained me the maestro's sympathies, and of these he gave me a tangible proof in the shape of a composition.

I never much cared to make a collection of autographs, but I treasure the album I have previously spoken of, which Mendelssohn gave me as a godfather's first present. It took me upwards of fifty years to fill the little book, its pages being devoted only to those celebrities who were also personal friends of mine. So I had not asked Rossini for his autograph, as most people did on first acquaintance, and I had no reason to regret the delay. "I must compose something for your horn," he said one day; "I will write the notes; that is easy enough, but I can't draw the staves, you must do that." I answered that I was proud to collaborate, and so two pages of my album were filled. He composed an allegretto-moderato of about thirty bars for the "Cor en mi," heading it: "Thème de Rossini, suivi de deux Variations et Coda par Moscheles père," and signing it "Offert à mon jeune ami Felix Moscheles, G. Rossini, Passy, ce 20 Août 1860."

He sat down to the piano and spared no pains to teach me how to perform it on the imaginary French horn—my vibrating lips. I introduced one of those little hitches, not infrequent when moisture accumulates in the tubes of the real instrument, a hiatus which the master graciously approved of. "But," he said, "stand so that the audience cannot see how it is done; you must keep up the illusion, and besides, remember this, you must never show yourself at a disadvantage to the ladies." I have never blown that horn of mine without thinking of his advice, however little I have succeeded in acting up to it.

My father, responding to Rossini's invitation, wrote two brilliant variations and coda of considerable length, which it cost me not a little trouble to learn. Once that I had mastered their difficulties, the piece became my *cheval de bataille*, and whenever I performed it, accompanied by one of the two composers, I invariably made a . . . But enough! Happily this is not a place where I am expected to blow my own trumpet.

I called one day to take leave of Rossini, when I was about to leave Paris for a short time on a visit to my parents in Leipsic. This was before Rossini had become personally acquainted with my father, and he enjoined me to deliver a message to him. "Tell him," he said, "that I am a pianist. I daresay he knows that I have written operas, but I particularly want him to understand that I am a pianist too, not, to be sure, of the first class as he is, but of the fourth."

"Très bien, Maestro," I answered. "Je ne manquerai pas."

" Yes ; but mind you deliver my message correctly," he insisted. " My ear is exceptionally good, and I manage to hear what is said at a considerable distance. I was not at all satisfied with the way Rosenhain delivered a similar message I had entrusted him with."

I promised that I would scrupulously repeat what he had said, but I added that I could not take the responsibility of stating that he really was a fourth-rate one ; he might be a third or a fifth rate pianist for aught I knew.

" Oh, if that is all," he said, " I will play you something, and you can judge for yourself." And with that he opened the small upright piano in his study and began improvising, whilst I settled down comfortably to listen to my own special fourth-class pianist. It was indeed interesting. His plump little hands moved over the keys with a delicate touch, suitable to the simple melodious vein in which he began. When presently he broke into a rapid movement, and the pianoforte player asserted himself, it was still with the touch of the good old legato school. His execution was masterly, but not brilliant ; whenever he introduced passages or figures for the pianist as such, these seemed commonplace and hackneyed. But when, on the other hand, the musical thought sought expression, it flowed as from an inexhaustible store, and took the dramatic shape, reminding one of his best operatic style and his most brilliant orchestral effects.

His manner throughout was simple and unaffected. There was nothing showy or self-conscious about him, no by-play of any kind, no sudden pouncing on some *ben marcato* note, or triumphant rebounding from it. In fact, there was nothing to see but a benignant old gentleman playing the piano; one wouldn't have been surprised if he had worn a pigtail like those pianists his predecessors, who were not in a hurry, and treated their little set of crowquills with loving care.

Rossini came into the world three months after Mozart's death, a fact perhaps worthy to be considered by those who believe in re-incarnation. It would be interesting to learn what may have been the temporary abode of Mozart's spirit during those intervening three months. Perhaps it crossed the Alps and found its way to Rossini, for the Maestro, imbued as he certainly was with the spirit of his great predecessor, never lost an opportunity of acknowledging his indebtedness to him, and was always ready to talk of his favourite master.

"Beethoven," he said to me one day when conversation had turned on German music, " I take twice a week, Haydn four times, but Mozart I take every day of the week. Beethoven, to be sure, is a Colossus, and one who often gives you a tremendous dig in the ribs. Mozart is always adorable. But then he had the good fortune to go to Italy at a time when singers still knew how to sing."

In answer to my question what he thought of Weber, he said, " Oh, il a du talent à revendre celui là!" ("He has talent enough and to spare"). And then he went on to tell me that when the part of Tancred was sung in Berlin by a bass voice, Weber had written some violent articles, not only against the management, but against the composer, and that consequently Weber, when he came to Paris, did not venture to call on the Maestro; he, however, let him know that he bore him no grudge, and that led to their soon becoming acquainted.

I asked if he had met Byron in Venice. "Only in a restaurant," he said, "where I was introduced to him; our acquaintance, therefore, was very slight; it seems he has spoken of me, but I don't know what he says." I translated in a somewhat milder form Byron's words, which happened to be fresh in my memory: "They have been crucifying 'Othello' into an opera; the music good but lugubrious, but, as for the words, all the real scenes with Iago cut out, and the greatest nonsense put in instead; the handkerchief turned into a *billet doux*, and the first singer would not black his face. Singing, music, and dresses very good."

The Maestro regretted his ignorance of the English language. He had been in London in his early days, had given concerts there, and had even taught aristocratic ladies, but nothing, he said, would ever induce him to cross the Channel again, and, for the matter of that, to trust himself to a railway. When he migrated from Italy to Paris, he made the journey in his carriage. He told me he had given much time to the study of Italian literature in his day. Dante was the man he owed most to; he had taught him more music than all his music-masters put together; and when he wrote his "Otello" he insisted on introducing the song of the Gondolier.

His librettist would have it that gondoliers never sang Dante, but he would not give in.

"I know that better than you," he said, "for I have lived in Venice, and you haven't. Dante I must and will have."

A companion picture to the crucified "Othello" was the performance of "Fidelio," which all Paris was talking about at that time. One Sunday morning I spent an hour alone with Rossini, and I had to give him full particulars of the proceedings at the opera. These were characteristic of the taste of the day. The libretto of Beethoven's opera was completely changed, Florestan being replaced by Jean Galéas, Pizarro by Duke Sforza. The Minister becomes Charles VIII., and Fidelio the Countess Isabelle; the whole story turned into a political intrigue, and Fidelio, the devoted wife, changed into a plotting and ambitious spouse.

A story in which a woman, actuated by her affection alone, nobly worked for her husband's deliverance, must have been thought too tame to put before a Parisian public, and so the stronger motives were introduced.

The press was unanimous in its condemnation of the work itself, not of the garbled version. "Cette musique est très ennuyeuse," said one; "Enfin c'est symphonique!" wrote another. "Si Beethoven n'avait pas senti la faiblesse de sa production, il aurait écrit un deuxième opéra."

"Yes," said Rossini, remarking on the press and the public, "that is just what I should have expected. Do you know what I owe my success to? To my crescendos. Ah, my crescendos! What an impression they made on them. Afterwards, to be sure, when I thought it well to give up that little trick, they said, 'He's no longer what he was; he's beginning to decline.'

"You know what happened to my friend T——i, the tenor. He went to F——o, and asked him how much he would take for a good notice in his paper.

"'Un billet de mille,'[1] said F.

"'Ah! I'm afraid I can't afford that,' sighed T.; 'couldn't you do it for 500 frcs.?'

"'Impossible, mon cher monsieur,' replied F. 'J'y perdrais!'"[2]

Who was responsible for the irreverent production of "Fidelio"? I am afraid it was, to a great extent, Berlioz and Madame Viardot. That I say with bated breath, for nothing could exceed my respect for those heaven-born musicians. But I wonder to-day, as I wondered then, why they should ever have planned this adaptation of "Fidelio" to the French stage. It was an unfortunate selection, if only because many numbers of the chief part had to be transposed to suit Madame Viardot's voice. She had but lately achieved one of her greatest triumphs in the character of Orpheus. A grander or a more beautiful rendering of Gluck's masterpiece cannot be imagined; the grave full-toned quality of her voice seemed to suit the part of the bereaved husband, who goes forth, lute in hand, to seek his spouse in the shades of Hades. From the first scenes, where she laments and implores, to the last, where

---

[1] A 1000-franc note.   [2] I should be the loser by it.

she succumbs to despair, she held her audience spellbound. How she had fitted herself for her task I well remember. Classical scholar as she was, she read her Orpheus in the Greek original, and the costume she wore was of her own designing.

I was much at her house in the Rue de Douai in those days, and it was made doubly attractive to me by Monsieur Viardot, who himself was a man of great artistic and literary attainments. His book on the "Galeries de l'Europe" is a standard work; he had formed a collection of pictures by the best Dutch masters, and he was devoted to them as only the true connoisseur can be. Amongst the many celebrities that I met there were Ary Scheffer, Tourgenieff, Saint Saens, and, on one occasion, Richard Wagner. He had come with his manuscript score of "Tristan and Isolde." Madame Viardot was at the piano reading it at sight, and mastering its intricacies with the grasp of the true musician; whilst Wagner stood by her side, turning the leaves and occasionally breaking in with a word or two.

"N'est ce pas, Ma*t*ame," he said, carried away by the grandeur of his own creation. "N'est ce pas, Ma*t*ame, que c'est su*p*lime?"

I chanced to be the only one privileged to be present on that occasion. Close at hand stood a casket in which a treasure was preserved, the original score of "Don Giovanni." No wonder I was fully impressed by the situation, actually in touch as I felt myself with the master of the past and the master of the present. If what I was listening to was well named the Music of the Future, might not the score enshrined in that casket be called the Music of Eternity ?

An event that was looked forward to with the greatest interest by the privileged group which enjoyed Rossini's hospitality, was the performance of the "Stabat Mater" at his own house. Those who wanted to be on the list of the invited did well to conciliate Madame; but that was not always an easy matter. She knew her own mind, and would give one a piece of it when she felt so inclined. The following is characteristic of her little ways :—I called one day to introduce a Mr. Mertke, a young musician just arrived from Leipsic, to Rossini. The master was busy conducting a rehearsal of that " Stabat," and so, remembering it was Madame's reception day, I thought I would improve the occasion by paying my respects to her and introducing my friend. She received us politely, but I noticed at once that she was not in the best of tempers and that a squall might be expected at any moment.

My friend and I seated ourselves cautiously on the edges of our chairs and awaited further developments. Happily the clouds gathering round her dark brow were not to burst over our heads ; the danger was averted by the appearance of a very handsome and elegant woman. She was a well-known operatic star, and swept into the room with all the assurance that success and an up-to-date Parisian toilette can give. With charming grace and affability she greeted Madame Rossini and beamed kindly on one or two friends. "I have come, chère amie," she said, " to

offer my services to the Maestro. I hear he is going
to perform his ' Stabat Mater,' and, if he wants a good
voice to join in the chorus, I am at his disposal."

" There you are," answered Madame Rossini in her
sternest manner ; " we have refused more than one
of that kind. It's an age one hasn't seen anything
of you, and now there's something going on, and you
want to be in it, you vouchsafe to reappear."

" Mais chère amie," answered the other, " you
don't for a moment believe what you say ; you know
what has prevented my seeing my dearest friends.
Empêchement de force majeure, n'est ce pas ?" And
therewith she proceeded to give us some interesting
details connected with her first experiences as a
mother, and with her consequent inability to make
afternoon calls—details so minute that they did
not fail to convince everybody present excepting the
obdurate Madame Rossini, who was about to retort,
when the primadonna managed, with marvellous
skill, to change the conversation. We soon found
ourselves talking of the latest scandal ; of a phaeton
which a certain lady had no business to show herself
in at the Bois, so soon after a certain duel which that
particular phaeton had led to. From that we got
quite naturally to the chapter of *robes et chiffons*,
and all went so smoothly that my friend and I soon
made ourselves more at home on our chairs. But
there was to be another brush between the ladies.
As the brilliant one rose to leave, she said with a
winning smile, " Adieu, très-chère ; vous êtes bien la
plus excellente des créatures, but really," she added
sadly, " just now you were not *gentille*."

" I did not mean to be," answered madame, "and I did mean every word of what I said." That was her parting shaft. But for all that the operatic star was not to be frozen out. She managed to get an invitation to the Easter performance, or came without, for aught I know ; she told that chère Madame Rossini that she positively adored her, and that she was captivated by her *franchise* and her *verve intarissable* (her plain speaking and her inexhaustible verve), sentiments which presently she translated for my benefit with the words : " Ah mais, cette chère Madame Rossini, elle est vraiment impossible " (That dear Madame Rossini, she is really impossible).

The " Stabat Mater," as we heard it on that evening, was the revised and remodelled work, very different from the one Rossini had written in his early days. The score of this he had given to a friend, a monk, after whose death it passed into the hands of some musician, who published it much to Rossini's annoyance. " On ne saute pas d'un coup du théatre à l'église " (One does not bound at a leap from the theatre to the church), he said one day to Kuhe the gifted musician and impresario, as he was alluding to the shortcomings of that early version and the necessity of revising it.

Madame Rossini could, when she chose, be an excellent hostess, and she was usually at her best on those Saturday evenings when she and the Maestro received, and when naturally all that was prominent in the musical world gravitated towards the salons of the veteran composer. On one of these occasions, I nearly got into trouble with her. A lamp was

slowly but surely going out, and any one else in my
place, just by the tail of the grand piano, would have
been prompted, as I was, to remove it. I looked
across the room at my hostess, my eyes respectfully
putting the question, "Hadn't I better take that
lamp out?" From beneath her dark Italian eyebrows shot an annihilating glance that made me
tremble in my dress shoes, and that plainly said,
"Move if you dare, young man—but if you do, you
will repent it." I did *not* dare, but the situation was
painful. The select circle of friends gathered around
that grand piano were one and all listening in religious silence, impressed by the music and the presence
of the Maestro; that irreverent lamp alone showed
unmistakable signs of collapse, and soon attracted
general attention. Would it or would it not hold
out to the end? It would not; Madame Rossini
had to get up, cross the room and carry out the
offender. She did it defiantly, majestically; I should
have done it meekly, apologetically.

But, to be fair, I must add in conclusion that she
could be very friendly too, and playful in her way.
It would be ungrateful of me not to record how she
greeted me with "Bon soir, cher amour," one evening.
But that was at Wieniawski's wedding, and I suppose
the darts of Cupid were flying about.

As far as I could judge, she made that illustrious
husband of hers an excellent wife; she knew what
he liked, and she took care that he had it, whether
it was a favourite dish or a favoured visitor; and,
what was more, she knew whom to keep at a distance,
a valuable quality in the wife of a man whom every

musician, good or bad, professional or amateur, wanted to know, and who was besieged by autograph-hunters, interviewers, and the host of nondescripts who are ever anxious to cling to the tail of Pegasus.

I have known more than one wife of that most useful genus, and have not always quite liked their methods; as when, on one occasion, I had run over to Paris, I called on an old friend, also a great composer. His better half, who always jealously guarded the approaches, espied me from the top of a high staircase. "Ah, c'est vous, Monsieur Félix," she cried with genuine delight. "Comme cela se trouve bien; justement j'ai un paquet à envoyer à Londres." I had a long and interesting chat with the master, in exchange for which I gladly took Madame's most undesirable parcel.

In the summer of 1860 my father made a short stay in Paris. He was most cordially welcomed by friends and colleagues, amongst these the Erards, Viardots, Crémieux, Auber, Ambroise Thomas, and Rossini. The Maestro was at that time staying at his villa in Passy. Referring to his first visit there, my father writes :—

"Felix had been made quite at home in the villa on former occasions. To me the Salon on the ground floor with its rich furniture was new, and, before the Maestro himself appeared, we looked at his photograph in a circular porcelain frame, on the sides of which were inscribed the names of his works. The ceiling is covered with pictures illustrating scenes in the lives of Palestrina and Mozart; in the middle of the room stands a Pleyel piano.

" When Rossini came in, he gave me the orthodox Italian kiss, and was effusive in expressing his delight at my reappearance, and very complimentary on the subject of Felix. In the course of our conversation he was full of hard-hitting truths and brilliant satire on the present study and method of vocalisation. 'I don't want to hear any more of their screaming,' he said; 'I want a resonant voice, full-toned, not screeching; I care not whether it be for speaking or singing, everything ought to sound melodious.'

" He then spoke of the pleasure he felt in studying the piano. 'And, if it were not presumption,' he added, 'in composing for that instrument. I find it hard, however, to make my fourth and fifth fingers do their duty properly.'

" Talking of the present style of playing, he said : 'How they maltreat the piano! Ils enfoncent non seulement le piano, mais encore le fauteuil et même le plancher!' (They smash not only the piano, but the chair and the very floor).

" Every instrument, he went on to say, should be treated according to its special character. Sor, the guitarist, and Vimercati proved the possibility of obtaining great artistic results with slender means. I happened to have heard both these artists, and could quite endorse his views. He told me that, arriving late one evening at a small Italian town, he had already retired to rest, when Vimercati, the resident Kapellmeister, sent him an invitation to be present at a performance of one of his operas. In those days he was not yet as hard-hearted as he is now, when he once for all refuses to be present at the performance of any work of his; so he not only went to the theatre, but played the double-bass as a substitute for the right man, who was not forthcoming. This reminded me of what I once experienced to the cost of my nerves at York, when the part of the viola in Mozart's D Minor Symphony was missing, and the bassoon was flat. I showed Rossini on the piano what the effect was like, and he laughed heartily. Then he wanted a little serious music. I improvised, and he said, 'Cela est il gravé? C'est de la musique qui coule de source; il-y-a l'eau de réservoir et l'eau de source; l'une ne coule que quand vous tournez le robinet, elle sent la vase, l'autre, fraiche et limpide, coule toujours. Aujourd'hui on confond le simple et le trivial; un motif de Mozart on l'appellerait trivial si on osait!' (Has that been published? That is music which flows spontaneously. There is tank-water and spring-water; one runs only when you turn on the tap, and always savours of mud, the other ever flows fresh and clear. But nowadays people do not know the difference between the trivial and the simple; they would call a melody of Mozart's trivial if they dared.)

"He was delighted to hear that encouragement was given to the serious study of the organ at the Leipsic Conservatorio, and he regretted the decay of church music in Italy. On the subject of Marcello's and Palestrina's 'sublime creations' he was quite eloquent. When we parted he made me promise to call on him once more before the day fixed upon to dine with him. I was happy to do so, and, when I next came, Rossini, yielding to my request, but not without modestly expressing diffidence in his own powers, played an Andante of his in B flat, beginning somewhat in this style :

in which, after the first eight bars, the following interesting modulation is introduced :

"The piece is what we Germans would call tame. He also showed me two manuscript compositions, an Introduction and Fugue in C major, and a sort of pastoral Fantasia with a brilliant Rondo in A major, which I had to play to him, and, when I added a missing ♮ to the MS., he declared it was 'worth gold' to him. Clara, who was with me, and had already mustered up sufficient courage to sing my 'Frühlingslied' and 'Botschaft' to Rossini's satisfaction, was obliged to repeat both songs before the singers, Ponchard and Levasseur, who had just come in. I accompanied, and, in answer to the Maestro's remark that I had enough flow of melody to write an opera, I said : 'What a pity that I am not young enough to become your pupil!' and when, referring to my playing from his manuscripts, he dubbed me 'King of Pianists,' I told him that whatever I was, I owed to the old school and the old master Clementi.

At the mention of that name he went to the piano and played parts of his sonatas by heart.

"On another occasion he would have it there were barricades in my 'Humoristische Variationen,' so boldly did they seem to assail time-worn traditions; and as for the 'Grande Valse,' he found the title too unassuming. 'Surely,' he insisted, 'a waltz with some angelic creature must have inspired you, and *that* the title ought to express. Titles, in fact, should pique the curiosity of the public.' That is a view uncongenial to me; however, I did not discuss it."

At the dinner my father spoke of, the conversation turned on Meyerbeer and on macaroni. He seemed much attached to both, more though to the latter, I thought, and to other productions of the Italian chef, than to the chef-d'œuvres of his Franco-German colleague. He would speak in very appreciative terms of Meyerbeer, but he did not seem displeased when disparaging remarks on the works of his rival were made.

One of the stories current concerning the two masters was this:—

Rossini was going along the Boulevards with a friend, when they met Meyerbeer, and exchanged cordial greetings.

"And how is your health, my dear Maestro?" asks Meyerbeer.

"Shaky, cher maître, very shaky. My digestion, you know, my poor head. Alas! I'm afraid I am going down hill."

They pass on. "How could you tell such

stories?" asks the friend; "you were never in better health, and you talk of going down hill."

"Ah, well," answered Rossini, "to be sure—but why shouldn't I put it that way? It gives him so much pleasure."

Another time the following short dialogue:—

"Eh bien, cher maître, que faites-vous maintenant?"

Meyerbeer: "Je me corrige toujours."

Rossini: "Moi je m'efface."

Whatever may have been the relative merits of the two masters in matters musical, it is certain that Rossini was acknowledged *facile princeps* in all concerning the cuisine, and we used to listen with due respect to his remarks on the mysteries of the culinary art.

Crémieux, the eminent lawyer, who was a guest at that dinner, had the reputation of being the plainest man in France, a sort of missing link. A story is told of him and Alexandre Dumas. The great novelist was unmistakably of the mulatto type, and Crémieux, who must have been addicted to making personal remarks, indiscreetly questioned him as to his descent. "Was your father a mulatto?" he asked. "Yes," answered Dumas, "my father was a mulatto, my grandfather a negro, and my great-grandfather a monkey; my family began where yours ends."

Quick at repartee as Dumas was, he did not always have the last word, as on an occasion when he received a letter from some playwright—I have forgotten his name—offering to collaborate with him in the writing of a play. " It is not usual," replied Dumas, " to yoke a horse and an ass together." " Comment donc!" retorted the other. " How dare you, sir, insinuate that I am a horse?"

That Villa Rossini I visited ten years later under very different circumstances. It was in May 1871, after the terrible events that marked the reign of the Commune. I had not witnessed these, but had crossed over from London shortly after the Versailles troops had succeeded in making themselves masters of Paris.

The villa stood in its own grounds. The municipality had desired to present Rossini with the site; he would not, however, accept the gracious offer unreservedly, and so it was arranged that he should occupy it on very advantageous terms.

As I passed the gates that led to the grounds I knew so well, the first thing that struck me was a notice posted up and signed by the military authorities, to the effect that all unexploded bombs and other projectiles should be buried underground, awaiting the time when they would be collected by competent artillerymen.

I left others to do the burying, and made for the house. There was no Madame Rossini on the lookout, as she used to be in former days, ready to guard the approaches to her husband's study with Cerberus-like fidelity. It was some time before I could find anybody at all. A man - servant finally emerged from the basement; he was the only soul on the premises, and evidently much shaken by recent

events.   It needed nobody to open the door, for
one could walk in through large gaps in the walls,
where the shells had done their work.   Part of the
staircase had been blown away, but enough of it
stood to take me to the upper floor, to the room in
which, three years ago, Rossini had died.   The house
until lately had been occupied by his widow ; now all
the furniture had been removed ; but a large iron
safe stood in the middle of the music-room, like a
solid island, surrounded by a sea of brick and mortar
rubbish.

I had looked round in vain for something worth
preserving as a memento of this my last visit to the
great Maestro's house, and had found nothing better
than fragments of wall-paper and pieces of a shattered
looking-glass.   As I gave a final look at the scene of
destruction, I descried a black-bordered paper all but
buried in a thick layer of débris.   Where all else
was destroyed, that paper seemed a living thing.   I
brought it to the surface, and found it was an old
copy of *The Musical World*, containing the obituary
notice of Giacomo Rossini.   When I returned to
London I gave it to J. W. Davison, the editor of
the journal in which it was published, so that it
might be preserved to record the incidents of the
master's life, and to attest the grievous disasters that
befell the villa he loved so well.

 **I** well remember Paris emerging from her trials. It is difficult to-day to realise the magnitude of the disaster which laid low the beautiful capital of France. When I arrived within its shattered walls, the monster conflagration that would have destroyed the whole city, had it not been for the timely arrival of the Versailles troops, was all but subdued. The firemen, however, were still kept busily engaged, for clouds of smoke and tongues of fire would at intervals burst forth from the smouldering ruins. Tottering walls on the one hand, huge *façades* of masonry on the other, marked the places where but yesterday glorious specimens of architecture, ancient and modern, had stood. There was the shell of what had been the Tuileries, that palace built in the 16th century, which had seen so much of the history of France. Mobs had pillaged and sacked it; within its state-rooms one crowned head had been forced to wear the cap of liberty, a humiliation which did not save it from the knife of the guillotine. Some fifty years later a bourgeois king had to fly for his life from the palace; and last, it was an unfortunate Empress who had to make

good her escape, and seek refuge on the shores of England.

There would be no more pillaging and sacking now; the venerable specimen of the Renaissance style was destroyed. To-day the stranger is just shown the place where the Tuileries stood; then, as the walls crashed down, burying treasures and relics of bygone days in their fall, one was appalled by the tragedy enacted before one's eyes. I had my little personal recollections too. I had danced there more than once with some of the fairest Parisians; I had drunk the future Emperor's champagne with a conviction that it was quite the best of its kind, and was evidently intended to make us understand that our host meant business, imperial business, pretty sure to be settled ere long, whether we liked it or not.

Well, one fine old building is gone, I thought, as I turned away from the ruins, but at least the Louvre is saved. That marvel of architecture was intact. The principal works of art it contained had been taken to places of supposed safety, and the whereabouts of the Venus of Milo were said to be known only to some few persons, who had dug a hole and therein buried her. Much else had been providentially saved; there were large gaps in the Rue de Rivoli, but the unique old Tour St. Jacques had escaped unscathed. At the Palais de Justice the fire had stopped short on the threshold of the exquisite Sainte Chapelle, one of the most perfect works of the thirteenth century. I had with some difficulty obtained permission to roam over the ruins of that Palais de Justice and the Prefecture de Police, and whilst the firemen were working to subdue the flames wherever they broke out afresh, I used my brush to make a sketch of the huge maze before me. There were bundles of official papers at my feet ; *Actes de Naissance* and *Actes de Décès*, charred only, and quite easy to decipher, but as I touched them, they crumbled to ashes. Some seemingly well-preserved parchments I consigned to my pocket, but a few hours later I found little more than dust in their place. The Hôtel de Ville, too, which had fallen a prey to the flames, had many an association for me. Henri Lehmann, during the time I was studying under him, had been commissioned to decorate the great hall with a series of pictures. I had lent an apprentice's hand, and had seen them grow under his brush, as, in an incredibly short space of time, he produced what was thought to be the best work of his life—work destined to hand down his name to posterity as one of the most fertile and distinguished painters of the second empire. Ingres, too, who in those days was considered the greatest draughtsman since the time of Raphael, had contributed a master-piece to the decoration of the hall, a *plafond*, " The Apotheosis of Napoleon I." This work I had also seen in progress. On the occasion of a visit to his studio I recollect a lady asking him, in effusive language, where he had found the models for the ideally classical horses attached to the triumphant car of the great conqueror. Ingres led her straight to the window. " There are my models, madam," he said bluntly, pointing to the cab-stand.

I wandered through Paris day after day, and

everywhere the ghastly traces of war, as it really is, confronted me; blood-stained flagstones, broken-down gun-carriages, barricades that had been stormed, and homes that had been wrecked. Everywhere the iron shutters of the shops were riddled with shot or broken open. One climbed as best one could over a heterogeneous mass of *impedimenta*, collected for attack or defence, or thrown away in precipitate flight. Every effort had been made to prevent petroleum being poured into the basement of the houses. The gratings in the streets had been boarded over and otherwise secured against those female fiends the Pétroleuses. Some of the wealthiest quarters of Paris were known to be undermined, and it was only in the nick of time that the Versailles troops arrived to prevent the execution of such written orders as, " Faites sauter le quartier de la Bourse."

The fashionable quarters and the suburbs of Paris had suffered terribly from the bombardment. I wandered for days over fragments of every mortal thing that had once been whole, past dismantled batteries, along the barren wastes of the Bois de Boulogne, and through avenues of wrecked villas. Costly furniture and works of art had been shattered to atoms by the enemy's bombs. In one place I came across a Louis Quinze sofa and chairs that had evidently been carried out for removal, and stood waiting so placidly, that they seemed to invite you to sit down and rest; and in one of the gardens there was a cottage piano, which appeared none the worse for its adventures; two coffee-cups stood unharmed upon it, showing that some two persons had taken their demie-tasse by the side of that piano.

The most striking effects of shot and shell showed themselves on the ornamental ironwork which had once enclosed those suburban villas. It seemed as if they had vented their fiercest passions on those beautifully designed gates and railings French art excels in producing. One could not suppress a feeling of pity as one saw them writhing in anguish and stretching out their weird iron arms as if in supplication. Here they were unhinged and started from their sockets; there their limbs, once so perfectly poised, were twisted into unsightly shapes, and stood out amongst the wreckage in fantastic and uncanny figures.

I had wended my way one afternoon to the revolutionary quarter of Belleville, and had got into conversation with a workman of more than average intelligence. Not feeling at our ease within earshot of the "Mouchards," as the growling, spying, myrmidons of the police are termed, and not liking the looks of the *gensdarmes à cheval* with their revolvers at half-cock, we had adjourned to one of the numerous establishments kept by the *Marchand de Vins, Traiteur*, which take the place of our public-houses. There my workman became confidential and declared himself a Communist to the backbone. He scorned the idea that the German was his enemy.

" If I'm to fight at all," he said, " let me find an enemy for myself. Let me shoot the *richard en face*, the capitalist who has been exploiting me and mine. We'll make him and the like of him disgorge his plunder, and then we'll start a fresh deal. As for the Germans, my dear sir, I dare say there are a lot of jolly good fellows amongst them, and plenty who would take a bumper, a *canon de vin*, with us, if they were here now, and drink to the perdition of the bourgeois."

"That is all very well," I answered, "but I'm pretty sure you were just like the rest, and went tearing along the boulevards and shouting 'A Berlin!' And you would have been only too jolly glad to get the Rhine, if you had had a—— "

"The Rhine, monsieur!" he interrupted me, "the Rhine! Do you think I know what the blessed thing is; and, supposing we had got it, do you think they'd have given me any of it?"

That was twenty-eight years ago, and since then many a workman has learnt that he does not get his share of the "blessed thing" he has to fight for. I wonder whether he will give up fighting, or whether he will see to it that he gets his share.

It was an impressive sight that met the eye in the Place Vendôme. There was the famous column lying prostrate in huge fragments like so many mill-stones, with the bronze legends commemorating the conqueror's march, battered and crushed out of all seeming in their fall. Those gigantic vertebræ of the mighty pillar made one ponder on the vicissitudes of greatness, and on the ups and downs of heroic symbols. One could not help marvelling at the audacity of the men who had ruptured that spinal cord of patriotic self-glorification.

It was an artist, and a great one too, who planned

and directed the destruction of the work of art, Courbet, the most uncompromising of painters and of demagogues. I was living in Paris at the time his first great works were exhibited, and I recollect what a storm of abuse they raised. His "Enterrement à Ornans," a large and striking picture, crudely realistic, depicting, as it did, mourners at the open grave, with reddened noses and swollen eyes, was considered a deliberate insult offered to all idealists, romanticists, and mannerists. His picture, "La Baigneuse," was simply derided by the critics; there was no drawing, no modelling. "C'est un sac de noix!" A bag of nuts, not a woman of flesh and blood.

Well, Courbet's work has outlived criticism; history remembers him as a *chef d'école*.

The only time I recollect meeting him was on the occasion of an international gathering of artists in Antwerp in 1861. He was quite a boon companion, and had a marked objection to retiring to rest before daylight. He would sing us jolly songs, one of which, "C'est l'amour qui nous mène,"[1] was a favourite of his.

The Commune went to work very systematically to bring down the huge column. An incision was made at the base in the shape of a notch; a double pulley was attached to the balustrade at the top, and another fixed to the ground in the Rue de la Paix, a rope passing through both to a capstan. When this was set in motion, after some preliminary difficulties had been overcome, the column oscillated

---

[1] 'Tis love that leads us.

for a moment, and then came crashing down in three colossal sections on to a bed of sand, fascines, and straw prepared for it, there to break up into a thousand smaller fragments.   The statue of the great Emperor had lost its head and one arm.

An act of vandalism, we say.   Yes, but of vandalism with a purpose.   We can fancy Courbet declaring: "The work of art must be sacrificed as a warning to those who would honour and perpetuate the memory of selfish aggressors."

It was History herself he meant to drag from her pedestal—History, ever crowning herself with wreaths of laurel and halos of virtue.   It was Art too he waged war upon, that Art which he deemed had too long served to glorify the rule of Force : sometimes in a picture or in a legion of pictures, as at Versailles, exalting Imperialism and inciting us to go forth and emulate the deeds and misdeeds of our ancestors ; sometimes in a statue of some clever organiser of wholesale slaughter, appropriately cast in the bronze of cannon taken from the enemy ; or, again, in a barbarous trophy, a triumphal arch—in fact, in a scalp of some kind, that, from generation to generation, we are taught to gloat over.

This was the wording of the decree which condemned the column to destruction :—

"THE COMMUNE OF PARIS

" Considering that the Imperial Column of the Place Vendôme is a monument of barbarism, a symbol of brute force, of false glory, an encouragement of military spirit, a denial of international rights, a permanent insult offered by the conquerors to the conquered, a perpetual conspiracy against one of the great principles of the French Republic, namely fraternity,

" Decrees :—

" *Sole article*—The Vendôme Column is to be demolished."

One day—it was a wretched day, the rain pouring in torrents—I went to see the ruins of Saint Cloud. People were discussing the question as to who had really done the work of destruction there—the Germans, the Versaillais, or the Communards. To the poor victims who had come forth from their hiding-places, returning only to find their homes and hearths ruined, it could really matter little whether the grim work was done by the six of one or the half-a-dozen of the other.

Wandering along the streets in ruins, I was struck by one piece of high wall left standing out against the grey sky to bear witness to the strange caprices of the destructive element ; a large red umbrella hung in its place on that wall, and a striped petticoat be-drizzled with rain was being blown about by the wind. The fireplace had kept its every-day appearance, whilst the floor beneath it had gone; on the mantelpiece stood some little household gods, bits of china, a clock, and various nick-nacks one could not distinguish at a distance. Close to me was a touching little group of victims. A woman with three girls, their ages ranging from eight to twelve years, stood gazing at that wall which had once been part of their home. They did not give vent to their feelings in tears or loud lamentations, as so many around me did; the mother was simply dazed, the children overawed. They had come back to Saint Cloud from I know not where, and were carrying their little belongings tied up in cotton handkerchiefs. I think they would scarcely have been able to identify their home, if it had not been for the red umbrella and the striped petticoat.

After a while I spoke to the woman and elicited with some difficulty that her husband had been killed early in the campaign, one son was maimed for life, and the other had not been heard of for two months. When I gave her a few francs she put them in her pocket mechanically; her thoughts were elsewhere. I passed on to witness more destruction and distress. When I returned, some half-an-hour later, to where the high wall stood, I found the mother and the three girls just where I had left them, still hopelessly gazing at the household gods that were mocking their misery from on high.

It was not till that day that I quite realised what we mean when we speak of blank despair.

The recuperative power of the French people is truly extraordinary, and, from the first day and hour of his deliverance, the Parisian gave striking evidence of it. Endowed as he is with indomitable pluck, infinite resources, and inexhaustible light-heartedness, he could set to work with a will, or dance and fiddle with a vengeance, whilst the ashes of his city were still glowing. It came quite natural to him to re-possess himself of that city, and to drop unconcernedly into his old ways of life.

There he was once more, the typical Parisian who must have his daily stroll along the Boulevards; he must sit somewhere where he can sip something and see somebody else sipping or strolling. He must watch his opportunity of saying something polite to somebody, and, at a given hour, he must call for an *absinthe* and concentrate his thoughts on the importance of an approaching meal.

And there he was again, the expert diner we all know, devoutly pinning his napkin under his chin, and thanking the gods that at last the sacred rites of the dinner-table could be duly performed.

One of the characteristics of the Parisian, I always thought, is that exquisite politeness of his. What a lesson to us, who won't even make room for a fellow-creature in a 'bus if we can help it!

In former days I used to say that I could always tell, if I wanted, to what nationality any particular man in the motley crowd of loungers on the Boulevards belonged. I need but tread on his toes, and he would use strong language in his mother-tongue. The German would invoke the "holy thunderweather," the Dutchman would be still more sacrilegious, the Englishman would damn something— probably the eyes I should have made use of; and so on—each would fling his pet wicked word at me. Only the Frenchman would raise his hat and say, " Pardon, monsieur."

Knowing and loving the amiable city as I did

—I had spent altogether about six years there—I
was deeply interested in her fortunes and misfor-
tunes, and now warmly welcomed the first signs of
returning prosperity.

The cannon's roar had ceased, people were coming
from their cellars or other hiding-places, looking
for their friends and congratulating one another
on being alive.   Crowds of sightseers filled the
streets and stood gaping at the ruins or commenting on the unique spectacle before them.   Barricades
were being demolished, and squads of men and women
were set to work to clear the roads of broken glass,
splintered wood, and other accumulations of nondescript rubbish.   Shops were being opened, and the
Dames de Comptoir, as correct and business-like as
ever, were getting out their books.   Goods and
wares that had been hidden away, were being
brought to light.   Shopkeepers were counting up
their losses and discounting their prospects.

Matters political were in abeyance.   Whenever
I asked, " What is to come next?   What Government would you vote for ? " I got the answer : " Cela
nous est bien égal, monsieur, pourvu qu'il-y-ait du
travail."[1]   One lived in a sort of interregnum, a
period of transition from lawlessness to order.   War
had ceased, but peace had only just begun to strike
roots.   There was no bragging, no cheap oratory—
nobody seemed to think himself particularly "*trahi*."[2]
There was no show of military rule.   Even the

[1] We don't care a pin, sir, as long as we can get work.
[2] Betrayed.

sentries chatted freely with the bourgeois, and there were no ominous cries of " *Passez au large*," coupled with the significant thrust of the fixed bayonet, as one used to hear in the days of the *Coup d'État.* On the contrary, thousands of soldiers, with their *Chassepots* slung carelessly across their shoulders, were sauntering along the streets, most of them evidently provincials, amazed at the grandeur of the capital they were visiting for the first time.

Cabs were about, and even the heavy three-horse omnibuses were resuming their well-regulated course ; but no private carriages were to be seen. In fact, the upper ten as well as the submerged tenth seemed to have disappeared, and the odd million about was made up of the *bourgeois*, the *piou-piou*,[1] the *badaud de province*, and other sightseers.

I scorned conveyances of any kind, and tramped along on foot from morning to night, for it was only thus I felt I was my own master. I could pull up, stumble, or climb as circumstances required, or I could turn in, stand drink, talk, listen, and argue— or, better still, hold my tongue.

In the evening darkness reigned, except in the neighbourhood of the cafés. There people were congregating as usual, seeking the light like so many moths, and settling like flies on the sugar that was to sweeten their *demie-tasse* or to be pocketed for home consumption. At eleven o'clock the cafés were closed, and nothing remained to do but to go home in the dark. The moths, by the way, must have

---

[1] The French Tommy Atkins and the country cousin.

had a dull time of it, for the graceful lamp-posts had suffered so severely that very few of them were fit for service.

The Commune had naturally produced a great quantity of scurrilous literature and vile caricatures, some quite unmentionable; but they are interesting historically, throwing, as they do, a lurid light on the events of those days and the passions they evoked. I bought whatever I could find of such papers and drawings, as also a few of the more respectable publications, and the collection is a pretty complete one, including, as it does, copies of the Père Duchêne, La Lanterne, Le National, La Vérité, &c., and some sixty caricatures of the Emperor, the Empress, Thiers, Jules Favre, and many other leading men, all furnishing abundant material for recording and illustrating the politics, hysterics, and erotics of those troublesome times.

Towards the end of my stay I went to Saint Denis. Peace and its blessings were really coming, and welcome signs of their approach were not wanting; even little twigs of olive branches were being held out where I least expected to see them.

Saint Denis was still in the hands of the Germans, and was not to be evacuated till a stipulated sum, forming part of the war indemnity, had been paid. Officers and men quartered there had made themselves very much at home, and some did not seem to be on bad terms with the inhabitants, as in one case, when a bright young fellow on the German side seemed on particularly good terms with an attractive young lady on the French side. He and I had got into conversation; he was evidently pleased to meet a countryman of his (I can be a German occasionally), and was disposed to be friendly and confidential. "Come with me," he said; "I will show you the prettiest girl in Saint Denis." I went to see "the prettiest girl," who, it seemed to me, had been watching for him at the window, and now came down to the door.

He was a non-commissioned officer in I forget which regiment. When not in uniform he was a lawyer—for aught I know, a rising young *Rechtsanwalt*, with plenty of clients. I hope so, for the sake of the young lady, who was charming, and was as much smitten with him as he was with her. He had taught her a few German words, which she could not pronounce without laughing and showing her pretty teeth; she again had lent him some books from her little library. He spoke French fluently, and was happy to be put through a course of French literature by his fair friend.

Love being thicker than blood, I feel sure they eventually got married; and after so romantic an opening, their story cannot but have proved interesting. Should anybody care to write it, I think the line to be taken should be this: They married, and lived "happy ever after"—as happily as their children would let them. They had four, differing widely in their tastes and convictions. One son enlisted in the German army; the other in the French. Both were deeply grieved to have fallen on evil times, when emperors and presidents were ever proclaiming the blessings of peace, and when even the people were beginning to question the desirability of attacking their neighbours.

Of the daughters, one loved the Germans, and was unhappy because she was to marry a Frenchman her parents had selected ; the other hated the Germans, and was broken-hearted because she was not to marry the Frenchman she loved.

It must all end happily, however, for it is essential that the moral should be pointed : Love your neighbour, if only to show you are unshackled by prejudice. Marry him or her, whether he or she is your hereditary foe or not, and settle down to a life of peace and happiness, that you may inaugurate, by your noble example, the blessed era, when the lion and the lamb shall no longer hesitate to go and do likewise.

But not often was it my good fortune to spend a pleasant hour as at Saint Denis and to imagine little romances built on slight foundations. The tragedy being enacted around me forced itself on my view more than once, when I met batches of miserable prisoners marched off, some to be judged by court-martial, others already sentenced to be shot. The Parisian looked on without exhibiting much interest in their fate. He had seen so much of bloodshed in every form lately that he had grown callous. The day of settlement had come, the murder of the hostages must be avenged, and the *canaille* must be cleared away, just as the broken glass and the wrecked barricades had to be.

The reign of terror continued ; it had only changed its name. Now it was called Justice. Shocking specimens of depraved humanity were those ill-fated prisoners, dragged from their haunts to be tried by the military authorities in Versailles.

I saw types such as only come to the surface when conflicting passions of the worst kind stir up the very dregs of society : dishevelled viragos, brutalised men, female fiends, men devils—hyænas, ready to spring and fasten their claws on you, were they not chained. I heard their howl of despair and their laugh of defiance, as they were led off to be shot.

And thus, whilst the beautiful city was smoothing her ruffled feathers and taking out a new lease of life, the poor wretches met their doom at the foot of the blood-spattered wall.

Wild beasts if you like—but men and women— our brothers and our sisters—alas! born in squalor, bred in vice, and tainted with hereditary ugliness of body and mind.

Who made them what they are? Let us try to find out, and, if we can, let us stand the guilty ones up against that wall, and clear them away with the other human wreckage. But no! neither you nor I would be left to do the clearing away.

CHAPTER XI

SOME INCIDENTS OF ROBERT BROWNING'S VISITS TO THE STUDIO

 well remember, and it is often a source of infinite enjoyment to me to recall, many a trifling incident connected with the name of Robert Browning. He was the kindest and most indulgent of friends, and, as such, I remember him with gratitude and devotion; and he was the most honourable and lovable of men, and so it was but natural I should honour and love him.

What I can record about him is mostly of a personal character, and I only trust that, if any member of a Browning Society happens to come across these pages, he will not resent my inability to add more than a few descriptive touches to what is already known of the poet.

He was well aware that I had never really studied his works, in fact that I had only read a small portion of them; but he made allowances for that, as for my other shortcomings. He also knew that when, by dint of perseverance, I did master some difficult pages of his writing, none could more warmly appreciate the subtle beauties they contained than his humble friend.

"Last night I read Bishop Blougram," I told

him on one occasion. "I went as far below the surface as I could get, but I need not tell you I did not reach the bottom."

"Try again," was all he answered; and when I asked who had been his models, he said that Cardinal Wiseman was his Bishop, and that Gigadibs was not sketched from any one particular person. The Cardinal, he told me, had himself reviewed the poem favourably.

I first met Browning at my cousins the Bensons. They occupied one of those unique houses in that finest of avenues, Kensington Palace Gardens. Notwithstanding the name, the houses really have gardens, and command an unlimited view over the grounds which extend from Kensington to Hyde Park. Inside the hospitable mansion all that was best in the world of art and literature would assemble, and men and women of note felt so much at home there, that they would just lay down their laurel wreaths and wipe off their war-paint, before they came in, and move about as if they were ordinary mortals. They ate and drank too, as if anxious to show their appreciation of Mrs. Benson's table; she certainly made a point of placing the best of nectar and ambrosia before the gods, her guests. And the chef saw to it, that the menus should be worded with due regard to historical truth. I recollect one occasion when he had introduced "Cotelettes à la Charles Dickens" on the programme.

"You had better change that," said Mrs. Benson, "and put 'à la Thackeray'; he is dining with us to-night."

"Oh, madam," protested the chef, "surely you don't mean that; everybody would at once recognise them as 'Cotelettes à la Dickens.'"

Dinner was usually followed by the most perfect music, for the gods loved to play to one another, and it needed no pressure to induce a Joachim to open his violin-case, or to lead the pianist of the day straight to the piano. But on one occasion, I forget why, there was some difficulty with Madame Schumann; she had certainly not taken one or two broad hints to the effect that she was wanted. I was, to be sure erroneously, supposed to be devoid of all shyness, and was therefore deputed to get her to the piano. I had known her years ago when, as a girl, she came to Leipsic with her father, and I remember exchanging knowing winks with my sisters behind old Wieck's back, when he held forth about his unique and incomparable method of teaching, as exemplified in his daughters Clara and Marie. He had a queer way of putting it, but he was certainly not far wrong in his estimate of the method and its results.

When I asked Madame Schumann whether she was inclined to play, I was very badly received. She was "particularly disinclined," so I changed the conversation. But presently — quite by chance to be sure—I mentioned her husband's "Carnaval." "There is one part," I said, "which I particularly love: the 'March of the Davidsbündler,' you know. If I could only hear you play just that page or two!"

"Page or two indeed," she said, boiling over with indignation. "Wenn man den Carnaval spielt,

spielt man ihn ganz!" (If you play the "Carnival," you play it from beginning to end.)

And an instant afterwards she was at the piano, throwing her whole soul into that wonderful piece of tone-painting.

Elizabeth Benson was one of the many gifted members of the Lehmann family; the two eminent painters Henri and Rudolf Lehmann were her brothers; so too Frederick, her husband's partner in the well-known firm of ironmasters, Naylor, Vickers & Co. And he, Mr. Benson, was a shrewd German-American who had amassed a fortune in business and lived in perfect style. Being a man of culture and refined tastes, he had a remarkably well selected library and had surrounded himself with many choice works of art.

Browning's son—he had but one child—was also a welcome guest at 10 Kensington Palace Gardens. He was equally gifted as a musician and as a painter, so much so, that for a time he seemed inclined to sit down between two stools and await events. This caused his father some anxiety, and it was evidently with a feeling of relief, that he came to tell me one day, that Pen had got up and made his choice of stools in favour of the one marked Painting. The decision was due to Millais. Pen had accompanied him on a visit to Scotland, and whilst Millais was painting his picture of "Scotch Firs," his young friend made a study of the same subject, which gave evidence of so much talent that Millais unhesitatingly advised him to devote himself to art. When Browning came to tell me of

Robert Browning.

the very satisfactory incident, he asked my advice
as to the best opportunity for study open to him.
In those days, very different from the days we can
boast of now, the best advice to give was that he
should go abroad. I suggested Antwerp, and further
recommended my friend Heyermans as the best
teacher I knew. My advice was taken, and it led
to so excellent a result that Browning never tired
of expressing his gratitude to me for having found
the right man and having put his son in the right
place. Under the guidance of that right man Pen
made rapid progress and soon produced very striking
work.

When he began to exhibit, no father could be
more anxious about a son's reputation or prouder of
his successes, than was Browning. Praise such as
came from the lips or pens of Leighton, Millais, and
other friends, warmed his heart, confirming, as it
did, his belief in Pen's powers. He could be very
sensitive too, when full justice was not done to that
son, as when his statue of Driope was refused at the
Royal Academy. Young Browning, not content with
using the brush to give shape to his artistic concep-
tions, had taken to the sculptor's tools. These he
had learned to handle when, after a prolonged stay
in Antwerp, he went to Paris and studied sculpture
under Rodin, an advantage of which to this day he
is particularly proud. This life-size figure of Driope
was the outcome of much study and thought, and
had been so warmly appreciated on all sides, that
it was deemed worthy of being cast in bronze.
When it was rejected at the Royal Academy,

Browning was indignant, eloquently indignant, and well he might be, for the work was a remarkable one, and as it now stands in the vast Entrance Hall of the Palazzo Rezzonico, many think as I do, that it can challenge comparison with some of the great masterpieces in Venice.

I need scarcely say that the adverse verdict of the rulers at Burlington House did not shake his confidence in Pen or in his first teacher. The poet's gratitude to the latter was expressed in ever-varying forms. He writes to him: "I have to repeat—what I never can be tired of repeating, however inadequately I make my words correspond with my feelings—how deeply grateful I am to you for your instrumentality in the success of my son, which I am sure he will have attributed to the admirable master whose true 'son' in art he is bound to consider himself." When, some years later, Heyermans settled in London, Browning never lost an opportunity of smoothing the artist's path among strangers, in the country which has since become the country of his adoption.

As I may presently allow myself to speak of some of my pictures which Browning liked, it may not be inappropriate to record here that there were others which he disliked. Such were some Japanese subjects, which my love of the newly imported art had impelled me to paint. At the time I am speaking of—in the early seventies—the work of the Japanese was only just coming to the front; there was no shop to display it in all London or Paris. The first things of the kind I can remember here

were some of those cheap paper fans on sale at a
very popular little shop in the Brompton Road,
Harrod's, now developed into one of London's
monster emporiums. In Holland I had previously
come across some wonderful specimens of Japanese
painting and weaving, and when I next saw a unique
collection of such work in the Paris Exhibition,
my admiration was fairly kindled into enthusiasm.
Shortly afterwards the same exhibits found their
way into the hands of those syrens with the ivory
hammer, known as Christie & Manson's, and on that
occasion my savings found *their* way into the same
hands. I was equally fascinated by Japanese art at
Farmer & Rogers', where I soon made friends with
one of their staff, a promising young connoisseur,
Mr. Liberty, the same who now rules supreme in
Regent Street.

Now Browning worshipped—I thought rather
exclusively—at the shrine of old Italian art, and I
do not think he ever really appreciated the Japanese.
Certain it is that he disliked the pictures I painted
when my Japano-mania was at its height; notably
one entitled " On the Banks of the Kanagawa," which
he condemned, perhaps not without good reason, for
I had never been on the banks of that or any other
Jap river, and my figures, although clad in the beautiful dresses I had bought, were more or less evolved
from my inner consciousness. In fact I would not
hesitate to say that the picture was bad, were I not
afraid of being thought wanting in respect to the
august body of Royal Academicians, who gave it a
very excellent place on their walls. As their judg-

ment is known to be infallible, Browning, for once in the way, must have been labouring under a misconception.

If so, he but too generously made up for it in later years when, on many occasions, he showed the greatest interest in my work. He became a frequent visitor at the studio, and the hours he spent with me are amongst the happiest in my artistic experience. To him it was a never-failing source of pleasure to visit his artist friends, and with more than one of them did he make himself thoroughly at home. He had the gift of putting everybody at his ease, sometimes exchanging a few pleasant words with the servant who came to answer the door, sometimes chatting with the models; he was quite unconventional, and would just as soon say, " He don't " as " He doesn't." A great friend of his was Jack Turner, a charming specimen of the London waif, a perfect little angel in his tenth year, but an angel, as it unfortunately proved, with a stumble and a fall, in consequence of which he had to do his growing up in a reformatory, and who asks for the price of a glass of beer when I meet him now. " Good morning, Mr. Browning." " Thank you, Mr. Browning," the little angel would say, for he had quickly realised that the name had a good sound, and the poet would stroke his curly hair and press the price of an ounce of sweets into his innocent little hand.

Then there was Laura, a model, who had one of the most sculptural figures I have ever seen. She had come to me in the regular course of business to get work, accompanied by another young girl; her features were not regular, but mobile and expressive, her eyes restless, and her hair rebellious as it hung in brown wavelets over her forehead. Her friend was a contrast—the regular blue-eyed maiden, fair-haired and fair-skinned. I took their names and addresses, putting them down as head models, for, in answer to my question whether they sat for the figure, Laura had replied, "No; certainly not." It was the close of the season, and I had much work to finish before I could leave town. I told my visitors so, and returned to my easel, but they were evidently disinclined to go; they looked around as if fascinated by the artistic surroundings, and after a whispered consultation, they hinted, carefully veiling their words, that they had no insuperable objection to unveiling. It was evident that they were fired with lofty ambitions of "the altogether" kind. (Immortal creation of my friend Du Maurier, that word, *the altogether*, which lulls suspicion and alarm in the breast of the Philistine, and checks the blush that would rise to the cheek of the British matron.) I bluntly told my would-be models that I was working against time, and that for some months to come I should not be able to use them, whether in sections or as a whole. But they were not to be dissuaded, once having made up their minds to qualify for *the altogether*.

Befittingly coy and shy, Laura's friend emerged from the dressing-room, the type of the English maiden, the rosebud of sweet seventeen. The milk of human beauty flowed in her veins, tinting her with creamy whites from head to foot; one only wanted some dove-coloured greys to model her forms, till at the extremities one would put in a few touches of pink madder or of Laque de garance rose dorée. It is a beautiful little type, "rosed from top to toe in flush of youth." Greuze could paint it, and others too; but whenever I attempted it, I have found that I was not good at rendering the girlish forms and the strawberry-and-cream colour.

Very different was Laura. She came into the room as if to the manner born, freely and easily. She had seemed rather short of stature and awkward in her movements. Now she was tall and graceful, and so sculptural in form that at first you would scarcely notice her colour. You could not render her dull bronze-like tints without mixing your light-reds with cobalt blue or with real ultramarine at a guinea an ounce, if you could afford it.

I did not break out into Pygmalionic enthusiasm, but I felt that I must leave all else and study the line that started from the neck, and went straight down to the heel, unimpeded by petty details or any of those non-essentials which just mark the difference between the real in Nature and the ideal in Art. The next day I began a picture of her which has since found its way to America. My friend Legros chancing to look in when she was sitting, so warmly appreciated her that I invited him to come and make studies from her at my studio occasionally; of those I have a very beautiful one drawn for his *bas-relief* "*La Fontaine*," which many will remember having seen at one of the early exhibitions in the Grosvenor Gallery.

Couldn't Browning be indignant when the British matron presumed to misinterpret the artist's glow of enthusiasm!   Doubly indignant, when the matron took the shape of a patron or the title of a Royal Academician with a vote on the Council of selection, or a hand on the Hanging Committee.

"The impropriety lies in the objection," he would say, "and I have put what I think of it in my Furini."[1]

Browning had a marked predilection for a certain chair in my studio.   It is a cross-breed between what the French call a *crapaud* and we an easy-chair. In this he was installed one afternoon, when Laura was perched on the model-table, artificially supported, as best she could be, to give me a flying position. I was at work on one of two companion pictures which, for want of a better title, I had called "The Cloud-Compeller" and "The Cloud-Dispeller."   In the first a deep-toned figure gathers the rolling clouds together ; in the second, a brighter child of the skies peeps out from behind them.

"You might take some lines from Shelley's 'Cloud' for those pictures," suggested Browning.

"Yes—Shelley's Cloud," I answered.   "To be sure—Let me see—Oh yes, it is one of those beautiful poems I know, but can't remember."

"Oh," he began, leaning back in the easy-chair —"Don't you remember?

> "'I bring fresh showers for the thirsting flowers
>   From the seas and the streams ;
> I bring light shades——'"

---

[1] "Parleying with certain people."—FRANCIS FURINI.

And once started, he recited the whole poem. Recited is scarcely the word. He simply told us all about "The daughter of the earth and the nursling of the sky," and he conjured up, with the slightest of emphasis, pictures of "the whirlwinds unfurled, the stars that reel and swim," and

> "That orbed maiden with white fire laden
> Whom mortals call the moon."

I went on painting—and listened. Laura kept on flying—and listened. She was an educated girl, and knew as well as I did that we might consider ourselves privileged listeners.

Laura had had quite a long spell of work, considering that the office of a cloud-compeller is not a sinecure, and she was well entitled to a rest. Browning said something to that effect as he rose to go, and, adding that she was a brave and conscientious model, he slipped half-a-crown into her hand. When I laid down my palette to go to the door with him, the usual little word-squabble had to be gone through. No argument of mine would ever persuade him that I had a right to see him to the door, but I often did so, heedless of his protest. On the other hand, no argument of his could ever persuade me that *he* was justified in seeing me to *his* door, but he always managed to do so, whether I was persuaded or not. He had stairs to go down and up again; I had not, so it was most unfair, but that was Browning all over—always afraid to give trouble, ever ready to take it.

When I got back to the studio, a new picture met

my eye. I found Laura giving vent to her feelings in a wild dance of jubilation, the half-crown sparkling above her head as she held it up triumphantly with both hands, whilst clusters of brown hair which had been carefully pinned up out of the way, for I was painting her back, now cascaded over her shoulders and down to her waist, suggesting new and original shapes for fashionable capes or opera-cloaks. When Nature's mantle had once more been pinned up and a drapery substituted for it, she settled down in the chair the master had just vacated, and proceeded to discuss the grave question as to what should be done with the half-crown. She scorned my suggestion that she should spend it on a pair of gloves, and then and there decided to have it made into a brooch as a memento of the memorable afternoon.

The next day I received a letter from Browning indicating the particular passages from Shelley's poem which he thought would be suitable to my pictures.

That Laura was a queer girl; it was not till months after her first visit to me that I chanced to find out she was a good pianist and had a pretty voice, and only when she had got quite acclimatised in the studio did I elicit the truth about that first visit. She had always put me off with the evasive answer that "a friend" had given her my address, but at last she confided to me that there was no friend in the case.

"We were walking down Sloane Street," she said, "Amy Stewart and I, when we saw your board up with 'The Studio, Cadogan Gardens' on it. Your dog was at the gate wagging his tail, and seemed like asking us in. I patted him, and said to Amy, 'Let's go in for a lark and say we are models.' And she said, ' Yes; you go first.' So we rang the bell and asked for the artist. You said you were busy and hadn't much time to look at us, and you didn't seem to want us—so we stopped." Her father, I then found out, was a well-to-do builder, much absorbed in his business. No, she said, in answer to my question, he was not aware that she was sitting; her mother was, but had never asked for particulars. Let well alone, I thought, anxious as I was not to lose my model. But not long afterwards I was much startled by Laura's announcement that the sittings must henceforth be given up. She was very sorry, but she was forbidden to come any more.

"What has happened?" I asked in dismay; "your father? your mother?" "Oh no." "Well, do have it out; nobody else surely has a right to interfere." "Well, yes," she said; "Father O'Brien has." I saw it all; she was a good Roman Catholic, and her father confessor had become alarmed, and had put in his veto. "Is that all?" I broke in, much relieved. "Well, Laura, you did startle me—thank goodness, it is only a priest; he of all people couldn't have meant it seriously. He wouldn't be so ungrateful after all we artists have done for the Church. Think of the old masters, Laura; you must go to Father O'Brien and remind him of Raphael and all the saints and Madonnas he painted. Why, to be sure, he must know that even the divine Raphael could not have given us their souls without their bodies, and that even he would never have draped his models till he had made a careful study of those respected bodies.   Oh no, there is nothing to be feared from a good priest; you must go at once, Laura, and speak to him."

Whether she went or not, and whether, having duly weighed my argument, Father O'Brien was struck with remorse, I do not know, but certain it is that Laura came, sat, and helped me conquer the difficulties yet to be grappled with in two pictures I had begun from her.

I was travelling from the sunny South back to the cheerless North.   It was in January, and I was returning from Italy, where I had spent some months, to my own home and hearth; back to the chimney that I knew would smoke, to the pipes that would probably burst, and the blacks that would certainly fly.   Serpentining along the coast of the Riviera, I awoke in the early morning and peeped through the window just by my side in the sleeping-car.   Farewell to the sea and to the sparkle on the playful little waves that were gently breaking against the shrub-covered rocks; farewell to the middle distance and to the distance, and generally to anything worthy to be termed a horizon.   Presently all that will be replaced by somebody's stone wall opposite my own stone wall, or by a growler or a Piccadilly lamp-post in a fog.   And I shall wear a thick overcoat out of of doors, and sit peacefully installed at my own writing-table in-doors.   And the organ-grinder will come to grind under my windows, and to remind me of the country I love so well—and he will keep on grinding till it is time to get up and conduct him to the nearest police-station.

Then, too, I shall meet my friends, and they will ask me where I have been, and tell me where they have been ; and, one and all, they will want to know what I am painting for the Royal Academy, and not have the slightest notion how insulting the question is, particularly if—*il n'y a que la vérité qui blesse*—I *have* been painting *for* the Royal Academy.

That is what I was thinking as we popped into tunnels and out again into the bright sunshine. Then—I don't know whether I fell asleep or whether I kept awake—but I certainly dreamt the most beautiful pictures ever painted. I could not put them on canvas to save my life, any more than I could put them on paper ; but there they were, just across borderland, and I saw them with my own eyes, and not as one usually sees them, cramped by ugly gold mouldings at so much a foot.

There was one creature of extraordinary beauty—a goddess she must have been—with tresses of molten gold ; she had got into a big shell which I had bought in Naples (they call it *terebra*), and, stretching herself full length in it, she had fallen asleep. Then other shells I had left behind in those stalls that line Santa Lucia came up from the deep, and a little lithe-limbed urchin—I felt sure I had seen him before—ensconced himself in one of them as in an arm-chair ; and next—such are dreams—two darling little nieces of mine came toddling along from Tedworth Square, S.W. London, stark naked, and straightway condensed themselves into one meditative water-baby, that loved the shells as I did, and cuddled them as I couldn't.

Dreams to be sure—fancies, mocking visions of beauty, not to be realised, I know it well, but to the artist life would not be worth living if it were not for the glorious excitement of hunting the will-o'-the-wisp.

So I began what I called the shell-picture shortly after my return to London. Browning was in sympathy with my subject, and often came when I was tackling it. In the afternoons he was a man of leisure, his mornings being devoted to his own work, which he would take up when he had read the *Times* and answered his letters. After luncheon he very rarely returned to his study. He would go out about two o'clock, perhaps to walk down to the Athenæum Club, where on Saturdays he was to be seen very regularly, reading the weekly papers, or he would visit his friends. Amongst those his artist friends were the most favoured, and more than one of them, I am sure, would be better qualified than I am to fill a chapter of reminiscences, headed " Browning at the Studio." He himself often speaks in his letters of the pleasure it gives him to associate with them.

" I scribble this," he writes on one occasion, " in case I should be unable to look in to-morrow afternoon—as I will, if I can, however : always enjoying, as I do, the sight of creation by another process than that of the head, with only pen and paper to help. How expeditiously the brush works ! "

And another time he says—

" As for the visits to your studio, be assured they are truly a delight to me, for the old aspirations come thickly back to memory when I see you at work as—who knows but I myself might have worked once? Only it was not to be; but these are consolations—seeing that I am anyhow

" Yours sympathisingly,

" ROBERT BROWNING."

The aspirations he speaks of he had in former years sought to satisfy. When living in Florence he had arranged the large corner room on the first floor of the Casa Guidi as a studio. There he used to make life-size drawings of the human figure from casts, working on a specially prepared canvas, which enabled him to rub out his studies and to replace them by others. He never painted; form had more attraction for him than colour. When in Rome he worked several hours daily in Storey's studio, and when he returned to England he intended taking up modelling seriously. He did indeed begin in War- wick Crescent, but he eventually abandoned the attempt, carried away by mightier impulses. The regret that he had not been able to cultivate his taste for the plastic art, would however often find expression in words.

What he might have done as an artist is a matter of speculation, but he certainly made a most obliging and excellent sitter, as I can vouch for, having been one of those who had the privilege of painting him. He sat for me in 1884, and my portrait has found a permanent place in the Armour Institute in Chicago.

As my shell-picture advanced, I became ambitious to find a better name than the one I had given it temporarily, and as usual Browning was consulted. Isaac Henderson, the novelist of " Agatha Page " fame, happened to be at the Studio, and between them the matter was at first facetiously discussed. On this occasion my name had the proud distinction of drawing from Browning the only pun I ever heard him make. " Why not call it *more shells* by *Moschels?* " he said.

Later on he quoted various passages from poems that seemed to fit my subject, but he felt himself that they were only partially suited to it. In the evening, recalling our conversation, I wrote to him that, knowing as I did exactly what I was trying to express on canvas, I felt sure it would be difficult to find lines quite adaptable to my meaning. " Why not," I asked, "in default of a real poet, sign an imaginary name, Grelice di Napoli, for instance?" Grelice was meant for an Italian version of the name which I had composed when I first met the *Gre*-te who was to link her name to that of Fe-*lix.* The pseudonym was adopted, and we are best known to our friends in every part of the world as "The Grelix."

I suggested then that Grelice di Napoli should have said something of this kind :—

"And as I walked along those lovely shores, and breathed the air of balmy climes, I waking dreamt of living forms that wedded opalescent shells ; of peace, and rest, and blissful harmonies."

I was at work the next day when the post brought Browning's answer, and as I read it I broke into a hearty fit of laughter. *He* had written five lines of poetry, and signed them : *Felix Moscheles.* They ran thus :—

> " And as I wandered by the happy shores
> And breathed the sunset air of balmy climes,
> I waking dreamt of some transcendent shape,
> A woman's—framed by opalescent shells,
> Peacefully lulled by Nature's harmonies."

A day or two later he came to bring me another version which, he explained, he thought I should "like better." This was adopted, and the picture was christened, "The Isle's Enchantress," and described by the following lines :—

> " Wind-wafted from the sunset, o'er the swell
> Of summer's slumb'rous sea, herself asleep.
> Came shoreward, in her iridescent shell
> Cradled, the isle's enchantress. You who keep
> A drowsy watch beside her—watch her well ! "

The day was approaching when, with other work, I was to show that "Isle's Enchantress." Picture show-day they call it. Soft-soap day would be more correct, for every artist expects his friends to give him as much of flattery as they can find it in their consciences to give. And as a rule consciences are elastic ; a little encouragement from the artist goes a long way, and, once he satisfies his friends that he is of an unsuspecting nature, they will lay it on thick in the pleasantest of ways.

To be sure the day brings its little trials too, but of those another time.

It had occurred to me that some of the friends I had invited to meet my Enchantress, might like to have a copy of Browning's lines; so I went round one evening to 29 De Vere Gardens to ask whether he had any objection to their being printed.

"None whatever," he said, in answer to my question.

I thanked him and added, "To be sure I want to put your name to them."

"Oh, you can't do that," he said; "they are not mine, they are yours."

"Mine!   Why, you know, *I* couldn't write verse to save my life."

"Ah, but you did; you sent me the substance and put it into blank verse."

"Blank verse!"—Blank was my astonishment, and I felt like the man in Molière when he was told he had been speaking prose all his life.

Well, we sat by the fireside in that drawing-room of his and discussed the matter, and he would have it that I was the author and that he had only put my idea into shape.

"If I had suggested alterations in your picture," he said, "or if I had advised you to introduce a coral-reef here and a dolphin there, would that have justified me in signing *your* picture?"

"No, perhaps not," I agreed, "but if you had laid on the last coat of paint, the one the public was to see, you certainly could have done so."

And so the skirmishing went on with varying fortunes, till, by some happy fluke, I hit upon an argument which settled the matter in my favour.

"Well," I said, "I can't give you a reason for it —in fact I have never been able to understand why it is so—but it is an undeniable fact that the public *will* make a marked difference between your style and mine, and if your version is to be adopted, it must stand in your name."

"Very well, then," he said, "have it your own way. I am sure you are welcome to anything I can do for you."

"Truly kind you are, and truly grateful am I, and plucky too I beg you to believe, for I don't care a pin if people do say : 'There goes Moscheles hanging on to the tail of Pegasus !'"

I meant it then, and I mean it to-day. You may laugh if you like, but I have the best of it ; it isn't everybody who can boast of having written five lines of poetry *together with Robert Browning.*

The picture I have now. It just fits a recess in my dining-room, measuring about five feet by seven. I daily sit opposite it at meals, and when I watch the golden rays of the sun as they come pouring through the garden-window, and steal across the canvas, I see a beautiful picture which I certainly never painted.

First the light plays on the flowing hair where it dips into the water, and gives it just the aureate tints I tried in vain to mix ; then steadily creeping on, it illuminates, first the closed eyes and the parted lips, then the body and the seaweed straggling across it, and presently it reaches the urchin in the Concha, and would fain make me imagine that I could paint an iridescent shell and a child of flesh and blood.

Those are moments of happy delusions and I

acknowledge it gratefully, for it is not vouchsafed to every one to paint his pictures together with the blessed sun, any more than it is to write his poems together with Robert Browning, or indeed to sit down daily to a square meal, and to have before him a canvas into which he can weave pleasant memories of the Past.

*   *   *   *   *   *

A portrait I was painting of Sir James Ingham, the Bow Street magistrate, led to the following incident. I was telling my sitter how great were the difficulties I had to contend with as a host and an impresario when I had a musical At home at the Studio.

Which of one's talented friends should be asked first? Should Signora Cantilena come before or after Madame Pianota? Singers to be sure are entitled to most consideration. They are invariably affected by the weather, whilst the pianists are only out of practice. If I want la Signora to sing at about eleven o'clock, I begin asking her to favour us at a quarter-past ten, allowing her from forty to fifty minutes to get over the insurmountable difficulties which, just to-day, stand in the way of her acceding to my request. But then, in the kindness of her heart, when once she begins, she is inclined to go on till she has successfully illustrated the wonderful variety of her talent. And there is Herr Thumpen Krasch, who is waiting all the while to get to the piano, and when he is there, he is naturally disinclined to play his best pieces first, and reserves his Monster-Rhapsody on Wagner's Trilogy, the success of the season, for what I call the after-end. As for myself, I forget my duties and go into raptures, delighted as I am to think that my friends sing and play their best in the genial atmosphere of the Studio. But oh, the other virtuosi who are waiting to be heard! "*Ote-toi, que je m'y mette*" is the motto of every true artist, and my friends are all true artists.

"Yes," said Sir James, "those troubles are as old as the hills. Don't you recollect the lines Horace wrote two thousand years ago?" and he quoted them.

"Splendid! I wish you would write them down for me; my Latin is rather rusty, and I should like to remember them."

So he wrote :—

HORACE, 3RD SATIRE.

"Omnibus hoc vitium
   Est cantoribus, inter amicos
   Ut nunquam inducant
   Animum cantare
      rogati
   Injussi nunquam
      desistant."

The same day Browning came in, and seeing the lines, he took up a pen and wrote without pausing to think—

"All sorts of singers have this common vice :
   To sing 'mid friends you have to ask them twice!
   If you don't ask them, that's another thing :
   Until the judgment-day be sure they'll sing!
       —*Impromptu Translation*, July 10, '83."

How rapidly his mind worked I had occasional opportunities of witnessing. He would let us give him a number of rhymes, perhaps twenty or thirty, to be embodied in an impromptu poem. This he would read to us just once, and, as he spoke the last words, he would ruthlessly tear it up into small fragments and scatter them to the winds. Nothing would induce him to stay his iconoclastic hand, and on such occasions it only remained for me to regret that I was not some sensitive plate, some uncanny Edisonian Poetophone, to preserve the spontaneous creation of his mind.

"Do you ever listen to Reciters?" my wife asked him one day; "I mean to Reciters of Browning's poems?"

"Oh, I do the Reciting myself," he said, "when I am amongst a few sympathetic friends. I will read to you with pleasure. What have you got?"

The few sympathetic ones were not wanting that Sunday afternoon; I gave him the volume of "Selections" from his poems, and turning over the pages he said, "As we are in an artist's studio, I will read 'Andrea del Sarto.'"

There was not a shadow of declamation in his reading. For the time being he was just Andrea talking to his wife, the "Faultless Painter" as they called him, who knew his own faults but had not the strength to battle with them. It was Andrea himself we were in touch with, his dreamy sadness that we shared. His yearnings for requited love, his longings for the unattainable in art, drew us to him, and we would have helped him had we been able. That sorry business with the King of France was disgraceful — there was no denying it. He admitted himself that he had abused the king's friendship and misused his moneys, but surely for such a man as was Del Sarto, something could be done to settle matters, and once more to turn his genius to account.

And that Lucretia, his wife ! his " serpentining beauty, rounds on rounds!" Why *will* she not answer ? The right words from her spoken now might yet make of him the good man and the great artist that a God may create, but that a woman must consecrate. One just felt as if one could give her a good shaking. if only to make her break the aggravating silence she so imperturbably maintains whilst he so pathetically pleads. As for the cousin, one would have liked to go out and give him a sound thrashing to stop his whistling once for all.

We were so impressed at the close of his reading that for a moment we remained hushed in a silence which none of us cared to break. He looked round at us, anxious lest he should not have brought home his meaning, and said, " Have I made it clear ? "

It is rather a sudden transition from Del Sarto to myself, and from " sober pleasant Fiesole " in the background, to the Royal Academy in Piccadilly ; but all artists of all times, the little ones as well as the great ones, have their grievous disappointments, and one place is as good or as bad as another to crush some of their fondest hopes.

Annually then, towards the end of April, when the judges at Burlington House had spoken, Browning had his visits of condolence to pay. How help-

ful and encouraging he would be, none of us, I am
sure, could forget. I thanked him on one occasion,
telling him that I valued his good opinion more than
any other man's, and reminding him of his own
words :—

> " And that's no way of holding up the soul,
>   Which nobler, needs men's praise perhaps, yet knows
>   One wise man's verdict outweighs all the fools."

The one wise man always found a word of
encouragement—

" Beware of despairing thoughts," he answered.
" The darkest days, wait but till to-morrow, will have
passed away."

In his ever simple, unassuming way he compared
himself to me, recalling his failures, and telling me
how for many years not a poem of his was read or
could boast of a publisher willing to take it, and
how now 3500 copies of the new edition of his
works had been sold in a month. " To be sure,
one must live long enough," he added, and quoted
Philip von Artevelde's first speech, in which he says
so many die before they've had a chance, and—

> " Then comes the man who has the luck to live,
>   And he's a miracle."

Unvarying kindness too he showed me when, as
he put it, I " entrusted him with a piece of business."
Such a piece was my preface to the Mendelssohn
Letters. In this he made six or eight corrections,
suggestions he insisted on calling them, when he
brought the paper back himself that he might explain verbally why he had substituted a word here

and added another there. At the end he had
pencilled : "Excellent. R. B.," and I felt as proud
as a peacock and as happy as a schoolboy.

When the book finally came out he was in Italy,
and I sent him a copy of it.

It was characteristic of him that his kind heart
prompting him, and his unlimited powers of expression aiding him, he would, even on the most trivial
occasions, write in the warmest and the most affectionate terms. So he did when he answered acknowledging the receipt of the book, and mentioning
the photo of a picture which I had painted for
A. P. Rockwell, a dear friend of mine and a great
fur-merchant in New York. It showed a life-size
female figure stretched on a tiger-skin and frankly
nude, but for the white Mongolian and other furs
thrown around and about her.

He dates from Casa Alvisi, Canal Grande, Venezia,
October, 29, '88, and after a few introductory sen-
tences, he says :—

" I concluded that on leaving Scotland you would
proceed elsewhere than homewards, and it seemed
best to wait till I was sure of finding you. Even
now—I am sorry exceedingly to be still far from
sure that this will go to you safely housed within
the old easy reach of De Vere Gardens—for there
shall I live and probably die—not in the Rezzonico,
which is not mine but Pen's : I am staying here
only as the guest of a dearest of friends, Mrs.
Bronson, who has cared for the comfort of my sister
and myself this many a year. No ; once missing my
prize of the superlatively beautiful Manzoni Palazzo,

I have not been tempted to try a fresh spring un-
baulked by rascality.   So much for the causes of
my tardiness in thanking you most heartily for the
charming Lady of the Furs : why not give her that
title ? Everybody here paid the due tribute to her
beauty and your skill.   You promised I should witness the beginning and ending of such another picture
—and it is not to be—if things are as I apprehend.
Wherever you go, may all good go with you and
your delightful wife ; my two precious friends !

"And now here is a second occasion of sincere
thanksgiving.   Your letter arrived yesterday—and
I supposed that the gift referred to had been consigned to the Kensington house : whereas, while I sat
preparing the paper whereon to write, came the very
book itself—the dearest of boons just now.   The
best way will be to thank you at once, and be
certain of finding plenty more to thank you for
when I have read what will interest me more than
anything else I can imagine in the way of biography.
Let me squeeze your hand in spirit, over the many
miles, this glorious day—a sun floods the room from
the open window, while an autumnal freshness
makes it more than enjoyable, almost intoxicating.
In half-an-hour I shall be on the Lido—perhaps in
a month I may cower by the fireside in Kensington.
Meanwhile and ever, my dear Moscheles, believe me,
gratefully and affectionately yours,

"ROBERT BROWNING."

He was with me one day when a distinguished
German officer, Graf D., unexpectedly came in.   The

count was in London to attend some grand military pageant organised for the benefit of the German Emperor. His Majesty, on a visit to his royal grandmother, was being entertained with a right royal show of death-dealing ships and other instruments of warfare. He seems to have enjoyed it thoroughly, and in return for attentions shown him, he was graciously pleased to raise the aforesaid grandmother to the dignity of " Colonel of the First Regiment of Dragoons, stationed in Berlin." As a specimen of the officers to serve under her, Graf D. was ordered to London. He told us that he had dined twice at the royal table, and that he had found the ceremonial on such occasions rather less exacting than in Germany ; the Queen herself was somewhat reserved, but the rest of the company were pretty free to talk or to laugh as they liked.

I had questioned him on the subject, recollecting how indignant Rubinstein was at the hushed silence prevailing in the presence of her Majesty. He could not and would not stand it, he said, and spoke out as he would have done elsewhere.

When D. had gone, I told Browning that the count was not only a gallant soldier, but a man to be held in great esteem, on account of his moral courage. It was a bold thing for a man in his position to side with the Jews at a time when the antisemitic movement was at its height. That an officer and a scion of a noble family should associate with bourgeois of the Jewish persuasion as he unhesitatingly did, was an unheard-of thing.

No wonder it should be commented upon amongst his brother officers. Whatever their prejudices may have been, he had once for all checked their utterance by stating in unmistakable language that he would tolerate no disparaging remarks on any one of those whose houses he frequented.

Browning was naturally in sympathy with the count's broader views and his chivalrous conduct. " Is it possible," he said, "that men should seek to sever themselves from those who are as *they* are—all made of mortal clay ! "

When I alluded to the difference in appearance, and especially in manners, so marked in Germany between the Christians and the Jews of a certain class, and sought thereby to explain the repugnance these so often inspire, he said—

"Naturally ; their characteristics would become more intensified through long exclusion from other groups of men ; their manners would be unlike those of others with whom they were not allowed to mix. No wonder if, hedged in as they were, those peculiarities took offensive shapes. Does not every development, to become normal, require space ? Why, our very foot, if you restrict and hedge it in, throws out a corn in self-defence ! "

On the 7th of May, it was in 1889, Browning came in after luncheon. " It is my birthday to-day," he said, "and so I came to sit with you and your wife for a while, if you'll let me."

I rejoiced, and at once thought of work in his presence, always a source of double pleasure to me. My wife thought of the pleasure it would give her to offer him some little present by way of marking the happy day.

"I have been out model-hunting this morning," I told him, "and have caught the very specimen I wanted for the boy lolling against the door of the public-house in the 'Drink' picture. I was in luck; for I went to Victoria Station with the definite purpose of finding a typical 'Cheeky,' and I found him. He is just having a square meal as an introduction to business, and I am burning to paint him and his cheek. Will you come in with me and let me start?"

"The very thing I should like to see you do," said Browning, and we adjourned to the Studio. Little Cheeky, the veriest young vagabond, uncombed and untamed, cap over ear and cigarette-stump in mouth, was happily transferred to canvas in an hour or two, and his effigy has ever since remained with me in memory of the friend who sat by me on that day. In the meanwhile my wife had bethought herself of a little piece of antique embroidery framed and under glass, which, but lately, we had picked up in Rome; that seemed worthy to be offered to Browning, and she pressed him to accept it, but in vain. Warmly she persisted, firmly he resisted. At last, and lest he should displease or pain her, he said—

"Well, my dear friend, let us make a compromise. You keep it for me for a year and give it to me on my next birthday."

We have it still! He was never to see that next birthday!

He died on the 12th of December in the Palazzo Rezzonico in Venice.

When Pen's telegram with the fatal news reached me I was standing by another deathbed.

On the last day of the year 1889 he was buried in Westminster Abbey. It had been proposed to transfer the remains of Elizabeth Barrett Browning from Florence to be laid by the side of her husband, but the idea was abandoned as not being likely to meet with the approval of the municipality and the English colony of that city. Browning himself had never expressed any wish on the subject of his resting-place, further than mentioning on one occasion the Norwood Cemetery as a fitting place, and saying that, if he died in Paris, he wished to be buried near his father.

Shortly after his death I painted a water-colour of his study in De Vere Gardens. Everything had remained intact. " All here—only our poet's away," as he says in " Asolando." The empty chair by the writing-table which bears his initials, the desk which he looked upon as a relic. His father had used it when a lad, and had taken it with him on his voyage to the West Indies. The poet possessed it from his earliest boyhood, and used it all his life ; everything he wrote in England, so his sister told me, was written on that desk. The little dumb keyboard I have already mentioned in the first of these pages ; it had five notes over which he would mechanically run his fingers. He had a way too of beating a tattoo on his knee, or he would just for a few seconds mark time, moving his arm backwards and forwards. Sometimes he would squeeze up his eyes and look out of the window, or he would take up some little object and scrutinise it closely, whilst his thoughts were busy elsewhere.

On his table lay a book he had shown me as one he treasured : a little Greek Bible. On the last leaf was written : "My wife's book and mine." Pictures by his son hung on the walls ; so too a portrait of his wife when a little girl, by Hayter ; one of Hope End, the house in which she lived, and one of the tomb in the English Cemetery in Florence where she lies buried. Another reminiscence of her is the low chair to the right of the table ; she at all times liked low seats, and this chair was a favourite with her.

Among the things on the walls was a pen-and-ink drawing of Tennyson by Dante Gabriel Rossetti. On the back of it Browning wrote—

"Tennyson read his poem of 'Maud' to E. B. B., R. B., Arabella, and Rossetti on the evening of September 27, 1855, at 13 Dorset Street, Manchester Square. Rossetti made this sketch of Tennyson as he sat reading to E. B. B., who occupied the other end of the sofa.—R. B., March 6, 1874, 19 Warwick Crescent."

μεταπιπτοντος
δαιμονος.

On the drawing is written in Mrs. Browning's hand—

" I hate the dreadful hollow
Behind the little wood."

The large bookcase which made up the background for my drawing, he designed himself. The fine old oak-carvings he had bought many years ago in Florence, where they had adorned the refectory of some old monastery; when he got them home, he put them together, with the assistance of an ordinary carpenter, according to his own design, chalked out on the carpet, and ever after he took great pride in the result. The bookcase held to the end of his days the many rare and beautiful volumes he prized so highly.

Another bookcase he wanted to accommodate piles of books he had brought from Warwick Crescent when he moved to De Vere Gardens. I suggested a certain one that had belonged to Sheridan and was now for sale at Joshua Binns's, then the king of dilapidators. But he preferred a severely useful piece of furniture in mahogany which we found close to my studio at Taylor's Depository. Books he would always handle very carefully. He would never leave a book open or place it face downwards—or, worst of all in his eyes, deface it by turning the corner of a page. His strong dislike of the imperfect was characteristic. Anything mended he objected to, and he would rather a thing he valued were broken outright than chipped or cracked.

The manuscript of "Aurora Leigh" was a treasure he guarded lovingly. It had been lost with other things in a trunk forwarded from Italy to England, but, when search already seemed hopeless, it was found in Marseilles. I have heard him say, referring to the incident: "She thought more of Pen's laces and collars than of that book." He wanted to have the manuscript bound, but could not make up his mind to part with it even for that purpose. Three times he replaced it on the shelf before he let it go. It is now in Pen's possession, as is the MS. of "Asolando," both eventually to be left to Balliol College, Oxford, as others already bequeathed to that institution.

After his wife's death, Browning took the house in Warwick Crescent, originally to find a place for the furniture which he had had forwarded from Florence; the neighbourhood was selected because a sister of Mrs. Browning's, Arabella Moulton Barrett, lived in Delamere Terrace, but he strongly disliked the house, and always had a wish finally to settle in the Kensington district. It was, however, only towards the close of his life that he left Warwick Crescent and made his home in De Vere Gardens.

Stiff staircases such as he found there he never objected to; in fact, whether at home or when travelling, he had a marked preference for being located in one of the upper storeys. So it was on the second floor he had established his library and study.

His sister, Miss Browning, to whom so frequent reference is made in his letters as Sarianna, lived with him and ever devoted herself to the task of securing his comfort and happiness. She would write out his poems and otherwise make herself useful as his amanuensis; frequent too were the opportunities the brother and sister took to travel together, and when abroad, they would enjoy nothing better than a walk of several hours.

The last time I saw him at the Studio, he had come to tell me that he was shortly leaving for Italy.

He spoke with enthusiasm of Asolo, describing its beauties in glowing colours, and he told me how, some forty years ago, as a young man, he had reached it when on a walking tour through the Venetian province.

> " How many a year, my Asolo,
>   Since—one step just from sea to land—
>   I found you!"

It was the old tower crowning the hills, the Rocca, at that time tenanted by hawks, that had made the most lasting impression on his mind. He had been there again in later years with his sister, and now he was elated at the prospect of once more revisiting it and the picturesque old city he loved so well. He went, and it was there he wrote his last work, " Asolando."

Prompted by the desire to ramble over the ground he had so lately trodden, and to gather what evidence I could of his passage, I went to Venice and Asolo in the following year, and painted a series of water-colours (some fourteen or fifteen) in illustration of notes I took during my stay in these places. Some of those notes may not be out of place here to complete my sketch of Browning.[1]

A couple of hours' ride by rail took me from Venice to Cornuda, two more by diligence to my destination. Leaving the plain an excellent road, cut into the flanks of the hill on which the town is built, soon brought me to the summit. I had only

----

[1] The following notes formed part of an article published in *Scribner's Magazine* in 1891.

risen six or seven hundred feet, but a magnificent view greeted me on all sides. "In clear weather you can see Venice," the driver told me; but I was anxious to look forward, not backward, and alighting at the entrance to a narrow street, I walked along the *Sotto-portici*, formed by a series of quaint thick-set arches supporting the upper storeys. A few steps brought me to the house in which, as the tablet on the wall says, had lived the "Somma Poeta."

"What a curious place to select!" was my first thought as I stood at the door of the old house. I walked up twelve or fifteen hard stone steps, grasping the banister to guide myself in the dark, and was soon warmly welcomed by Signora Nina Tabacchi, as, passing through the kitchen, I was ushered into the sitting-room. "Scrupulously clean and neat," was my next impression, but how plain! The room was only a piece of the kitchen partitioned off, a glass door and window separating the two. The thin cotton curtain might possibly screen the mysteries of the culinary process from the poet's eye, but his ear must have been caught by occasional sounds of hacking and chopping, and certainly no kettle could have boiled, no wood could crackle, or incense arise from that adjacent hearth without making itself distinctly noticeable. Such was his study and his drawing-room, a *multum in parvo* about twelve feet square.

I had ample time to study my surroundings, for I spent some weeks in the rooms vacated by the poet. The furniture was of the good old lodging-house type. In the centre of the little sitting-room was a round pedestal table, half of which was devoted to Browning's papers; on the other half, luncheon was served for himself and his sister. A full-length sofa, uncompromisingly hard, took up the greater part of one wall, and a kind of sideboard stood opposite. On the chiffonnier, between the two windows, rested the looking-glass, and half-a-dozen mahogany chairs, cane - bottomed and severe backed, completed the arrangements. On the flesh-coloured walls hung a series of prints, illustrating the history of Venice. Doges disporting themselves in most conventional attitudes, the vanquished kneeling before the victors, gave one the impression that history involves a great amount of bowing and scraping. In pleasant contrast with such triumphs were the domestic joys as depicted by the photographer. Looking up from his papers, Browning's eye must have rested on that shell-adorned frame which encircled the usual specimens of family portraits. There were the inevitable aunts and uncles, the young man pressing into the focus, to meet the clever dog seated on the table by his side, and a typical presentment of the mother and child as conceived by the lens.

To Luigi, the landlady's son, Browning was from the first very friendly; but how this lad, ever on the alert to make himself useful, could have kept any length of time in his good graces, is a mystery to me. He owns that on one or two occasions the sturdy master sent him flying, when he would imprudently insist on opening the door for him, or on lighting him down the dark staircase.

On his arrival Browning had bought a plain glass

inkstand and a few wooden penholders; they were still there, on a blue-patterned china plate, just as he had left them. I reverently put them aside, but I might as well have used them; for just as he would never allow me to make the slightest fuss of him, the living friend, so he would not have expected me to stand on ceremony with the inanimate objects that survived him. A pen was just a pen, as "A flower is just a flower."

Asolo boasted of a theatre, and the performances must have been none of the worst, for, out of twenty, Browning only missed three. He would sit in his friend Mrs. Bronson's box, and follow the actors as they told the story of Hamlet, Othello, or Mary Queen of Scots, or as they played Goldoni's popular comedies. The performance usually wound up with a short farce. From that he would escape, leaving Gigi (that is Luigi), who was his frequent companion, to do the screaming laughter. About half-past eleven or twelve he got home, and by five or six in the morning he was up again. His bedroom was about 16 feet by 9, and 10 feet high. A really good rococo design, speaking of an artistic past, embossed and picked out in grey, decorated the whitewashed walls. Rafters brought out the irregularities of the ceiling, and bricks, very much wrinkled and worn with age, paved the floor. Signora Tabacchi had offered to procure a carpet, but had met with an energetic refusal. There was a funny little looking-glass, and a wash-hand stand with a diminutive basin, and over the glass door a towel was neatly tacked to insure privacy.

And what in this land of vistas greeted the poet's eye as he opened his shutters? A blank wall and another set of shutters. They would be opened presently to be sure when the sun left the neighbour's wall, and then a flood of light would burst into the centre corridor of his house, and the reflections from the marble floor would carry the quivering rays along to another window beyond, through which you caught a lovely glimpse of the hills on the other side of the valley. In that particular glimpse Browning delighted. When his son came to Asolo, he was struck, as I was later, by the uncongenial outlook.

"Wait, Pen, till they open those shutters," Browning had said. Pen waited and was duly impressed and pleased. It was well so, for had it been otherwise, his father's pleasure would have been incomplete.

The people of Asolo are of the kindliest nature; simple, peaceful folk, hard-working and contented. Perched on high in their picturesque dwellings, they seem raised above at least some of our terrestrial troubles. They live sheltered by solid masses of mediæval stone, and surrounded by the gardens they cultivate; the vine is here, there, and everywhere, zig-zagging along rough stone terraces and gliding down the slopes, or creeping into the windows. A tangle of massive foliage springs from one knows not where, large leaves that dwarf all else elbow their way to the front, and here and there in their midst a big yellow gourd comfortably rests on a stone cornice or on an artificial prop.

The fig leaves, though certainly overshadowed by their bulky neighbours, hold their own in the universal struggle for air and space. And somewhere in the distance is a little graceful figure stretching upward to train the vine in the way it should go, and right or wrong you straightway jump to the conclusion, if you are an artist, that that figure belongs to a beautiful girl.

The children are out of doors ; so are the pigs. Whilst the latter always seem grumbling and dissatisfied, the former are as happy as sunshine and *polenta* can make a child. The sight of an approaching stranger carrying the artist's paraphernalia, at once suggests to a sturdy urchin the idea that he should rush for a chair, and to the woman at her door, that she should offer you a hearty welcome. No wonder if some of these good people were destined to entertain an angel or a poet unawares. Browning might not have manifested himself as such, but there was something about him that endeared him to all he met. Faces brightened as I spoke of him ; voices deepened as they answered, "*Ah poveretto!* how kind he was—*proprio buono!* Here he used to sit and chat with us ;" or, "I showed him the way to the Rocca eleven years ago." This last remark came from the postmaster, who took the deepest interest in everything concerning Browning. He was very anxious that I should paint a picture of the post-office, as being the historical place the poet had many a time visited. "It was over that counter of mine," he said, "that his last work, the immortal ' Asolando,' was handed.

On me he relied to transmit it with the greatest care, for he assured me he had kept no copy of it. Yes, it went per book-post, registered and addressed, I well recollect, to the publisher Mr. Smith, of London, and he was surprised it should cost so little—only seventy centimes; it weighed 450 grammes, you see, and so that was the postage."

I may add that the manuscript thus sent, and since returned to the poet's son, is written in Browning's neatest and distinctest hand. There are but few corrections or erasures. Of these one has perhaps a special interest, as applying to the last line he ever published. The "Epilogue" he first ended thus :—

> "'Strive and thrive' cry 'God to speed,
>   Fight ever there as here.'"

This he changed to—

> "'Strive and thrive' cry 'Speed fight-on,
>   Fare ever there as here.'"

On hearing that the manuscript had safely reached its destination, Browning's kind thoughts at once reverted to the postmaster, good and true, and he went to thank him for his share in the transaction.

Little can have changed at the Rocca since Browning visited it. The stones roll down the narrow path from under your feet, as you ascend through vineyards and orchards, past stray poultry and groups of sleeping ducks. In a few minutes you reach the crest of the hill, and find the old stronghold, turret - flanked and loopholed, that had for generations frowned upon the valley below, as was the way of citadels in the bad old times. Now it is all smiles, garland-wreathed and happy in its green old age.

During his stay in Asolo Browning and his sister spent much time in the house of Mrs. Bronson, the Mrs. Arthur Bronson to whom the poet dedicated his last book of verses, and whom he thanked in his preface for "yet another experience of the gracious hospitality bestowed on me for so many years." In the afternoon they would all take long drives together.

It was on one of these occasions that Browning hit upon the title he would give his volume of poems. His son suggesting that it should in some way be connected with the name of Asolo, he bethought himself of the verb *asolare*. "Have you a good dictionary?" he asked his hostess. "I feel sure it was Cardinal Bembo who used the word, but I must look it up." He did, the well-known result being the adoption of the title and the explanation given in the introductory lines.

At Mrs. Bronson's it was quite understood that he should come and go as he liked, and that he should consider "La Mura" as much his home as he would his own house. A spacious loggia had recently been added to the old building, virtually forming a new room, roofed in, but open to the air on three sides. Here Browning spent many hours walking up and down or reading, or he would sit in the arm-chair and "drink in the air," as he used to say.

From that point of vantage he would watch Nature's ever-varying moods, and muse over the historical recollections evoked by Caterina Cornaro's palace and the other old buildings on the hills opposite. Often he would hurry back to the house, anxious lest he should miss the sunset as viewed from that loggia.

A constant source of enjoyment to him **was** an old spinet, marked and dated, "Ferdinando Ferrari, Ravenna, 1522." Knowing how much pleasure this little instrument had given him during former stays at her house in Venice, his hostess had had it brought to Asolo, and, here as there, he delighted in playing upon it of an evening, simple, restful melodies that had been familiar to him for years, or quaint scraps of early German or Italian music.

From the spinet he would go to the books. "What have you got?" he asked on the first evening of his stay. "What shall I read to you? Shakespeare? What! You don't mean to say you haven't brought your Shakespeare! I am shocked."

On this, as on other occasions, he was always most deprecatory when asked to read something of his own. But the new edition of his works which he had presented to his friend, being at hand, he would take down a volume and relate, in his own words, and with his unaffected intonation, the story of a Paracelsus or a Strafford. And that would afterwards lead him to speak with ever fresh enthusiasm of the historical associations connected with such names. In the course of the exhaustive studies that always preceded the composition of any work of his, he made himself intimately acquainted with every fact concerning the lives of those whom he was about to pourtray. Whatever detail history had preserved he made his own, and what his mind had once assimilated, his memory ever retained.

The pilgrim to Asolo would naturally look about for some clue to the poems written there. He would hope to meet with some of the models, animate or inanimate, that might have suggested one or the other of the " Facts and Fancies." But, reticent as Browning always was concerning his work, even with those nearest to him, he has left no trace to guide us.

It was quite exceptional when, one day returning from a drive, he said, " I've composed a poem since we've been out; it is all in my head, and when I get home I will write it down."

" What is it about?" very naturally asked his companions.

" No, no, no; that I won't say. You know I never can speak of what I am writing."

" Ah, but now you have told us so much, you must tell us all," pleaded Mrs. Bronson; and as she resolutely declared she would not take No for an answer, he gave way, and said—

" Very well then, I will tell you. It is all about the ladies wearing birds in their hats. I've put it pretty strong, and I don't know how they'll take it."

The proof-sheets of his book of poems he had given to Mrs. Bronson. " Did you understand them all?" he asked. " Did you understand the flute music? Ah, not quite. Well, some day I'll tell you all about it." But the day never came! He little knew that he was postponing it for ever; on the contrary, he was planning pleasant things for the future.

"If I were only ten years younger," he said, "I should like to have a place here in Asolo. Now the Asilo Infantile; if I could get that, I would complete it and call it Pippa's tower. It is more for Pen. I may not enjoy it long; but after all, I do think I am good for another ten years."

The Asilo Infantile he spoke of was a large unfinished building, originally intended to do service as a schoolhouse. It stood opposite the loggia on the ridge of the hills that push forward into the valley.

Pippa and her sister-weavers were often uppermost in the poet's mind, and he would tell how formerly the girls used to sit at their work in the doorways all along the *Sotto-portici* and weave cheerful songs into their web. Now the trade had gone to Cornuda and elsewhere. He had visions of what he would like to do for the poor girls thus dispossessed, should he come to live among them— visions that were in a great measure to be realised by those who bear his name, and who have inherited his world-wide sympathies.

Negotiations were opened with the Town Council with the view of acquiring the building and grounds to be dedicated to Pippa. It was the first time that municipal property was to be sold, so the matter had carefully to be considered by those in authority.

The negotiations took their due course ; but alas ! they came to a close too late. The intending tenant was never to obtain possession.

The day and hour that a favourable decision was arrived at, was also the day and hour of the poet's death.

THE END

Printed by BALLANTYNE, HANSON & Co.
Edinburgh & London